A Fallen Sword

A Fallen Sword

Book I in the Wolf and Viper Series

KAVEN HIRNING

This book is dedicated to my dice.
Every action, every encounter, every reaction...
Everything in this book was decided by the luck of the roll.

If characters make weird choices, or act outside of themselves:
Blame the dice.
I probably rolled pretty low.
Don't hold these poor people in the story accountable.

Enjoy!

This book was written and inspired by DND.
A d20 was used over two hundred separate times. Rolls were also made for damage.
This book is *not* affiliated in any other way with Dungeons and Dragons or other campaigns.
Only by dice... And spirit.

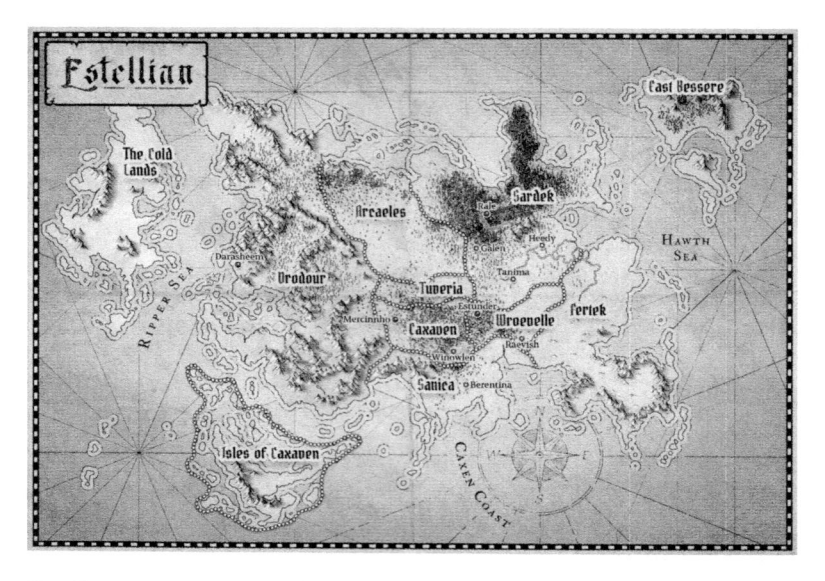

Estellian is composed of seven territories and kingdoms.

Sardek, the High Crown, remains the most powerful of these under the rule of the Caston line.

All trade and agreements with Caxaven and Sanica are facing termination by the High Crown unless they submit to the Allies.

Drodour will remain untouched by ownership, as will any outposts and ships to the unexplored Cold Lands and East Bessere.

Estellian is home to many Arcanen users. Magic given by the High Pantheon of the gods.

Sorcerers are gifted spell casters; becoming a wizard makes one a *master* of them.

Mages tamper with elemental magic.

Clerics are given the ability to bless and heal.

Warlocks are masters of wards and can sometimes even manipulate time.

There are other Arcanen powers that have not been identified by the Kingdoms and Territories.

Be wary of these; they are a threat. Some can change the way they look; others can control the mind.

They bend the established rules of the Arcanen and worship no gods; they claim no masters.

Be wary of these.

The Gods of Estellian:

THE HIGH PANTHEON:
Rashawe, God of Wish and Want
Deleon, Goddess of Fire and Sun
Raenin, God of the White Fire
Vaste, God of Sea and Salt
Idenethor, goddess of Tree and Soil.

LOWER GODS of Estellian:
Radina, goddess of Beauty and Temper
Degolian Murks, Lord of Death and Sorrow
Audrina, goddess of Truth and Hidden Things
Pastrege, God of the Overlooked
Nerillian Coève Algeras, god of The Gentle Touch
Ocal, Our Lady of Heathers (often associated with lust and pining)
Maji, The Fluent
Lady Idalia, Maiden of Light

There are hundreds of other deities and lesser gods that are recognized and worshiped in Estellian.
Listed above are the most commonly practiced.

Table of Contents

The Bitch and The Half Breed 2
The Dame and The Cart 10
The Nelimen 18
The Deal 24
The Open Road 28
The Veravant 36
The Little Fox 44
The Mission Begins 49
The Storm of Ice and Fury 53
The Rogue and His Ass 69
The Goddess of Truth and Hidden Things 76
The One Bed 84
The City That Burned 93
The Rectory 97
The Blacksmith and His Blade 101
The Vote 119
The Little Foxes Run 127
The Decision 134
The Sun Criers Temple 142

The Night Beneath the Stars of Estunder 152
The One Problem Solved 178
The Sorceress Returns 184
The Mountains of Drodour. 200
The Divide 219
The Jedarei and The Zonderi. 229
The Messaging Gem 240
The Ash of Hands and Many Mouths. 249
The Scorn and the Skin 261
The Vaenir 283
The Wolf. 294

THE FOX RING

To the Ring we serve.
Swift, death on the wind.
Some, death do deserve.
Some, death may bend.
Little foxes run with cunning and deceit.
Little foxes run, light upon your feet.
Little foxes hunt alone.
Little foxes have no home.
To the Ring we serve.
Some, death do deserve.

One does not simply become a Fox.
The Ring must agree and take a vote, but the decision still ultimately lies with the Veravant.
Do not break the code or suffer to become a Wolf.
They are exiled. They are alone.

The Bitch and The Half Breed

Mirevra was a bitch.

Or at least, that is what most would call her. Some referred to her as an assassin, others a fighter. Still, her favorite had to be *a no-good, dirty, rotten thief*. She did not care. They were all true, anyway. Mirevra thought most people were a bunch of idiots, so why should their opinions offend her?

Sometimes, she would listen to those around her prove their loquaciousness, rambling on and on about how the gods or their fate had shaped who they were. She did not believe this for a moment. Mirevra was under the firm belief that people are born just as they are and will always end up being. How they got here was irrelevant. Fate did not shape a person; their will did. Those with weak wills were always destined to become weak people. When Mirevra first joined the Fox Ring, this became even more evident. What began as a guild of fifteen rested now at a humble five, not including the Veravant.

Only five Foxes proved themselves worthy, strong, and capable. Those before them folded; they gave up or died pathetically. Save one, Cage

Mastrosis. He had defected from the Ring, disobeyed the Veravant, and was subsequently marked as a Wolf. None of the remaining five had ever met him. After telling Cage's tale as a warning, the Veravant did not mention his name again. Mirevra had altogether shaken the thought of him from her mind. She was not to even think of a Wolf. There was no return once you were marked as such. The guilds forever sullied your name; your face was known for shame alone. Not just to guilds, either. Your name leaked into cities and towns, villages and hamlets alike. As a Wolf, your life was one of absolute rejection.

They are exiled. They are alone.

The Veravant had sent two of his Foxes, Mirevra and Bagah, to the desolate town of Beretina to deal with a shady merchant who had foiled an entire shipment to the Ring. At least twenty hand-forged ruby blades, due for delivery six days ago, had never arrived. The Veravant did *not* take the misplacing of his things lightly. So, Mirevra made sure she told the merchant just how unimpressed her boss was before she slit his throat and Bagah cleaned out his shop.

Now Mirevra and Bagah stood outside one of the town's taverns, their stolen cart filled with pilfered goods ready to be returned to and divvied by the Ring. However, they had not found the ruby daggers, which Mirevra knew would ruffle the Veravant greatly. Likely, highwaymen had stolen the daggers en route, or the Nelimen had intercepted the shipment. *Or another guild, another pest.* But that was a problem for another day and would be dealt with then.

For now, Mirevra only wanted a strong drink. She sauntered into the tavern and, for a second, was thrown by the absence of *any* patrons. However, she dismissed her shock as she surveyed the fully stocked bar and the busy keep. He stared at her with obvious lust. Mirevra was used to such lascivious looks. Her job kept her figure rather shapely, and her tan skin was striking compared to the pale denizens of Beretina. Her long, sand-colored hair was pulled back tightly, splashing down her backside, sweeping just above her rear. But it was her eyes that captured the most attention, Mirevra knew. Molten gold. Dangerously seductive. And right now, they were pulling the barkeep into a familiar trance. That is until Bagah entered behind her. Immediately, the barkeep turned up his nose and spat.

"Filth!" he cursed, his once captivated stare now overcome by disgust. "What is *that* kind doing in Beretina?" Mirevra turned her chin to catch the other Fox in her sidelong view. As always, Bagah seemed unfazed by the insults and moved to sit on one of the bar's stools. She followed slowly, taking smooth, careful steps. How would this night go, she wondered. She always wondered.

Despite his repulsed look, the barkeep slid Mirevra a drink, which she then slid to Bagah. This greatly displeased the barkeep, and he smacked his lips to convey his dissatisfaction. Mirevra ignored this, pointing to a tankard behind him. Reluctantly, he poured her another drink and returned to cleaning the other side of the bar.

The two Foxes quickly drank their fill, and covertly, Mirevra observed Bagah. She watched as he used his sleeve to wipe his mouth, how his eyes lingered too long on the base of his empty mug. She hid it well, but the truth was that Mirevra *did* pity him. Wherever they went, whatever they did, she would always be a forced witness to people's unfortunate ways of coping with a Teruk in their presence. Bagah might be only a half-Teruk, but usually, he was treated just as poorly as a full-blood. Teruks looked like creatures from a story told to frighten children. A large, brawny breed, their faces were often twisted and mangled. Their breaths were rough, nasty gales tearing across the sea, chopping the waves, tipping over boats.

A full-blood Teruk's skin was an unnatural jaundiced yellow; their eyes matched this sallow hue. The bridges of their noses, often sharp and jagged, dropped farther down the face than a human's, leading to a distinctly small nose. In fact, it was hard to call a nose. Just two uneven nostrils resting over a pair of thin, crooked lips. When and if they were present, their teeth were said to be rotted, polluting their mouths with a distinct sour smell. Mirevra had mused that Bagah's breath was foul but only as rank as any man she had met. She often wondered how many rumors that swirled around the full-bloods were true and how many were false.

Nevertheless, the Teruk did not concern themselves with petty matters such as vanity. They did not trouble their minds with trivial whines and complaints that most humans flank themselves with daily. The Teruk were as terribly simple in self-regard as they were utterly devastating in battle. If they liked, one Teruk could take on entire troops of heavily armored soldiers and Mirevra knew this reality was where the *true* hate for Teruks sprang from. And that this strength was precisely why they were hunted.

Half a century ago, the Teruk were a free people with territories spreading far and wide across Estellian. They forged good, hearty blades, the best in these lands, save for weapons cast by Gerelland Nerth.

But when King Kallias Caston, the Root Puller, usurped Syhther Vethari's throne in the kingdom of Sardek, he saw the Teruk as a threat. He knew that should the Teruk ever rise against the High Crown—his crown—they would surely win. They were a brute force, far too powerful, and they did not bow to the customs and traditions of humans.

Power and greed are often intertwined. As they both devoured the new King and starved all compassion from him, he quickly realized he would remain vulnerable if the Teruk and their weapons ran free. The King gave the Teruk an ultimatum. Either fight for him and become the most potent force in all Estellian or perish.

Nothing was in it for the Teruk but servitude; they declined the King's *offer*.

And so, the Root Puller achieved his moniker. He laid waste to the Teruk's homes in the middle of the coldest night of the season. Legions of soldiers, some cloaked in the armor of Gerelland, descended upon them in great fury. The Teruk were ambushed, startled, and bewildered by the attack. Yet, they fought hard and true for their homes. And they may have won that damned battle, even with the element of surprise acting against them, if not for the clerics that Kallias had summoned to aid his troops. His soldiers' weapons were blessed, and as they were of Nerth, it made their armor too tough to penetrate. And when his soldiers were wounded, they were healed almost instantly. The fight was unbalanced, the scales always tipping in favor of the King.

In the end, after an all-night, hard-fought battle, the Teruk surrendered. Kallias and his legions destroyed their land. Their homes and family names, all were plucked away like trees pulled up from their roots. Most of the Teruk were forced into the King's armies. They were caged in the murky catacombs beneath the castle, living worse off than rats, waiting to be called when the war horns sounded. Many were sent to the outskirts of the kingdom to work as free laborers for the highest nobles. Others fled, though no one seemed to know where. As long as they stayed away, nor did anyone seem to much care. They have not been heard from in fifty years; surely, no threat lies in the few who escaped. Besides, the number of Teruk doing the King's bidding would be far too many for a few disbanded rebels to take on. The Teruk were now a fallen, miserable kind. And Bagah knew this sad truth all too well.

He never spoke of his heritage; he did not need to. His eyes, swimming in yellow, and lack of a nose gave him away. Not even his lustrous head of silky brown hair or full rows of white teeth could hide his Teruk features. Though every day, he silently prayed to Rashawe that they might.

Bagah never spoke of his family, either. Even now, Mirevra did not know if it had been his mother or his father who had passed down the Teruk line. She did not know if he had siblings. Or a lover. Bagah had never spoken of his life before the Ring. Not once.

Bagah was a complete enigma, and Mirevra did not ask questions. Their friendship was a silent one, for the most part. Rather than with words, they spoke with gentle nods of the head and specific eye movements. They communicated well enough, Mirevra thought as she raised her chin slightly. Bagah signaled for another drink.

The barkeep snorted at the young male and turned his attention to Mirevra. "Another round for you, Miss?" Annoyance dripped from his tongue. Clearly, he had no intention of asking Bagah the same and even less intention of serving him. *"Filth,"* the barkeep breathed again, his eyes darting between the half-Teruk and Mirevra.

Currents of dark brown pulsed through Mirevra's golden eyes. She did not like it when her friends were treated poorly, but *oh*, how she delighted in an opportunity to teach an asshole a lesson. A smile crept across her face, and Bagah released a heavy sigh. He moved first, of course. Slower than he ought to have, but Mirevra knew that had little to do with stamina and more to do with boredom. How many times had they had to teach this lesson in the last six days alone? Too many. Not enough.

"That tongue is cruel," Mirevra said, her voice hardly above a whisper. This raised a brow and twisted lips from the barkeep. He braced his hand against his hip as he leaned in closer.

"What was that?" His voice was flat; he did not really care to find out. Oh, but he was going to, regardless.

"So, very cruel," Mirevra continued, her small fingers drawing an invisible pattern on the bar. The barkeep noticed Bagah had left his seat and strode toward him.

A Fallen Sword

"Aye, you there! Filthy Teruk! No one is allowed behind my bar, especially not the likes of—"

Mirevra struck, and the barkeep's eyes widened. Before his hand could leave his hip, his tongue was pulled from his mouth, and the tip cut clean off. He howled in pain, and when he moved to swing his fists at her, he found his limbs immobile. Bagah, that *filthy* little Teruk, held them pulled behind his back with one large hand. His face held no expression, and he appeared wholly disinterested in the altercation. Even as the barkeep squirmed with all his might to break free, Bagah did not feel challenged. Humans were weak, and this man particularly so.

Mirevra rolled the tip of the barkeep's tongue around her flattened palm. "Funny," she scoffed before flicking her eyes back to the keep. "It does not seem so cruel now that it has been removed." Quickly, almost invisibly, her hand covered his mouth. He wailed into her palm; tears filled his angry eyes. "Perhaps next time you will think before you speak, *Jedarei*," she instructed.

Bagah breathed heavily through his nostrils, a laugh of sorts. His only show of humor came when Mirevra spoke a jest in his native tongue. *Jedarei* was one of the first words he ever taught Mirevra, and only because he loved to call her one when she pissed him off. She preferred it over *bitch* any day. Though, she quite liked them both, for they suited her. The man shook under her hold, and Mirevra clicked her tongue three times as she moved her dagger side to side. "I would not do that; you might choke."

"Mir," Bagah said mildly. "Tell me you did not put it back in his mouth."

She smiled again, that vicious smirk that reminded Bagah of a feline ready to pounce. "Of course, I did, Bagah," she said. "I had no further use for it. And now, neither will he." After shoving the barkeep to the floor and leaving him to wobble about while spitting half his tongue into his trembling hands, Mirevra and Bagah grabbed three bottles of ale and a clear liquid housed in a nice-looking decanter. As they headed for the exit, the barkeep shouted at them, his screams almost impossible to comprehend.

"You Bith! I wih have yeh hea-th foh thith!"

Mirevra turned to see Bagah grinning widely. "Judging by its color, this ale will likely taste like piss," he said, shaking the bottle in question in rough circles.

The barkeep still hurled insults at them as they walked out of the tavern and into the cold, empty streets. Mirevra glanced over her shoulder at her friend. "I know you do not like questions, so I will not ask how you know what piss tastes like." As they walked toward the tree line, Mirevra heard the barkeep faintly in the distance, calling her a dreadful bitch over and over. She smiled.

Yes, it was a title that suited her just fine.

The Dame and The Cart

The air was cooler than on most summer nights in Estellian. A crisp breeze offered even more reprieve after the day's heat. There was no mark or even a trace of death on Mirevra's fingers as she surveyed them in the dim moonlight. The cart was just a few rows of trees away, covered by a tarp she and Bagah had sewn myriad foliage onto. The leaves did not match those of the woods, but Mirevra was not concerned. Beretina was a crossing village, one made for quick stops. Water pouches refilled, a flagon of ale, and a bite to eat, and visitors were on their way. If the tavern, which of all places should be teeming with passersby, was empty, the woods likely would be too. Distracted by her own nails and how stunningly clean they were for someone who had just slit one man's throat and sliced off another's tongue, Mirevra did not see a distant shadow lurking by their cart. Bagah never noticed such things since he usually stared at his feet as he walked. He would kick a small pebble, wondering if he had separated it from a family.

Did rocks feel? Would that pebble ever see its rock friends again? He walked, and he wondered.

When Mirevra finally did look up from her delicate fingers that one would never guess were those of a killer, the shadow was gone. She pulled sharply on the tarp to secure it before whistling at Bagah. "Do you want to sleep? Or shall we begin pulling tonight?" The half-Teruk shrugged, and Mirevra sent him a subtle nod in return. "The nearest town is Tarelste, only a few hours away. Once there, we shall steal a horse and make the rest of our travels much easier. We will return to the Ring by the week's end–."

The golden-eyed assassin's words ceased abruptly. Bagah immediately braced himself, flexed his muscular arms, and held his fists before him like two mighty boulders. Mirevra knew she was a second late and that it would cost her. *A second is often the difference between life and death, little Fox,* she heard the Veravant's cold whispers in her ear. She had no time to even mumble a curse before a wisp of dark mist surrounded her. Her eyes bled black, her nose filled with smoke, her mouth smothered by a thick fog. She could not breathe. *A Binding Spell.*

Confronted by an Arcanen, a person capable of wielding the magic their patron deities bestowed, Mirevra knew two things. One, she could not win by a trick of hand. Arcanens were quite wise; unfortunately, she was not. Two, Bagah was going to really fucking hate this Binding Spell. The bastard loathed closed-in spaces, and this spell felt like the entire force of the world was squeezing them into a corner. One in which they did not fit.

There was only one option, the worst of all the tactics Mirevra had ever employed. Yet, she knew there was no time to be picky. She closed her eyes against the spell, letting it sting her like a thousand wasps and waited. Usually, there would be a break in the magic. A small moment where it waned ever so slightly, though most people were too distracted by their own anguish to notice. Mirevra had been trained to sense it, and when she felt the break in the magic's wall, the tiny slot just big enough for a small snake to sliver through, she reached for it with all her will.

The second the binding receded from her tongue, she swallowed her pride with a large gulp and succumbed. She begged for mercy.

Her cries filled the night air; cold, hungry puffs of smoke exited her lips. She begged and begged while, in her deepest thoughts, she scowled. One moment of mercy, one more second earned back, and she would gouge out the eyes of the sorcerer who placed this spell on them. Bagah, keeling over as air dissipated around him, heard the other Fox's shrieks and a glimmer of hope flashed through his pain. Only once had Mirevra used this plan, a few years after Roman, the newest member of the Ring, had joined. The Veravant had placed Mirevra and Roman both in the fighting ring. Roman would have to best her or draw a tie to be a part of the guild. The hand-to-hand fight did not last long. Mirevra was a skilled fighter, the best in the league. Roman, not so much. He was strong, yes. He had size and weight on his side but was not quick, and his moves were all too predictable. Then, just as Mirevra was about to land the final blow, Roman changed shape. Where once stood a rather rotund man with rosy, red cheeks and a jovial demeanor, there was a bear, a harrowing, black-furred beast with sharp teeth and terrifying claws. The bear released a vicious snarl and swiped, and Mirevra gained a wound whose scar she still carried. She was not all out of luck, though. Three punishing pummels to the bear's side, a chunk of its ear sliced off by a dagger, and Roman had had enough. He slammed Mirevra to the ground and held her there. No matter how she writhed under his massive weight as the bear's saliva poured onto her face, she could not move.

It was then that Bagah learned the trained assassin's last resort maneuver. Mirevra cried out to the man-turned-bear to take pity on her. And Roman, gods love him, obliged. Almost instantaneously, he appeared in his plump form, apologizing profusely. Mirevra flashed that cat-like grin that alerts her prey to make peace with its gods, swung her feet, and swiped his legs out from beneath him. He fell on his back, and she straddled him, pushing the tip of her dagger to his chest. Roman yielded seconds later. After that defeat, Mirevra still convinced the group to let Roman join the Ring. For whatever reason, the Veravant had let him.

Bagah heard Mirevra's cries and felt the magic waver. If he were not in the throes of suffocating, he might have grinned. Because that single moment was enough. The pleas soon became a grunt, and then the clang of iron meeting iron and two women hissing at each other filled the air. Bagah gasped for breath even as the binding spell ebbed its way back into the hands of whoever cast it. He allowed himself a few short seconds of coughing, enough time to regain his composure and not reveal how terrified he had been of the spell's confinement. But as soon as he took a deep, solid inhale, his veins began to protrude from every inch of his body. Sickly black rivulets, as dark as ink, gorged beneath his skin. Teruk blood coursed through him, feeding him life, feeding his anger. Bagah knew that the two were often one and the same for him. "Do not give way to the rage," he heard Mirevra say distantly, but his ears were already so hot and the pounding in his temples too loud. He felt rage overtaking him. That tiny glass jar he kept well hidden, shoved into the deepest depths of his sorrowful heart, was overfilling, ready to burst. It was almost impossible to pull him back when it got like this. Yet, Mirevra tried. Over and over, she repeated the mantra. *"To the Ring we serve."* But the anger wanted her to stop talking, too. *"Do not give into the rage, Fox. To the Ring we serve."* Should she keep at it, he could smash her beneath the weight of his boulder-like fist. *"To the Ring you serve, Bagah! And... and I need you..."*

The pounding stopped. The burning sensation subsided. When Bagah looked at his friend and accomplice, she was straddling another form. A tall, toned woman with rich auburn hair lay beneath Mirevra, a sour look on her face. *A glorious face at that. Was this Radina in the flesh? The very goddess of beauty and temper?* His companion's waspish voice broke through his reverie. "Well, Bagah? Do you mean to stand there until this foul creature gains enough strength to cast another heinous spell upon us? Or will you help me tie her up?"

"Upon my word," the woman said with a frown. "Tie me up? Do I look like cattle to you?" Mirevra tilted her head, ready to answer in a way the beautiful woman would not enjoy when Bagah spoke instead.

"Nothing of the sort. Apologies on my friend's behalf," he said quickly as Mirevra shot him a nasty look. Bagah waited till his veins had retreated back into the safety of his fair, not-quite-yellow skin and dipped his head low. "You used Acarnanian magic against us. This rather wretched choice to tie you up only ensures that will not happen again."

The woman squared her eyes on him. Shimmering green like the forest trees after rain. Bagah's favorite color. Who was this lady? *"Teruk..."* she breathed the word as if she had not meant for it to escape her mouth. Or as if she were holding back other words she wanted to say. *"Are you him?"*

Bagah was confused. *Him?* Could a beautiful woman like this be looking for him, of all people? No. Instead of entertaining such a foolish thought, Bagah replied briskly. "Best not to worry who or what I am, Lady. You will not be able to remember my face by the sunrise in two days' time." *A shame indeed,* he thought. *For I will never forget a face like yours.*

Bagah felt utterly naked under the woman's gaze. Yes, he was very much used to being the conspicuous *thing* in every room he stepped foot in. His looks had always prompted hateful and confused stares, but this was different. *Hers* was different. She regarded him in a new way, one he had never experienced. Not during his time in the Ring or ever before...

"I am afraid my asinine friend is correct," Mirevra broke in, tearing Bagah from his trance again. The feisty Arcanen grimaced as the golden-eyed assassin's knees pushed into her arms to keep her pinned. Mirevra pulled a coarse rope from her satchel. "You see, you will have to travel with us for a few days, which is punishment enough; trust in that." She pointed back at Bagah with a mocking expression. "He snores. *Loudly.*" Bagah resented the comment but remained silent. It was not his fault he did not have a nose. "By the way, we will take you to meet our lovely friend, Tilly. You may not like her at first, though she is also an Arcanen. She specializes in all things memory befuddlement and general mayhem. One cup of tea with her, and you will forget all about this encounter."

The woman did not struggle as Mirevra tightly tied her wrists and began the same procedure on her ankles. Still, she directed a pointed question at her captor. "What makes you so important that I must forget your face?" Instead of answering, Mirevra grunted as she fastened the rope around the woman's legs. So, again, foolishly, Bagah responded.

"What is your name, then?"

The woman's shapely brows arched, and a smile pulled at her perfect, full lips. "You want my name, Teruk?" When Bagah said nothing, she continued in the same sardonic tone. "Whatever for?"

"I–I only wonder. You seem to have taken great interest in us. Can you blame me for doing the same?"

"I suppose not."

"So, what is it?"

"What is what?"

"Your name."

The woman cracked a broad smile and did not appear to mind as Mirevra dragged her to the rear of the cart. "I am afraid that even if I told you, you would not remember. I will tell you after you wake up."

Bagah immediately tensed, every muscle in his strapping body flexed as he longed to argue and further interrogate this woman. But she only released a laugh, one harsh and full of secrets. "For I also have a lovely friend."

Pain spread across the back of Bagah's skull. The fall to his knees was quick, yet looking at the mysterious woman felt like an eternity. He knew he was about to black out. He understood that someone had fired on him from behind and that he and Mirevra had been too preoccupied to take proper note of their surroundings. Even through these thoughts, he could not take his eyes off her. The way she tore through the rope with ease and with a flick of her wrist blasted Mirevra back. He watched as she approached him, cupped his cheek in her soft hand, and smiled. His eyelids flickered. He was close to that dreadful sleep he would most assuredly awaken from in a far worse predicament than this, but he heard her. Her mesmerizing voice, her cool, plummy accent as she whispered into his ear.

"They call me The Dame, Teruk," she said. Her voice warped as he faded into sleep. "The Dame of Disaster."

The Nelimen

The Mountain is inevitable.
A worker, a scholar, and a warrior will all eventually face one.
The worker will climb it.
The scholar will find their way around it.
The warrior will cleave it in two.
Become the warrior.
Sturdy as the earth beneath our heels.
Never to yield, never to kneel.
Break the rock.
Break the seal.
Never to yield, never to kneel.

One does not choose to become a Nelimen. The Nelimen choose you.
To decline is to choose death.
Do not break the code or suffer to become a Wolf.
They are exiled. They are alone.

The Nelimen

When Mirevra opened her eyes, she did not understand the light that poured into them. Her mind could not wrap around where she was, who she was with, or why she was lying flat on her back on a table. She turned her chin to find Bagah, but her neck whined and urged her to keep her head straight. *Where in Degolian was she?* The last she remembered, she had just sliced off one pitiful man's tongue and walked back to the cart with Bagah. Had they been attacked? Had she suffered some sudden ailment? Her eyes shot in every direction, taking in all they could. Two lanterns lit with white fire swung above her. A cleric's fire of Raenin. To the right, a large, arched wooden door. *Not at the Ring, then. A place unknown.* To the left, an armory wall. Only two blunted blades hung there and one decrepit shield. Still, if she could reach those blades, she might be safe. Before the Ring, Mirevra did not carry weapons; she found they weighed her down during her travels. The dagger and the short blade she now carried were a compromise at the Veravant's request. Which she did not really mind anymore, for how she loved to cut things.

When it came right down to it, Mirevra was all fists, legs, and feet; she would face a god with nothing but her bare knuckles, foolish as it was. But the Veravant had insisted she learn swordsmanship, convincing her that sharp things quelled foes faster; both tongue and sword. The blades she eyed on the wall were not sharp, but even if they could not pierce a body, Mirevra was strong. Bludgeoning was always an option. Now, only to find Bagah. She wiggled her fingers, lightly grazing her legs just above her knees. She was not under paralysis, which meant whoever or whatever had struck her had aimed for her neck. One last quick scan of the room, her ears perked for any voices, footsteps, or breathing, and mumbling an apology to her body, Mirevra threw herself from the table. Her neck hissed violently, but she ignored it and drank in the rest of the room. *A healer's quarter.* This much was obvious. Whoever had placed her here had relieved her of her weapons. But the two dull swords were quickly within her tightly clenched palms. Next to a roll of bandages and herbal gauze, miscellaneous tonics and ewers were strewn across the cabinets. Mirevra would have scratched her head if she had a free hand to do so. Why would someone knock her unconscious and then heal her? And in a room with weapons, albeit poor ones? What in the Degolian had happened on their way to that damned cart?

No time to search for any more answers. Mirevra approached the door, touching the dark wood lightly before gently placing her ear against it. She drew a large breath, closed her eyes, and listened. Nothing... Nothing... Nothing... *There.* Footsteps, about thirty feet away. Boots, worn leather, stone floors. Twenty feet away. Ten. Five. Mirevra drew back from the door, positioning herself so that when it opened, she could come out from behind it for a sneak attack, but the footsteps paused just outside the door. She did not move a muscle. She stopped her breathing. One blade was braced in front of her, guarding her chest and abdomen, the other at shoulder height, ready to descend on whichever poor soul dared to turn that knob. But the knob did not turn. Instead, a deep voice called out to her.

"I am sure you found the blades. I told Shiln not to leave them there, but she insisted." A deep sigh. "She said we must test you and see if you will try and fight. I assume you are right next to the door, ready to clobber me as soon as I walk in?"

Mirevra assessed the phantom voice. Male, thirties, *cocky*. She waited, unwilling to concede. She held her breath firmly, ready to strike. "Really, there is no need for a fight," said the thirty-something-year-old, cocky male voice. *There is always a need for a fight.* "We have your Teruk friend in the room next to yours. He is already up and eating. You took far longer than he to heal from a simple Binding Spell."

Binding Spell? So, Mirevra and Bagah had encountered a sorcerer, then? It was no wonder her memory was little more than a hazy vision. Tilly, another Fox and member of the Ring, was an Arcanen and oftentimes proved it by wiping the Ring's memories after a night of foul debauchery. Only after she and Mirevra became close did Tilly give the fighter a choice to keep her memories. Armed with the group's memories, Mirevra and Tilly collected interesting information on each of their Foxes, except for Bagah, who, even drunk, abstained from degeneracy, at least amongst the Ring. Mirevra had wondered if his abstinence was simply in his character or due to his Teruk blood. She often pondered if Bagah considered himself worthy enough of a good lay.

The assassin puffed her chest, still full of air, and twisted her lips into a snarl. To her, Arcanen powers, in most cases, were a weak way to shirk a proper fight. Had Tilly been there to counter the Binding Spell, Mirevra would have torn the limbs off the caster. She heard a dark chuckle. "You are still standing there," the voice said. "Like a statue. You are holding your breath, too, aren't you?" Startled, Mirevra almost released that air, but she held fast. "I will bet fifty silver you look wholly ridiculous right now. Please, you must let me see it." Before Mirevra could even think of her next move, the door blasted open, sending her back a few steps. But she instantly recovered and braced for a fight. She lunged toward the open door, masterfully flourishing both blades. A woman stood in the hallway. Her skin was pallid but radiant. Mirevra had never seen such an unblemished face. Her hair was long and straight, and inky black strands fell gracefully over her shoulders. Her eyes were angular, dark brown, and piercing. She bore an untroubled smile on her heart-shaped face, and her fingers gleamed with Arcanenian purple light. *This must be the sorceress.*

Mirevra did not wait a second longer; she charged.

The Arcanen user lifted her glowing violet palm. Her smile widened as her eyes narrowed in on her target. But Mirevra caught it, the slight bend of the woman's elbow, the way her eyes moved slightly beyond Mirevra's shoulder. Her magic was a feint. Zigzagging, just in case the sorceress did intend to blast her backward with another spell, Mirevra launched herself into the air. Mirevra saw the sorceress's eyes widen— shock becoming her—as she turned her body and brought the blunted blade down on the attacker behind her. Black hair, light stubble framing a sharp jaw, thick eyebrows. A man in his thirties smiled arrogantly as their blades kissed.

Here was the voice from behind the door. "Well, this certainly is one way for an introduction," he said, smirking. Mirevra only bared her teeth, her expression entirely primal. With a quick parry, their blades sang free. She struck again. He countered, and his brows shot up high. "Although, I do not seem to mind this way. Nice to meet you." With that, he pushed his weight against his blade and released, spinning twice to the left before swinging his blade to slash her leg. She stifled her yelp and buried it deep down beneath her anger. She knew he had not sliced too deep, but she wasted no time to wonder why. Impulsively, Mirevra tossed one of the blades far to the side, wielding her remaining one with both hands.

Now, this dark-voiced stranger was *fucked*. Even as her neck rebelled at her sudden movements, Mirevra moved with skilled agility. She brought her sword down over and over until, finally, she broke his defense. The tip of her sword sliced through his white, ruffled shirt. Blood stained his ribs. *Good, but not good enough.* He took a quick second to glance down and sighed as if annoyed, as if this fight meant nothing to him, as if it were a mere inconvenience. Flashing his eyes, their hue a deep gray storm rolling over the hills, he frowned. "What a shame. I really liked this shirt." He shrugged and attacked. She blocked, but their weight was equal as they pushed against each other. When she tried to parry, his blade caught hers and would not give way. She would have to step back to release this hold, but there was still a sorceress in the room, no doubt summoning the strength to cast another spell. Mirevra scanned the corridor with her peripheral vision. There was indeed another door, as the cocky male had said. But was Bagah actually in there? Eating, no less?

Mirevra took her chances and took two steps back. Her neck clawed at her; her muscles groaned. Her vision blurred, and her shoulders slumped. How was she this tired? The fight had barely begun. "I think the elixir is beginning to take its toll," said another voice, perhaps the Arcanen woman. But the tone sounded much too masculine to belong to the lithe sorceress. "Or maybe she is just terribly bad at fighting." Mirevra longed to turn and hiss at whoever had insulted her, but the world was folding. The stones beneath her felt like waves ushering her into the deep and unknown.

"Trust me. She is very skilled," said the dark voice, but where was the speaker? She could no longer see her opponent. She could no longer see anything. This did not feel like a Binding Spell; this was not Arcanen magic. She had been poisoned. *Gods damn it all to Degolian. To the Murks!*

"Well, at least now we know it works," said the deeper voice. "It is activated once the heart rate rises to a certain level. Judging by how quickly it takes her under, she exceeded that level and then some."

At war with her own eyelids, Mirevra fought against the poison. She cursed them, vowing that she would cut them off should they close. She heard the clang of iron hitting stone. She had dropped the sword, her only protection save for her bare fists. *Where was Bagah? What was happening?* "Do we take her to Briatriel? Or should we put her back in Shiln's quarters with the beast?" The voices bled together. The world distorted further, and she felt the cold stone under her cheek. She could not remember if she had fallen over.

"Let her rest. When she sees her friend is all right, she will be much more willing to play nice."

"Those damned Foxes. Such brutes, the whole lot of them."

"Aye." Then, Mirevra's eyelids proved they were just as skilled fighters as she, and slowly, they closed. She stared blankly into the dark, unsure if someone's arms had gathered her up or if her body was unraveling like thread spilling off a rolling spool. "But this one? She does not fight like a Fox. This one here strikes like a viper."

The Deal

~~~~~

This time, Mirevra woke up chained to a bed. And the owner of that dark voice beyond the door was watching. Mirevra grit her teeth and desperately shifted her shoulders from side to side. She wiggled her fingers about to see how much freedom they bore, and her eyes made a quick swipe of the room to see if there was anyone who might help her. But there was only him. He sat in a red chair shoved into a corner of the dimly lit space. There were no windows here and only one door. Black, likely made of iron, and hard to break down should she need to. He laughed, a rolling chuckle that filled the space like a torrential downpour breaking free from the clouds.

"Careful, Viper. Neeps' elixir is still well within your system. Struggle too much, and right back to sleep, you go." Mirevra ignored him. She had rarely found herself in a situation like this. But, if there was one thing that the Veravant had taught her, it was to be a fox. *Cunning. Deceitful.* Feigning utter defeat, she continued to squirm. While the male was distracted by her movements, her eyes located the lock. On the bed frame, to her left and hidden from his view. She wiggled her fingers again, and they released a small pin from the edge of her tunic.

It was nothing more than a hairpin to the untrained eye, but it was a key for those who knew how to use it. She had to act quickly; the male rose to his feet, his lips pressed into a hard line. He took a step toward her; three more steps, and he could see her left hand moving toward the lock.

"You know, I am actually quite upset with you. Do you see this?" The male pointed to the blood stain on his white shirt, whose sleeves billowed dramatically with his broad gestures. "I acquired this shirt—not easily, might I add—from a notorious pirate. It is one of my, if not *the*, favorite articles of clothing. And you ruined it without a second thought." Mirevra glared at him, her stare a warning. He shrugged and flashed her a mocking frown. "That is the dichotomy of Arcanen magic, I suppose. It can heal a wound, but it cannot heal the true damage," he lifted the shirt to show off his chest, which should have been marred with a shallow cut. Yet, there was nothing there but tan flesh that reminded Mirevra of the desert sands. Their cleric must have healed him. He took another step the moment Mirevra's fingers found the lock. She began to pick it quietly, allowing the cocky sort's rambling to cover the sound. "Unless you know of a way to get blood stains out?" Click. Click. *Click.* Mirevra wanted to smile when she felt the latch give way; instead, she schooled her face into neutrality and narrowed her gaze on the male.

"Has anyone ever told you that you speak too much?" Her question gained a pair of raised brows above his stormy gray eyes.

"Has anyone ever told you that you do not speak enough?" he countered. As he was about to take another step, Mirevra acted. *Little Foxes run.* She slipped out of the chains, lighter than she thought they would be, and gathered them in her hands. The man did not jump back; instead, he almost *let* her break free. And when she wrapped one of the chains around his throat and pulled his face close to hers so that the last thing he would see was the golden eyes of a killer, he smiled. *He fucking smiled.* "Truly, we must quit meeting like this, Viper."

The door burst open to reveal the sorceress from the corridor, and next to her... Bagah? Mirevra's mouth hung slightly ajar for a moment. There was her half-breed friend, a linen hand towel clenched in one palm and a greasy, half-eaten leg of meat in the other. "Mirevra?" His yellow eyes raced between her and her target.

"So, that is your name," the dark-voiced fellow commented, then flashed teeth in a broad smile. "It is so nice to meet you, Mirevra. I am Lars. Lars Dellary. And if you do not mind, my balls got a little twisted when you wrapped this around my throat, and I would dearly like to free them. Please, unhand me."

Mirevra did no such thing. Her golden stare locked on Bagah, and she tilted her head slightly. He returned half a nod, then took another generous bite from the meat. Lars Dellary's face was reddening; a few veins bulged on his brow. Mirevra smelled tobacco and vetiver. It reminded her of something, but now was not the time to try and place it. She released the man but raised her fists in front of her for protection. "If you wish to hold a guild's trial over the merchant and his belongings, I regret to tell you we are not interested," she said. Perhaps her latest victim was more important than she had assumed, so these nuisances were after her. Lars glanced at the sorceress and raised his upturned palms.

"Merchant? Belongings? Shiln, what is she talking about?" He focused back on Mirevra. "What are you talking about?" Mirevra, in turn, looked to Bagah, tempering her bewilderment.

"Where in the Murks are we, then? And what do you want?" Her eyes caught the dim light dancing off of Lars' ring. She did not know how she had missed it before. A signet, blue and gold. Her nostrils flared. "Nelimen?" No one could tell if she had hissed an insult or asked a question. But Shiln, the sorceress, answered.

"Yes. We are two of the Nelimen, and you two are from the Fox Ring. We do not care about the merchant, nor do we care about your cart full of junk. We only chained you to the bed so you would not try to slit one of our throats again." Her raspy voice grated, and Mirevra would not have been surprised to see smoke billow from the woman's mouth after her words.

"Then what?" She pinned her glare on the sorceress, examining Shiln's skin for any vestige of purple light. There was none. Good.

"We only know that our Head ordered us to collect the two of you and escort you safely to an agreed-upon location. It is part of the deal."

"The deal?" Mirevra almost spat, an incredulous smirk creeping up her face. Did they really think she would not kill every last one of them? Why should their Head's orders mean anything to her?

"Yes, the deal," the sorceress repeated. "Between our Head and the Veravant."

The Open Road

～∞～

The assassin shifted in her seat. The ride was long and far too bumpy. The wheels' wood spokes were worn thin, the coach's door almost fell clean off its hinges, and the roof hung lower than it ought to. Still, Mirevra sat in silence. This was likely a trap, but when Shiln spoke of the Veravant, Mirevra knew she had no choice but to ride along. If anything, she would accompany them to learn what else they knew about the Fox Ring. The Veravant's name was hardly ever mentioned outside of the Ring, so this alone meant these Nelimen knew more than they should. That was dangerous. Mirevra had to discover the extent of their knowledge. Did they know the location of the Ring's den? Did they know of the other members?

It did not make a lick of sense that the Veravant and his Fox Ring, mainly composed of unwanted criminals, would strike a deal at all. Especially with the obnoxious, self-proclaimed *heroes guild*. The Nelimen? She could not wrap her head around it.

Bagah sat beside her, seemingly untroubled. The Nelimen offered him slab after slab of roasted meats, so, by the looks of it, he was perfectly content. Had Mirevra not known the depth of Bagah's loyalty, she would have already given him a swift kick to his cock and one more to the head for being so easily bought. Seated across from them were the sorceress and the halfling —they called him Neeps—who had poisoned her. He had yet to apologize for it, which was a good thing. Mirevra would have lost any respect she may have held for him had he done so.

Neeps' skin was darker than hers, his hair a thick, wild black patch. His eyes were shifty, constantly bouncing from object to object, and such a dark brown that they appeared black as coal from a distance. And his accent, perhaps he was from further north. He spoke rapidly as if his tongue could not keep up with his thoughts and substituted the sound of a z for an s. Mostly, he mumbled to himself, always tinkering with vials he kept in a jingling knapsack. Shiln's eyes did not move from Mirevra. At one point, she thought to ask the Nelimen sorceress if there was a problem but resolved to stay quiet. Lars and the tall, auburn-haired woman she had tied up near the cart led the horses.

Heral, they had called her. Or was it Hecta? Helen? Maybe Harlowe? Mirevra could not remember and did not care enough to ask. Finally, Shiln broke the silence. "Your eyes," she said as her brows pushed toward the lean bridge of her nose. "I have not seen their color in quite some time. Tell me, where do you hail from?" Mirevra almost laughed but kept her expression void. The sorceress studied her further, raking her curious eyes over Mirevra's hair and skin. "The Northeast, perhaps? Somewhere near Calabena?" Again, she remained silent. The sorceress might know about the Veravant, but that knowledge was already too much. Mirevra would not disclose one fact about herself to these... these... *mosquitos*. Shiln hummed, leaned against the rough wood seat, and drummed her fingers across her thigh. "I must say, I *do* wonder how the Fox Ring came about a Teruk–"

"Half-Teruk," Bagah interjected through a mouth filled with meat. Shiln tilted her head in resignation.

"Of course. My apologies. *Half*-Teruk."

This seemed to appease Bagah, and with a single grunt and nod, he returned to carelessly munching away. But Shiln pressed on. "Even so, it is hard to imagine a human wanting to ever breed with a Teruk. So, who was it then? Your mother or your father?" Mirevra had heard enough. She spread her legs wider and rested her elbows on her knees as she leaned forward.

"If you wish to keep your tongue, I suggest you stop moving it," she cautioned, and a chill ran down her arms. It had been one day since she had cut something, and she was feeling the itch to return to that pleasure. Shiln only smiled at Mirevra's warning.

"So, she *does* speak."

Mirevra slowly moved her head from side to side, like a predator sizing up its prey. She leaned back but kept her legs spread. "Only when necessary," she answered. "Unlike some."

This elicited a laugh from the sorceress, who quickly pulled out Mirevra's dagger and twisted it between her hands. Mirevra glowered at the sight of her stolen weapon. The itch to cut begged harder to be scratched. Shiln flipped the blade flawlessly, weaving it through her fingers with ease.

"If you cannot tell me where you are from, then perhaps you could tell me why a beautiful woman like yourself would deign to join a guild dedicated to such crass assignments? Surely you thought of other leagues to join before the Fox Ring?" When Mirevra only snorted, Shiln continued her line of questioning. "Unless you were rejected by others?"

"I only tried for one guild and was sworn in two months later," Mirevra snapped. She pulled her lips into a firm line, but pride gleamed in her stare. Two months to join any guild was an amazing feat, as most members needed at least six, if not more, to prove their worth.

"I would say I am impressed," Shiln's raspy voice mused. "If I thought stealing from old merchants and scrawny barkeeps was difficult." She took a deep, derisive breath and shrugged her shoulders. "I am afraid that a life of petty crime is not something to be marveled at. And two months actually seems excessive…"

"And parading around like Estellian's saviors because you defeated one lousy leviathan grants you bragging rights?" Mirevra quipped, allowing her contemptuous smirk to show itself. The sorceress stopped spinning the blade. Her eyes seemed to grow thinner as they fixed themselves on Mirevra like a hawk on a mouse.

"The Nelimen are *not* saviors. We are warriors."

Bagah and Mirevra scoffed in unison. Neeps finally looked up.

"Sturdy as the earth," he added before peering back at his glass bottles.

"Warriors who require aid from lowly criminals specializing in petty crime, apparently. Your leader must either be desperate or know you cannot do his charge alone," Mirevra said, staring at the Arcanen while not losing focus on her dagger.

"*Her charge,*" Shiln corrected. "And we do not ask our Head why she chooses what she does. We simply honor it." Mirevra blew a raspberry and shook her head. "You laugh at honor?" The sorceress asked. "I suppose I should not be shocked. You are Foxes, after all. Honor must be a foreign concept." She rocked forward and grinned. "The Nelimen have never had *a Wolf* in our den. Can the Ring say the same?"

Bagah stopped eating. Mirevra's brow arched, and the two women glared at each other for some time before the coach became an arena.

Mirevra dove from her seat, her knee driving into Shiln's stomach. The sorceress groaned. Mirevra then twisted the blade from Shiln's hand, which was beginning to glow violet, and gripped its hilt firmly. Before Shiln could cast any spells, Mirevra lightly pressed the blade against the sorceress' fair throat.

"What did I say about that tongue, witch?"

Neeps jerked up to his feet and grabbed his satchel. Bagah sent the halfling a look that told Neeps this was not their fight. Neeps gulped, nodded, and sat down.

"I did not take you as the overly sensitive type, Fox," Shiln almost laughed. "I see now that I was wrong." The coach ground to a halt, throwing Mirevra off her balance enough for the sorceress to bring her hand forward and touch her opponent. Mirevra felt as if a thousand bolts of lightning were piercing her skin. She threw herself back, grabbing her own throat as tiny, malevolent prongs repeatedly stabbed her body.

"What are you doing?" Bagah cried out. "Stop it now!"

As if opening an invisible door, Shiln turned her outstretched hand, and Mirevra grunted louder in pain. "It is merely a Spell of Pricking, nothing special," Shiln remarked. "Quite simple, actually. Although I have no doubt that those on the receiving end would call it anything but."

"I said stop," Bagah implored, watching his friend flop like a fish on dry land.

"She threatened my life, Teruk. I am only returning the favor."

Bagah's veins began their restless pulsing. "Stop," he ground out between closed teeth. But the sorceress did not.

Mirevra's eyes strained wide, and her tongue hung from her mouth. Neeps curled himself into a corner, hugging his satchel. Bagah knew he could safely assume the halfling was not a fighter, but whatever rattled about within that bag could surely cause damage. Then he felt it, the discomfort oscillating through his limbs. He knew it was the elixir Neeps had forced down their throats. His heart pounded faster as his anger grew and, with it, the agony of the serum. He looked down at Mirevra and saw tears streaking her cheeks. Under the Spell of Pricking, there was no telling what strain her heart was enduring. *Double damage.*

"Shiln...," Neeps muttered quietly. The halfling's eyes grew wide as he watched Bagah try to rise fully upright in the coach. As he crouched against the ceiling, a massive threat of black veins and eyes cold as stone, the doors swung open. Lars on one side, Heral on the other.

"What is the meaning of this?" The auburn-haired woman who made Bagah's throat tighten when she spoke demanded. Lars was already pulling Neeps from the gig.

"Alright, ladies, that is enough," Lars said. He pulled on Shiln's arm. "Release her. We are almost at the inn."

Bagah tried to steady the lump swelling in his throat and swallow the heat and fury. But Mirevra was still under the spell, and the elixir kept stinging his skin. He could not hear his friend's voice; he did not feel the calming wave that flowed in precisely when he needed it. The glass jar was breaking.

"Bagah," another voice cut in. Not Mirevra's. His yellow eyes flitted to her. Heral. The goddess divine. She did not say another word but bore her dark green stare right into him. He stared back with the same intensity as his veins continued to fight to break free from their fleshly prison. He could have sworn he saw a twinkle in those green eyes, not as eyes glimmer when they catch the light, but something else entirely. It was as if her pupils had become two suns, and roaring fires encroached upon every inch of green. When she blinked, the fires disappeared. Bagah was filled with confusion. So much so that he hardly realized that his bafflement had instantaneously replaced his anger. Drawing in a shaky breath, he rolled his shoulders and heard Mirevra gasp.

He dropped to his haunches and cradled her body. She had been released from the spell, and Lars had pulled Shiln from the carriage, and the sorceress was now lying flat on the rocky road cursing her dark haired comrade.

"There was no other way to stop you, Shiln. You could have killed her."

"Good. She is a Fox! She is a RAT!"

Bagah looked at Heral, but she was no longer standing there. She was gone. Neeps peered into the coach with fervent interest. "Where is your cleric?" Bagah demanded of the halfling. "Your sorceress did a number on her; she will need healing."

Neeps' dark eyes widened. "The Nelimen do not have a cleric. Well, I suppose not technically..."

"Do not be a fool, halfling. I saw the white cleric's fire when I awoke in your den." The half-Teruk stated firmly.

Neeps raised a stiff finger.

"Indeed, it was a cleric's fire, but not of a cleric."

Bagah had no patience left for riddles. He showed his teeth and pulled in his chin.

"If not a cleric, then who?"

"A sorceress." Shiln was back on her feet, dusting off her rear. "I am trained in Arcanen sorcery but was raised near a temple of Sun Criers." Bagah searched his mind for any memory of Sun Criers but came up short. "When they saw me, an orphan of no station or worth, they took me in. I learned their ways and lived by them, too. I am Arcanen favored, but I also dabble in healing and blessings."

Bagah scratched his head. "I do not know much of Arcanen; this much is true. But is it not known that only one power is granted to each vessel? How then can you both spell cast and heal?"

Shiln shrugged.

"She likes to say she lives by the Sun Criers way, but how many Gentle Touch serving healers do you find casting damage spells on people?" Lars broke in, a dashing smile crossing his face. "Go ahead and mend her, Shiln. We do not want the Viper waking up too angry. We do not want either of them too angry." With those words, he sent Bagah a look that said, *'I know what you are capable of.'*

Lars patted Shiln on the shoulder. "I cannot afford to lose another good shirt."

The Veravant

It took almost an entire day's travel to reach the inn nestled in the small town of Reavish. Mirevra switched positions with Heral and sat in the driver's box with Lars. He spoke a lot of trivial matters and made japes that only he found humorous, but he did not press or ask her personal questions. So, she did not try to attack him. At the very least, that was all they could hope for on their journey. When they reached Reavish, one by one, they dislodged themselves from the coach. "We will need to use discretion," said Neeps, recklessly slinging his jingling pack over his shoulder. "No one can know we are here."

Mirevra grumbled a curse under her breath. "You will find that my colleague and I do not exude the bravado the Nelimen so often do," she said. "Discretion is a key characteristic of the Ring."

Shiln shot Mirevra an annoyed look but only moved past, knocking Mirevra's shoulder as she sauntered toward the inn. Mirevra smiled, living for how her words could prompt a rise from the sorceress while trying to ignore that her foe could easily do the same to her. She knew she would need to work on that, but that was another problem for another day. What she did know was that she would definitely not show a hint of agitation in front of the Veravant if he *were* actually here. She let the Nelimen walk ahead and grabbed Bagah's arm before he followed suit. They spoke no words. She only dipped her brow towards him, golden eyes simmering. He squinted, then nudged his chin upwards. She then leaned her head ever so carefully to one side. His thick brows lifted high, but he nodded.

If it is a trap, give way.

Mirevra turned to go to the inn, and Bagah bit his tongue, chewing on the silent command. *If it is a trap, give way. Give way to the rage.*

Once inside the inn, a small, nothing-to-boast-of three-story structure missing dozens of its wooden shingles, Lars did all the talking. He spoke briefly with the innkeeper, making the old woman dressed in a wooly frock laugh heartily. He spun to face the group. "Perrie will take you to the third story, where our leaders await. I have been instructed to stand guard outside with one other. Will it be you, Heral?" Then, he scanned the rest of his league. "Shiln? Neeps?"

They all looked at each other and waited for the first to speak up. When no one did, Lars threw up his hands. "Oh, please. You all could not possibly leave me lonely out here! All by myself? Think of all the trouble I will get in. I am sure we passed a brothel along the way…"

"I will stay out here with you," Shiln said flatly. "Only because I do not wish to be in the same room as those *leeches* when I do not have to be." Mirevra was grateful for the rejection; she felt the same way about being near Shiln. She directed another look at Bagah, and the pair of Foxes followed Heral and Neeps up two spiral staircases. Mirevra readied herself to strike the moment Heral opened the small wood door. She steadied her breathing and felt her cheeks burn with heat. Two Nelimen leading them upstairs, two others standing guard below? It was a trap. It had to be.

"There is my *little Fox.*" His voice was as smooth as honey, as lethal as venom. His accent curved and moved like water. Mirevra's shoulders slumped a bit as she realized she and Bagah had not, in fact, been led to their deaths, but her heart continued to pound hard against her ribs just the same. The Veravant sat at one end of a long, rectangular table. As always, he looked straight at her when she entered a room. His spectacular green tunic was tied up the front to the base of his throat, decorated with intricate gold designs; even the sleeves were edged with golden leaves. His long red hair fell over his shoulders, and two gold branches twisted around his head into a small crown. His fingers tapped against the arm of his chair, and he smirked. "I have been waiting for you." At once, Mirevra and Bagah dropped to one knee and lowered their heads. They waited for him to give permission to rise, and when he did, Mirevra walked to the chair next to the Veravant and sat down. She had not even glanced at the Head of the Nelimen. She needed answers from her leader first.

"Why this?" Her voice was strained. "Why them?"

The Veravant raised his large, fair-skinned hand. He is a Fox, she thought. Cunning and light and death on the wind.

"I know it was a rather unruly method of bringing you here, but when Briatriel wrote to me, I had already sent you and the half-breed to Beretina. When she told me her Nelimen were nearby, I had them bring you here. Were they nice to you, little Fox?" Mirevra scowled, and the Veravant laughed. His laughter, as polished as his speech, was like velvet against her skin. He placed his hand near hers, and her heart roared faster and faster until she felt a pang. *The leftovers of that fucking elixir.* She would kill the halfling and the sorceress, too. "Were you nice to them?" The Veravant asked her, with that goddamned knee-buckling smile on his face. Mirevra cut him a sharp glance in answer. "I did not think you would be," he answered in a sing-song tone. "That's my girl," he whispered.

Kaven Hiring

The Head, Briatriel, cleared her throat from the other end of the table. "Heral, Neeps, sit. Join us, for we have much to discuss." When Mirevra finally did turn to observe the Nelimen's Head, she was met with wild raven curls, two rosy plump cheeks and dark crimson stained lips. Briatriel boasted very large breasts and a calming and humble demeanor. Not what Mirevra had expected in the least.

The two Nelimen sat at the table; Bagah stood next to the door and looked down at his boots. Mirevra wanted to ask him to sit too but knew it would be useless; Bagah preferred a degree of separation from the Veravant and vice versa. The Veravant began. "I am sure you are puzzled as to why your Head and I have brought you all together, exposing your identities and our own faces. But I am afraid this is a dire situation we have on our hands. As much as we might seek to remain separate, the time has come to unite." He moved his hand away from Mirevra's, and she withdrew hers from the table.

"The Veravant is right. We face an extreme threat, and most guilds are pulling together to come and stop it. Not all can be trusted, but the Veravant and I once had a solid and true friendship, and I am sure he wants what I do," Briatriel said.

"How extreme?" Neeps asked, his eyes ever racing.

"The end of Estellian. The end of the world," Briatriel answered matter-of-factly.

Mirevra's eyes darted to the Veravant for confirmation. His smile had disappeared. The slight downward curve of his lips told her what the Head said was true. No one from either guild dared to speak. Briatriel resumed. "As you can see, this is no small problem. The Veravant and I agree. Neither of us wishes to die. So, here you are. Or at least, here are some of you. The others in our guilds have been informed and are on their way. Some will arrive as early as tomorrow morning. Be prepared to get...*cozy* with one another."

Heral scanned the table; her gaze lingered on Mirevra and returned to Briatriel. She folded her arms over her chest. "What are we dealing with here? A mad king? The High Crown's army?"

The Veravant clicked his tongue before responding. "I am afraid it is worse. Estellian faces a lich."

For the first time in a very long time, fear coursed through Mirevra's body. She could almost feel it rattle the others in the same way. Everyone's face had gone pale. Even Neeps' was drained of color.

"If what you say is true," Neeps chimed in hesitantly. "Then there is nothing we can do. Not even the guilds—not even us."

"He is right," said Heral. "A lich cannot be defeated. Even I do not possess enough power to..."

"Do you take your leaders as fools?" The Veravant cut in. "Do you think we summoned you to tell you we have no plan?"

Heral fell silent. Neeps leaned in. "What *is* the plan?" he asked.

The Veravant slowly pushed back his chair, and its legs ground harshly against the floor, sending a hideous screech through the silent room. He placed his hands behind his back and tilted his chin up. Mirevra knew he often did this to ensure everyone knew he was looking down on them.

"Maji," he answered a bit too coyly. Mirevra's brows shot up. *Maji?!* What did Maji, God of the Fluent, have to do with this? Studying his audience's confused faces, the Veravant spoke again. "It is as if I can read your minds," he sighed. "What could Maji, The Fluent, the god of all genders and languages, possibly offer to fight against a lich?" Mirevra swallowed her embarrassment. This was not the first time the Veravant saw right through her, and it would likely not be the last.

"The truth is, we are not entirely sure," the Veravant conceded. "But there have always murmurs from city to city, and from coast to coast, about the gods and their knowledge. If any god were to know what humans were up to and if any god were to know all the ancient tales, it seems only natural it would be the one who can understand us all."

Mirevra thought back to her studies of the gods. Maji, a deity subscribing to no gender, was always depicted in paintings surrounded by humans. They were known as an accepting, loving god who, above all else, offered two things to the humans who served them: stories and translations. "In Mercinnho, the Tajeh lives in the rectory of The Maji," the Veravant continued and Mirevra inclined her head. The Tajeh was Maji's most dedicated follower. They held all the stories the Maji collected, so the tale goes. "You will go there and ask what they know. You see, rumors of a glorious weapon abound in Estellian. Some call it a holy blade; others, a fallen sword. Regardless, it is said to be strong enough to slice through a god, mighty enough to kill a lich." The Veravant straightened his shoulders, removed his hands from behind his back, and rested one on the viridian hilt of his own blade. Mirevra understood at a stroke.

"Gerreland," she breathed quietly. But the table somehow still heard her.

"Gerreland Nerth?" Neeps inquired. "The almighty blacksmith?"

"Indeed," answered the Veravant, stroking the hilt. "It is said this weapon was forged eons ago by Gerreland Nerth and buried with him in death."

"Surely, we would have heard of such an object," Neeps interjected, his mouth twisting in quick thought. "Gerreland forged the most outstanding weaponry and armor that has ever existed. Estellian has scourged the lands to find all his pieces. If there *were* a blade strong enough to bring harm upon a god, the world as we know it would have been scrambling to find it. King Kallias would have–" Neeps grabbed his throat and choked. His eyes turned a deep red; sweat crested his brow.

"I do not take well to being interrupted," the Veravant scolded, his eyes locked on the halfling. Briatriel's nostrils flared, and she slammed her hands against the table.

"Enough! Release your hold on him now."

The Veravant smiled, cocked his head to the side, and allowed a moment longer of suffering before Neeps gasped for a full breath and nearly fell out of his chair.

"May I finish?" Briatriel looked at the Veravant with a sorrow Mirevra could not place. When she nodded, the Veravant grinned. "Thank you."

The Veravant paced the small room, his hands again placed neatly behind his back. "Just as many guilds have remained hidden for centuries, so can many secrets. Gerreland knew this sword was too precious and dangerous to be in the hands of just *anyone*. Only his apprentice would have known of the weapon, and only his apprentice…" He lifted his chin to the table, a sage teacher amongst his slow students, awaiting an answer.

"Would have known where he was buried," Mirevra answered. Her cheeks flushed when he sent her that nod of approval. Deep in his brown eyes, she saw a look of pride. *His favorite student, his little Fox.*

"And we know who his apprentice at the time was, do we not halfling?" The Veravant turned sharply on his heel to face Neeps, who still sat panting. Neeps nodded quickly.

"Yes," he acknowledged hastily.

The Veravant eyed him rigidly. Neeps perked up as he realized the Veravant's question warranted a complete answer. "The Tejah of Maji, of course."

"Precisely," the Veravant concurred, the word slowly rolling off his tongue. "The Tejah of Maji served as Gerreland Nerth's apprentice until his enigmatic death. Of course, it will not be the same Tajeh you will visit, but the current one. Each Tajeh holds all the stories passed from line to line in their archives. They hold the truth of these rumors in their hands. So we must pray to Rashawe that the Tajeh holds it still. For without that sword, Estellian is lost," he said, looking to Mirevra. "Work together to find it, or the world will become ash."

The Little Fox

After ensuring Bagah had secured a room and faced no trouble from the innkeeper, Mirevra entered another chamber. There was nothing eloquent in the small room with pale green walls and a bed big enough for two. Nothing save for the Ring leader. The Veravant stood beside the bed with that half-smile on his face as he watched her move toward him. "I am sorry I had to put you through the misery of suffering their company, little Fox," he said softly. "But rest assured, I am prepared to make it up to you." He did not wait for her answer but unbuckled the leather belt that held his weapons, including the viridian blade forged by Gerreland Nerth. He meticulously placed this blade in its case, a black onyx box lined in green velvet and warded by his most impenetrable spell. Mirevra had never asked him how he had acquired so valuable a blade; she likely never would. She knew the Veravant was a man of many stories that should not concern her.

"Well?" His brown eyes swept over the assassin's form with feral delight. At once, Mirevra began to strip off her fighting leathers and take down her hair. She did not mind the smell of her sweat or the dirt on her arms. The Veravant also did not care about such things. He proved as much with the noise he made when the last article of her ensemble dropped to the floor, and she stood naked before him. He drank her in quickly, closing the distance between them with a few long strides. "Oh, my golden-eyed little Fox. You do serve me so well," he purred into her ear.

Chills covered Mirevra's body, and the hairs on her arms stiffened as he brought his lips to her neck. He peppered rough kisses against her skin as she undressed him with a practiced expertise that came naturally to her. His body was very lean but surprisingly muscular. His skin was fair, *illuminated,* and blessed by Radina. In return, Mirevra went for his neck once it was bare, careful to move his hair away, pushing the red strands to fall behind his shoulders. His hands cupped her ass, then pulled upwards, and her body groaned in anticipation. His teeth tugged on her earlobe, one hand smacked her ass roughly, and then the two were on the bed. Mirevra assumed her usual position on top. She did not have to tell the Veravant why she never lay beneath him. She would never lie beneath a man. She would feel too vulnerable, too out of control. But the Veravant knew just as well as she did that it did not matter what position she claimed; he was always in control. *Always.*

Mirevra kissed his cheek, his chin, every part of his face she could devour except his lips. There was an unspoken rule of their encounters: they would never kiss upon the mouth. *'Too intimate, little Fox,'* the Veravant would say. *'I do not want to confuse your mind.'* With one hand pressed firmly against his chest, she flipped her long, sandy blonde hair to one side of her face. Her stare roved over his eyes, nose, neck, and torso. He brought his hand forward and clutched her chin harshly. His eyes narrowed.

"You are mine, little Fox. You belong to me." And then, he slid his cock into her so quickly, so deeply, that she gasped. It always started like this, the illicit encounters with the Veravant. First, there was a shock of pain. But then, if she concentrated, a wave of pleasure would come soon enough. He was buried in her now but held her face firmly and did not let her move. "Pledge yourself to me again," he instructed.

Mirevra swallowed, feeling his cock pulse within her warmth with restrained desire. "I am yours. I pledge myself to you," she vowed. He pulled himself out from her ever so slightly, then thrust back in. She kept her mouth closed and breathed heavily.

"In whatever way I want you, I can have you. Swear it. Your body and your soul, all *mine*," the Veravant commanded. Mirevra had promised this hundreds of times, often wondering if her services in and out of the bedchamber would ever be enough to persuade him. She responded as he expected.

"I am yours. In this way. In every way."

Another thrust, then complete stillness. It was not a tease; it was torture. "I own you, forever," the Veravant asserted, his guileful brown eyes staring hard into hers.

This was the part she hated most. *Forever.* That word had stained her heart like black ink spilled onto a canvas for as long as she could remember. Each time she heard it, she was taken back to a different time, place, and version of herself.

She understood the Veravant. She knew why he could ask her for things she could not ask of him. He was one of the most powerful warlocks in Estellian, the chosen leader of the Ring. To become genuinely intimate was too risky. It could jeopardize her position in the guild and make her a target of clever enemies. So, it was only sex; it was always only ever sex. But *forever,* no matter the context, made

Mirevra's chest deflate. It meant too much. The Veravant squeezed her chin harder, and she stopped herself from flinching. He raised a brow. "Forever?" he asked. She knew it was not a question.

Her head bowed, Mirevra muttered beneath her breath, speaking barely over a whisper. "Forever."

He unleashed himself, her reward for her answering correctly, and her body bounced against his lower waist and thighs as he plunged stroke after deep stroke into her. Her chin remained grasped in his hand, but she did not gasp when he clutched it harder or when his nails dug into her cheek. She let him do whatever he needed, whatever he wanted, without complaint. She was his. To do with as he pleased...forever.

The inn's other occupants could likely hear the slaps of their flesh and the wood headboard pounding into the wall. Still, their sleep would not be interrupted by any moans of pleasure from her. Long ago, the Veravant had expressed that Mirevra needed to stay her emotions, remain in control, and never let pain or pleasure best her. While his own face contorted, twisted, and stretched, Mirevra's remained blank. Her golden eyes fluttered, but that was the extent of her reaction to his thrusts. She could tell this pleased the Veravant; his body tightened beneath her, and she felt his cock grow taut. Then, with one final push inside her, he released his hand from her chin.

Her chin ached, but the slight smirk on the Veravant's face was enough to quell any pain. He placed his hands behind his head and raked his eyes across her breasts. With a deep inhale, his lips moved to speak, and she thought for one second that he might compliment her.

"Your room is downstairs. There is only a small cot, but I know you would much prefer it to sharing a room with one of those *Nelimen*," he said. His words fell heavy in her ears. Of course, she knew she would never sleep next to him. He would never permit such a thing, but just once, she wished he would allow her to stay a little longer after the deed was done. Not even to speak...just to be near.

A foolish, ignorant thought. As Mirevra dressed, her mind became cluttered with other, more unnerving thoughts. Why had Briatriel looked at the Veravant with that sorrowful expression during the meeting? What solid and true friendship had they ever shared? Did the Veravant even keep friends at his side, and if so, what did he consider Mirevra?

"Goodnight, little Fox," he said, and did not wait for her to leave before blowing out the candle near his bed and plunging the room into nothingness. Darkness flooded Mirevra's mind, as well. And she knew that no amount of light could pierce it.

The Mission Begins

As Briatriel had said, more members of the guilds appeared the following day. From the Ring, Roman and Beldon, who had traveled three endless days to arrive at the inn. They asked for beds before Mirevra could greet them and quickly fell asleep. It was probably best; they would be on the road toward the Tajeh and without beds for a time. Another member of the Nelimen entered the inn as Mirevra was finishing her midday meal. Jardin, they called him. He did not speak much; his mouth stayed nervously clamped shut. He was completely bald, boasted a thick, burly beard, and his eyes of steely blue matched his ring. He was handsome, Mirevra thought. Those blue eyes against his rich, dark skin made him stand out from the crowd. But *he was a Nelimen*, she reminded herself. Jardin did not introduce himself to her, but after speaking with his Head, he sent Mirevra and Bagah one head tilt as a greeting. It was enough.

The sky was clear, and the sun shone bright as they loaded the coach. Neeps had procured potato sacks from the inn and stuffed them full of apples, dried meats, and seeds. It was determined that Shiln, Neeps, and Heral would travel inside the coach, and Jardin would ride the tailboard. Mirevra, Beldon, and Roman were mounted; Bagah would walk. "Where is Tilly?" Mirevra asked Beldon. He first settled on his horse, patted its neck with authoritative confidence, and then turned his bright blue gaze on Mirevra.

"The Veravant had her remain at the den. The Ring will need some form of protection there." Absently, Mirevra bobbed her head, wishing Tilly were part of the mission; her Aracen powers could have come in handy. Mirevra would have felt better if someone who could counter Shiln's nasty spells traveled with them.

"What, am I not enough for you anymore, Mirevra?" Beldon's voice was crisp as the morning air. With his commanding demeanor, shining hair, and speckled ginger beard, he could easily be mistaken as a King's Guard or even a knight. In truth, the cleric was a foul, cursing scoundrel. Which was what Mirevra loved him best for. Beldon had joined the Ring before her; the two were the longest-surviving members. She considered Beldon a proper friend, as did all her fellow members of the Ring.

"You are far too much for me," Mirevra corrected. "This much, you know."

"Aye," he agreed with a wink. "I would not worry; I am sure once we find this miraculous weapon, Tilly will be on hand when we deliver it back to the Veravant." Mirevra's eyes raked over his face like sharp fangs. Beldon winced. "Oh, right. The Nelimen do not know we will deliver the weapon to the Veravant." He laughed. "I did not mean to say that part aloud."

She quickly surveyed the others. Still loading the coach, none of the Nelimen appeared to have heard Beldon. Lars sat on the driver's box, munching away on an apple. He hopped off and headed behind the inn, declaring that he had to take a piss. She rolled her eyes. How that was anyone else's business, she did not know. She did not understand these kinds of people at all.

Beldon was a skillful cleric but an absolute buffoon in almost every other way. The Veravant had given the Ring careful, *secret* instructions that morning. '*Work with the Nelimen until you retrieve the sword, but leave as soon as it is within your grasp. Say nothing and go. Bring it to me. If they try to stop you, turn them to bone and dust.*'

"Do you think it is real? The sword, I mean." Beldon asked as Mirevra finished her examination. She turned back to him.

"I do not know," she said plainly. "But it does not matter. If a lich is coming for Estellian, we are dead whether or not we look for it. At least this way, we may stand a chance."

Beldon nodded and gave his mount a final pat. "I suppose," he mused. "And if there is one thing I could teach you, it is to take the chance. *Always* take the chance."

His face shielded by a gilded fox mask, the Veravant stepped out of the inn. *Well, so much for discretion,* Mirevra thought. He looked like a goddamned deity walking across the cobbled courtyard, and when he turned to face her, she steadied her mare and took in a pained breath. Though she could not see his eyes behind that mask from this distance, she knew they were trained on her. They were always on her. He practically glided in her direction.

"Oh, Mir. Tell me it is not so! The two of you are not still—" Beldon muttered, but Mirevra shushed him harshly. When the Veravant reached them, he rested one hand on Mirevra's leg.

"I leave leadership to your stead, little Fox," he said, handing her a small ametrine. The Messaging Gem. She gripped it firmly and stowed it in a small, removable pocket in her leather tabard. The Veravant's hand slowly raised to brush her cheek. "It is for whatever information you collect," he said. "And if—*when*—you find the sword. Between us, the gem can be used five times." His hand then traced the thick braid draped down her back. "Choose wisely." Mirevra had no idea where or when the Veravant had acquired this artifact. Able to send and receive missives across any distance, Messaging Gems were almost as rare as Gerelland blades. After its magic was depleted, the ametrine would turn gray and resemble an ordinary rock. But for now, it pressed against her chest, almost burning through her garb.

Mirevra nodded, and the Veravant smiled. "Do not disappoint me," he said, then strode to Daemon, his black stallion. He gracefully threw himself into his saddle as he did most things. He did not give her another look before kicking the horse's ribs and riding away. The Veravant was gone, but his voice stayed with her. *'Do not disappoint me.'*

Loud shouts from Neeps and Shiln snapped Mirevra from her thoughts. She grimaced. The two were squabbling over how many vials Neeps could bring on the journey, and their voices grated against Mirevra's ears. She would not disappoint the Veravant. She *would* retrieve the sword for him, and she would kill anyone who got in her way.

The Storm of Ice and Fury

※

Three days passed, and the Fox Ring and the Nelimen had made it to Caxaven without stabbing each other to death in their sleep. It was a small victory, particularly on the part of the criminals. That was not to say that Mirevra had not imagined piercing a dagger through the throats of each of the *heroes*, as they ate their rations, slept, or sat silently. She wanted them dead, especially Shiln, who had reluctantly returned Mirevra's dagger and blade. Shiln was no mere annoyance; she was a threat. Mirevra noticed how often the sorceress's eyes followed and studied her. As a result, Mirevra slept restlessly, one eye always willing her to wake in case the Nelimen tried to snuff her out. The lousy sleep made her crabby during the day, sending her into a foul mood at nightfall. Fortunately, the fellow members of the Ring tolerated her bitchy attitude, as they were used to it. What surprised her was how well Lars handled it, *curse her luck*.

Mirevra had noticed that the obnoxious bastard's gaze also trailed her. And from what she could ascertain, Lars' eyes held a far different message than Shiln's. Mirevra detested how he would observe her with a gleam in his gray stare that turned them the color of blades at night. It was a different look than she was used to receiving from men. Lars' stare was not lustful; it was amused. When she grunted, rolled her eyes, or scowled at Shiln, she caught his sideways smile that was never far away. He sent her one now as she braced her elbows on her knees by the campfire and tore into an apple.

Bagah had snagged a rabbit to roast and offered to share it with Mirevra, but she declined. His stomach needed it more than hers, and the rabbit was no bigger than his hand. The fruit would suffice for the night. Mirevra squinted with distaste at Lars before turning to Beldon, who spoke animatedly about elixirs with Neeps. She jabbed her elbow into her friend's side. The cleric turned at once. *"Ow!"* It was an exaggeration, but Beldon was certainly dramatic when it suited him. "That hurt, Mir."

She curled her lip. "Not as badly as listening to the two of you drone on and on, I can assure you. Making fast friends, I see."

Beldon huffed.

"Not everyone is a grump, like you. And do not mistake my interest in elixirs as friendship. I can *assure you* that Neeps and I have not."

"It is true," the halfling said. "I do not consider this man a friend in the slightest."

Mirevra would have been delighted to hear this, but when Beldon and Neeps turned to each other and grinned, she blew a sharp breath and stood. Bagah lifted his chin and flashed concerned eyes, but when she raised a flattened palm, he returned to roasting his game. Shiln and Heral stood talking near the coach and as curious as Mirevra was about the green-eyed woman and her skills, she wanted to avoid Shiln at all costs. Her headache was only just starting to subside; she did not wish to egg it on further. Jardin stood near a tree, gazing into the distant horizon. He held his large arms in their cobalt-blue bracers, crossed. She decided she would not disturb this man who spoke less than Bagah. That only left Lars, who stared at her with a sharp grin, or Roman, hunkered down by a pair of twisted trees a few paces from the camp. *The druid it is.*

She did not try to conceal her footsteps, and he craned his neck to greet her. His plump cheeks flushed their usual bright red.

"Ah, Mirevra," he greeted her, his smile as broad as ever. He patted the ground next to him. "Sit with me, will you?" She sat but did not cross her legs as he did. Instead, she crouched and rested her elbows atop her knees, twiddling her fingers in an intricate pattern like a spider weaving a web. "How are you faring, considering our most unusual predicament?" Roman asked. Mirevra thought her comrade's smile was too broad and easy for their unusual predicament. Many times, as she and Roman fought side by side, all the fat, jolly man would do was smile. She would never say it aloud, but *deep* down, Mirevra found Roman's grin a great comfort. If Roman was smiling, she did not fret, even if the odds seemed stacked against them.

"Not well, I am afraid," she answered honestly. "I am not in the business of teaming up with heroes. Lo and behold, in my short time with them, I have found that I dislike it. My patience grows thinner each day."

"Yes, well, you do not like teaming up with anyone. So, this information does not come as a shock," Roman said. He looked her in the eye, and soon enough, his infectious grin spread to her own face.

"I fight well alongside you, do I not?" Mirevra protested, straightening one knee to rest on the grass.

Roman's hazel eyes widened.

"Of course you do. Fighting has never been your issue; it is all the time *in between* those fights that you struggle with. Why, it took us months to even become acquaintances! Even after I washed all your dishes, your clothes, your bedding! I even cleaned the den!" Roman laughed as he recounted his efforts, and Mirevra smiled again. Yes, Roman was a marvelous addition to the Ring. His ability to shape himself into wild beasts was a help, of course. But he also kept the den tidy and clean; without him, there was no telling how foul it would be.

Mirevra shrugged. "Making friends has never been a desire, but my heart is with the Ring, and to the Ring I serve. I am less inclined to make friends with...*them*," she said, tossing a viscous look over her shoulder at the coach. Roman squawked with laughter.

"Would it truly be so hard, Mirevra? To open your heart a little to them?"

"Yes," Mirevra grimaced. "It goes against my very nature."

"And me being a criminal? What does that say of my nature?" He prodded her shoulder with a finger. "Do you not remember my story, Mirevra? Have too many seasons passed for the tale to stay fresh?" One corner of Mirevra's mouth curled.

"Of course, I remember, Roman," she said. And it was true. Mirevra would never forget. Roman was once a simple baker in the bustling city of Tanima in southern Sardek. He had lived a simple life, one made for him, flourishing in creating little cakes and scones. Then, another guild had torn through the city, prepared to slaughter anyone who would not abide by the new law of the High Crown. By order of King Dern, his citizens would pay increased taxes to fund an even larger army. This was a silly proposition since the kingdom of Sardek already *had* the largest army after The Root Puller had acquired the Teruk. Roman tried to pay the exorbitant taxes, but when he ran out of money, the collector seized almost everything. Everything but his sister Tilly, who had been away at the time, *thank Rashawe*. Now, they both served the Ring.

Perhaps some would wonder how a gentle, convivial man like Roman could become a Fox, a criminal, a no-good, dirty, rotten thief. But Mirevra did not. She knew a person could be pushed only so far before they must push back. She knew this better than anyone.

"Let my story be one of inspiration then, my friend. For if I learned to love criminals, perhaps you can learn to love the heroes," he said. Mirevra frowned and spat, earning raised palms from the druid. "All right, perhaps not love... but *tolerate*. It is a start, at the very least," he amended. Mirevra studied his plump cheeks, thinning brown hair, and bright eyes. She nodded.

"For you, I will try my best."

Roman smiled and laid a gentle hand on her shoulder. He squeezed and rocked her back and forth playfully. "Then we shall have no trouble, for *your* best could bring kingdoms to their knees." They eventually returned to the fire. The guilds had agreed that it was safest if one Nelimen and one Fox stood watch together. Roman volunteered for the first shift. The Nelimen drew straws, and Neeps lost.

Roman and Neeps positioned themselves on either side of the camp while the others slept. Mirevra dreamed of her usual nightmares. The murky lake, a dark stone viaduct, her hands slipping, slipping, slipping... *'Forever.'*

"Mirevra," Roman said, shaking her shoulder. She jerked upright in a cold sweat, her dagger at the ready. He laughed as, with a steady hand, she lowered her weapon. "It is your turn on watch. Did you rest well?" In answer, Mirevra dragged her hands down her face. Roman shook his head. "I suspected as much. Would you like to go back to sleep? I can take your—"

"No," she replied quickly and touched his arm. "I am fine. You rest, sweet friend. Hopefully, you find greater reprieve in it than I did."

"Quite an easy feat, I am afraid," he teased.

Mirevra stood, dusted the earth and grime from her rear, then looked across the fire to see who she was paired with. She allowed a slight groan to escape her. Lars Dellary. Who else would misfortune have offered? Lars lifted his hands high and shrugged.

"Better than Shiln," he offered. Mirevra rolled her eyes and stomped in silence to her position. She did not know how long it took, but it was certainly not long enough before Lars made his way closer to her. "So," he started, and Mirevra immediately felt exhausted just hearing his voice. "Wonderful weather we are having, would you not say?" She registered his ridiculous smirk in her peripheral view and remained silent. "Yes, wonderful weather indeed. You know, last I camped with Heral, we were caught in a torrential downpour. It was the worst! Oh, you should have seen Heral's face when her hair got—"

"I do not know how the Nelimen usually keep watch, but talking loudly instead of surveying the perimeter is a quick way to find death," Mirevra snapped. "I suggest you take your loud mouth and obnoxious ruffled shirt back to your side and do what we were called to do. *Watch*."

Lars glanced down at his dark blue ruffled tunic with billowing sleeves and feigned offense. "This shirt is *not* obnoxious. And I look quite good in it, thank you." She eyed him slowly, her derision clear, then turned to face the tree line. Lars did not take the hint; he completely disregarded it. "You are not very good at this whole *working together* thing," he said, positioning his body to face the same trees Mirevra watched. Her head remained perfectly still, but she shifted her eyes to look at him. "It is not so bad, you know? Partnering up with people in an attempt to save the world. It is not as if the stakes were small."

"I am well aware of the stakes and that we must work together. But, I do not have to like you or entertain your vexatious conversations. So, if you do not mind—"

"What is it like? Being a Fox, I mean," he interrupted. Her brows perked up in interest before she cursed herself and drew them back down. *Do not let him see you are interested in anything he says. You will only encourage him to keep talking.* After a small, gods-given silence, his dark voice continued. "You know, I did not always see myself as a Nelimen. When I decided to join a guild, I thought long and hard about my choices. There are just so many options. It is like...shirts." *Oh gods. One cannot find peace in sleep or anywhere else. Rashawe, help her.* "You think you will like one, but how will you know unless you try it on? The guilds, of course, are not like that. You can try for any, but once you get selected, that is it. No changing, no going back. You're stuck with the outfit you chose. Never can you leave one guild to join another, and if you act against your guild...*Well."*

Despite herself, Mirevra turned toward him. "Some would consider your words deeply treacherous. What is the matter, Ruffles? Are you rethinking your choice to be a Nelimen?" Her eyes flicked to his ring with its engraved mountain. "Not feeling as *sturdy as the earth*?" This earned her his genuine laugh. She whipped her face back to the trees.

"No, I am not rethinking my guild, Viper," he said cheerfully. "I was born to be a hero. The free drinks, the cheers, the laud, and the women..." Lars sighed, lifting his eyes to the sky as if reminiscing about his encounters. She scoffed, but he ignored her. "But curiosity does get the better of me sometimes. What would it be like? To become something different, to *be* someone different. A criminal, for instance. I think I would be quite good at it; I am known for getting in and out of places undetected. Or, taking things that do not belong to me," he said, and his smile stretched. "I am sure the Fox Ring would appreciate someone with my skills."

"I think you would find that your skills could not compensate for your mouth, which moves far too often."

Another laugh. Mirevra's cheeks grew warm.

"Come, Viper, do not tell me you have never felt the call to do something else? Have you not once wanted to save someone simply because it is the right thing to do?"

Mirevra did not respond. She gulped down the lump in her throat. *'Forever, forever, forever...'* Lost in her thoughts, Mirevra did not hear Lars move closer. He sat next to her, a hand and foot apart. Too close. *Too fucking close.* Yet, she did not move.

"I do what the Veravant tells me to do," she said. "If he finds someone worth saving, I will save them. If not, I will let them die." Her eyes fell to the ground. "Death comes for us all regardless."

Lars let out a low whistle. "Grim," he said. "Is that the way all criminals think? Maybe I do not want to be a Fox then."

"You would never make one."

He did not seem to take that as an insult; he only nodded his head. "I think you are right," he said. He pulled an apple from his pocket and rubbed it against his shirt. "Would you really do *anything* the Veravant asks of you?" Cold rage crept up Mirevra's spine.

"Yes," she snapped. "Anything."

Biting into his apple, Lars spoke through a mouthful of fruit. "What if he asked you to kill your Teruk friend?" He swallowed. "Would you obey him even then?"

Instantly, her cold rage turned to heat. Fire raced up and down her limbs, and the itch to cut something roared back. Mirevra rolled her shoulders with a controlled confidence to settle herself.

"He would not ask me to do that," she stated, struggling to control her expression. The Veravant had not ever been kind to Bagah.

"How are you so sure? He is half Teruk," Lars volleyed.

"Why should that mean anything?" Mirevra seethed. "Do *you* have a problem with him being a half-breed? If so, we can settle that now, Ruffles." Lars raised his hands in mock surrender.

"Of course, I have no quarrel with him being Teruk! I think it is fantastic, actually. I only wondered. Should the Veravant command this, for whatever reason, could you do it?" Mirevra was unsure why she allowed this annoying male to keep speaking, but she contemplated his scenario. *Could* she kill Bagah if the Veravant ordered it? She knew this was well within the realm of possibility. The Veravant had noted on more than one occasion that the Teruk were a brutish kind who could not be trusted. Mirevra believed that Bagah was the most fiercely loyal person she knew, not just as a Fox but as a friend. But she also knew there would be no convincing the Veravant of this. Whatever he believed was the truth. Immovable.

Mirevra could hear Bagah's loud snores. No, she did not think she could kill him. So, she lied.

"Yes," she responded with the stone-cold face of an unfeeling killer. "If the Veravant ordered me, I would kill Bagah."

Lars halted mid-chew. His gray eyes swirled with an emotion Mirevra could not place. Was it shock? Disappointment? He lowered the fruit, and his shoulders slumped. "That is a distressing answer," he said softly. "I would rather become a Wolf than kill someone I cared for."

Mirevra's body went rigid. She had never heard someone speak so recklessly. To even breathe the word Wolf was considered taboo; to say you would willingly become one... Mirevra studied Lars. Who was this man? This horribly irritating, flamboyant, *handsome* man? She straightened, not daring to let these wildly inappropriate thoughts consume her.

"What you say is both perfidious and despicable. Not to mention completely disloyal to your guild and your Head," she said. "To openly admit you would go against your sworn oath already makes you enough of a Wolf." Her tongue seemed to swell as that last word escaped her lips. Wolf.

Wolves are exiled. They are alone.

Lars laughed, shook his head, and took another generous bite of apple. "Perhaps that is the difference between heroes and criminals," he said. "For *real* treachery is going against who you are in here," he said, pointing at his chest. "I will follow the Head's orders unless they compromise who I am. I honor Briatriel. I honor the Nelimen, but they do not own me." One last bite, and he threw the core into the trees.

"Here," he added and tossed her dagger—that she had last seen when she placed it snugly in its sheath— at her. Her mouth hung open even as she reflexively caught it. How in the Murks did he steal this from under her nose? Lars stared at her in open disappointment. "You are right, Viper. Even with my skills, I could never be a Fox." He clambered to his feet and returned to his post.

Mirevra's heart pounded, and her gut twisted. Her vows and pledges to the Veravant echoed through her head. The Ring she was sworn to. The Veravant. Who owned her. She longed to run to a sleeping Bagah, shake him awake, and beg him for forgiveness for her lie; she would never harm him. She wanted to chase down that ruffled-shirt asshole and knock his teeth out for making her feel shame. Instead, she hugged herself against the cooling night air and repeated the code. *To the Ring we serve. To the Ring we serve.*

To the Ring I serve.

She shook as a cold wind swept across her face and cradled herself tighter. Her teeth began to chatter, and she dropped her arms and stood straight.

It was summer. Where was this cold wind coming from?

She had no time to think before they attacked.

A blast of freezing wind slammed her to the ground. Her eyes snapped open, and she wiped moisture from her face. *Ice?* She did not waste another second to solve the mystery. Launching to her feet, her dagger in one hand, her short blade in the other, she shouted for the Ring to wake up.

"What in the Murks was that?!" Lars called from the other side of the fire as another blast swarmed their camp, and small sleet pellets dampened their skin. Bagah leaped up, and the others followed suit. "Viper, did you see anything?" Lars called as he pulled a pair of matching swords from the sheath strapped to his back. Mirevra drew herself into stillness and silently scanned the trees. Something was out there assessing when to attack. The increasing cold was proof enough.

A few seconds later, she heard a grunt and turned her cheek, only far enough to glimpse Roman shifting into one of his beasts. The white

A Fallen Sword

fox. He scurried past Mirevra and ran into the woods. *Do not die, you fat, rotten bastard. Find the threat and come back immediately.* She would have preferred if Roman had entered the wood as the black bear or even the brown horse. But she knew he could best evaluate a threat—and report back—in the fox's guise. A dim purple glow lit the camp. Shiln must be preparing herself to summon a spell if needed. Mirevra felt her jaw relax a tiny bit and for the first time, she was thankful for the sorceress' powers.

A yelp cut the night. It came from the woods, and Mirevra struggled to keep her muscles still. She could not run in alone; she must wait. For Roman, for anything. Unflinching, she lowered her chin and glared at the very trees themselves. She trusted nothing.

Silently, the others joined her at her post. "Should we go in?" Neeps whispered, clasping two vials to his chest.

"Absolutely not," Beldon replied. His face was already illuminated by a cleric's bright, white gleam. "Unless you want to face the unknown with only your tiny tonics."

Neeps shook his head at Beldon. "I assure you, you will not think these so tiny when I activate them."

Beldon nodded absently. Bagah stood next to Mirevra and matched her stance. They looked at each other just once and then faced the trees. Finally, Mirevra saw the white fox racing away from the tree line, a trail dogging its every step. She heard a crack as the grass under her feet began to freeze, ice covering each blade within seconds.

Roman had no chance to shift back and alert them. Seven figures emerged from the windowed trunks. Mirevra stiffened. Four women and three men, their dark hair blowing in the crisp wind, each wrapped in a celestial blue cloak. Mirevra began to shiver. Even from this distance, she could see only clear, pale blue...ice where their eyes should be. Pure ice. The woman in the group's center held her hands straight out, formed them into a triangle, pushed them away from her, and then pulled him back into her chest.

"Mages!" Heral's voice sounded from behind her, and Mirevra made the mistake of looking back at the woman who cried out. Her eyes were...*changing*. Her hands were outstretched towards the fire, and Mirevra could not be sure, but it looked like the flames began to swirl towards her palms in a fiery vortex. Then, she felt a sharp sting so cold in her chest that her breath was stolen. A frost-bitten ache splintered across her entire torso. Bagah released a barbaric howl as she turned her attention back to the trees. Her torso was now covered in that same icy blue of the mage's eyes. It spread quickly, spidering towards her neck and limbs. She felt her body begin to resign to paralysis.

"Beldon," was all she managed before the ice crept up her throat and into her mouth, freezing her in place. At once, the cleric ran to her side. Neeps sprinted ahead and launched two vials directly at the line of mages, then spun quickly, heading for refuge behind the coach. The vials spiraled through the air; one hit a tree and exploded viciously. Fire erupted, disputing the cold; the other vial hit a mage on one end of the formation; yellow smoke erupted from the shattered glass. The mage dropped to his feet and choked.

Mirevra thought she heard Beldon mumble that he was impressed, but all she saw was white, white, white. A cleric's fire. Then she felt its white warmth seeping into her frozen skin.

While she was being healed, Bagah stood before them should any of the mages attack. Shiln ground her teeth as the purple light swelled around her hands, and then she launched a spell at the center mage. At the same time, Jardin, who stood on top of the coach with his bow

A Fallen Sword

trained on the mages, released an arrow. The reed whistled as it sliced through the air and hit the center mage. Weakened by Shiln's Binding Spell, the mage fell to her knees. Flanking her right, another female stepped forward, throwing her arms as if chucking something at them. Icicles, sharp and ruthless, whizzed through the air towards the archer. He jumped from his station, but not fast enough. One of the ice daggers slit his arm, and he grunted. Another mage moved forward, this time contorting his fingers in maze-like movements. The woman next to him wove her fingers like yarn was strung between them.

The white fox darted in their direction. He bit and gnawed their legs while Lars chased after them with his two blades. The final male mage engaged with him, forging a blade of ice. Lars fought hard and true, but it would not be enough; Mirevra was aware of that even in her debilitated state. The two mages with the winding and twisting fingers were creating something, conjuring a spell that simple swords could not combat. They looked at her and raised their hands to the sky in unison. An ice formation began to climb from their fingers, sprawling into the night sky like streaks of frozen lightning.

Beldon pressed his hand harder onto her chest until she could at least wiggle her fingers and toes and move her eyes, while Bagah launched himself at the mages. He felt the anger whispering in his ears, the glass jar beginning to shake. He slung a fist, but with a nimble step, one mage dodged it. He turned, swinging at the other, but something caught his wrist in midair. Another mage held him in an ice-cold grasp. No, one of their hands would not be large enough to encircle his wrist. Ice shackled him, frozen manacles of considerable strength. A blow to his gut nearly knocked his breath away, but he flexed and roared, and the icy cuffs broke clean away. They shattered into a thousand jagged pieces, slicing his skin with shallow cuts as they fell. But Bagah barely noticed. He grabbed the wide-eyed female mage still on the ground by her neck and flung her into the nearest tree with full force.

Her back slammed against the bark, and her body went limp and crashed to the floor. When Bagah looked back at Mirevra, he saw luck and time were not on his side. Multiple trees surrounding the camp had caught fire, and the ice formation was morphing. Its solid black substance was no longer ice, or maybe it was; he did not know. Pulsing purple bolts splintered through it and towered to the sky like a chilled obelisk. It leaned and fell, but the black ice did not break. With serpentine movements, it sped towards Mirevra and Beldon. Bagah knew he could not reach Mirevra in time or smash it.

This was a mage, elemental Arcanen; he was only a half-breed barbarian.

"Heral!" Lars shouted and slammed his boot into the mage's chest, then sprinted toward Mirevra.

Heral strode forward quickly, hands held before her, flowing in circular shapes as a transparent ball formed within them. Bagah saw the fire in Heral's eyes, the same he had seen in the coach, and it flashed brighter as the ball grew larger and larger. Bagah could not move; he was entranced by Heral's hands. Lars was now at Beldon's side, but the Teruk's eyes remained fixed upon the tall woman. He only moved when the remaining six mages formed a V formation. Heral stood as if turned to stone, and her eyes burned like the brightest stars against a still, black sky. She released her hands with a furious scream.

It all happened too quickly for Bagah to understand. One moment, a blinding light hurled towards him and the mages, and the next, he was on the ground a safe distance away, watching the mages burn alive. But it was not fire that consumed their bodies; it was nothing he recognized. His eyes dropped as the mages' shrieks intensified.

Mirevra? Was she safe? Did everyone make it?

A Fallen Sword

Bagah's mind was scrambled; he did not know...he did not understand. The last thing he saw was Heral's face, this auburn-haired beauty blessed by Radina. Softly, she told him to sleep.

So, he did.

The Rogue and His Ass

The sun rose in a cloudless blue sky. The members of both guilds were tired; almost no one slept after the battle with the mages. Mirevra still clutched her aching chest, free from all ice but now filled with recrimination. She could not shake the looming sense of failure that encumbered her. She had missed Heral standing near their cart in Beretina; she had been unable to best the Nelimen in their den—although she *had* been poisoned—and last night, the mages would have killed her if not for...for... Slowly, she swallowed an acid lump in her throat. She knew Beldon had done his best to mend her during the battle, and she owed her life to him a thousand times over. But when they had returned to camp, the cleric had stated that Mirevra would not have lived, the mages' strange magic would have killed them all, if not for the Nelimen. Mirevra was shaken when she'd heard this and still did not know what to do with the information.

"Lars called on Heral to protect you. Without that command, you and I would not be here," Beldon said as he settled near her. He had rarely left her side since their return to camp and had even mended her every few hours during the night to be on the safe side. "And protect you she did. I have never seen anything like it," he said, shaking his head. "What do you think she is?"

Mirevra eyed the Nelimen. Neeps was eating, and Shiln was healing Jardin's wound. Heral sat on the carriage's driver's box, her chin tilted toward the sky as she soaked in the morning sun. Her eyes were closed as the light splayed across her face. Lars had gone to a nearby stream to clean up. Looking straight at Beldon, she shrugged. "I cannot say what she is," she answered truthfully. "I am not sure it will do us any good to find out, either."

The cleric brayed his laugh that Mirevra hated. "You are not nearly curious enough for my taste, Mirevra."

"And you are too nosey for mine," she countered but felt a swirl in her stomach. Beldon was mindlessly obsessed with other people's affairs, while Mirevra usually could not have cared less. But she felt something strange pull at her spirit. She wondered if Lars was still bathing. She wondered what she might say when she saw him next. To her dismay, their conversation last night still rattled her.

"I know you do not like the Nelimen much," Beldon smirked. That was an understatement. "But I urge you to remember that you are only alive because of them." He laid a hand on her knee. "It is all I ask, Mir. Just remember that. Besides, Lars is as generous as he is handsome. We should thank him not only for our lives but for giving us something so nice to look at on this journey."

Mirevra wanted to stick out her tongue and pull away, but under his brash remarks, Beldon's sincerity rang true. Say what she would about the Nelimen—and she could draw up quite a list of negative things—her life *had* been spared by the very trait she found the most annoying about them: their heroism. Especially Lars.' She needed to speak to him, so when Beldon released his hand, she rose and stomped towards the grove of trees.

Mirevra watched as Lars bent and dunked his head into the flowing stream. As he straightened his naked body, he threw back his head, and a water trail followed. He slicked his hair away from his face, and she noted it was long enough to cover his neck. He continued to smooth his hair, displaying his impressive arms and chest. Mirevra had not noticed *these* parts of him before, covered as they always were in his ridiculous ruffled shirts. His shoulders were broad, his neck thick and sturdy. Even when his arms relaxed, their muscles bulged. His broad chest narrowed as it reached his waist. Just below, the deep furrows that outlined his hips plunged into the water... She shook her head. He was ridiculous. And so was she for entertaining her curiosity. Why should she care how fit his body was?

She descended the mild slope to the stream with quickened steps. She needed to talk before her silly mind redirected its thoughts. Lars flashed that half-way smile she loathed. "Come to watch, have you?" He splayed his arms wide for her to take him all in. She had done no such thing. His smile shifted as she sat on the bank and yanked off her boots.

His thick, black brows rose high. "Come to *join?*" There was hope in his tone that she hated even more. She ignored it and pulled her tunic over her head without changing her expression. Lars' mouth dropped open as he marveled at her breasts, her midriff, her everything. He was no different than any man.

Mirevra did not find shame in the naked form, especially her own. It was only a body, after all. One that had kept her alive and had won her a thousand fights. Why would clothes, or the lack thereof, change her feelings about it? Of course, she knew its effect on those attracted to her, and she had used that effect to her advantage on her missions more times than she could count. But that was not why she now undressed. The truth was, she told herself, she smelled disgusting and needed a wash. And if staring at her breasts, kept his garrulous mouth shut long enough for her to say her piece and be done with it, so much the better. She walked toward him without pausing to check the water's temperature. The river wrapped around her ankles, shins, and thighs, past her navel, until she mirrored his stance. Her breasts sat just above the water's surface; his eyes did not lift from them as she predicted. He gaped.

"I came to say two things," Mirevra began, not squandering a second. "First, to thank you. My cleric told me that you saved my life last night. Well, you and Heral." Now she wondered why she had not thought to first thank Heral, who had done more to keep her alive than Lars and had been sitting on the coach back at camp. Well, she was here now. No time to ponder too much about it. Finally, his eyes found hers. Total bewilderment scored his features. *Was he more nonplussed by her thanks than her breasts?* This had never happened before. She pushed her shoulders back and shoved her torso forward so her nipples nearly touched his chest. Still, he did not look down.

"A Fox thanking a Nelimen? Could I be dreaming?" Lars splashed water on his face and shook his head, spraying Mirevra's cheeks and nose with tiny droplets. She frowned.

"A Fox and a criminal, I may be. And a killer, of course. But these titles do not prevent me from knowing how and when to give thanks when necessary. I do not withhold my gratitude on account of pride," she said with a touch of scorn. It was true; she had always thanked those who did right by her. She would have felt indebted to them if she had not thanked them, a price she could not afford. Lars' face still betrayed utter shock. "Do you not believe me?" Her cheeks flushed warm despite the cool water. His lips curled down, and he slowly shook his head.

"I do not take you as a liar, Viper," he answered smoothly. Her nose scrunched.

"Then why do you not seem to be able to accept my appreciation? And why do you call me that?"

Lars brought one hand to his mouth, pulled at it, and sneaked a glance at her breasts before his lips twisted into a smirk. "I also did not take you as one who would give thanks, to a *hero* no less. Maybe you are different from the woman I thought you were," he explained. She scoffed.

"I did *not* say you were a hero."

"You did not have to. I am a hero."

Mirevra rolled her eyes. Arguing with him would be of no avail; she would get further into a conversation with one of the pebbles beneath her feet. "And as for Viper," Lars continued. "I do not have to call you that if you do not wish it." She cocked her head and considered this.

"If you prefer, I could call you little Fox." Mirevra's breathing ceased, her body froze, and her heart may have stopped beating. "It that not what he calls you? The Veravant?"

"How...?" She trailed off, dumbfounded and unable to think clearly. He had not been in the meeting at the inn; he could not have heard the Veravant utter those words. The thought of the Veravant suddenly made her feel sick to her stomach, and she did not know why.

"How did I know he calls you that? The same way you knew to find me here. I eavesdrop. Quite a lot, actually." With that, Lars dunked his head into the water again. When he jolted from the surface, he shook his hair, flinging fatter droplets onto her face. "Now, what was the second thing you wanted to tell me?" he asked.

Beneath the water, Mirevra's fingers flexed, and she grinned. Lars beamed back and moved closer, confusing her smile for an invitation. Her breasts now touched his ribs. A rush of sensation tingled down her spine as his warmth pressed against her. Slowly, she raised her hand from the surface, and Lars' eyes gleamed in anticipation as he watched the water stream from her fingers. She curled those fingers into a fist and swung with all her might. Her knuckles collided with his cheek, and she knew they would leave a mark. *Good,* she thought. *Let it be a reminder.* Lars grabbed his face, hissed, and squeezed his eyes shut. When they popped open again he shook his head. "What in the Murks was that for?!" he exclaimed, nursing his wounded cheek. Mirevra gnawed the inside of her cheek and slipped under the water. When she rose a few feet away, she smoothed back her thick hair and eyed him with feline precision.

"You may have helped save my life, but you also put it in danger," she called, her golden eyes simmering in delight at his pain. Lars stared at her, his jaw slack. "When we were on watch, you could not tame your tongue. You distracted me. I would have seen the mages if not for you. Our conversation was a mistake that almost cost several lives. We must ensure we never make it again." Despite the discomfort she knew Lars felt across his jaw and cheekbone, the arrogant male smiled. *He smiled.*

"Ah," he said with a nod. "There she is, the woman I thought you were. The Viper."

Mirevra bit her tongue as Lars waded back to the river bank and forcibly pulled her stare away from him as his body cleared the water. His ass, in all its glory, was on full display. Another part of him swung freely and hung low enough for her to catch a glimpse. She bit down harder on her tongue. *What in the Degolian Murks was wrong with her?* Lars dried his hair with his linen tunic, then flapped it in the wind to dry it. He turned to face her, and despite all the willpower she tried to summon, her curiosity bested her, and she looked at him.

"I suppose we are still where we started then, me and you," he said. The levity in his tone confused her. She had just punched him *hard*, so why was he still smiling at her? He should be calling her a bitch and moving on with his day; instead, he shook his head with that damn smirk and said, "Little Fox does not suit you. I shall keep Viper." He picked up his trousers and climbed the bank. He called out over his shoulder. "Only now, I really do not give a damn if you like it or not."

When his form was lost between the trees, Mirevra seethed. Her cheeks burned, but not from the anger she was accustomed to. He elicited something else from within, and it infuriated her. *"Jedarei,"* she whispered and dunked her head again to try and douse the fire in her bones.

The Goddess of Truth and Hidden Things

Two more nights passed. At sundown on the third night, the guilds readied themselves; pressing hard, they could reach the Mercinnho and the Tajeh of Maji in one more day. First, they argued over which route to take. Lars suggested a hidden path through the woods, assuring them it was a short cut. Shiln demanded they find a town where they could all rest before reaching Mercinnho. The sorceress was the victor, and near nightfall, the guilds entered a small village. Winowlen boasted two taverns, one inn, a blacksmith, a stable, and a temple to the goddess Audrina. Mirevra's eyebrows rose as she rode past the temple; the people of Winowlen must highly value candor to have a temple for the goddess of Truth and Hidden Things and not a commonly worshiped deity like Rashawe or Idenethor. Like most people, Mirevra preferred holding her secrets.

Heral and Shiln had no issue paying the young stable hands a pretty coin to care for their horses. *How tired the creatures must be*, Mirevra thought as she dismounted. *How tired they all were.* When Lars suggested they visit the tavern before they rested, Jardin, Neeps, and Roman declined and walked toward the inn instead. Mirevra almost joined the trio, but Bagah tilted his head to the side, so she sent her companion a slight shrug and followed him into the tavern. There might be another tongue that demanded slicing, and besides, a nice flagon of ale did not sound so bad after almost being frozen alive. Despite her healing, that memory was stuck with her. She settled at the bar and allowed Beldon to buy her a drink. She supposed a Fox's standard tavern etiquette—stealing drinks—would not be the right call, surrounded as they were by a band of heroes and their attempt to keep their identities hidden. When the bar wench placed her drink before her, Mirevra stared at the goblet. She glanced around to reassure herself. She was in familiar enough surroundings. Well-worn tables scattered across a scratched, none-too-clean floor, creaky stools, a bar wench dressed in old wool, and a ripped apron. Yet she had been served ale in a silver goblet. She flicked her finger against it, lifted it to her face, and observed it thoroughly. Yes, it was pure silver. Yes, she *would* be stealing it. The bar wench noticed Mirevra's furrowed brow.

"We get them looks a lot," she said, her accent disjointed and thick. "No one expects such fine silver in a place like this." She shrugged a shoulder. "Who could blame ye? To Audrina," she said, tipping her cup toward Mirevra before returning to her task and filling another silver goblet for the next patron. Mirevra watched Shiln and Lars drink their fill. Bagah and Beldon were already on their second drink. Ankles crossed, Heral leaned against the doorframe and inspected her nail beds. She did not drink. Now that she thought of it, Mirevra realized she had not seen Heral eat or drink a damned thing on their journey.

She took her own advice and reminded herself it was best not to pry too closely. As long as Heral remained true to their mission, her abstaining from sustenance, albeit *quite* peculiar, was her business. Returning to her drink, Mirevra caught the stare of a pair of gray eyes honed in on her. She looked away quickly and downed her drink with one generous gulp. The first few minutes after her hefty swig were genuinely delightful. Mirevra hung in that sweet balance between sober and intoxicated.

The rest of the night was her worst fucking nightmare.

Had an hour passed? Two? Seven? Or had she finished her drink only seconds ago? Mirevra did not feel drunk. Or maybe she did. Or maybe she felt somewhere between drunk and dead. She shook her head vigorously to combat the effects of whatever the bar wench poured her. Poison was her best guess.

"Do not be startled, Mirevra," a voice hummed above her. She craned her neck to see who was speaking and tried to grab her dagger but could not move her limbs. They were now liquid.

"Who are you? How do you know my name?" Mirevra almost foamed at the mouth as she struggled to form words. A woman, or a silhouette of a woman, dipped in pure light, stood before her. A white dress hugged her body, and her white-blonde hair fell past her waist and pooled on the floor. Through her blurred vision, Mirevra met the silver eyes glittering back at her. Desperate for clarity, her brain frantically pulled at every strand of her hazy thoughts. Something...something echoed in the back of her brain and began unraveling, but she could not tie the strands tightly enough. But when the woman spoke, Mirevra knew precisely who she was.

"You hold many secrets, Mirevra of Galen, Yahelle of Sardek." Mirevra's eyes shot to the side, fighting to avoid the gaze of the goddess Audrina. "The harder you try to escape the truth, the worse it will become," the goddess said in a breathy whisper. *Goddamned village and their goddamned temple.* Mirevra grimaced; she should have known. The well-kept temple, the silver goblet. She had drunk Faerabidia. To become priests and priestesses of Audriana, her worshipers imbibed reams of the liquid. Mirevra had heard Faerabidia called the goddess' very essence as it forced your mind to divulge all hidden thoughts and your tongue to speak the truth.

Mirevra had always steered far away from anything resembling the concoction. Through her haze, she berated herself. Why had she let down her guard? Exhaustion from the fast journey? For whatever reason, she had willingly accepted a glass, and now Faerabidia—and the goddess—held her in their secrets-hating clutches. Blinking, she searched her scrambled mind. What else did she remember about this goddess and her hideous drink?

"You know the truth is the only way out of the Faerabidia," Audrina answered. Mirevra's body grew rigid. Had she spoken aloud? "No," the goddess answered again. "I am not in the tavern, Mirevra. I am in here. *I am within you.*" The form vanished like a wisp of smoke. A thump slammed through Mirevra's chest. It ached and throbbed, and though she squirmed and almost groaned out loud, Mirevra could not escape the discomfort. "There is so much anger and guilt in here. Loneliness abounds," the goddess said. "But you are also afraid. What do you fear, Mirevra? Tell me." Mirevra ground her teeth so hard she thought they would turn to dust. *Fuck this goddess.* Audrina had no right to Mirevra's thoughts, name, or fears. She writhed for what felt like hours before the goddess' voice broke in again. "Do you fear the coming end? That the holy blade does not exist?" Mirevra steeled her mind and steadied her breath. She was a fortress, an iron vault. She would neither bend nor break, especially not for someone who had not earned it. "Do you fear the Veravant will never love you as you love him?" A silence rippled between them before Audrina continued. "Ah, you do not love him, I see. You do not know what it is to love or be loved. That also frightens you."

"Godsdamn you," Mirerva spat. If only she could move her feet, she would run away and never look back.

"No. No, that is not it. There is a truth that lies deeper and that you fear even more. It will go easier for you if you confess it, Mirevra." The thud in Mirevra's chest quickened, and she moaned.

"Confessing will release you from the pain," the goddess said, her sweet voice nowhere near matching the unfounded anguish she produced.

"Go to the Murks, you bitch," Mirevra said.

The goddess of Truth and Hidden Things's face remained unperturbed, but Mirevra felt Audrina's incorporeal form slide into her. Her limbs became Mirevra's limbs. Mirevra's mouth, the goddess's mouth. *No. No. No.* Mirevra flung herself off the stool and hit the floor hard. Her ribs hurt, and she coughed up a small amount of blood. She tried to rise to her hands and knees; she would crawl away if she had to. Audrina would never get her. "It does not work like that, and you know it. Only one thing can unbind you," she heard Audrina say. Mirevra cursed and began to crawl. Her legs shook, and her arms wobbled. As if through a warped cloud, she saw Bagah fighting, too. Lars stood next to him with the sorceress to his right. All of them were locked in this *bullshit* they had not consented to. "Wait! What is this?" Audrina's voice was now octaves higher.

Mirevra slid one hand and one knee forward. "Get the fuck out," she grunted. "You have no right."

"The Murky Lakes. I see them!"

Mirevra released a guttural cry. *Please, no.* "Who are they? On the bridge?" Audrina demanded.

She would beg and plead if she had to, as long as she could keep that memory buried.

"Siblings? Parents?"

Mirevra slumped, and her chin hit the floor. She did not even feel it; the agony within felt powerful enough to kill her. Death by too many cuts. Mirevra did not have the strength left to fight the goddess. Her mind was all but mush; her body water. She closed her eyes and saw what Audrina saw.

The Truth. The Hidden Thing.

A young Mirevra ran as quickly as she could across the bridge that led south. The riders were now so close that she heard hooves pounding behind her. Her mother's hand slipped in and out of her own as the rain poured and poured over their heads. A crack of lightning, a roll of thunder, and the men were upon them.

Writhing on the filthy tavern floor, Mirevra scratched at her throat. *Mercy, Audrina. Do not make me watch! Mercy, I beg of you!* The memory flashed against her closed eyes like a beacon of hot light burning every crevice of her mind. She knew there was no escape. Audrina was the goddess of truth, not mercy. The images sharpened.

The slick, wet stone of the bridge. The men's muffled curses. They grabbed her mother first, and her scream tore through the thunder and still haunted Mirevra all these years later. Mirevra threw her tiny body at the assaulter's legs and pounded her fists. Another guard, dressed in gold and black, kicked her off. She fell hard on the wet stone, and pain arched through her back. Above her, her father drew his sword, his golden eyes darkening as if melting. Through the sheets of rain, she watched him fight. But there were too many soldiers, and she heard more horses galloping closer. A grunt drew her attention from her father's battle, and she turned to see her mother, twisting with all her might, held between two of the guards. Those dark brown eyes that Mirevra had only ever seen filled with warmth and love were now shrouded with fear and anger.

'Mama!' Mirevra shrieked... *'No!'* She ran toward the guards as one drew a Gerelland blade and sliced her mother's throat. She was too late. Her mother collapsed to her knees and, choking, grasped her throat as blood flowed over her hands. Mirevra stood frozen. She felt nothing, heard nothing. She could only stare at her dying mother. Weakly, pathetically, she stared and did not fight. She could only watch as all the life drained from those brown eyes.

A pair of hands landed on her shoulders. She suddenly felt the rain and wind on her face again and heard the low rumbles from an angry sky. Plumes of smoke flew from the horses' nostrils as they stomped on the stones and huffed temperamental breaths. The hands pulled her up, and a pair of strong arms held her taut... She gnawed at the man's fingers and fought her own true fight. Her father's voice finally broke through, and she stilled within his arms. It was he who carried her.

'I need you to trust me, Yahelle. Let the water take you east. Then go south, as far south as you can. Find a place and hide. Do whatever you can to survive. You must live, my Yahelle... Live.' Mirevra's heart pounded against her ribs as she pleaded with her father to let her stay with him. She knew she was prepared to die with her parents. *'They will kill you if you stay in Sardek and hunt you wherever you are. You must go far away. Will you do this for me?'*

Will, her father said, not *can.* He knew she could; he believed she could do anything.

Her father placed her tiny body onto the bridge wall as four soldiers closed around them. She looked up at him but could find no words. His gold stare softened as he gazed upon her for the last time. *'Live, Yahelle. You must. It does not end here. Remember, I will be with you always... Forever.'* He shoved her as the guards delivered their fatal blows. Some stabbed, others hit, others sliced. She tried to catch herself on the bridge, *but her tiny fingers could not hold her weight. They were slipping; she was slipping. Her father called out to her one final time: 'Forever...'*

Mirevra inhaled a clear, full breath. Her eyes snapped open, and she was on her back, staring at the tavern's thatched ceiling. She rolled over, stood straight, and then frantically patted herself, assuring herself she was whole and free of Audrina. She was here, not at the bridge. Bagah, Beldon, Lars, and Shiln were also coming to; she watched them rub their eyes and stagger. Their clothes were soaked in what looked like the cold, clammy sweat that finally broke a fever. The bar wench continued to serve patrons and go about her business as if nothing had happened.

Mirevra met Bagah's eyes, and when he nodded, she left the tavern. Once on the street, she faced the goddess' temple and glared. The impulse to burn the goddamned thing to the ground flared. But a faint voice stopped her. It was so very distant, yet it whispered in her ear as if the goddess was still within.

'Thank you for your truth, Mirevra. For it, I shall grant you one in return.' Audrina's lyrical voice filled her ears. *'Beware the Wolf, Yahelle Vethari. It is closer than you know.'*

The One Bed

~~~

Back at the inn, they crowded on the tiny second-floor landing and argued for so long over who would sleep in a bed that Mirevra thought it would be easier to stay awake the entire night. Sunrise was only a few hours away and still shaken from Audrina's foul play, she was unsure she even wanted to sleep. Unless their squabbling had awaked them—and all the inn's guests—Jardin and Roman slept in their room. Neeps had an empty bed in his room and the remaining room held two. Three beds, six assholes.

"It is only fair that I get one of the beds," Shiln pleaded with a vexed look. "I require a good rest for the Arcanen magic to regenerate. Where would we be without my spells?"

Beldon scoffed, and Mirevra held back a smile. "If protection is the priority, surely Heral should claim a bed. Her magic has kept our lives intact," Beldon retorted.

Shiln only shrugged. "I cannot argue that point. Heral and I will take the open room."

Beldon blanched as if the sorceress had cursed his family. "I absolutely was not suggesting that."

Bagah and Mirevra exchanged glances. Both leaned against the wall, arms folded across their chests, their blank expressions perfect portraits of boredom. Lars rubbed his temples as if to drain the sound of the quarrel. The Faerabidia must have wreaked havoc on him too, if even *he* was annoyed, Mirevra thought.

"Fine," Shiln conceded. "Heral and I take one room, and Beldon sleeps in Neeps' room. The two of you are becoming fast friends anyway."

Beldon raised a finger, ready to protest, but Mirevra kicked herself off the wall and spoke first. "Sounds like a plan. Now, let us all just shut our mouths, please. This night has done a number on my skull and it is still too fragile for all this squawking." Bagah pushed himself off next. He brought two fingers to his brow in a mock salute, bid the group farewell, and walked down the stairs.

"Where is he going?" Lars asked, brows raised.

"To sleep in the coach," Mirevra answered. "Or on the ground outside."

"How do you two do that?! Speak without speaking?"

The assassin sighed heavily. "It is a skill the likes of you would do well to learn. Everyone, go to your assigned rooms. Ruffles and I will find a place to sleep. We'll be just fine." Shiln scowled at Mirevra and curled her lip. But, when she looked at Lars, he waved a hand in dismissal.

"She's right. After the night we had, sleeping on the ground sounds more appealing than arguing for one second longer."

Mirevra touched her brow, still trying to stop the memories Audrina had shown her from respawning.

A Fallen Sword

"Yes," she agreed whole-heartedly. "What Ruffles said."

For a moment, Beldon and Shiln appeared ready to keep arguing. But apparently, sleep beckoned them into her sweet, tranquil arms and their squabble did not last for long. "If you need me," Beldon said, placing a hand on Mirevra's shoulder and nodding his head at Neeps' room door. She nodded and patted his hand twice before walking down the stairs. Lars followed her.

"*So,*" he practically sang from behind her. "Where will we sleep?"

"There is no *we*, Ruffles. You will find a place to rest your head, as will I. Separately," she barked.

Lars clicked his tongue. "What is the matter, Viper? Afraid you might like sleeping with me too much?"

With all the strength she could summon, she refrained from backhanding him.

"I would prefer the ice mages over you."

"Methinks the lady doth protest too much," Lars quipped.

Mirevra stopped, combed her fingers through her thick hair, then spun on her heel to face him. She was fed up with their banter, which she feared had become too familiar.

"Is there any particular reason you pick at me? Have I done something to earn your ever-constant teasing?"

"I suppose there is something about you that is easy to annoy," he said with a shrug. "And frankly, I enjoy it too much. After all these years, Shiln ignores me."

"Is it that easy? I pay you no mind, and you stop your incessant talking?" she queried. Lars smiled, and she again had to restrain the urge to slap him.

"But you do not want me to stop annoying you," he stated matter of factly. "As much as you hate it, something else in you desires it. I see the war between the two in your eyes. You cannot decide if you loathe me or like me." Mirevra stepped towards him with a grimace, but her breath caught. She had never stood this close to him; even in the dim light, she saw lines crinkling around his eyes. He had to be at least ten years her senior. Though this feature did add to his good looks... She shook her head. *Those lines come from making himself laugh,* she reminded herself. *Because only a jackass like him would find his japes even remotely funny.*

"I can assure you, such a war does not exist in me, nor has it ever. I *loathe* you. I hate your voice. I hate your snarky jests. I hate your unwarranted arrogance. And most of all, I hate your ruffled shirts," Mirevra said, her voice bitter with venom. But Lars did not back down. To her surprise, he stepped forward to tower over her. His chin was level with her forehead, but he lowered himself so his lips were only a hair's breadth away from hers.

"Say what you will about my tactless jests, obnoxious voice, or even my confidence that you find so revolting," he said with equal menace. "But you leave my godsdamned shirts out of it."

She met his stare. Astonishment seized her as she realized she could not think of one biting insult. Instead, her mind was busy calculating whether Lars was taller than the Veravant. He was. Next, she breathed in his scent. *Tobacco and vetiver.* From this close, it intoxicated her. It was indeed familiar.

"I would leave the shirts out of the discussion if they were not so horrible," she said. It was a *shit* comeback, but her mind spun from his closeness. Perhaps it was the long journey, the mages, or even the lingering effects of the Faerabidia, but Mirevra could not find her footing. She struggled to pull words from the depth of her mind.

"I could always take it off," he suggested with a wink. "If you prefer."

The itch roared back. This time, Mirevra did not know if it called her to cut Lars' throat or the shirt from his body. Derision simmered in her bones; she knew he saw it happening. That war he mentioned earlier. She was in full struggle with it. *Fuck.*

"Oh, hello! Do not mind me," a small voice broke in. Lars and Mirevra spun and saw the old innkeeper making her way down the hall. She raised a tired arm. "Not used to my guests waking up so early; I need to grab the broom," she said, reaching behind Mirevra to open a small closet door. "Sun comes up in less than two hours. Have to make sure this place is ready for breakfast. Ready for another day to get dirty," she explained. Pulling out the broom, she inspected Mirevra far too closely for the assassin's comfort. "Why, your eyes are heavy, child. Pray tell, did you rest at all?" she asked with one eye squinted. When Mirevra did not answer, Lars cut in.

"I am afraid there were not enough beds to go around. We were just on our way to find another place to rest." He paused and swept his gaze over the keeper. "Oh my... dearest me, look at your face," Lars said, resting a fanned hand on his chest. "It is striking. Your eyes–they are spectacular. They remind me of the most glorious sunset." Mirevra had no idea what the bastard was talking about; the innkeeper's eyes looked like nothing of the sort. "I've never seen such a pair of eyes. What a marvel! What a wonder!" The innkeeper's cheeks flushed scarlet, and Mirevra pressed her lips together so as not to laugh. Lars shook his head. "Again, I apologize for being so bold. My friend and I need to find a place to rest. Not to worry, we think there may be room in our coach with the Teruk. We'll just be on our way..."

"Nonsense! A handsome bloke like you cannot be fittin' in no coach to sleep! The two of you can take my room, so long as you promise to tidy up after yourselves," the innkeeper said.

"That is not necessary..." Mirevra began, but Lars pulled her behind him and gently placed his large hands on the innkeeper's shoulders.

"What a generous offer from such a delightful woman. Truly, I say, your kindness and beauty know no bounds." Mirevra shook her head; the prick flattered the woman well enough. "How much more will it cost us?"

Her cheeks still stained red, the innkeeper fluttered a frail hand. "Oh, not a single coin! So long as you are sure to say goodbye before you leave."

Lars released one shoulder to grab her hand. He leaned down, almost snapping his body in half to gently kiss the top of it.

"I would never dream of leaving without seeing your pretty face again," he said in a low voice. Now wholly flustered, the innkeeper used the broom to shake him away, and then she and Lars laughed. Mirevra swallowed hard to prevent herself from throwing up in her mouth. The innkeeper strolled down the stairs, her giggles echoing behind her. Wearing a grin that threatened to split his face, Lars faced the assassin.

"You see, Viper? Some women cannot get enough of my incessant remarks." Mirevra ignored him and pushed past to follow the foolish innkeeper.

The innkeeper opened a door that led off the front hallway. Mirevra stopped at the threshold. The room was... *quaint*. There was a small hearth and a tiny white vanity with a washbasin crammed catty-cornered against a wall. A narrow bed took up the rest of the space. Mirevra did not tarry. She yanked off most of her clothes and climbed in, spreading her legs and arms wide. "Goodnight, Ruffles," she said, curling a hand under one of the two flat pillows. It was filled with only a few measly goose feathers, but Mirevra had slept on worse and was not about to complain. Her peace was soon interrupted by *him*.

"Excuse me, why do you assume that you got the bed?" Mirevra flipped over on her side to see him standing beside the bed, his hands braced on his hips. "I must have missed the part where *you* got us the room." She smiled and fluttered her lashes.

"You mean, how you coerced that poor, lonely old woman into letting you have it? Seriously, Ruffles. That was *not* very heroic of you." She was proud of her jab until he stalked to the other side of the bed, and the mattress sagged under his weight.

"Move over," he demanded, pushing his legs beneath the quilt. His skin grazed hers. He was shirtless. Mirevra froze. Apparently, their proximity did not faze Lars, as he immediately began complaining. "Gods, these pillows are worthless! Let us hope Rashawe fills them as we sleep, or I am sure to get a crick in my neck."

Finally, Mirevra could again move her body. She sat up but did not look at him. "What. Are. You. Doing?" Each sharp word was laced with the threat to slice his throat, but of course, he was unfazed by threats, too.

"Trying to catch whatever sleep I am afforded," he answered. "What about you?"

Mirevra's jaw muscles ticked as she ground her teeth. "I do not sleep with others," she said, ignoring the tightening in her chest. *Not even if she wanted to. Not even if she wished to do so many times.* Lars lifted himself and smacked his pillow before sighing and resting his head on it again.

"Of course, you do not. Just ignore me, as you said you would earlier, and sleep. Night is fleeting," he said. Her face hardened, and he laughed. "Really, Viper! You will not even notice I am here." A lie. Mirevra always noticed when he was near, just as she always noticed when he was not.

"I am not going to touch you, Viper. I am going to sleep. You do not need to worry." Mirevra unclenched her jaw, turned, and assessed him with a cold stare. His face was severe, stoic as a rock. Then, that slight smirk cracked through the stone. "Unless you ask me to touch you, of course." She yanked most of the quilt from his hold, settled on the pillow, and faced away from him.

"Touch me, and it will be the last thing you ever do, Ruffles. I will kill you where you lie," she warned. She closed her eyes, but her body remained stiff on the narrow bed. She felt his body heat; she could almost hear his heartbeat. If either moved an inch, their bodies would be pressed together. Mirevra knew how to remain still, though. If anyone moved, it would be him, and she would make good on her promise. Lars yanked the quilt back, and she heard him whisper.

"Well then, that would not be such a bad way to go."

The hours both flew and crawled by for Mirevra. She was exhausted and could barely keep her eyes open, but she was disoriented by Lars' body next to hers and could not sleep. Eventually, against her better judgment, despite her mind signaling off every warning–his heat became a source of comfort. The sound of his breaths pulled her into the most tranquil rest. It was the best sleep she had in a very long time.

A Fallen Sword

The clatter of dishes and the delicious scents of sausage and butter woke her, seducing her senses. A smile etched across her face. What a wonderful smell for a wonderful morning.

Then she felt it.

His arm was across her waist. Her muscles screamed at her to move, but she stayed completely still. She glanced down at his arm and the black hair covering almost every inch. She turned her head and watched his chest rise and peacefully dip with his slow breaths. He did not snore, thank the gods. Gold sunlight spilled through the window, and she looked at his face closely. He was not so bad when he was unconscious. His full lips were a light pink, and he had a strong nose. She noted his full, thick eyelashes. This had been the first night she had ever slept beside a man. When she settled for the night with Bagah or Beldon, they slept a few feet apart, and their arms never found their way to Mirevra's body. She allowed herself a few moments to drink in the feeling of being held. She liked it. Maybe.

Then, she threw off his strong arm and slapped him awake.

"It is morning," she announced, rising and dressing. "We must eat and be on our way. The Tajeh is close."

Lars said nothing as she dressed, but she felt his gaze on her. He watched her closely with sleepy eyes and a slight smile. Mirevra opened the door and sent him one glance.

A glance that said *tell no one of this.* She slammed the door closed behind her.

The City That Burned

~~~

Tales of Mercinnho always centered on its extravagance and its inhabitants, swathed in the finest clothing, leading lives of leisure and luxury. *A place of dreams.* As they rode into the city, Mirevra thought it looked more like a place of nightmares. It was what she imagined the Murks, the ultimate destination of those who lived evil lives, looked like. The destination for Foxes after their deaths. At least this Fox, Mirevra thought. The town had been burned and razed. The air was heavy with smoke, lingering ashes, and the stench of charred flesh.

Shiln knelt, swiped a finger through the ash, and then held it high to examine it. "This destruction is fresh. I suspect it was done in the last few days," she said. "Someone else must be looking for the blade." Grumbles and exclamations broke out, but Bagah and Mirevra only exchanged intense stares. Mirevra's gut roiled, and her mount shied. She straightened in her saddle to ease her discomfort, patting the horse's neck while trying to make sense of this. Perhaps another guild knew of the blade, and their leader was even more determined to find it than the Veravant and the Head? Mirevra glanced down and saw the charred corpses of small animals tangled together under a scorched tree. Or had the Sardek army pillaged this city? The swirling discomfort intensified, and a wave of bile rose in her throat.

"Beldon!" Shiln called. "Help me look for survivors to heal. The rest of you look for the Tajeh. Let us pray there are survivors," she said as she walked away. Soon, Beldon was peering into what was left of the homes and shops while Shiln raked her eyes over the charred rubble for bodies. Lars held his nose. Roman and Neeps shook their heads in sorrow.

"There is nothing left," Jardin whispered. "We would do well to return to our leaders and report this news."

"We should investigate first," Lars advocated, his thick brows furrowed. "We cannot leave without knowing what happened."

"Look around, Lars," Jardin said. "This place is nothing but embers and bones. We need to leave quickly, lest we wait for whoever or whatever did this to return and finish us off, too."

Bagah glared at Jardin for suggesting such cowardice. Mirevra knew very little of Bagah's story. But this scorched city and its smell could not be dissimilar to what his people experienced. The Teruk lands had been destroyed, and the Teruk people had endured an unimaginable carnage. Bagah would never leave without first searching for survivors. He would not leave until he found the Tajeh.

Mirevra dismounted as Heral addressed Jardin like a mother to a child. "We must look for the Tajeh, at least. If you prefer to wait in the coach, so be it. We will not force you to wander about with the rest of us," she said. Neeps raised his finger.

"I will search the shops for any surviving ingredients," he said, scurrying off without explanation.

"What is he..." Mirevra started. Lars looked at her with a wry smile that did not meet his eyes.

"He wants to make more potions," he said. "Neeps only cares about two things: his vials and what goes in them."

Jardin huffed a rough exhale. "Do as you wish. Search for corpses if you must. I smell nothing but trouble here. A sinister act is in play." His blue eyes snapped to Lars before they caught Mirevra's golden ones and held them. "Something lingers here. Death. Betrayal," he said. It was not a question.

Mirevra could taste fear on her tongue. And death and betrayal were apparent scents. Jardin waited for her response, but she did not know what to say. Yes, she could smell it, *feel* it even; did everyone not share this? The city was razed, burned, and desecrated.

Jardin tore his eyes from hers and fixed his bow upon his back. Mirevra felt instant relief. "I will tend to the horses," he said.

Heral nodded, but Mirevra was confused. The Nelimen were heroes, or so they said. Why would one of their members not want to look for survivors? Why did the rest of the guild allow it? Did this not go against their code?

She watched Jardin walk back to the carriage. Another feeling was moving in her now. *'The Wolf is closer than you think,'* Audrina had said. Mirevra shook her head to clear her thoughts.

"There are two in here!" Beldon cried from inside one of the houses. Shiln hopped over fallen pillars and rubble to meet him, and Mirevra watched as white fire flared through what was left of the windows. Roman turned to her.

"There may be others. I will scope the perimeter," he said and wild-shaped into the white fox. He slithered across her ankles and trotted quickly away on his little legs. Mirevra, Bagah, Heral, and Lars stood quietly, each assessing the situation. Lars stroked his chin.

"I suppose the four of us could search for the Tajeh while the others look for survivors?" he asked.

Mirevra nodded, then scoured her memory for what the Veravant and Briatriel had told them. "They live in the rectory of The Maji. That should be easy enough to find," she said. Heral frowned and reached into a pocket. Mirevra braced herself, for this woman used magic that did not operate under Arcanen laws and there was no telling what she was reaching for.

She blinked a few times as Heral offered her a piece of cloth. "To cover your mouth and nose," Heral said. "Unless you want to breathe in the smoke. It does not matter to me either way."

Bagah declined the offer. He did not need it. His lungs worked differently; it would take more than ash and smoke to weaken them.

Mirevra snatched the black cloth and promptly tied it around her head, covering her nose and mouth. Lars and Heral did the same, and the unlikely quartet suddenly resembled a team. Mirevra was not sure what she thought of this. She ignored the subject as they began their search for the Tajeh of Maji. She was acutely aware that there were more pressing matters than whether or not she blended in with heroes.

The Rectory

For once, Lars was quiet. Hours had slipped by as the four walked down every winding street searching for the rectory of The Maji. They found countless ruined structures charred black from the flames and pillaged shops. But they saw no one. Surely, whoever or whatever had stormed through here was not searching for the blade. If so, there would have been no cause for this carnage. The more destruction she saw, the more Mirevra believed that those responsible had burned this city to a crisp as a message to the territory of Caxaven. Sardek, the High Crown, was known for boundless greed. After extracting the Teruk army, Kallias laid siege to several empires and territories. Wrovelle, Arcaeles, and Fertek had surrendered to Sardek. They now called themselves the Allies, but the whole of Estellian knew this simple title did not convey the truth. Everyone in these territories now existed as the absolute servants of the High Crown and were ready to do its bidding whenever summoned.

Only Sanica, a thriving southern kingdom that had rejected Kallias and even rebuked his genocide of the Teruk, and Caxaven, remained free of Sardek. There was also Droudor in the west and closest to the

Cold Lands. But Droudor remained unclaimed in a tacit agreement between the powers, none of which saw any use for it. Tales of Droudor suggested it was not a place anyone would want to claim.

Mirevra stepped over a headless doll and swallowed her bile as she glimpsed a scorched crib through a broken window. This *was* Sardek's doing. The Allies would never stop until Sanica and Caxaven conceded. She sucked the fabric in and out of her mouth as she breathed deeply.

"There," Bagah said and pointed a finger. She followed his eyes and gazed at the hills that surrounded the city. She narrowed her sights but saw nothing, save for rolling knolls and thickets of trees. But when Heral thanked Bagah for his keen eyesight, Mirevra knew something was there.

"What?" Lars asked, and Mirevra was grateful that he could not see anything either.

"They blend in well, but the temple and the rectory are there," Heral said.

The four made their way toward the hills. On foot, it took them another hour, and the heat did not let up; shade from the trees offered little reprieve. Mirevra's dry throat ached, and she cursed herself for not bringing water. When they reached their destination, her tongue felt like she had been licking cotton cloth. The rectory was a humble structure of unevenly stacked stones marked by two large chimneys. Heral did not stop to knock on the arched doors. She kicked them, and they blew open.

As Mirevra entered the main room, bright paint covering the walls assaulted her eyes and made her slightly dizzy; portraits of every god and deity she could think of crowded the colorful walls. Limestone and marble statues filled every corner and surface, and the books.... Gods, there were enough books for every soul in Estellian to start a library. She hadn't the slightest clue of how they all fit, books were crammed into every inch of the floor-to-ceiling shelves. Even more sat in neat piles lining the hallways leading from the main room. And more than a few were sprawled on the floor as if flung down hurriedly. Mirevra straightened her shoulders and assessed the room. The archives were more disorganized than she had expected. Still, she acknowledged that if she were the keeper of every story, her mind would forget her surroundings and be even more scrambled than it was. "Stay vigilant," said Lars, taking in the chaos. "We do not know what we may find here."

The four searched until the sun prepared to descend below the horizon. The rectory did not hold the secret to the mysterious Gerreland blade. The Veravant would not be pleased, Mirevra thought. Lars and Heral shook their heads in defeat and proposed leaving the group. But Mirevra watched Bagah and saw him flare his nostrils and then squeeze them together. Their eyes met, and she tilted her head toward her shoulder. Bagah nodded. "Where?" Mirevra asked. Bagah pointed to the books strewn in front of a large fireplace that ate up most of one wall. She took off in that direction.

"What just happened?" Lars asked, following her back into the room.

"Bagah smelled someone. He said it came from this fireplace. Look for anything that could open a trapdoor," Mirevra answered as she began to toss books in every direction. Lars scratched his head.

"When did he say that?"

Heral returned to search the bookcases, Bagah overturned the furniture again, and Lars scanned the heavy curtains and windows. Mirevra stood quietly and stared at the fireplace mantle. *If I were the conduit for The Maji, what would I value?* Books and pieces of hemp were too obvious. She knew she was not the wisest soul in Estellian, but she had survived this long; she knew how to think through a problem. If there were a hidden room, the Tajeh would want something they valued highly in return for entry.

A remnant of a memory formed then careened through her mind. *Her old quilt stitched with the heavenly designs of the constellations...The smell of her mother's favorite tea... Her father reading a bedtime story.* She blinked. A small, feathered quill and a piece of hemp paper rested on the mantel. She gripped the quill and began.

"What are you writing?" Heral inquired, stepping closer. *What* she was writing did not matter so long as she wrote.

"A story," she responded plainly. "A new one for the Tajeh to discover." It was a simple tale of two criminals and two heroes working together to find a missing blade, but it was enough. She heard a crack, then the sound of stone grating against stone. Lars whistled.

"Quick thinking, Viper." A small entrance in the stone wall split open. The opening was just wide enough for a narrow spiral staircase. Heral led the charge down, Bagah taking up the rear. With sconces lighting the rock walls, Mirevra could at least see the next step. At the bottom of the stairs, they found themselves in what seemed to be an endless labyrinth of books. Unlike the books upstairs, these were color-coded and organized. Mirevra almost felt suffocated by how neatly fashioned it all was. Now, this was how she had pictured archives. *Wonderful, awful, and massive.*

The band of four wandered through the bookshelves filled with dyed leather books and stacked codices until, finally, somehow, they all met in the center.

There was a small hearth, a violet chair with a teetering stack of books beside it, and on the chair's plush cushion sat...the Tajeh.

The Blacksmith
and His Blade

※

They were short. Their legs dangled off their chair and did not reach the floor. When Heral approached, they did not startle or display much emotion. With a loaded exhale, they placed their current read atop the stack and looked up. "So, you have come to ask for a story. Make it quick. Which one would you like to hear?" Mirevra blinked rapidly. It could not be easy to find out what they needed, could it? She studied the Tajeh's slight build, their orange hair, and the freckles splattered across their young face. Long lashes, thin lips, sharp cheekbones. A gaudy medallion draped down their chest. They were lovely, but not a day over their twentieth year; they were far too young to be in such a high position for The Maji.

Heral was all business. "We are here to ask about the holy blade forged by Gerreland Nerth. Rumors say he created a sword mighty enough to kill a god and that it was buried with him. Can you tell us if he did create this sword, and if so, where Gerreland is buried?"

A Fallen Sword

Lars stepped closer, more interested in the Tajeh's answer than in anything Mirevra had seen. The Tajeh jumped to their feet and stretched their hands to the ceiling. "I *could* tell you," they said. Mirevra waited for the Tajeh to continue, but apparently, that was all they would say. Their round, light-blue eyes gazed at the four, and they smiled. "You did not think you could come here and receive a story for free, did you?" The Tajeh laughed. "A bunch of fools you are, if that is the case."

"What do you want as payment?" Mirevra asked quickly; she had no patience for their humor. "We will offer whatever it is you require."

"Let us not get ahead of ourselves," Lars interjected, flanking Mirevra's side. Her skin flushed with warmth as she recalled how they had woken only just that morning, and she stepped away. "We would like to know how to pay you, though we cannot make any promises," Lars said. He looked at Mirevra, his brows lowered. "Some prices can be too high." Mirevra swallowed the *fuck you* she wanted to blurt and nodded instead. Lars was right, godsdamn him. What if the Tajeh wanted something they could not give?

The Tajeh laughed again. "Is it not obvious?" The four looked at each other.

"Coin?" Lars questioned and reached deep into his pockets. The Tajeh mumbled, looking quite annoyed at Lars' guess and gesture. They crossed their arms over their chest.

"What use would The Maji have for coin? You are lucky you are so disrespectfully handsome, or your stupidity would eat you alive," said the Tajeh. Mirevra choked down a laugh. *Disrespectfully handsome* was one way to describe Lars; *stupid* was even better.

"Then what?" Heral broke in, her eyes dancing with intrigue.

"The same way you gained entry to the archives, of course. The Maji will tell you a story—for a story."

Mirevra took another step back. A story for a story. A truth for a truth. She longed to curse out loud. These damned gods with their damned bargains.

"Easy enough," Lars said. "Once upon a time, there was a small bear who could not climb a tree," he began with dramatic gestures. "Day in and day out, he tried..."

The Tajeh held up a stiff hand. "Not just *any* story," they reprimanded. "The Maji already knows far too many fables." Their voice dropped to a mutter. "And more fables *will* keep coming. Yes, they will. And I will have to record them." They looked at Lars sternly. "Most are dull and ordinary," they said.

"I am sorry," Lars apologized brightly, and Mirevra wanted to roll her eyes at his patent insincerity. "You did not specify. Tell me what kind of story The Maji wishes to hear, and I will supply it."

"Tell us a story from your life," the Tajeh said. Mirevra blanched. She would do no such thing, especially after Audrina had already torn through her precious memories. She now quietly moved behind Bagah.

"A story from my life?" Lars' dark tone came close to mocking the Tajeh. The Tajeh nodded.

"One of deep value," they added. "The Maji loves tales that make Their heart swell—like romance. *Oh! Oh!* Do you have a story about the matters of your heart? Tell us when you first fell in love!" Lars' face went blank, and he shook his head.

"I have never been in love. Afraid I cannot help you there," he snapped. Mirevra cocked her head. Surely, a man as handsome and charismatic as Lars had been in love? Then she gulped. Did others assume the same of her? Would they also be surprised to learn she had never shared love either? The Tajeh dropped their head, and their delicate lips twisted as they scrutinized Lars. They clutched the medallion hanging from their neck and squeezed it hard.

"The Maji says you lie," the Tajeh called out.

"How do They know if I lie?" Lars snapped. The Tajeh laughed.

"The Fluent gathers stories in any way they can be told. Conversations, whispers, stories told in songs and literature," they said, gesturing at the thousands of volumes surrounding them. "Every story ever told is here, and The Maji knows them all by heart. Stories are what They love and who They are. They know you lie because They have heard many stories about you. Many whispers, giggles, and hushed words in the night. The Maji says you lost a great love."

Lars' face turned ashen. He stumbled backward and would have fallen over if Heral had not grabbed and steadied him. Mirevra stepped away from behind Bagah's protective bulk to inspect the rogue. She sensed the fear emanating from him, the trepidation that bound his tongue. The Tajeh hopped off their chair, moved closer, and waved their finger at Lars. "The one you loved is dead."

They said it so plainly that they may have been remarking on yesterday's supper. The fear on Lars' face morphed into anger. He marched to the Tajeh and loomed over them.

"It seems The Maji knows plenty about me. Why do They need my story?" His question was anything but a threat, yet Mirevra sensed the chaos and pain laced through it.

"They do not know *your* story. They only know the tales They heard. Stories *about* you spoken by other mouths and to other ears."

"Speak plainly," Lars demanded. The Tajeh nodded and giggled.

"It seems you will not speak of your first love. But it has been told by another," the Tajeh mused and again clutched their medallion. "Hmm, yes. The Maji has heard some of this tale. There is a dark room. Ships are preparing to sail, and your beloved...her hair was long...a chestnut brown... Another man..." the Tajeh looked up at Lars with wide, sad eyes. "A guttural cry is born of heartbreak."

"Enough!" Lars seethed. His sword sang as he freed it from its sheath. Heral hurried to Lars and pushed his arm down. The Tajeh simply laughed.

"The Maji says the oracle was right. They say this is why you are so afraid."

"One more word, and I swear to Degolian–" Lars began, but the Tajeh cut him off.

"If you do not wish to speak of your heartbreak, perhaps someone else here will speak of theirs. Trust that eventually, The Maji will learn all your stories. If there is one truth about mortals, you *love* to talk. Humans exist in stories. When a person's story dies, so does their memory. It is as if they never existed at all. But The Maji remembers. The Maji has never let a story fade." They clutched their medallion and studied Heral, Mirevra, and Bagah in turn. "Now, who will tell me of their heartbreak?" Mirevra held her breath, praying to whatever gods would listen that the Tajeh would not choose her. Yet she felt only slight relief when their eyes settled upon Bagah. "Half-Teruk," they said and pointed at him. "The Maji would like you to tell your story. For it, I will tell you of the Gerreland blade, *if it is real, and where it can be found....*" Their voice drifted off like a raft on the sea, and their blue eyes glimmered with anticipation. Without moving a muscle, Bagah held the Tajeh's stare for a long, silent moment. Mirevra had begun to wonder if her friend would attack them when Bagah spoke.

"Many mouths have certainly told my story. The bastard child of Droudor, the oddity in the village. Ask The Maji; They will tell you," he said. Mirevra's heart pounded and ached. She had never asked Bagah where he hailed from, had never poked into his past. Yet from the moment Bagah had appeared at the den and pledged to be a Fox, Mirevra had sensed the pain engulfing him. He did not need to speak of it. When they met, they had looked quietly at each other, reaching an unspoken agreement. Their history was off-limits. Both had endured sordid pasts but would not let these determine their futures. Mirevra now gazed at her boots, rubbed her hand over one vambrace, and did anything to spare her friend another pair of curious eyes. The Tajeh squeezed their medallion and shut their eyes.

"Mmm. Oh, yes. They have heard. There are still voices that speak of it today. The Maji can hear them."

Bagah winced, but the Tajeh pressed on. "Some consider your birth a tragedy. They call your father a monster. He took a human woman and did with her what he pleased," they said. The Tajeh squeezed their eyes tighter and gripped the medallion with fresh force. Bagah's nostrils flared, but he did not recoil from the Tajeh's words. "The Maji says this is a lie. Your father and mother chose their fate together before the Root Puller..." The Tajeh cocked their head as if The Maji were next to them, whispering in their ear. "There is an unfortunate canard that the Teruk are nothing but beasts, but The Maji know it is untrue. The Teruk were happy when free; they were not the angry barbarians the kingdoms know today." The Tajeh's eyes snapped open and met Bagah's. "Tell me your story, half-breed. The Maji has heard it from others, but They now request your own."

Bagah shifted. He glanced at Mirevra, and she shrugged. *It is your choice.* Heral inched closer to Bagah, keen interest marking her striking features. "To learn the truth about the blade, I must ask you that you do this," she whispered, her eyes heavy. Lars spoke next, his expression still pained from when the Tajeh spoke of his life.

"Heral and I will leave. The Maji may need to hear your story, but your business is not ours. If we return upstairs, will you speak freely?"

Bagah could still smell the freshly torched city below, his mind filled with scenes of rampant destruction and corpses. He pinned his yellow eyes on Lars and nodded. Lars threw a hand on Bagah's shoulder and, with tight lips, nodded back. He then gestured for Heral to follow him upstairs. Mirevra moved to follow, but Bagah's arm blocked her.

"Stay," he said. Mirevra clenched her trembling hands and shook her head to dispel her rapid thoughts that fired in every direction. Bagah had asked her to stay; he had invited her to hear his story. Stepping back so she remained out of sight, Mirevra studied her half-Teruk friend as he readied himself. His face was impassive. The Tajeh released their medallion.

"The Maji thanks you. Wait here. I must retrieve an empty codex to write your story." The Tajeh scampered around a corner of a bookshelf and disappeared. Bagah and Mirevra did not speak or look at each other. Here was a dreadful moment that neither had ever wanted. But for their mission and for the Ring, they would endure it. When the Tajeh approached, their footsteps sounded heavier. A large older male rounded the corner holding a codex. Their skin was bronze, their hair a raven's black. When they spoke, their voice was many octaves deeper. "Begin," they said and plopped down in the chair. Mirevra trembled.

A Fallen Sword

The Tajeh had taken a new form, which they often did, a large detail she had forgotten in her study. But that is not what made her shake. Something else now haunted her. *Bagah's story.*

Bagah breathed deep and readied himself to speak more than he had likely ever spoken in his lifetime. He closed his eyes and began.

"Forty-eight years ago, the Teruk owned territories in every known land, though most were in Sanica and Drodour. My story began in the mountains of Drodour. A Teruk man named Gegaret and his wife, Everarda, had just given birth to a boy." Mirevra felt a jolt run through her. Now she knew where Bagah was from. She knew his parents' names, that his father was the Teruk, and most astonishing, Bagah was in his fortieth year. She had always assumed he was perhaps approaching his thirtieth year. He appeared no older than her, all things accounted for. Her eyes darted to her friend, then back to her boots.

"Though not common, it was not unheard of for a human and Teruk to have children. My father loved my mother. I remember this clearly." Bagah's eyes snapped open, and he stared at the Tajeh. "Be sure to write that down," he said firmly before continuing. "My father.... He had his issues, but he was kind to her. The Teruk are good-natured–in our hearts, we do not wish to fight. But because our bodies are strong, Kallias saw us not only as a threat, but as a weapon. Rumors spread from Wrovelle and Arcaeles that Kallias had an *offer* for the Teruk: to become his soldiers or suffer punishment. My father was not the Xadaet, but he was a prominent figure. His word held sway with the people. He declared that we would never bow to Kallias and that the Teruk would remain on our land. Yet, he took no chances. That night, my mother and I left our home for Tuvaria. My parents knew my mother would be safe from the Sardekian army as a human, and perhaps I, a half-human, might have a chance at life. I was only a babe; these words are what my mother told me as I grew into a boy. But somehow, I remember them. I cannot explain..." Bagah stumbled but then cleared his throat. "Two nights later, Sardek attacked. The Teruk lands were destroyed. My father turned coward and fell to the Crown's sword."

The Tajeh wrote incredibly fast, their quill never seeming to lift off the hemp. Mirevra felt the walls close in, and she rolled her shoulders. She should not be here and should not be listening to this story. She lifted her gaze and met Bagah's eyes.

Bagah's lips quivered. "Does The Maji need more?" He did not break his gaze on Mirevra. The Tajeh quickly looked up, stroked their facial hair, and squeezed the medallion.

"The Maji says the blade is not a myth. It exists. It was forged by the legendary blacksmith, and indeed, it can be used to kill a god," they said and then winked. "Or a lich."

Mirevra stepped forward, her eyes wide. Their chance for survival had just grown tenfold. "It is real," she breathed. The Tajeh nodded, then placed their quill back on the paper.

"For where it is buried, The Maji needs more," they said briskly. Bagah blanched a sickly pale yellow. His giant hand curled into fists and squeezed until his knuckles bled white. Mirevra realized it was not the destruction of his lands, nor was it that he and his mother were forced to flee that haunted his heart and soul. It was what had happened afterward. Whether she wanted to or not, she knew the turmoil Bagah felt. The Tajeh squeezed the medallion. "The Maji knows much of your father but very little of your mother. Especially after she left Drodour. Very strange. Unfit. Not the way a story should be," they said, their brows arched in anticipation. "Will you tell us of her?" Bagah swallowed hard, his fists still clenched.

"You will tell us exactly where Gerreland is buried?" He bargained with the Tajeh, though his eyes never left the ground.

A Fallen Sword

"Yes. We will tell you where Gerreland is buried," they promised. Bagah's neck constricted, and his nostrils flared. The half-breed took in anxious puffs. Eventually, his breaths slowed, and his voice filled the room once more.

"Twelve years passed. My mother and I lived quietly in Tuvaria. We took care not to bring any attention to ourselves. We kept our heads down and lived humbly. She sewed and tailored coats for a shop in a nearby town; I tended to the chickens and our few crops. We scarcely left our house except when Mother needed to drop off her work or sell eggs." Bagah's voice waned in and out. He cleared his throat. "My mother told me that being half-human would save me from Teruk's fate even if we were found. The Sardekian army could not force me to join their ranks, nor could they ship me off to be a free toiler. But she knew I was not completely safe. A new world was born under the Root Puller, and everything had changed for the Teruk. As a half-Teruk, human society would never accept me, much less be treated kindly. It was a pain and burden she wished she could have taken from me. I understood. But for as long as I can remember, anger grew in me. It could not be satiated; it could not be quelled. My mother feared it. She told me...." Bagah brought a hand to his brow where the veins on the sides of his forehead bulged. His lips twitched, his voice shook. "She told me to keep my anger locked away. She told me it was not *my* anger that stirred within me and that I could not claim ownership of it. She... She told me I had not been born with this hate in my heart," Bagah whispered. He wiped his nostrils and blinked hard.

Memories flashed before Bagah's eyes. His mother's warm gaze and her gentle spirit. The times she had urged him to control the anger. The way the sun shone on her as she lifted a glass jar, ready to fill it with her fig jam. "But she could not understand. *All* I felt was hate. *All* I knew was anger. My home was gone, my father was gone, and I... I was this," he said, waving his hands over his body. "This *thing*. A beast, a monster. My very existence was and is still a mistake. Everyone knows it. I know it. My anger knows it, too." Bagah siphoned a deep breath and looked at the Tajeh. "There were times I could not control the anger. It devoured me. It controlled me. It *became* me.

"One morning, my mother sent me to town to return repaired coats to the tailor. I wore a cowl, and it shrouded most of my features. But boys were walking along the road, and they…" Bagah grimaced, and Mirevra's face tightened. She forced herself to watch her struggling friend. "They noticed my height and my build, and they knew. Most had heard of 'the oddity from down the way.' They taunted me with the tales they had been taught and accused me of terrible things. They said I had gobbled up babies, ransacked homes, and made deals with Degolian. They tore off my cloak and set fire to my mother's work. They threw rocks at me and called me a demon. I wanted to kill them. I should have killed *them*." Bagah stopped, his entire body shaking now. The Tajeh scribbled down the story with no compassion in their eyes. It was just a story. One of millions.

Mirevra stepped quickly to Bagah's side and rested her hand on his wrist.

"That is enough," she snapped at the Tajeh. "Tell us where Gerreland is buried." She could not stomach hearing her friend's pain. Let Bagah say the word, and she *would* learn the names of those boys, kill them, and make their families watch as she did so. Nasty souls who made another being suffer simply because they looked different. Mirevra wondered how Bagah managed such fury in his bones; her anger now was almost too much to bear. The Tajeh laid their quill neatly in the spine of the open book and smiled tautly.

"The Maji says that we cannot tell you where the blacksmith is buried," they said. Mirevra practically growled.

"You *promised you would*. Bagah has told you his story, and you said–"

The Tajeh lifted a finger high in the air.

"Because the blacksmith is not dead," they added calmly. In an instant, Mirevra's eyes turned from a feline on the prowl to its spooked prey. Gerreland Nerth was...*not dead?*

"That cannot be," Mirevra mumbled. "Gerreland Nerth died eons ago. He cannot still be... He could not..."

"But he is. Gerreland Nerth *is* alive," said the Tajeh. "That is why we cannot tell you where he is buried."

Questions roared like a cyclone through Mirevra's mind. She bit down hard on her cheek and grabbed the closest one.

"And the blade? Is *it* buried?"

The Tajeh grabbed the quill and looked down at their pages. "Finish the story, and The Maji will tell," they said calmly. Mirevra longed to grab that damned book from the Tajeh and clobber them with it. Her body tensed as she moved to take a long stride toward the chair, but Bagah grabbed her hand.

"To the Ring we serve," he muttered. "The Veravant sent us here to do one thing. And we will do it, whatever it takes." Mirevra looked into Bagah's eyes and shook her head.

"You do not have to say another word. I will tell them something about my life."

"It is fine, Mir," Bagah assured her. "My mother's story should be known. At least by someone. It is unfair to keep it hidden because of my mistakes." He released her hand and turned to the Tajeh. "I will tell you the rest, but The Maji must promise to relinquish all that They know of the blacksmith and the blade. Do They give me Their word?"

A squeeze of the medallion and in seconds, the Tajeh nodded. "All will be told of Gerreland Nerth and his fallen blade. They promise."

Bagah bobbed his head and strode forward. "When I returned home, I was too angry to see. Anger blinded me, and my veins burned within my skin. My heart punched and kicked, and my ears were filled with the sound of rushing water. I was wholly consumed by the rage."

Mirevra swallowed. She had often urged her friend not to give way to the rage, but in truth, she had never seen it. Only a handful of times had she witnessed Bagah approach that anger. Still, it was close enough for her to understand that it should be unleashed only in extreme cases. "My mother tried to calm me. She desperately called out to me. I felt her hands push me away. Then I heard her cries, her screams–I heard her heart beat so fast. I heard the glass jar break." Bagah choked, and his knees wobbled. Mirevra grabbed her throat as comprehension dawned. She now knew why Bagah had never spoken of his past and why The Maji had not heard stories of his mother. Heat stung her eyes. "When I came back, she was gone."

"When you came back?" The Tajeh looked up and asked.

Bagah dipped his head. "When the rage receded, and I could see again, she lay on the floor, her body mangled by my hands. I had killed her. My mother was dead. *Gone.* I had murdered her, and I do not even have the punishment of remembering what happened. All I remember is that I returned home, and everything was red. My entire world was bleeding crimson. And then after..." Bagah brought a hand to his mouth, and his brows puckered. "I pray daily to Rashawe that I can remember! I should be plagued by the memories! It is what I deserve. My penance should be to always know exactly what I did. My mother was light, and I am darkness. I gave way to the rage, and she is gone. I took her soul."

Bagah no longer looked sad. Mirevra recognized the rage rearing its insidious head. She grabbed her friend's hand and rested her head on his arm. His furious panting slowed as his fingers squeezed gently around hers. The Tajeh dotted the page with one last exaggerated flourish and snapped the book closed.

"The Maji thanks you for your story. Now, Everarda's name will live for eternity in the pages of the archives. Her life will be known, and her death understood. Her story shall never fade. May her spirit finally rest," they chirped, almost merrily. Bagah inhaled slowly, and his heartbeat steadied. Maybe, just maybe, he would find some peace in that. Mirevra wondered if she would feel the same if Bagah knew her whole truth, name, and story.

"Now, about the blade," the Tajeh said. "You may wish to sit." He gestured toward two plush cushions, but Bagah and Mirevra declined. As tired as her legs were from the journey up the hills, Mirevra's body was still lanced with too much nervous energy to rest in a sitting position. The Tajeh clasped their hands neatly in their lap. "Gerreland Nerth, the legendary blacksmith of Sardek, forged twenty-seven blades in his lifetime. This would be a paltry number and nothing to boast of for an ordinary blacksmith. But as we know, Gerreland's blades were not ordinary. He made the most explementary weapons known to our lands, dangerous in more ways than one. His armor found its way into the world and spread far and wide. It was a sought-after accouterment for soldiers in battle. While he was alive, Gerreland Nerth received great rewards for his creations. Too much coin to know what to do with; elixirs and potions and whores abounded. His life was, shall we say, overly comfortable. He grew bored. So, as men of great status do, Gerreland sought what he did not already have. He traveled to the temples of Ashe and, for seventeen seasons, practiced the way of the Belcerdites."

Mirevra's head drew back. Belcerdites had been a legendary practitioner of Arcanen. Under the way of the Belcredites, a sorcerer could become a wizard, a master of Spells.

"Gerreland Nerth practiced wizardry?"

"Practiced? No, no. He perfected it," the Tajeh stated. "The legendary blacksmith's palms now teemed with Arcanen magic. He became more powerful than any sorcerer or warlock known in Estellian. This was when pride replaced curiosity, and he began plans to forge a new blade. The Vaenir, he called it. A sword powerful enough to defeat a god! Many tried to stop him. They pleaded with him to consider the true cost of such a weapon. But he ignored all admonishments. This is the way of arrogance; it loves to speak, do—and become! But it fails to listen. Gerreland forged the blade. The deed was done." The Tajeh paused dramatically and scanned their audience's intent faces. "And indeed, its cost was too high. The Arcanen was too strong! Gerreland's soul was ripped in two. Half his soul—the portion that, before pride overtook him, had been filled with wonder, creativity, and honor—was absorbed into the Vaenir. But the other half—blackened and sullied by pride, greed, and chaos—remained in the husk of his body. That very husk now roams the world, seeking the blade."

Mirevra cocked her head and tapped her chin. "Does Gerreland seek his blade to reunite his soul?"

The Tajeh contemplated their answer for a long moment. "Yes and no," they finally said. "The Vaenir indeed carries half of Gerreland's soul, and it is desperate to reunite with its other half. A soul broken in two cannot find rest! And Gerrelend is tired; he longs to sleep. He cannot enter an afterlife of peace until he is killed while possessing his whole soul. But the dark half of his soul seeks the Vaenir for reasons much more grim than finding peace in death."

"What happens if the two are reunited?" Mirevra asked.

"It all depends," the Tajeh said. "If the husk that is now Gerreland finds the blade first, he will obliterate Estellian. We will all become cold ash, the fallout of evil incarnate. But life can be saved if the Vaenir is wielded against the husk. The Vaenir's power will force Gerreland's soul to reunite, and he will pass on to whatever the gods have planned for him in the next life."

"The Vaenir can kill the husk..." Mirevra's thoughts seemed to bleed together. Then her eyes snapped the Tajeh's. *"The lich."*

"Precisely, child. The husk, that half of Gerreland Nerth's soul *is* the lich." Bagah recoiled and stomped backward a few paces. Mirevra held strong.

"Where is the Vaenir?" Mirevra demanded. "If we find it, we can bind Gerreland's soul and kill him." The Tajeh frowned, held a finger beneath their chin, and sent Mirevra a subtle nod.

"I suppose one could. Though I must warn you, the blade was never meant to be wielded by a human. That is why Gerreland Nerth met such a fate. It is too powerful for your mortal bones. A human is not meant to be hoisted up as a god."

"A problem for another day," Mirevra said, dismissing it with an airy wave. "Something we will resolve *after* the blade is in our possession. Tell us its location so that we may go at once. If the lich is searching, he is getting closer by the second. We cannot waste time."

The Tajeh shook their head. "I am afraid it is not so easy. The blade has been lost since the day it was forged."

Kaven Hiring

Mirevra grimaced as the hope tingling through her limbs ebbed and was replaced by a nervous agitation. "Are you saying there is *no* chance? You have no notion of where it could be?" Her voice cracked, and annoyed at herself, she drew up straighter.

The Tajeh stroked their chin, then put a finger to their lips. "Wait here," they said and again disappeared around the corner. Mirevra turned and faced Bagah.

"Do not fret, friend," she said. "We will find something. Anything! That blade will be in our grasp in no time at all." She did not believe her words, and to judge his expression, neither did Bagah. But it did not matter what they believed. Finding the Vaenir was their only chance for survival. She stood still as a voice echoed in her mind. *"Live."*

When the Tajeh returned, they bore rich dark skin and dark ringlets that fell to their shoulders. A long dress of sheer lilac tulle hugged their shapely hips. Gorgeous gold eyes—rivaling her own—watched Mirevra. Their voice was still low when they spoke, but now a sultry accent spilled from their tongue.

"Stories are always shared," the Tajeh said. "In whispers around a tavern table, loudly over a hot campfire, in soft tones before bed." They lifted a leather-bound volume. "In here, you will find all The Maji has ever heard of the Vaenir. Every rumor and story lies within these pages."

Mirevra reached to grab it, but the Tajeh pulled it back to their chest. Mirevra scowled. "Do not tell me The Maji requires another story," she said.

The Tajeh smiled. "The Maji rarely parts with a volume from Their archive. To receive this is the highest honor, the greatest privilege The Fluent has ever granted a mortal," they said. Mirevra tried not to roll her eyes. "But rumors and stories are spreading like wildfire. The lich is in pursuit of the Vaenir. The fate of Estellian now rests in the hands of whoever can find and wield that blade," the Tajeh said.

They now offered the volume to Mirevra, and their tone softened. "The Maji has heard many stories from the dawn of our age, from across the world, and back. Still, They find *your* story particularly interesting, child. Do take this lightly; The Maji believes you can find the blade. They believe you can save the world."

As Mirevra grabbed the leather-bound pages, she heard voices and loud noises. It was time to go. "Thank you," she said gravely. "And thank The Maji." Bagah and Mirevra whirled around, sprinted through the maze, and raced up the spiral staircase into the rectory. They found Lars and Heral bent over and panting laboriously, but Mirevera did not ask why, instead, she held the newly acquired volume high in the air.

"Who is the fastest reader?"

The Vote

By the time they returned to the scorched city, it was well into the evening. Roman, engulfed with sweat and his cheeks blazing a deep red, greeted them. "Did you find anything?" he asked Mirevra. She nodded, held up the book, and asked him the same question. He bobbed his head and handed her a patch with a gold and black insignia. Mirevra's stomach dropped as she examined it. *So, it was the Sardek army.* She handed it back to Roman as he continued his questions. "Why do you think they did this? Do you suppose they are looking for the blade? I mean, assuming the rumors are even true?" Mirevra shook her head.

"We found the rectory untouched. The Tajeh is safe. If King Dern was looking for the blade, he would have no need to burn a city for it." She gestured at the horrific ruination carnage them. "This is the mark of the Allies. As long as Caxaven remains neutral, the Allies' hatred will spread. Such is the way of the Root Puller's line." She motioned for Bagah, Heral, and Lars to follow her, then took long strides to where Neeps sat, tinkering with his glass bottles.

Roman stumbled as he tried to keep up with her. "You think Sardek will keep attacking the southern kingdoms until they bend their knees? What will he have left to rule but smoke and bones!?"

"Land ruined is still land to own," Mirevra shrugged. "Greed is boundless. Madmen have an unquenchable thirst to conquer. Especially Dern," she said. She threw the book in the halfling's lap. "They tell me you can read quickly."

"This is true," said Neeps, thumbing through the pages. "What is this?" His voice and features were a blend of excitement and puzzlement.

"If we have any chance of finding the blade, the answer will be in this book. Read it quickly and tell us what you find," Mirevra ordered.

Neeps scowled at her tone. Heral bent and met Neeps' eyes. "Mirevra speaks the truth, Neeps," she said quietly. "Read."

"The blade is real?!" Roman gasped.

"So says The Maji," Lars answered. He nodded at Mirevra and Bagah. "According to what They told these two, the blade and the lich are bonded. Two parts of the same soul–".

"Save it for the entire group, Ruffles," Mirevra broke in and squinted into the dark. "Where are the others?"

"Beldon and the sorceress—pray forgive me, I cannot remember her name—are leading the survivors toward the road," Roman said. "They found a few men, some women, and even children. Not many, though. It seems the Sardek army showed little mercy."

"Where are they taking them?" Mirevra bit down the rest of her response. *The Sardek army shows no mercy. They never have.*

"The sorceress said there is a city two days east of here with a cleric's temple and a place of–"

"We do not know in which direction the book will lead us," Mirevra interjected, her eyes simmering. "We cannot promise to lead them to refuge if we are on a different road."

"Of course. It is just... These people...they need help," Roman sputtered.

"These people—and we—will all die if we do not find that blade, Roman."

Bagah nodded in agreement. "It is true, Roman. You know it. We cannot save them and the world. Let us pray to Rashawe that the blade lies in this city's direction. If not? Unfortunately, the survivors are a sacrifice we must make."

"But, there are children!" Roman's hazel eyes gleamed with tears, and he did not bother to wipe one away as it trickled down his cheek. "Even if the blade lies to the west, we *must* go east. It is only two days!" *Curse his soft heart,* Mirevra thought as she drew a steadying breath.

"We face the world's end, Roman," she said flatly. "Two days is too long. We must find the Vaenir."

Roman blinked rapidly, and Mirevra realized he had not yet heard the sword's name. But rather than ask about the weapon, he pushed Mirevra one last time.

"So, we will let them die?" His voice shook at the end of his question, and Mirevra felt her chest cave a bit. She gently touched his round cheek and looked into his damp eyes.

"We are not heroes, Roman. We are Foxes," she said. Roman tried to turn his face away, but her hand held him firm. "We do not tend to the injured birds." *We eat them.* She could not say the rest of this sentence aloud, either. Not to Roman.

Roman pushed Mirevra's hand away, turned, and ran into the darkness. Mirevra met Lars' gaze. He looked her up and down, shook his head, then followed Roman. Mirevra felt heat flood her, and she looked to Bagah for support.

"To the Ring we serve," Bagah said firmly, and his voice and the words soothed her. At least someone understood! She might have sounded like a monster, but she was a monster that intended to save the world.

Mirevra repeated their mantra and prayed to every god that Neeps could read as fast as Heral claimed. The lich was also pursuing the Vaenir, and it searched without human constraints. It had no need to eat, rest, or argue about what to do with survivors. It was on the move; Mirevra felt it in her bones. And if the Vaenir desperately called to its other half, the lich was much closer to finding the blade than they were.

She rubbed her temples and, for a moment, let her shoulders slump. Jovial, compassionate Roman had never before pushed back that hard against an order. Roman knew the Veravant had left her in charge; arguing with her was arguing with the Ring's leader. *Unheard of.*

At that very moment, the skin next to the hidden pocket throbbed, causing Mirevra to startle.

The Messaging Gem.

She turned to Bagah. "Find the others and relay to them what the Tajeh told us. I will meet you at the crossing outside the city. If the halfling needs more time to read, we will make camp. If he has learned anything, we will not waste time with sleep," she said.

Bagah nodded, flared his nostrils, and charged after Roman and Lars. Mirevra scanned her surroundings, then hopped over charred wood and fallen stone until she was behind a burned home and out of sight. She pulled out the gem and held it between her thumb and finger. It did nothing. Though she had never used one, she knew it needed to emit a glow to send a message. She shook it. The gem did not react. She rubbed it against her tunic, held it up to the night sky, and blew hard on it. Still, nothing. Frustrated, she smacked it three times against her vambrace and almost jumped as suddenly the stone glowed. Granted, it emitted only a dull light in the dark, but it gleamed. Her eyes flared in wonder and fascination; Mirevra brought the gem to her mouth and disclosed all that had happened on the journey, omitting the memories Audrina had shown her and the story Bagah had told the Tajeh. She closed with the news that all the Foxes were alive. She tapped the gem thrice more—this time gently—and watched it closely until its glow flickered out. Once it was back in her hidden pocket, she patted it gently and walked to the crossroad.

Jardin stood atop the carriage, staring at the stars, his bow strapped across his broad back. Heral sat inside the carriage with Neeps, lighting her hand over the pages so he could read. Lars sat across from them, watching closely. Neeps looked only a third of the way into the book, which irked Mirevra. However, she grudgingly admitted that this was an outstanding accomplishment, considering how little time had passed. She would likely only be on the second or third page if the task had been left to her. Bagah stood next to a silent Roman near their horses. Shiln and Beldon hovered over a small group of survivors. Mirevra caught the eye of a tiny, bedraggled girl who stood a bit apart from the group. She jerked her gaze away, but not quickly enough. They had made eye contact.

Mirevra's breathing sped up, and her chest felt heavy. Beldon jogged to her side.

Dejection and worry had replaced his usual mischievous expression. "We did our best to heal their wounds, but many are weak," he said in a low voice. "Especially the children. They will need more healers and blessings to stand a chance." Mirevra did not reply. Her patience was thin and she knew it would not withstand another quarrel amongst the Foxes. Beldon narrowed his eyes as he watched her. "Shiln was raised in this area. Two days to the east, we can find aid. The Sun Criers could help these people." Mirevra remained silent. Beldon's shoulders pulled back. "Will we not help them?"

"Not if our mission takes us elsewhere," she said without emotion. Beldon frowned but nodded.

"I hear the blade, the Vaenir, truly exists. It seems our luck has not yet run out."

Mirevra braced her hands upon her hips. "Thank Rashawe," she said. Her eyes were fixed on Neeps, who was flipping through pages but not fast enough for her comfort.

"Aye, thank Rashawe," Beldon said. He looked toward the survivors and sighed. "Had I known these people might face an even crueler fate than death at King Dern's hands, I would not have healed their wounds."

"We have been around the Nelimen for far too long. We are starting to sound like them," Mirevra scoffed.

"It is not such a bad thing to care about others," Beldon said with a shrug. "After all, we *are* trying to save the world, are we not?"

"We are trying to save it for our own lives. Everyone else is merely benefiting from that."

"Yes, I suppose. However, I sense there might be a possibility you are doing it for more than just yourself... Perhaps a small chance?"

Mirevra thought of Bagah. She thought of the Veravant and Roman and Beldon, too. She thought about Tilly, her Arcanen friend, back at the den. She did not answer Beldon. She watched as Lars stepped out of the carriage and stretched. He stared at the huddled survivors, then turned to examine the outlines of the ruined city. Next, he looked toward her, and even in the dark, she knew he had met her eyes. She held his gaze for a moment before turning back to Beldon.

"I suppose there is a *small chance* I could be doing it for others," she sighed. Then she smiled wickedly at the healer. "But it is only because I would rather be the one to slit their throats instead of the lich."

Beldon flashed his toothy grin. *"Always take the chance,"* he said beneath his breath.

Neeps and Heral hopped out of the coach. "Neeps thinks he found something," Heral called, and Mirevra sprang forward.

The halfling's eyes shifted in all directions as he pointed to a page. "The stories do not give a concise course," he said. "Many are jumbled and are more riddles than actual tales. But a few lines lead me to believe the blade can be in one of three places."

Mirevra scowled. "One of three?" she bit out. She did not like the odds.

Neeps straightened. "Yes. One of three. I have not finished reading yet, *Fox*," he seethed. Mirevra kept a straight face, but a small huff of laughter escaped her nose. She could not understand why the Nelimen believed calling her a Fox was an insult. "We can look for one of these places now, or we can take the survivors to Estunder and the Sun Criers temple while I finish the book and see if I can make better sense of the clues," Neeps concluded.

Fucking Sun Criers. She might have to cut some flesh if she heard their name again.

"What are the three places?"

"Nothing is certain, of course. But my best guess—so far—would mean that we search in the Fertek deserts, the Isles of Caxaven, or Drodour," he said. Mirevra did not have to look at Bagah to feel his discomfort. She resolved that she would not make her friend suffer returning to that land unless the halfling was positive the sword was located in Drodour.

"Shall we leave it to a vote?" Shiln called out. Everyone but Bagah and Mirevra mumbled their agreement. "Good," Shiln said. "All in favor of saving these people and allowing Neeps to read further, raise a hand."

Mirevra watched as Roman, Beldon, Shiln, Jardin, Neeps, and Lars raised their hands. Mirevra eyed Heral closely; the woman seemed hesitant, but Shiln clapped her hands loudly before Heral could vote. *What would her vote have been,* Mirevra wondered, but Shiln's voice broke through her thoughts. "Then it is decided," the sorceress declared. "We leave for Estunder."

The Little Foxes Run

'*No tears for the dead, little Fox,*' the Veravant had instructed Mirevra after her first kill. '*Those who die by hand or blade are not so different from those who die by age or sickness.*'

The road to Estunder led through the woods, and the guilds tried to travel as quietly as possible. The survivors coughed through much of the night and kept the clerics busy until sunrise. Mirevra still could not look into the faces of the few who had survived the Allies' carnage. There was no point. '*Death comes to all. We do not cry for what is inevitable.*' She schooled her expression to remain neutral, even as she heard the little girl call again for her mother. It was a familiar cry and far too close to home. '*We do not mourn. Death is natural, no matter the cause.*' It was a male who was Mirevra's first kill. He had supplied the Veravant with the necessary information, and the Veravant no longer found him useful. So, he had ordered Mirevra to cut the man's throat. Had her victim been a father? Someone's brother? It did not matter. Everyone was someone; everyone was no one. Mirevra had sliced and ended him quickly. She had not cried. '*No tears for the dead.*'

A Fallen Sword

Estunder was still a day's journey away, according to Shiln. It might have been a bearable distance if the guilds had packed rations for eleven extra people. But helping keep the survivors alive had depleted their resources. And though the team still had water, their food sacks were empty, and everyone was growing hungry. Even Mirevra's belly soured with hunger. Bagah, who required more food than any of them, grabbed his grumbling stomach. "We need to find food," Mirevra said, pushing her horse into a trot. She slowed to a walk next to the lumbering coach. "Find a place to stop. We need to hunt," she called to Lars, who was in the driver's box. He nodded. Sitting beside Lars on the box, Neeps ignored Mirevra and buried his nose in the book.

She glanced over her shoulder at the four male survivors who had walked the entire journey. Weaker survivors had taken turns riding inside the coach or on horseback and had been able to rest. These four were now reaching their limit. Their dry coughs shook their bodies as they shuffled forward, drooping their heads low. Mirevra tried to push down the pity that rose and twisted in her chest, but she failed. It was not the survivors' fault they were now homeless and sick. They were simple people who had met the same cruel fate she had; the Sardek army had destroyed them for reasons they had no control over. She opened her mouth to call one of the men to take her horse for a time, but by the gods, she was saved when Lars called the party to a halt.

The travelers stopped in a large clearing, rested, and drank water; Beldon tended to children's wounds, and Roman entertained them. The druid changed one of his arms into a bear's and another into a horse leg while the children laughed and clapped. Mirevra jerked her eyes away from the momentarily happy children. She would not let herself feel even more sorry for them. Her pity would not help and it would certainly not fill their stomachs either. "Who will hunt, who will stay?" Lars' voice in her ear interrupted her brooding. She looked at Bagah, who stepped forward.

"I will hunt," he volunteered. "And bring Roman and the ranger along."

"Those three are our best chance at finding game," she told Lars.

"I concur," Lars said. "But perhaps someone should go with them and forage for some berries and herbs."

"I suppose," she said with a shrug. Lars stared at Mirevra without blinking until she pulled back. "Well, do not look to me! Do I look like someone who gathers berries?"

"If you could ever wipe that gods-awful snarl from your face, you might," he laughed. Mirevra stood, her face impassive. Lars lifted his hands. "Easy, Viper. *I* will go forage. You stay here and perhaps get to know these people you care so much about." She offered him a counterfeit grin in return for his mock sincerity and pushed past him to alert the others of their plan. In a short while, Mirevra watched as the hunters disappeared into the treeline. She gazed absently into the trees long after they left, replaying their journey in her mind. It had only been a week, yet Mirevra felt like time was slowing, but changes were occurring rapidly. One week ago, she would have killed any Nelimen on sight. She would have accused them of stealing the Veravant's ruby daggers and would not have hesitated to deliver harsh blows. Her memories of losing her parents were buried deep, and she knew nothing of Bagah's past. She would have left the survivors to fend for themselves. But most vexing, one week ago, her mind was not racing with the thought of a sleeping man's arm flung across her waist. Such a silly, ignorant thing to be preoccupied with. One week was a lifetime ago, and Mirevra no longer recognized her thoughts. She hardly recognized herself. She breathed deeply in the pleasant summer air, but her chest throbbed. She slapped a hand across her heart; were sadness and confusion finally tearing her apart? As the throbbing continued in regular beats, she looked around. No one seemed to care what the Murks she was doing, but she called to Beldon that she needed to relieve herself in the woods. He waved a dismissive hand, reminding Mirevra there were details not even his curiosity did not hunger to know. They had definitely been around the Nelimen too long.

She walked amidst the trees until she no longer heard voices from the camp. Concealing herself behind a thick trunk, she pulled out the gem and felt it pulse within her grasp. It was not yet glowing, but she felt a spark lace up her fingers. Deciding to be gentler this time, she tapped the gem three times and held it close to her ear. *'Greetings from the den, little Fox.'* She jerked the gem away and clutched her throat. His voice, the smooth, intricate, lovely sound of his voice, shrouded her in guilt. She had slept near another and harbored too many thoughts of the rogue. She belonged to the Veravant. Her hand shook as she returned the gem to her ear. *'It is no shock that the blade is real, but I am pleased to hear it confirmed and that you are on your way to finding it. I knew I could bet on you, my little Fox. I count the days impatiently until I can see you again.'* Mirevra closed her eyes and let a small smile etch across her face. The Veravant missed her. How could she not feel that she had missed him too? The stone flickered. *'We have only three messages left. Make them count.'* His voice died out with the gem's light. She clutched it in her palm and took two deep breaths before shoving it back into the hidden pocket and returning to the camp.

Mirevra heard children wailing and women screaming even before she glimpsed Shiln's raging purple light through the trees. Sprinting into the camp, she braced herself for an enemy, even the lich itself. All she saw were the survivors crowded in a tight circle. Mirevra shoved her way between them, and her breath stopped. Roman... He was... He was...

"What in the Degolian Murks happened to him!?" she shouted, throwing herself beside him. The druid was mainly in human shape, although one leg resembled a bear's. But his other leg was missing altogether. Shiln was frowning in concentration as she worked to seal the gaping wound. "Roman! Can you hear me? Tell me what happened!" If Roman could hear Mirevra, he did not show it. His body convulsed, and he stuttered incoherent words. His usually warm hazel eyes were glazed over and empty as he blinked at the sky. Mirevra slapped a hand over her mouth and forbade herself tears. "Heal him! Now!" She was screaming at the sorceress, but Shiln only hissed.

"I am trying! These wounds... They are not normal," she said breathlessly. Mirevra touched Roman's cheek.

"Stay strong, Roman," she muttered under her breath. "Where is Beldon? Why is he not helping?!" She was shouting again, and as she whipped her head around, she only saw the children's frightened faces.

"He is helping another," Shiln said. "They were attacked in the woods."

"By what?" Mirevra did not remove her hand from Roman's face.

"I do not know," Shiln admitted. "I only know that my blessings are not countering whatever it was."

"That is because you are *not* a cleric, not truly," Mirevra growled. "Your power will not be enough." Shiln's eyes slit like a cat's, and her lip curled.

"I am *trying* to save your friend, Fox. Do you not realize that!? I am trying to help!"

Mirevra glowered, but she knew Shiln spoke the truth, and her heart thumped in appreciation.

A Fallen Sword

"Who else is hurt?"

"I do not know," Shiln said again without looking away from Roman's wound. "Roman only said there was another, so Beldon raced to find out who." Mirevra's stomach flipped. It could be Bagah. Gods. She stared down at Roman, whose eyes roamed the sky as if seeking something.

"Mir... Mirevra..." His voice was weak, but she heard it. She leaned in close, her eyes wide.

"Yes, Roman. I am here," she whispered, smoothing his hair from his sweat-soaked forehead. She held his cheeks gently between her palms. He placed one of his hands atop hers, and she winced; it was as cold as ice.

"I tried. I tried to protect... It happened so fast," Roman stammered, and Mirevra shushed him.

"Save your energy, friend. Let us heal you, and then you can tell me everything."

His chest convulsed, and she placed a hand on it to steady it.

"It was... It is...," His voice was even more strained. A sharp pain spread across Mirevra's cheeks, and her eyes grew heavy. She forced her lips to twitch and willed her friend to smile. Silently, she prayed that his mouth would twist up in that familiar curl. But Roman did not smile. Not this time.

Roman was dying.

Mirevra turned her head away from her friend and screamed at Shiln, demanding that the sorceress use everything she knew to heal Roman. The druid's hand fell from Mirevra's, and she leaned in closer. *No, no, no. He could not die. Not Roman.*

"Mir," his voice was barely a breath. "It was... Th..Th.Wo–" Mirevra's golden eyes filled with hot tears. She grabbed Roman's hand and pressed it hard into her cheek. He stared at her, and she knew her face would be the final thing those kind eyes would ever see. She knew he could not find anything else to hold on to; nothing remained to keep his soul tethered to his body, this life. So, she smiled as best she could down at him. She smiled and told him that everything was okay.

He took in a breath, and Mirevra felt his spirit leave. That light in his hazel eyes was gone, and Mirevra saw nothing natural about it.

The assassin held Roman's lifeless hand against her cheek for a long moment. The muffled sounds of Shiln clearing the crowd were like a pebble tossed into a churning sea. She could not see through her blurred vision. *'No tears for the dead,'* she heard the Veravant whisper. But despite his velvety voice playing through her mind and everything she had been taught, Mirevra rested her head next to Roman's still form and cried.

The Decision

~~~

Mirevra sat with her back against a coach wheel, her arms draped over her bent knees and eyes trained on the ground. She heard the rest of the party return but dared not look up. She could not take the sight or even the thought of another friend injured—or worse. Especially not Bagah. Mirevra knew she could not stomach the pain if she lost him, too. She dipped her head lower and prayed. She thought Rashawe had answered when she heard his voice. "Did Roman make it?" Bagah asked. Mirevra slowly lifted her face. Tears still clung to her eyelashes, but Bagah did not judge them. His lips flattened into a bloodless line, and his nostrils flared. "Neither did Jardin," he said. The assassin and the half-breed stared at each other. Mirevra did not have to say death had come to the group because of the vote to save the survivors. Roman would still be alive and smiling if everyone had only listened to her and Bagah. But they did not, and Roman was dead.

Bagah shook his head slowly and looked into her eyes. "He would not have wanted you to think that way," he said. "Roman wanted to help them. That was his heart." Bagah dropped to his haunches in front of her. "Even if he had been able to see what would happen to him, Roman still would have voted to help. That was his way. The best way to honor him now is to ensure we see it through, Mir. They need aid. You know it just as well as I." Mirevra wiped her nose with a bare hand and sent him a simple nod. Bagah offered his hand, but she did not take it. She rose and wiped the earth from her rear and gazed wistfully into the distance.

"Do you think he is truly gone? Or do you believe a soul like his will live on, somewhere else, somewhere better?" Her voice was hushed and almost ashamed, like a child asking their parent something foolish. But Bagah only squinted and looked up at the sky.

"Yes. I believe it is somewhere better," he answered, then smiled briefly. "Maybe he is where my mother is."

Mirevra moved close to her friend's side and followed his gaze. "Then perhaps we shall see them again. *Soon,* if we do not find the Vaenir," she added dryly. Bagah huffed a quiet laugh.

"We will not be going wherever they are, Mir. That much is certain."

Mirevra released a stark, hard laugh and rested a hand against her belly. "You are right," she agreed. Her lopsided grin was a mix of grief and humor. "They are certainly not where *Jedaries* like us are sent to rot." She wiped her nose once more. "How reassuring."

Bagah raised his chin. "At least we will rot together in the Murks," he said. They walked slowly toward the rest of the group and had almost reached them when Mirevra finally remembered to ask.

"What attacked?"

"I wish I knew," Bagah said. "It was too quick. I was walking near Jardin, and he simply dropped to the ground. Gashes marked his entire body."

"And Lars? Was he hurt?"

Bagah nodded. "A slash in his arm. Beldon healed him quick enough. However, according to Beldon, Lars begged him to save Roman or Jardin instead. I do not think he is taking their deaths well."

"None of us are," Mirevra said, annoyance dripping from her words.

Bagah grunted in agreement, then looked down at her. *Yes, but they are heroes, and we are lowly criminals; they do not expect us to hurt as they do.* She inclined her head in agreement. "We will need to check on Beldon," she said. "He may blame himself for not getting to Roman in time."

"I did not see it either," Lars was well into his story as Mirevra and Bagah approached. "Roman had wandered off in his bear form, calling out that he had spied a rangale nearby. I heard a snarl and a snap. I assumed he had killed a deer, so I walked toward the sound. Then I saw a wisp, a blur, a *something*. Suddenly, it was upon me. I felt claws digging into my skin. I tried to draw my sword but could not see what loomed above me! How does one fight a ghost?" His voice rasped low and dark; all the arrogance was gone. "Then I saw Roman limping in pain. He was shifting back into his human body, and the last I saw him, he was crawling toward the clearing. I got up and ran; I just followed the shouting. That is when I saw..." Lars stopped and rubbed his mouth roughly. "Jardin was... He was gone. Nothing left of the poor bastard. The next thing I know, Beldon is there and healing me. I told him to heal Jardin first and find Roman," he choked out. "It was an ambush. A calculated one at that."

Neeps inched closer towards Lars. "Do you think it was the Teruk?"

That did it.

Mirevra was on the halfling in a second, her dagger at his throat, her mouth twisted into a primal snarl. Neeps yelped, and Heral's hands lit up in defensive flames.

"Do not do it, Fox; he only asked a question," Heral warned.

Mirevra seethed as she watched Neep's shifty eyes focus. They did not move from hers, the killer, the Fox, the Viper. "Release him so we might talk about this like adults," Heral urged.

"You will never accuse Bagah again, do you hear me?" Mirevra demanded. She could see red at the edge of her vision. "A Fox is dead. The Ring is in mourning. Bagah may be many things, but he would never betray or hurt one of his own. Do you understand?" The halfling did not respond, so she pushed the blade deeper. "Do. You. Understand?"

"Yes! Yes! I understand!"

When Mirevra pulled the blade away. Neeps hopped to his feet and rushed toward the coach. Heral's fists dimmed. The fighter saw Lars watching her–studying her–and as she sheathed her dagger, she spat.

"No one else needs to die today," Shiln interjected. "Both guilds have suffered plenty. We need to pack and keep moving. These woods have proven they are too dangerous. That is twice we have been attacked within them. The first may have been a fluke...I thought we had camped in mage territory, a stroke of misfortune. But after this afternoon, I am no longer convinced. This was no accident; this was planned."

"But why would someone attack us? And how would they know where we are going?" Lars asked.

Silently, Mirevra thought of the answer, though a shaken Neeps, who had crept back to the group, answered.

"My best guess is the blade," he said. "Think about it. It is the only reason our guilds have joined hands. There is no other reason to want us dead. Others seek the weapon, and likely not for the same reasons we do."

"Yes," Shiln nodded. "It makes sense that the lich has its own assembly searching for the weapon. Or King Dern and his forces are also searching. But that still does not answer how they know where we are going."

"Maybe we are being followed?" Mirevra asked, looking over her shoulder to scan the woods. Shiln shook her head.

"If we were being tracked, the attacks would be different," she explained. "As Lars mentioned, these seem to be planned ambushes." Her eyes passed slowly over the remaining members of the Fox Ring. "It is like they are always a step ahead...*waiting*."

Mirevra felt heat bubble in her veins, and her gold eyes glared. "Why do you look to us? Do you suggest one of us is to blame?" This would be the second time a Nelimen accused a Fox of such heresy, and she would not let it pass so easily. Puffing her chest forward and flexing her arms, Mirevra strutted toward the sorceress. Shiln did not back down.

"Try and use the little mind you have sequestered in your thick skull," she snapped at Mirevra. "You are criminals and work for the Veravant. He is known to be sneaky, suspicious, and selfish," she began. Mirevra caught a movement in her peripheral vision and noted Lars shifting his position.

"Roman is dead," Mirevra seethed. "Despite what you think of the Ring and our activities, we are not heartless–"

"I am not so sure," Shiln interjected, her thin brows arched high in contempt. "Lars said you would be willing to kill one of your own."

Mirevra heard Bagah roughly suck in air. She did not face her friend but the rogue, whose face had gone pale.

"Did he now?" Of course, the insufferable male who wore ruffled shirts and a crooked grin could not shut his mouth.

"It is not surprising," Shiln resumed. "As much as it is pathetic. But that is exactly what the Fox Ring is known for."

Mirevra whipped back to Shiln. "If it is a fight you are searching for, look no further," Mirevra snapped. She was not being smart, and she knew it. There were only three Foxes, two without Arcanen magic. They would face four Nelimen, one a sorceress and another whose power was still a mystery. Mirevra knew she could only take one of them out before death greeted her. Still, her fingers traced the hilt of her short sword. It would be worth it.

"There is no reason the Veravant would want his own dead," Lars said, his arms extended toward each simmering woman. "He would not let the Fox in charge deliberately take out one of his best. It wouldn't make any sense, would it?" He looked at Mirevra, his expression apologetic, then back at Shiln. "She nearly killed Neeps for even accusing the half-breed. Do you truly think she is responsible for the death of another Fox?" He shook his head. "She would not do that. No matter what she said before, it is not in her."

Mirevra did not give a damn what he or any of the Nelimen believed her capable of; her eyes did not move from the sorceress and her sparking fingertips. "Whoever is responsible obviously wants us all dead; let us not do their job for them," Lars said.

"And if we live? Then what? Are we not leading our hidden enemy right to the blade?" Mirevra demanded. Bagah's head tilted back and forth as he considered Mirevra's question. Beldon chewed nervously on his fingernail.

Lars pushed his hand through his dark hair before offering her a defeated shrug. "What other choice do we have, Viper?"

She hated that he was right. Each second they wasted here, their chances of retrieving the blade dwindled. "Has the halfling discovered anything new?" She faced Neeps and glowered.

"I am narrowing down the options," he answered quickly. "But I need more time."

Mirevra's body felt as if it had been set aflame. How desperately she wanted to tell all the Nelimen and the survivors to fuck off. She considered returning to the trees and using the Messaging Gem to plead with the Veravant and beg him to release her from working with these *heroes*. This was not the way of the Ring–missions should not be walked into blindly.

"One more night, Viper," said Lars. She looked at him coldly. "We travel one more night to Estunder. Neeps will have finished the book. We will deliver the survivors to the temple, buy food, and wash ourselves before we set off in whichever direction the codex takes us." He approached her slowly. *He looked afraid. Good.* "It will not be so bad. We will figure this out," he said reassuringly to her. "You are in charge of the Ring. The Veravant put you in this position for a reason. But, he also put the Ring with *us*. There must be a reason for that, too." Gritting her teeth, Mirevra grunted a sort of agreement.

Later, Mirevra sat beside the fresh mound where the Foxes had buried Roman and rested her hand atop it. No more tears came, but she still felt coldness in her chest. It was a different kind of anger than the red, hot heat she usually felt. If an enemy awaited them, she would welcome them with her fists and blades. Mirevra would avenge her dead friend.

As for Estunder, perhaps the detour to the city was not all bad; she could smell her natural odor growing with every passing day, and being near Bagah was almost unbearable. A city would likely have a bathhouse, a tavern, and a place to buy a good meal. If she was to avenge Roman *and* save the world, she would need a good washing—and an even stronger drink.

The Sun Criers Temple

Mirevra began her morning by sending a prayer of thanks to Rashawe and Idenethor. The camp had not been attacked during the night. They had taken no chances. Three were on watch at a time. Mirevra, Shiln, and Neeps took the first shift; Beldon, Bagah, and Lars took the next. Mirevra did not know whether Heral had slept, and she did not intend to ask her. The habits of a woman who did not need food or sleep and held the sun's power in her eyes were no business of hers. At the start of the day's journey, everyone in the group was weary, slow, and quiet. Even the horses seemed to drag their hooves through the dust in the road.

In the late afternoon, as the group crested a hill, they saw Estunder spread out below them. The buildings were colorful, gleaming in warm lights. Even the Foxes were smiling as the survivors of Mercinnho's savage destruction summoned what was left of their energy to cheer. The men pumped their fists into the air; the women shed tears and clapped their hands. As the children hopped and danced around the coach, one small girl, the girl she had made eye contact with, bumped into Mirevra's shin. The girl's eyes grew wide, her breathing hitched, and she cowered behind her hands.

"I am sorry! I did not mean to touch you! I–I–" Mirevra cocked her head and watched as the girl scrambled to apologize. She knew why the youth was afraid, of course. Mirevra had made it clear she had wanted to abandon the survivors and had made no effort to get to know any of them. As the child's voice warbled in fear, she remembered doing the same as she cried out for her mother. Mirevra knelt and raised the girl's chin with a stiffened finger. Light green eyes stared back at her from a face stained with dried tears and dirt and drawn thin from hunger and fatigue. A familiar haunting swam within them. The ghosts of her dead family left so many miles behind lived in this girl's eyes. Mirevra's chest softened. The child whimpered, and Mirevra resolved to give the girl a moment of celebration, she knew the happiness that swelled now would be short-lived. Estunder would offer the girl a slight reprieve, a chance to realize she escaped death. But soon, memories would flood her, and she would realize she had not evaded anything. Anger and grief would imprison her soul for the rest of her life. But not today. It did not have to be engulfed by these things today. Mirevra smiled, and it reached her eyes.

"You need not apologize," she said, and the girl quieted, her brows raised. In fact, everyone seemed to have fallen silent, witnessing this odd encounter between the assassin and the child. "You have come so far, traveling all this way alone. A brave, strong girl like you should never apologize. Be proud of how far you have come. I know I am proud of you." Mirevra swallowed hard before she could finish. "Your mother would be proud of you, too."

The little girl's mouth curved into a mostly toothless grin, and he threw her arms around Mirevra's neck. The assassin stiffened and gave the girl's back an awkward pat.

"My mother would have liked you," the child said as she pulled back. Mirevra nodded with a tight smile. *No, your mother would not have.* The girl grabbed Mirevra's cheeks in her tiny hands and studied her closely—too closely. "Mother always said the golden eyes would come back and save us. She was right. Mother was always right. Here you are." The girl skipped off as if she had not said the very thing that would make Mirevra unable to hoist herself back up, but thankfully, she did not have to. A pair of large hands pulled her to her feet. Lars, of course. His face held a tender expression she had not yet seen.

"What?" Mirevra hissed. Lars shook his head, frowned, and held his palms out.

"Nothing. *Nothing,*" he said, his voice teeming with sarcasm. "I am simply observing."

"Are you so shocked, Ruffles? That this criminal might have a heart?" Lars' eyes held hers, and she saw how, in the afternoon sun, a subtle blue tinted the gray. Two storm clouds guarding a brilliant blue sky.

"Oh no, Viper. That does not shock me at all. *I always* knew you had one behind all that armor," he said, then dropped his voice to a whisper. "But did you?" Before she could answer, the rogue joined the children in twirling.

She turned away and saw Beldon beaming at her with pride. "Gods," she groaned. "It is not like I gave the child a sack of gold and a home. Why must everyone look at me that way?" Beldon only smiled wider.

"I do not know what you mean," he said, struggling to stop smiling. "I did not see anything at all." She knew it was a lie but appreciated it nonetheless. Together, they viewed their destination. "Just there," he pointed to something in the city center. "The Sun Criers temple. I have always wanted to see one. They are a mysterious clan. They do not call upon Raenin's white fire. They only serve the Gentle Touch. Is that not fascinating?"

"Who cares?" Mirevra answered with a laconic shrug.

Beldon guffawed. "Still not curious enough for my taste," he teased.

As they descended the hill, Beldon nudged her shoulder. "Roman would be happy they made it," he said quietly. "That is what I tell myself, or else I will fall apart," he said. Mirevra felt the part of her that had softened now ache. The cleric was silent for a long time, then added, "We should find a way to tell Tilly." Mirevra only hummed in agreement.

The one good thing about having a bunch of heroes around was their sickening generosity. The horses were left at a stable to rest and be adequately fed on the Nelimen's coin, and the coach rested on the city's outskirts, chained to a post. As the group made their way to the Sun Criers temple, Mirevra found herself constantly turning her head. Everywhere she looked, she saw shops to visit, buy, trade, and sell. There was too much for her eyes to settle on any spot for long. Bards walked the streets strumming melodies, women bustled by in big hats and puffed skirts, and they passed too many taverns to keep track of. She also sensed Bagah's confusion and underlying surprise. As they walked together, she noted that passers-by paid him little to no mind. Maybe their group was too large for anyone to notice him, or the locals were too busy going about their business to care about a half-Teruk walking their streets.

Shiln walked through the city as if she had never left it. She led the way, pointed at almost every building, and briefly explained its history. Mirevra noted when Shiln skipped over a worn stone and timber framed house. The Estunder native had only blinked emptily at it, swallowed, glanced at her feet, and moved the party along. Mirevra fell back a few paces and scanned the structure. Four windows on the first floor, four on the second. A dilapidated dark oak door rested crookedly on its frame. Other than not being well cared for, Mirevra saw nothing amiss with the house. But she knew how it felt to have sordid memories flood your body. The sorceress could not hide that much from her.

The pale gleam of an ascending moon illuminated their destination. The Sun Criers temple. Mirevra was definitely not a woman who frequented temples, especially those of clerics, but she was not unfamiliar with them. However, she had never seen anything like this one. It looked like it could have been plucked straight from the heavenlies. Constructed with an unfamiliar ivory stone that shimmered in the growing dark, its enormous base supported spires and turrets reaching high into the sky. Mirevra would have believed it a castle if Shiln and Beldon had not told her otherwise.

Shiln spoke with five women at the temple entry, a spectacular pair of doors that curved into the shape of an elm leaf. The sorceress then waved for Beldon to join them, which he did quickly. The two Arcanens spoke with the women until the city was dark. Everyone was exhausted, and the excitement of reaching the temple waned. The children grew restless. Mirevra's own legs groaned, and her stomach grumbled, pained with hunger. Just as the children's whining became too much for Mirevra to bear, Shiln whistled, and the entire group whirled to face her.

"The Sun Criers welcome you all by way of *Nerillian Coève Algeras. Our Souls Are All, and All Are Mine,*" she said with a broad smile. "Come."

Mirevra squinted at the temple's sheer opulence. She had certainly walked corridors flush with riches, but the Sun Criers temple eclipsed them all. Never had she been surrounded by so much exquisite art, and she had stolen many a portrait in her day. Tapestries and paintings lined the hallways, the ivory splendor of the stone peeking out to shimmer between them. The group's footsteps echoed on the polished marble floors. The ceilings were so high that Mirevra estimated it would take at least twelve of the guild members stacked on each other's shoulders to touch them. And the chandeliers hanging from these ceilings? Utter decadence. Could they be cast from pure silver? Likely so, Mirevra thought as she considered all the other objects.

The group finally reached the prayer room, where Sun Criers sat quietly. They did not open their eyes or unclasp their hands as everyone barged in after Shiln and their guide. A tall statue of Nerillian Coeve Algeras, saint of The Gentle Touch, sat atop a large plinth in the center of the room. The god lifted one hand to the heavens charted on the room's dome; the other was lowered and opened into a flat palm. *'The hand of Collection. Gently, I welcome the souls of the injured or dying,'* was carved into the plinth. A woman stood on the platform steps leading up to Nerillian. She had radiant dark skin, and an intricate braid peeked out from beneath the hood of her white robe. Shiln exchanged bows with the woman. They each lifted a hand to the sky, then to the floor, and then embraced.

"It has been many moons since we saw you last, Shiln. Welcome home," the woman said. Her accent drew out the words in long, elegant strokes. Hers was a fluid song, not a tight and clean voice like the Veravant's. It was a voice and accent Mirevra thought she could listen to again and again.

Shiln bowed again. "An honor to be back. As Levelle may have told you, we come with many injured souls, all requiring the hands of the Sun Criers and the mercy of The Gentle Touch. My guild and I have brought gold to–"

A Fallen Sword

The dark-skinned woman raised a hand. "We do not accept coins as payment here, Shiln. You know as much." Mirevra stifled a laugh and looked around at the grandeur crammed into every inch of the room. It seemed clear that the Sun Criers temple collected *a lot* of coins.

"Of course, Verone. I only meant it as a kind gesture. An appreciation of the temple and Nerillian's generosity," Shiln said, her head lowered. Verone extended a flattened palm.

"Then we shall gladly accept your gesture, but only half of what you intended to give. As is the mercy of The Gentle Touch." Mirevra snorted, earning Beldon's glare and a slight smirk from Lars.

Shiln dropped a blue pouch into Verone's hands and straightened. As soon as the purse touched skin, the praying clerics stood in unison, collected the survivors, and led them from the room. "I hope it would not be too much to ask, but we all desperately need food and rest. If the temple has more generosity to spare, we would be most thankful," Shiln added.

Verone gazed at each member of the guilds. She inspected Mirevra for a good while and then Bagah for even longer. She then lowered her hood, fully exposing her exquisite beauty. She nodded and gingerly took Shiln's hand. "As is the way of The Gentle Touch, you shall have meals and a place to lay your head for as long as you are in Estunder. Thank him for his mercy." Verone pulled a silver pendant from beneath her robe. She kissed it, raised it to the heavens, then dropped it beneath the fabric again. "Shall I escort you to the dining hall? Food shall be prepared at once." No one in the group protested, especially not Mirevra, whose aching stomach twisted and banged against her flesh.

The cleric led them into a room as luxurious as the others. The group sighed in unison at the sight and smell of roasted meats, steaming vegetables, and plates and plates of rice and legumes. As they began their meal, Mirevra briefly wondered how this temple managed to come by such an incredible variety of food, then decided she did not care to know. The food was delicious and filling; that was all she needed to know.

She instead listened absently to the conversations around her. Neeps and Heral discussed the book; Shiln and Lars discussed where the group would sleep. The only conversation interesting enough to tear her away from stuffing food into her mouth was a quiet one between Beldon and Verone. Beldon never spoke quietly, it peaked Mirevra's interest.

"Shiln says you took her in as a child blessed with sorcery Arcanen," Beldon said. "But tell me, how did you teach her healing and blessings? Was it difficult? Is she special?" Mirevra dug her teeth into a piece of bread and pricked up her ears. She knew only a few things about Arcanen magic. What she did understand was that sorcery, mage work, wizardry, and warlocks all sat under the Arcanen sky as different skills. Sorceresses and warlocks received an Arcanen magic of spell casting; mages usually received an element to control, and clerics were given healings and blessings. A cleric's white fire of Arcanen was meant for only two things: to heal a body and bless a weapon. How Shiln could both cast spells and heal was quite the mystery. She was a sorcerer and a cleric. Verone smiled and took a delicate sip of her wine before responding.

"The gods of the white fire are merciful and good. Many others have mastered more than one type of Arcanen magic; if you teach them young enough, and if their heart is pure, there is a chance to acquire multiple pathways," she said with her glass still on her lips. "Such is not a secret. You may know plenty who can wield more than one type of Arcanen. However, doing so taxes you physically and extracts a fearsome mental toll. This is why Shiln can only do so much with her healing. She is a far greater spell caster."

Beldon gulped down the entire contents of his glass and did not bother to wipe the spillage on his chin. "Interesting," he said with a far-off look. "I have always been fascinated in the wards of a warlock; perhaps I too can practice and become well-versed in double Arcanen. I am still quite young, after all!" He turned to beam at Mirevra.

"Simply because you act like a child does not make you one," she said dryly. "And you are hardly pure."

"I think the gods would say otherwise," he corrected her with a wink.

"I think the gods are laughing at you," she countered. They grinned at each other, but Verone frowned.

"Have you dabbled in the arts of the Arcanen?" Verone asked Mirevra.

"No. Never wanted to."

"I thought that would be your answer; you do not seem the type," she quipped. Verone pointed to the assassin's hands. "Calloused and bruised. You fight with flesh. You strike with bone and think it the honorable way." The cleric's light brown eyes regarded Mirevra intently. "You believe it is the *only* way."

Mirevra did not argue. She swallowed the rest of her bread and washed it down with sweet, red wine. "The body is flesh. The heart is guarded by bone. It seems right to die by the same if one must," she answered.

"Have you seen a heart?" Verone broke in, barely affording Mirevra enough time to finish her sentence.

"Yes," Mirevra said curtly. "I have held many a bleeding one in my *calloused and bruised* hands," she said. She knew better than to trust an interrogation. "Hearts are also flesh. There is no magic."

"Hmm," Verone mused, lifting her glass again. "So, you have not seen one. Not truly." Mirevra shrugged, not feeling like playing the cleric's word game, and returned to eating and drinking until her belly was full. She pushed back from the table, allowed the Sun Criers to lead her to a room with a quilted bed, plopped down and promptly fell asleep.

She dreamed of many things.

The Murky Lakes, of course. Bagah standing on a road with boys throwing stones at him, her friend's poor and savage life before he joined the Ring. Lastly, she dreamed of gray eyes.

She dreamed of them looking right at her before the storm within them broke.

The Night Beneath the Stars of Estunder

※

The temple's breakfast was less filling than its dinner. The Sun Criers believed the body should not always be comforted, nor should the hunger in one's belly always be sated. *Then, one could genuinely appreciate The Gentle Touch's mercy and gifts.* Hearing this, Mirevra was tempted to point to the paintings and tapestries and shout that the clerics' facade was not fooling anyone. As she walked out of the temple with Bagah and Beldon flanking her, she was greeted by the warm morning sun. As a pleasant breeze blew by, Mirevra shifted uncomfortably. Her leathers felt tighter, and her body smelled rank. It was time for a wash and then a city tour while Neeps read the codex. She turned to Beldon. "Shall we go our own ways or stay as a group?" The cleric frowned as if an idea was rattling around his skull, but he was unsure how to express it. Mirevra narrowed her eyes, urging him to spit it out.

"I think we should split up: one Fox and one Nelimen," Beldon said as Lars, Shiln, and Heral caught up to them. Seeing Mirevra frown, he continued. "It is only that, well, I was up praying last night while the rest of you slept. I could not stop thinking about Roman, about Jardin, either. Their lives were taken in an instant. We do not know if we can trust one another. If we split up, one Fox to one Nelimen, and something happens, we will have a clearer indication of who could be working against us."

Heral spoke first. "You assume one of us is a traitor?"

Beldon shrugged. "I do not think so, but how can we be sure?"

Lars scratched his head. "What if an accident happens? Do we blame the partner if one of us trips and falls off a ledge? It seems like this idea could get messy fast," he said.

"It sounds like I would be responsible for a Nelimen," Mirevra said. "And I cannot have that on my hands. Especially because I do not care if any of them die." Shiln rolled her eyes, but Mirevra felt Lars's stare bore into her skin. She held firm. "I think we should split up. The Foxes go one way, the Nelimen another. We take the day to care for ourselves, then meet here at sundown. If Neeps still believes the sword is in one of three locations, we can go in separate directions to search."

"We cannot do that," Shiln protested. "Our Head was clear that we must stay together. If we face more ice mages—or gods help us, the lich—our guilds on their own will be doomed. By staying together, we have a small window of hope; this is why our leaders pushed us to work together in the first place."

"We do not work well together," Mirevra stated. "The Foxes and the Nelimen are different breeds."

"Then we *should* listen to Beldon's plan," Shiln said, throwing up her hands. "We must learn to work together and perhaps even develop trust. However small it might be. *This* is our mission."

Bagah, whom Mirevra expected to only huff a nasty breath at this suggestion, broke in. "If we do this, we must agree that one cannot be held *entirely* responsible for the other," he said. "If one of us dies, the other will receive a guild's trial," he said somberly and turned to Lars. "I have already been accused by a Nelimen, and as half-Teruk, I probably will be again. I cannot take that risk."

Lars bobbed his head. "Alright, by me. So, how do we decide who goes with whom?" Mirevra shook her head. She still believed it best to keep the guilds apart.

"Do you agree to the terms? It is your call, Mir," Beldon said.

"It is not my call, Beldon. It never has been," Mirevra said with a short laugh.

Everyone stood in silence as she kicked at the stones beneath her boots. If she continued to argue against pairing up the guilds, the Nelimen would likely think she was the traitor if they did not already. Also, her team would push back as they had been this entire week. She flung a good chunk of her hair behind her shoulder. "I do not care what we do," she lied. "I need a bath. If getting one means splitting the guilds, so be it. Divide up, and let me be on my way."

Beldon siphoned a deep breath and released it with a wide smile. "If it is not a problem, I wish to partner with the sorceress. I have so many questions I want to ask…"

Shiln scowled. The specter of being pounded with inquiries for a full day did not seem to please her. But she smoothed back her glossy black hair and nodded sharply.

"Fine. I will take the cleric," she said. She raised three stiff fingers to Beldon. "But you get three answers, and that is it. Do you hear me? I refuse to spend my day with you barking at my side the entire time."

Beldon placed his hand on his chest with a dramatic flourish and pledged his agreement. Heral craned her neck in Bagah's direction.

"The half-Teruk will be my partner," she said without further explanation. Bagah nodded, but Mirevra swore she could see his cheeks blush under his light yellow skin, which never happened. She didn't think it was even possible.

The cocky grin appeared at her side.

"Looks like it is you and me again, Viper," Lars crooned. Mirevra was flooded with too many threads of emotions to untangle. Disgust, annoyance…and excitement all clotted into a tight knot. Today would be interesting, if not anything else. She did not betray an ounce of her confusion, holding her face completely blank as she walked down the cobbled street and ignoring the obnoxious brute calling out for her to wait up.

A few inquiries of the passers-by revealed that Estunder did boast several bathhouses. Mirevra quickly set off for what sounded like the cheapest and kept a few paces ahead of Lars. As they neared the bathhouse, her body grew eager. She longed to feel the warm water flow across her skin, coaxing her to relax. Her hair was in desperate need of oils.

She was so immersed in her thoughts that she almost ignored a loud gathering nearby as she approached her destination. The bathhouse sign squeaked as if welcoming her, but she gave in to her curiosity and worked her way into the crowd. Beldon would be proud.

A man wrapped in red linen and black lace stood on a rickety platform. The colors of Rashawe. With an open text on the platform beside him, he closed his eyes and preached to the onlookers. Mirevra pitied those in the crowd who stretched their hands toward the priest and cried out their needs. She believed in the gods and often prayed to Rashawe, but to do so openly? To let others learn of your deepest desires? She felt her skin crawl at the thought and suppressed a shiver.

Rashawe, The Patron Lord of Wish and Want, was the most worshiped deity in Estellian and regarded as a god in the higher echelon of the heavens. His name was likely the most uttered in all the world. It was no wonder he attracted both worship and infamy. Mirevra glanced at the people calling out to the priest. Many needed so much, and those who had enough still wanted more. The priest called for a woman to step forward, and as she reached the platform, she handed the priest a bundle of bloody rags. She had lost another babe, she said through sobs.

"Tell Rashawe I cannot lose another, I beg you. I cannot," the woman choked out. "My heart cannot take it. My body will give out. I will never truly be with child. I–I...I cannot have another ripped from my hands."

"You wish to carry a babe until birth?" The priest leaned eagerly toward the woman. Mirevra shifted and longed to spit at the priest. What in the Murks else would the woman have brought her rags for?

"But I say to you, you shall not need this wish," the priest cried. "Rashawe is capable of many great things! Let your wish be instead to *resurrect* what once was, my child! Let Rashawe grant you the miracle of what was lost now returned!" The woman stared blankly at the priest, but he did not let up. He pressed his palm against the woman's brow and muttered a prayer in an old language, perhaps a made-up one; Mirevra could not tell. She only knew the common tongue and a handful of Teruk words.

Next, the priest told the woman what she would need to do for the god of Wish and Want to hear her pleas. The standard instructions, Mirevra supposed, as the priest rattled them off. Pray multiple times a day, eat only light-brown rice, light votive candles at sunset, and then he added a long list of ingredients for an offering. The assassin felt her cheeks grow heavy as she stared at the woman's face, her shaking hands still clutching some of the rags soaked in the blood of another lost child. The woman turned to the crowd, her eyes searching. She was not looking for a person or a miracle, Mirevra realized. What the woman sought was comfort. She did not need a wish; she needed an embrace. A hand to hold hers and someone who cared and would listen. What the priest suggested was impossible and Mirevra shook her head in disgust. No power on the earth below or the sky above could bring back the dead. Not even Rashawe. Mirevra shook the thought as she saw Lars approach. This woman's sorrow was not her problem. It was not as if she were going to commiserate with the suffering woman; her words would not help any more than those of the babbling priest.

"This is not the bathhouse," Lars said, stating the obvious into her ear. "Unless something else has taken priority? What is it, Viper? Do you need a wish?" Lars' mouth coiling into his devilish smirk was enough to make Mirevra forget about the woman. She faced the dolt and glowered.

"Yes, actually," she snapped. "I wish for all your shirts to burn, Ruffles. Better still, that they burn with you still in them."

Lars shook with laughter as he grabbed her arm. Heat coursed through Mirevra's body in jarring pulses. *What did he think he was doing?* "My attire may make me look like a jackass," he breathed softly. "But you smell like one. Come. Let us bathe."

Mirevra gave the bathhouse her usual swift assessment before relaxing. There were only a few customers in the four pools. Two old fat men sat together in the corner of one, a woman and a man, two more strangers, in another. A wall of hedges with dried leaves separated the other two baths, and Mirevra suggested they each take one. To her shock, Lars did not argue.

She peeled off her clothes, carefully concealing the small pocket beneath her tabard. She watched as Lars pulled his tunic over his head; his rippling muscles beckoned her to join him in his pool. She resisted and unpinned the hidden pouch with the Messaging Gem nestled inside. A quick search offered two viable hiding spaces: beneath the rocks that lined the steaming pool or behind a giant palmed plant in the corner beside the hedge. She shoved the pouch and her weapons behind the plant and piled her clothes near the pool's edge before stepping into the water.

It was hotter than she expected, but her body sang in relief as she submerged herself. She spread her arms and paddled through the water, letting her skin enjoy the liquid coating. With a sigh, she stretched her arms across the rocks and settled into a corner of the pool. Lazily, she kicked her legs and watched the water ripple before her. She leaned back, smiled, and closed her eyes as deep relaxation seeped through her.

But not for long.

The splash hit her full in the face, and she whipped her head, her eyes blazing. Mirevra snarled.

"What the fuck are you doing?"

Lars settled against the wall and extended his arms as she did. "I got lonely," he said with wide eyes. It was all Mirevra could do to not attack him. "Besides," he added. "I *so* enjoyed our last bath, did you not?"

"No," she bit out, sinking lower under the water, wrapping her arms to cover herself.

"Oh, come now, Viper! Do not tell me you are suddenly shy!" He threw back his head and laughed loud enough for the entire bathhouse to hear, but Mirevra was unamused. Her cheeks burned at the truth that she would never admit out loud. Some part of her *was* suddenly shy around him, at least when she was naked. She did not understand what had changed, and that made her angry.

"We agreed to our own pools," she seethed. Lars only chuckled and pointed.

"It seems they did not understand that," he said. A group of women were now swimming and chattering happily in Lars' pool. How had she not heard them approach? Being around Lars, especially while naked, made her feel uncertain and foolish, and Mirevra detested it. Lars sighed loudly, closed his eyes, and rested his head against the rock. "We are supposed to be learning to trust each other, are we not? We cannot do so if you are determined to be where I am not."

"I will never trust anyone outside of the Ring," Mirevra declared. "Least of all, you."

Lars peeled open one eye and squinted at her. "That hurts, Viper. Truly."

Mirevra scoffed and began to rub her arms and legs briskly. She longed to leave but was unwilling to do so without scrubbing herself clean. Lars settled deeper into the water. "I trust you, after all," he continued. "Even if you are somewhat of a...a..."

"A what?" Mirevra cut him off and sent him a sharp glare.

Lars's grin stretched. "A bitch," he finished.

Mirevra's smile was involuntary. It was actually quite nice to hear that word leave his lips. She did love the title, and it would trouble her if Lars thought her soft and kind. The water suddenly rippled as Lars dunked his head, brought it up, then shook it. It was quite a sight, she had to admit.

"You are unwise to trust me," she warned, wiping droplets from her face. "I am not someone who holds your best interest at heart; In fact, I don't care about your best interest at all." Lars swam towards her, and her breath hitched. When he was far too close, he grinned.

"You do not want to hurt me," he said. "Maybe you did at first, but not anymore. Your eyes have changed." Mirevra frowned and blinked as if she could erase whatever he saw.

"Trust me, I *do* want to hurt you. Often," she snapped.

"Oh, so now you *do* want me to trust you?"

Mirevra glowered and ignored him. Silly games of a silly, insane man. Lars laughed and threw up his hands. "Alright, I concede. You may still want to injure me, but you will not."

"Are you certain?" Mirvera asked as she leaned her head against the rock and sealed her eyes shut, feigning the serenity she longed for when she entered the bath.

"Deadly certain," he swore, holding a hand to his heart. "If it were not, I would have the scars to prove it by now."

Mirevra gave up her feigned serenity, squeezed her eyes tighter, and frowned. Godsdamn him, Lars was correct. "The first few days, I thought you might kill me in my sleep," he continued. "I could see it plainly enough in that golden stare of yours. You wanted me dead." She heard the water slosh as he moved closer, but she refused to open her eyes. He was now so close she felt his warmth shroud her. "Then something changed," he almost whispered. "I am not sure what. You watch me a lot." Embarrassment coursed through Mirevra, and she concentrated on taking even, steady breaths.

"You are loud," she said with a shrug. "I sometimes study you because I cannot understand how one person can talk so much." He laughed, and she felt his breath on her neck. How close *was* he?

"You know, I was wrong about you the last we bathed," he said, and she heard tiny splashes as he lazily flicked the water's surface. "I said I did not take you as a liar. Yet here you are, lying to yourself." Mirevra refused to take the bait. Instead, the edge of her lip tugged upward.

"You watch me too, Ruffles. There is scarcely a moment I do not feel your eyes on me," she said. "And I am not loud. What is your excuse?"

"No excuse," he answered. "I enjoy looking at you. You are mean and attractive. I like it." Lars lifted a pruned hand to rub his sharp jaw. "And unlike you, I do not feel any guilt to lie about it."

Mirevra gulped. She was used to men falling prey to her charms, but Lars was different. With him, she never felt in control of their exchanges. His charms were a formidable adversary. What would the Veravant say–*fuck*. Her heart raced, and she felt the pulse pounding at the base of her throat. She felt his warmth grow stronger as he sidled even closer.

"I do not think you know how to separate yourself from him," Lars murmured. Mirevra *definitely* felt his breath on her neck, but she was debilitated by something else. There was a hollow note in his voice. She willed her eyes open and was caught in his stare. Her dreams come to life. The stormy gray eyes held, bewitched, and scared her.

"What do you want from me?" She heard the bite in her voice, but the question was sincere. She felt compelled to make sense of the strange feelings he birthed in her. The way his eyes roved over her face kept her paralyzed. He did not peer down at her breasts as he had in the stream, he was only fixated on her face. His eyes darkened as he drank in each freckle, followed every fine line, and studied how her eyes ran with streaks of brown when she was angry...or nervous. It seemed he saw everything. Lars shifted and leaned in. Her heart raced even faster, and she could not hide how her chest rose and fell in tandem. What was he doing? What was *she* doing? Why was she letting him get closer and closer and–

She caught a flash of movement beyond his shoulder and shoved him far enough to see two boys picking up her clothes. *"Hey!"* she yelled, and the pair snapped their sights to her.

"Go!" One shouted, and they ran with her tunic, tabard, and trousers in hand.

"Come back! Come back here, you little bastards!" She swam toward the opposite end of the pool, but it was too late. The boys—and her clothes—were gone, and she was stranded here naked. *"Fuck!"* Only her boots remained at the pool's edge. The hidden pouch, thank the gods, was still hidden behind the plant with her blades. She ground her teeth. This happened not only because she had chosen the cheapest bathhouse in the city but because she had let Lars distract her *again*. "Fuck! Fuck! Fuck!" She smacked the water with each word and heard Lars break into laughter. Hearing his amusement, her anger grew; she would drown him.

Before she could swim over and force his head under the water, the male pressed two palms on the rock and lifted himself from the bath. Mirevra's hand stopped mid-air, and she stared. His body was unreservedly perfect. She could not tear her eyes away even if she wanted to, and so much of her did not wish to do so. He had to have been sculpted by Radina. This was no human body. Not even the Veravant, in all his dripping appeal, could compare. Neither could his cock, gods save her, for whatever hung from Lars' lower half was not the size of any she had seen. She gulped down her anger and desire and looked back at her boots. She was so fucked. She could not walk around Estunder naked! Mirevra's head ached as she treaded water and tried to devise a plan. Just as she considered drowning herself as the best alternative to this ridiculous situation, Lars coughed. She turned and saw he now wore his trousers but was shirtless. And dangling a god-awful, ruffled, billowy shirt from one hand.

"I know you are not one for ruffles," he said, fighting back a grin. "But I believe you are all out of options."

They exited the bathhouse and joined the crowds on the streets. Lars was topless, and his longsword hung from trousers that hugged his hips. Mirevra, her long hair slicked back, wore nothing but his huge, painfully ruffled shirt and her boots. She had shoved the pouch with the messaging gem into one boot, where it rubbed against her foot with each step.

Without their sheaths, she was forced to hold both blades before her like an idiot. Lars stopped and eyed her up and down. "Let me buy you clothes," he suggested. "Though, I do like seeing you in mine."

"I will not let you buy me anything," she snapped and swiveled her head to gauge how much attention they were attracting. Some people were staring, but most seemed too preoccupied with their tasks to give a damn, thank Rashawe. "I will not be further in your debt than I already am. I will not owe you anything."

Lars's haughty scoff soon turned into a belly laugh. He rested his hands on his hips and shook his head. "You are something else, Viper. Do you know this?"

"I do, actually," she said. She raised her chin and tried her hardest to ignore how his damp chest and carved muscles glistened in the afternoon sun.

"A deal then," he said. "Because you have no coins, I will buy you clothes. Then you can steal me a few drinks from a tavern to make us even." She lifted a brow and considered his offer warily. He chuckled. "I know, I know. It is not very *heroic* of me. But the way I see it, the city stole from you first. It is only right to steal back. Fair is fair, right?"

A smile tugged at the corner of her mouth, and though she remained silent, she followed him around three corners until he picked a suitable shop. She tried on many outfits, some heinously ill-fitting, and modeled a few puffed skirts and ridiculous hats for good measure. Eventually, they exited out of the shop just as the sun set. Lars had also purchased new clothes and now wore a black tunic. Mirevera noted that it had fewer ruffles, but these sleeves billowed all the same. Mirevra had chosen a short-sleeved, burgundy tunic. A leather sheath now held her blades firmly around her waist, and she walked comfortably in a pair of nicely fitted trousers. She had drawn the line at allowing the rogue to buy her expensive new vambraces, so she opted for bandages and wrapped the cloth around her calloused and bruised fingers. He purchased an entire roll so she could discard and wrap them anew each time. Mirevra considered her new clothes and figured she would now have to steal an entire cellar to make their deal even. They chose an inconspicuous tavern on a sparsely occupied road leading out of the city.

The bar was half empty and quiet, save for occasional belches and distant mumbles. A few men sat near the door, but the rest of the tavern's patrons were gathered in the back and, from what Mirevra could hear, engrossed in an intense card game. The barkeep was a young man, handsome and blond. His beard was thick and burly, his eyes so brown they appeared maroon. Lars waved him down, and two flagons of ale were in their hands soon enough. Mirevra led Lars to a corner table, where they sat and drank. Then, they had another. And another.

Halfway through her fourth drink, Mirevra slapped the table and informed Lars it was time for her to invest in the card game. He followed her as she dragged her chair to the game table and asked to join. One of the men playing, her age, stammered his response. "You? Of course, you can join... You can do more than that!" He continued to stare at her until a large hand squeezed his shoulder.

"She will just be playing the game. Nothing more, nothing less," Lars said. The man whirled around, and he flashed an awkward gangly smile.

"I did not realize the lady was taken. My mistake, sir. We do not see many women around here looking like... Looking like...*that*." He gawked at her again, as did a few other men around the table. Mirvera gave an inward shrug; she was used to the attention and thought little of it. Lars patted the gawking male's shoulder roughly.

"You do not see women looking like *that* anywhere, friend. Now, explain the rules so she can play."

Mirevra was mortified to feel herself blush. She shook her head to fight off the effects of her previous drinks, then downed the one she still held. It was the alcohol that made her blush, she thought. *Not* Lars' assessment of her looks. Alcohol and nothing else. Nothing else at all.

The male's chair legs scraped against the floor as he eagerly scooted closer to Mirevra. He spent far too long explaining the rules and delving into excruciating detail about the very simple game. But Mirevra held her tongue; her silence could only be advantageous as she played drunkards.

After even more explanation, the game began.

Lars kept the drinks coming as Mirevra demolished every player who dared face her. Even in her intoxicated stupor, she could not be bested. Winning this game did not require much thinking, as it depended on her reflexes. She did not need to be sober to move more quickly than the men who challenged her. She was sipping drink six, and her eyelids started to feel heavy when she agreed to a final game. She placed half her silver coins on the line. If she wanted to at least pay Lars back for tonight's ale, she could not lose. She shook her head and slapped her cheeks. Her last challenger was a dreadful sight, even for her drunk eyes. Brawnier than even Bagah, his vast, puffy eyebrows almost covered his eyes. His massive, pale, bulbous nose rested above a pair of thin lips, and a snaggle tooth poked out from the bottom one. He leaned his mace against the table and sat heavily in the chair opposite Mirevra. He did not speak; he only pointed to the cards. Mirevra deduced his native tongue was grunts. She won two rounds. Three. Four. But the brute still demanded another chance. Lars sat her seventh drink down, then twisted his chair to lean against its back and watch her.

The giant competitor threw down a small burlap sack rattling with coin. "Everything I got is here in this bag. We play one more round," he proposed. "Winner takes all." Mirevra did not know if it was the alcohol, her pride, or the way Lars kept smiling at her, but she quickly agreed. Her challenger was big, but his size slowed him, and he apparently had not learned this. If he wanted to lose all of his money tonight, that was a problem he would have to face come morning.

The male, who knew more of the game's rules than Mirevra had needed to know, set a deck of cards on the table. Mirevra waited for him to flip the card she wanted. She waited. Waited–*there!* Her hand slammed down simultaneously as her competitor's, but only one covered the card. The giant lifted his palm and growled. She stared at her hand. It was beet red from the force of his play and stung, but she had done it. She won again. She reached for the burlap sack with a satisfied laugh, but the giant grabbed her wrist. At once, Lars stood, his fingers tickling the top of his hilt.

"I would not," he cautioned the behemoth.

"Ha! What's a bloke like you gonna do about it?"

Lars sucked in a heavy breath. "Not me..." he said with a wink. It was quick. It was easy. This buffoon had already proven that he did not possess quick reflexes. Mirevra yanked her wrist from his hand, pulled back, and struck; her fist collided with his massive jaw with a loud crack. The man flew back, and though Mirevra's vision was hazy, she pushed her chair back and stood braced for a fight. The male grunted incoherently, but Lars's laughter filled her ears. *"...her,"* he finished with a pinch of pride in his voice. He rubbed his own jaw. "I know that fucking hurt," he added with a smirk, and Mirevra grinned.

It should have ended there. The brute should have nursed his swelling wound and let them walk away with their spoils. But Mirevra was ready. If there was one thing she had learned in her countless hours spent in seedy places, it was that drunk men were the most ignorant fools of all and consistently overestimated their abilities. This one was no different. He scrambled to his feet and yelled. "You will regret that. I will kill you right dead, you filthy *bitch.*" She whirled to see him balling one hand into a fist while he swung his mace.

Lars stepped before her and plunged his blade into the man's belly. Mirevra blinked as something became very clear. The Nelimen rogue may have called her a bitch earlier at the bathhouse, but apparently, he did not take it kindly when another did the same. The man sputtered and gurgled curses as his eyelids fluttered. Lars pulled his blade out, and blood splattered over the floor. After staggering as he tried to stay upright, the beast of a man crashed to the floor. Mirevra's breath quickened.

"Leave before anyone can catch us," she hissed. Instead, Lars grabbed her by the waist and pulled her close.

"Where are you off to, Viper? We are not in any trouble," he said. She scanned the room; no one looked at her as they usually did after witnessing one of her kills.

"It is true," one man called. "Drakven was gonna' whack you with that there mace of his! He done it before! We've all seen it! Your suitor here was only actin' in self-defense!" The rest of the tavern cheered in agreement. Mirevra stood stock still while her brain whirled. She had no idea how to react to applause, to being the person in the right and not on the run. And she most certainly did not know how to react to Lars being called her suitor.

Mirevra used most of her winnings to pay their extravagant bar tab, figuring it was best not to steal after causing such a show. She tried to give Lars the rest, but he refused to accept it. Unwilling to argue in her drunken state, she pretended to concede but vowed that one day, when he was not looking, she would somehow sneak the coins into his trousers. She would *not* owe Lars anything.

They meandered through the streets on the city outskirts, arguing over which turns would lead them to the center and the temple. Mirevra was confident that she could find the temple if she were alone.

However, seven drinks in, Mirevra was drunk. Her heel wobbled as she stumbled on the uneven cobblestones, and she held her arms out to the side to prevent herself from careening into Lars. He was doing the same and with a smile spread across his face. Suddenly, he grabbed her arm. "Look!" Mirevra craned her neck but did not see the temple, only a small grassy hill behind a building. Lars pulled her along, and she did not have the strength or sobriety to fight him, especially as they climbed up. At the top, he dropped her arm and spread his own wide as he spun. "Look at this!" The male certainly sounded delighted, Mirevra thought, but she had no idea why. She folded her arms, turned her head slowly, and reassessed her surroundings. Just as she had thought, there was nothing. Only a hill surrounded by more hills outside of the city.

"There is nothing here," she stated. Lars's shining eyes met her aimless gape, and he grabbed her shoulders.

"Gods, Viper," he breathed. "Do you ever drop the scowl to just *enjoy* things?"

Mirevra shook him off. "I often enjoy things," she corrected. "When there are actual *things to enjoy!*" She clamped her mouth shut at the sound of his deep laughter. The way it made her cheeks burn. The alcohol was playing with her mind. This entire evening had not been wise. *Foolish! You fool of a girl!* She could not shake his scent. Tobacco and vetiver. She hated how the timbre of his dark voice rattled her and even how she was beginning to find his half-witted jests somewhat humorous. The images of Lars stepping in front of her and quickly killing that boor of a man flashed through her mind. It made her body flare with excitement. Her scowl deepened.

Still laughing, Lars sat on the grass and patted the soft ground beside him. Against her better judgment, she settled next to him.

"Here, let me show you something to enjoy," he said, pointing to the sky. "See there? The moon and her glow? Look how she covers everything in her pale light. Gorgeous, no?"

"*She?*" Mirevra asked, resting her chin on her shoulder to look at him. "You think the moon is a woman?" She laughed, but Lars was more serious than she had ever seen him.

"Not only the moon. The stars, the dark blanket of the sky behind them. All of it," he answered. "Night is a woman," he said as if it were a known fact. "The day is a girl, if you were wondering."

Mirevra shoved a thick lock of hair away from her face and faced him. "I was not," she said. "But now I suppose I am." She knew she should look away, but it was too late. The rogue's eyes deadlocked on hers. She could not break his stare.

"You remind me of the night," he said. "You can be ruthless and filled with a yearning to kill, but that is only the half of you. The stars are proof."

"Proof of what?" She had asked before she could stop herself, then she started to pull away. This conversation was ridiculous and should never have started. Then Lars reached out and tucked her rebellious hair that was floating in the wind behind her ear. Mirevra's breathing hitched. She no longer felt like a woman with more than a dozen kills to her name; she felt like a child. She felt... *afraid.*

"Proof that even in darkness, something shines," he answered. "We all have our dark parts, Viper. Even the heroes. But the night is not all black and gloom. That is what I wanted to show you, *remind* you of. There is light," he said quietly and pointed to her chest. "There is always light."

Mirevra felt a tic start in her jaw. Murks, the rogue was handsome. Too handsome.

"Even heroes have dark pasts, you say? Tell me, what is yours, Ruffles?" Lars did not answer. "Well?" She leaned in with a raised brow. Lars studied her face, smirked, then shrugged.

"I forgot what I was talking about."

Mirevra held her belly and laughed. *Genuinely laughed.* She could not remember the last time she had done that. Laughter felt awkward coming out, but also quite lovely. Lars draped an arm over his bent knee and watched her. She tried to stop; those damned gray eyes watched everything she did so keenly. "I love that sound," he whispered. "You should laugh more often."

The wave of joy swung into nausea, and the world started slowly spinning. Was her sudden dizziness the effect of his words or the ale? Mirevra briefly considered both but could not come up with an answer. Desperate to distract herself, she peered at the blue stone in the Nelimen's ring.

"You—You asked something yesterday," she stuttered. "If I had forgotten that I have a heart. What did you mean?" Lars' serious expression was back. "Are you not drunk?" She demanded and released a deep burp. His lips widened into a smile.

"Oh, I am drunk," he laughed. "Though I must have more experience than you with the feeling. You know, the victor's spoils and all that."

Mirevra only burped again and pounded a fist against her chest.

"Maybe I said the wrong thing yesterday," he mused, returning the conversation to her question. "I do that often. I am a man of many words—as you can probably tell—I am bound to mix up a few every now and again."

"So, you do not think me a heartless wench?" Mirevra blurted out. The second the question left her mouth, she longed to snatch it back, but Lars appeared to take her drunken sentiments in stride.

"Of course, I do not think that, Viper. It is only... We hear so much about the Foxes. Your guild is not known for showing humanity or kindness. Most call the Ring cold and empty."

Mirevra felt pressure growing in her ears but answered clearly. "That is mostly true," she said.

Lars shook his head slowly. "That is what I thought of the Foxes until I met you and the others. You cannot convince me that Roman was cold or that Beldon is empty. Honestly, they both would have fared better as a Nelimen. Even Bagah! He could lay us all flat, yet he has the temperament of a dove. How in the Murks did the Ring ever acquire such a selfless soul?" Mirevra had no idea if she was nodding, but nonetheless, she agreed. Bagah was the best of them, and she was glad someone else could see it. She was glad Lars did not see her half-Teruk friend and think the worst.

"And what of me?" Mirevra asked as she swayed. "You said I 'cannot separate myself from him.' You meant the Veravant, right?" She studied Lars as he shifted. She remembered far too vividly what he looked like naked. *This damned alcohol and these damned involuntary thoughts!*

"The Veravant," Lars began, shaking her thoughts free. Mirevra hated hearing the title from Lar's lips so much that the nausea returned. "He treats all of you as if you are his to play with, to do with whatever he pleases," he said. Oh gods, the bile was churning relentlessly in her stomach. Memories floated through her mind. She was atop the Veravant, his body rolling beneath hers, his cock deep inside. *'You are mine,'* she heard.

"It is wrong. He treats you as his property, as a weapon."

"I *am* a weapon." Had she said that out loud?

Lars handed her his water skin, and she gulped it down without question. Her stomach still rippled, but her mind cleared a bit.

"That is what he would have you believe, Viper. That you are nothing more than a blade at his disposal. One he can wield at his will; one that he can use to cleave the world in two."

When Mirevra handed him back the skin, he abruptly grabbed her wrist and pulled her to face him. "What makes him so different from the lich, then?" The skin fell to the ground. When Mirevra remained silent, Lars drew her in until their noses nearly touched. "It does not matter that you cannot see it. You are not a blade. You are not cold, hard, and empty. As much as you might pretend to be, as much as you wish it were true. You have choices, Mirevra. And you are free to make them. No one owns you." His eyes trailed down to her lips and lingered there. His hand warmed her skin.

She certainly had a choice now, and she had to make it.

Desire would not win.

She tugged her wrist away from his hold and pressed her face into her palms. "The Tajeh said you lost a great love. Who was she?" The mood was too close to want and desire. *Cursed Lady of Heathers.*

Lars' expression was stunned; his features stilled as if the ice mages had frozen him in place. "I–" he started, then looked away. When he turned back, he wore a familiar cocky grin. "Why? Are you jealous? Trust me, Viper, you need not worry. As I am sure you saw in the bath, there is more than enough of me to go around."

"Why do you do that?" Mirevra asked, her brows knitted in frustration.

"Do what?" he volleyed, the grin still strong.

"Use humor to hide how you truly feel?" Lars' smile disappeared, and Mirevra's nausea returned.

"Likely the same reason you use anger to do the same," he said, but his voice sounded far away. Mirevra's eyelids fell, and glimpses of Lars and the rolling hills wove in and out of her vision. He leaned toward her and called something, but Mirevra felt her mind swirl as the world tilted. She grunted as something pushed into her stomach. *Are those hands on me? Am I being carried somewhere?*

Through her thick haze, she cursed herself for letting down her guard. Her cheek fell against something soft. The rest of the night passed quickly.

Mirevra awoke, glanced at the table beside her bed, and grimaced. *His water skin.* She could not recall how she got back to the temple or how she came to be tucked snugly under a warm quilt, her hair pushed back from her face. What she *could* remember mortified her. *Lars, naked in the bath. Shopping with him for new clothes. Drinking, then playing cards in the tavern. Her laughter.* She pulled the quilt over her head and ignored the knock at her door. She knew it was Bagah but could not summon the will to tell him to enter. After several more knocks, he did so anyway.

"We were supposed to meet back here at sundown," his deep voice filled the room, and she winced. Her whole body felt fragile. She lowered the blanket enough to meet his gaze. It was Bagah, but something was different. Was she still drunk? "You look like shit," her friend said.

Scowling, Mirevra shoved the quilt aside, jumped out of the bed, winced again, and took two long strides to meet him face to face. It had not been her excruciating headache or a trick of the light. Bagah had changed. His skin was still fair, his hair still brown, but his eyes were much less yellow, and his nostrils, well, they had cartilage. Bagah had a full nose. It was a tiny snubbed one, but a nose, nonetheless. Mirevra reached toward his face with a curious finger, but Bagah swatted it away. "Stop that," he ordered. She dropped her hand but not her eyes. They held fast to his new feature.

"How?" Her voice cracked; her tongue was dried out. Bagah only lifted his brows.

"Where are your leathers?" He asked in return as he pointed at her burgundy tunic. "What in the Murks are you wearing?"

They walked slowly to breakfast, which Mirevra assumed would be another scoop of bitter oats and a stale roll. Bagah was silent; his eyes lingered on the intricate tapestries that lined the corridors. One depicted early clerics gathered around a white fire, feeding off its healing light. Others depicted more frivolous activities. Eventually, feeling her stare burn through his skin, Bagah stopped and turned to Mirevra.

"Heral," he answered quietly. "I am not sure what she did. I felt nothing. She asked me about the Teruk. Honest to Rashawe, I have never found anyone so interested in my kind before. I was not able to ask her a single question about herself, where she comes from, or what she is—"

"But the nose..." Mirevra's voice trailed off as she tried again to touch it. Once more, Bagah swatted away her hand.

"Is that the only part you care to hear about?"

She nodded. It was, in fact, the only thing that she could think about with her skull pounding in her ears. Bagah sighed but nodded. "Well, after we spoke about the Teruk, she asked me how it felt to be a halfbreed."

"And you told her?!" Mirevra's mouth fell open. She and Bagah had never spoken of his feelings, she herself only knew his story because he had told it to the Tajeh. Why had he told his story to this woman who was practically a stranger?

"Yes and no," Bagah said. "It seems you may not be the only one skilled at reading my face." He flashed her a grin as he resumed walking, and Mirevra marveled at how devastatingly *human* he looked. "Heral asked me if I had the power to change how people treated me, would I use it?" They paused at the dining hall entrance. He rubbed his nose between his large fingers. "I said I would. That I would do anything to not be what I am... then without warning, she touched my face. Her touch...was quick and delicate, and when she removed her hand, this was here." He gently squeezed his nose and then released it with a bright smile. "Something so simple, and yet, it has changed my life already. We walked through Estunder, and you cannot imagine the difference. People saw me as one of them, not something to hate."

"I always saw you as you were and did not hate you," Mirevra said, feeling her gut roil from the night's alcohol. "Your nose was fine." She tried to wrap her muddy thoughts around what had happened to her friend. Heral had no right to change Bagah's appearance. And the fact he welcomed it!

"You are not the rest of the world, Mir. You did not have to face it," Bagah said gently.

"It made you strong to face people's stares; it made you part of who you were."

"That is easy for you to say," Bagah said dryly.

"Not as easy as you may think," she said and let out a long sigh. "I only wish you would not bend to them, Bagah. You *are* half Teruk. It is your blood. You should be proud of it, regardless of what this cursed world thinks."

"I can be strong without the world hating me, Mir," he said gently. "And you can be strong without hating the world." He offered her a wistful smile. "Let me have this, Mir. Please?"

The doors opened. Everyone else was already seated at the table. Lars caught her eye, and she looked away quickly. Shame stitched its way through her chest. She grabbed a bread roll and sat at the other end of the table. Beldon turned from his conversation with Shiln and flashed her a crooked smile.

"My gods, Mir. You look positively disheveled!" He smoothed a hand through his immaculate ginger hair and laughed. "Do not tell me the impossible happened? It cannot be! Did you actually have... *fun?*"

"A mistake I will not soon make again," Mirevra snapped, digging her teeth into the hard bread. Her eyes swept across the table, and she noted Lars' grin. She hated it, *detested* it, but she could not stop the corner of her mouth from curling up in response.

The One Problem Solved

Neeps flipped the last page of the codex before roughly slamming it shut. "It is done," he announced to the group. Except for Shiln, who was praying inside the temple, they gathered in a courtyard beneath a red-leafed tree. The halfling flung himself off the stone wall where he had sat crossed-legged. He clutched the book to his chest. "I have finished. I read it twice," he declared. In the silence after his pronouncement, Mirevra struggled to remain calm and practically ground her teeth into dust.

"Twice?!" She was almost shouting. "You mean to tell me you had already finished the damned book and said nothing?"

The halfling turned up his nose. "Anyone who knows anything about reading would tell you it is important to review the material more than once. *Especially* when understanding said material is crucial. I do not know what you Foxes consider important, but an all-powerful lich taking over the world is high on my list." Mirevra said nothing, but her flaming cheeks matched her new tunic.

"Well? Did you pinpoint a location?" Lars cut in. He wore his new black tunic, and the fabric billowed over his arms before stretching tight across his waist. He had left the garb unlaced, exposing the wild curls of his chest hair. Mirevra fought to keep her eyes on his face.

Neeps inhaled deeply. "I can safely assume that it is not in the Fertek desert. The stories seem to toss the desert in as a feint."

"How can you be sure?" Mirevra demanded. Neeps' nose wrinkled.

"I cannot be sure. That is why I said I *assumed* Fox. Keep up."

Heral stepped between Neeps and Mirevra and took up the questioning. "Why do you think the Fertek is not a viable option?"

"For one, the stories are clear that the hiding place is in one of many tall rocks," he said.

"Tall rocks?" Bagah asked and cocked his head. Mirevra frowned as she looked his way. She was still not used to his nose. She never would be.

"My first read was confusing, to say the least. The book is filled with tales; only a few can be true. During my second read," he said and paused to send Mirevra a haughty stare. "I began to deconstruct what was a rumor and what could put us on the right path." He held up a finger. "I started with one small fact: the Vaenir rests in a place most high. On my first read, I thought this place most high could mean a temple or the home of a king. Then I realized the tales that spoke of its true location were simple. The obviously counterfeit stories droned on forever and were filled with complexities, but the Vaenir is *literally* in a place most high. The Fertek desert is flat, with only a few dunes. Even an untrained eye can see for miles and miles." Neeps paused again and flipped the book open to a marked page. "Here, the book says, *'The holy blade's light is high above and too far, a small sun in the distance, a twinkling star.'*

Mirevra felt Bagah's discomfort and turned to see him blanch. "That sounds more like a riddle than directions," said Beldon, seated on a stone bench a few paces away. Neeps held up a hand.

"At first, I thought so, too. But then I noticed a pattern. The false tales each differed from one another. Even if they led to the same location, their telling was off, even by a line or two. This indicates that whoever told these tales had only *heard* of the sword, not seen it. I searched the text for stories from people who may have had access to the blade itself…only *one* story across all the tales remained consistent in how it was told." Neeps thumbed to another place in the volume. "*A place most high but regarded as low…,*" he read and flipped to another page. "*Ash so heavy it appears as snow… In a place unowned, caught in a lover's quarrel…,*" Neeps closed the book and finished. "*The fires of the sun and all the land's soil.*"

Mirevra rolled her eyes and glanced at Beldon and Bagah, hoping they were equally unamused, but they appeared to take the tinkering halfling's words seriously. Finally, Lars spoke.

"Great. We are chasing a children's riddle, then."

Neeps opened his mouth, but Beldon cut in. "If these *are* the lines you believe will lead us to the Vaenir, then so be it," the cleric said. "But we still do not know where it is."

"The Isles of Caxaven are unowned; so is the territory of Drodour," said Neeps. "The Isles have cities that rest on hills. *High, rocky* hills. They also have beacons on these hills. What kind of fire do they create? Could they produce ash so heavy it appears as snow?"

Lars nodded thoughtfully, but Bagah stepped forward, shaking his head. "The Vaenir is not in the Isles of Caxaven," he said firmly. "It is in Drodour." Everyone turned to stare at him. Heral smiled.

"Are you sure?" Mirevra asked before one of the Nelimen could interrogate him. His brow creased in thought, Bagah gazed at his boots and Mirevra understood. Bagah longed to say he was unsure and that they should stay far away from Drodour, but he could not. For the look on his face told that he knew precisely Vaenir rested. "Then we shall go to Drodour," she said.

"Because the big brute says so? I am the one who read the book!" Neeps was openly sneering at Bagah.

"Yes, but you said it could be in Drodour–" Mirevra began.

"I said it *could* be! There is a dearth of evidence for its location... and think of the cost! Drodour is a dangerous world. The mountains are home to many myths and foul creatures. Why do you think Sardek does not bother to conquer that land? It has not been touched since the time of Kallias Caston! We would be fools to go there on a whim. The Isles of Caxaven is just as feasible and does not boast the same peril."

"That is true," Bagah said. "But the Vaenir is not in the Isles. It is in *'a place most high, but regarded as low.'* Drodour is home to the Teruk, or at least, it once was. What land could be regarded lower?" The group fell silent. "And the ash, I have seen it. Yes, I was only a babe, but the memory holds true. I cannot say where it came from, but it was there."

"So, say we go to Drodour," Neeps said. "How do we know which mountain it is? The shore is covered with them."

Bagah sighed, his eyes narrowed as if he were swept up in another memory. "My mother used to tell me a fable every night before sleep. The one of the rock and the sun," he said and inhaled deeply. "It is an old legend of our people. 'The dawn of time began with a single rock' is how it begins." Bagah closed his eyes. "The rock was alone in the valley and stayed that way for centuries. Its only companions were the sun and the moon high above it, taking turns in keeping the rock company. As time passed, the rock wept at night and told the moon that though it appreciated its pale glow, it could not think of anything more marvelous than the sun. The rock had fallen deeply in love with the sun's warmth and light. So, one night, the rock asked the moon if there was any way it could be with the sun, for it could not stand being so far away from its one true love. The moon told the rock that if the sun came down, the world would be swallowed by fire, but if the rock went to the sun, they might be able to be together. So, every day, the rock grew. It grew until it became a mountain, but it still could not reach the sun. So, it keeps growing and growing." Bagah's eyes snapped open.

"The Develdeon," he breathed. "It is the tallest mountain in all of Drodour. They say it still grows, not giving up on its love for the sun, still hopeful to unite. *One of rock and one of fire, who could not be no matter their desire.*' The Vaenir is in the Develdeon. It has to be," Bagah said in a flat voice.

"A lover's quarrel," Lars whispered.

Heral eyes flared. She reached high and rested her hand on Bagah's shoulder. "Then we shall go to the mountain. And you will lead the way," she said, her voice sure and comforting. Neeps looked nervous but said nothing. Beldon rose as Shiln entered the courtyard. She surveyed the group, and her eyes lingered on Heral's hand on Bagah's shoulder.

"What have we discovered?"

"The Vaenir's location. Maybe," Lars said, his expression wary.

Shiln's brows shot up to her hairline. "Well," she said. "That is one problem solved." Throbbing filled Mirevra's body, and she grabbed her head, swearing to herself that she would never drink alcohol again. But the throbbing was in her boot as well. She straightened. The Messaging Gem. She must tell the Veravant. *The guilds are set for the lands of Drodour.*

"And many more problems born," she whispered.

The Sorceress Returns

It would take at least six days to reach Drodour, and the rations the temple priests had given Shiln would not hold them over. Once again, the guilds split into pairs, and Mirevra and the fiery sorceress were tasked with buying what they would need for the journey. The afternoon was swiftly upon them, and Mirevra spent her hard-earned silver on a fine pair of peaked greaves to cover her legs. They did not match her new tunic, as Shiln pointed out repeatedly, but Mirevra did not care. The sorceress did not buy armor or weapons; instead, she spent her coin on a rich, velvet robe of violet. Its lantern sleeves hung loose and were adorned with elegant silver veining that twisted intricately to meet on the hood. Mirevra thought Shiln looked an absolute fool, but when the sorceress pulled the hood over her head, Mirevra fought to repress a shudder. A fool Shiln might be, but a mighty fool who could still Bind Mirevra's mouth and send lightning through her limbs.

They proceeded to the butcher's market to acquire dried meat for the road. The butcher was a brawny woman with a crooked nose and missing teeth. She had no time for small talk and her hands were stained with dried blood and dirt. Shiln emitted a repulsed noise as the butcher packed the meat into a sack. Mirevra offered her extra silver, and they made their way back to regroup at the temple. They were mostly silent until they walked past the house Mirevra had seen Shiln wince at a few nights prior, with eight windows and a ruined door. Mirevra could not help herself. "What is your history with that place?" she asked casually, nodding her head at the house. Shiln's face hardened, her eyes betraying nothing.

"I have no history," she snapped. A lie, Mirevra thought. How often had she told the very same one?

"It is obvious," Mirevra countered. "But you do not have to tell me. I only asked out of boredom."

Half true. Mirevra was indeed bored; the day was dragging long, and the anxiety over what lay ahead was slowly constricting her gut. But she also felt genuine curiosity. Shiln was one of the people she would likely face the most powerful being in all Estellian with, and knowing something about her might make the coming battle easier. Without breaking stride, Shiln eyed Mirevra.

"If it is so obvious, then surely so is the rest of the story," she said, cutting a corner sharply. Mirevra nearly tripped to follow in stride. "An abandoned child with nowhere to go and no one to turn to grows up in an orphanage and eventually finds a temple where she is raised by clerics. The end." The cloaked enigma rounded another corner with Mirevra hot on her heels.

"You do not know if you have any kin?" Shiln stopped mid-step, turning to the Fox with a fierce scowl.

"Do you?"

"None that I am aware of," Mirevra said.

Shiln's piercing stare roamed Mirevra as if she were looking for the most vulnerable place to strike. "Why do you bother me with questions? I thought you found solace in silence."

At that, Mirevra snorted. "Indeed, I find reverence in it. But these last few days have afforded me almost no time for quiet, and I am afraid I have been too ingrained with the senseless words of your guild to stop now."

"Too much time spent with Lars, no doubt," Shiln said with a wry smile.

"How long have you known him?" Mirevra asked, and for a moment, Shiln's face softened.

"Almost three years. Lars and Heral were the last to join the Nelimen, right after one of our own died in a glorious battle serving alongside the raiders of Fertek against a Midde Death Worm," Shiln said. Mirevra grimaced. She had heard of such worms, as large as a building and with the teeth of a lion. "He was always a gregarious sort; Heral not so much."

"What is she?" Mirevra did not want to seem too eager, but she pulled at the back of her neck as she waited nervously for the answer.

"What is Heral? A question for the gods to answer, I am afraid," Shiln answered with a rueful smile.

"Surely you have an idea. You have been bonded through a guild for three years; you have seen her power. As an Arcanen who can both cast spells and heal and bless, you would be the one to know most about it–"

"I do not," Shiln broke in. "I know that she does not operate under the usual Arcanen laws, but I also do things that most find uncommon.

Kaven Hiring

Heral's Arcanen is unlike any I have ever seen," Shiln continued. "What I do know is that it has only been used to serve the Nelimen, and for that, I am grateful enough," Shiln said. Mirevra squinted and grudgingly admitted to herself that perhaps she and the sorceress were not so different after all. When the temple crested the cobblestone road and came into view, Shiln turned her chin towards Mirevra. "Ask Lars if you are so interested. He and Heral scarcely ever leave each other's side. If anyone might know what she is, it would be him."

Mirevra felt heat course through her as the blurry events in the tavern and on the hill played through her mind. She barely heard Shiln's soft laughter. "Besides, the two of you seem to be growing....close," Shiln added. Mirevra growled and sent Shiln a warning glare. The sorceress lifted both hands, those ostentatious sleeves waving like two violet banners in the wind. "No judgment will come from me, Fox. Lars is a handsome sort and skilled with words."

"Lars is a nuisance and does not know when to hold his tongue, silver as it may be. I would not call that a skill."

They were closing in on the temple now, and Mirevra saw Bagah and Neeps already at the door. Beldon and Lars were likely still in the city. Gods knew how late those two would be. "Well, if that is not his skill, then wearing a person down surely is," Shiln said. "I did not enjoy him at first, either. But he grows on you. Careful, Fox, for even the strongest of wood can be whittled down in time." Shiln had a coy smile on her face, and Mirevra frowned. Was the sorceress threatening her or being friendly?

A shout sounded off behind them, and glowering, the two women whirled to face it. Beldon and Lars were racing up the street, carrying bags and bags of who knows what with obnoxious grins plastered across their faces. Their yelps and laughter echoed across the city.

"Putting those two together was a mistake," Mirevra scowled, lowering her arms and resheathing her weapons.

"We should stab them," Shiln said, straightening up and gathering her glorious cloak around her again. Mirevra grinned and noticed how Shiln fought back a smile as she watched Beldon's gangly sprint.

"Careful, witch. Beldon is also known to get under one's skin. Not even your thick cloak could prevent it."

Shiln only rolled her eyes as the men bounded past, but Mirevra caught levity in them just the same. Mirevra would not describe the day with the sorceress as a friendship forming. Still, she did not want to kill Shiln as severely as she did yesterday, and that might be a good thing.

Neeps' eyes shook more quickly than usual as Beldon pulled assorted jars and herbs out of his bag. Unable to wait for the following item, the halfling snatched the bag from the cleric and practically dove in. Meanwhile, Lars emptied the contents of his bag in front of Bagah. A sickle, an old machete, and a dark club. He handed the latter to Bagah and winked. "It is heavy."

Bagah lifted the club high above him and studied it in the late afternoon light. Mirevra was glad to see a smile spread across her friend's face, and despite being again distracted by his nose, she found herself matching his expression.

"It *is* heavy," Bagah agreed, lowering the giant block of wood to his side. Lars slapped his back as if Bagah were a colleague or an old friend.

"It is a good thing you are so strong," Lars said.

"The horses are fed and rested. I sold the ones we no longer need in order to buy more rations. Let us load the coach and head west." Heral spoke.

Like the others, Mirevra spun to face her. She searched the strange and beautiful woman's green eyes for the fire that she had seen consume them, but those eyes were calm now. Heral's power was curled inward, a sleeping beast, and well hidden. Heral peered at the men and their new toys. "Good. We will need all the weapons we can carry. Whether for the enemy who follows or the enemy who lies ahead, we must be prepared."

As they loaded the coach, Heral's words played in Mirevra's head. *The enemy who follows or the enemy who lies ahead.* What was it about Heral that made her feel so uneasy? The woman *had* saved her life when they fought the ice mages and gave Bagah a nose, but Mirevra could not shake the feeling that something else was at play. What Jardin had said in Mercinnho sat like an acidic lump in the back of her mouth, one she could not seem to swallow. *'Death and Betrayal.'* And he died not two days later. Remembering Jardin's words, Mirevra's skin crawled. Then she grudgingly admitted that part of her unease could stem from how deeply Bagah was taken by the auburn-haired beauty. It was as if he saw Radina herself. Heral had enraptured the poor male, and Mirevra worried for him. *Well, then, that is it*; the reason she was so wary of the woman. She simply feared for Bagah's heart. Nothing more, nothing less.

Lars raced up to Mirevra and tapped her shoulder. She jumped slightly and braced to strike, he only laughed at her reaction.

"Do you still have my water skin?" he asked. Mirevra did not answer. "It is fine; in fact, you should keep it," he said, then pulled himself onto the driver's box and stared down at her. "Let it be a reminder of our date."

"Our *what?!*" Mirevra nearly choked, and Lars laughed harder.

"So tense, Viper. It was a joke," he teased, and something in his eyes, the misty color of the sea in the morning, swirled with delight. "You know you *can* laugh every now and again."

Instead, Mirevra snarled. She caught Bagah eyeing her cautiously. From the look on his face, she knew she was not the only one worried for a friend's heart. The stone thrummed in her boot, and her face twisted. The gem was more of a reminder of her truth than the water skin could ever be. Just because she did not hate the Nelimen as badly as she once had, she did not belong to them. She did not belong to anyone but the Veravant.

Night came and went three times with no troubles. When Mirevra awoke on the fourth day, she allowed a few moments of relief to wash over her before shaking it off. Alive, they all still might be, but anything could change in these woods. The trees did not boast deep green leaves and brown trunks as she was used to. Instead, leaves the light yellow color of lemons feathered the tops of skinny gray trunks. The beaten trails were carved out of dull green grass. Plants growing in circular shapes had spikes poking out from them and some even jumped and stuck against clothing if you passed too closely. Mirevera avoided them and made sure the group made camp in clearings. Upon feeling the morning sun splash against her face, she sat up and saw everyone was awake, save for Bagah and Neeps.

The half-Teruk slumbered with his head resting against the coach, his arms folded over his lap, and his new club leaning against his arm. Neeps was inside the coach, for he was the only one small enough to sleep comfortably within. Likely, the book rested in clenched hands. Lars was roasting something over a small fire, and Mirevra's mouth watered. Heral and Shiln were walking the perimeter of their campgrounds. This was her opportunity. She had felt the damned stone in her boot the second her eyes opened. Saying nothing, she rose and made her way towards the thick of trees. She and Lars exchanged tight nods, and she played her nerves as morning grogginess. Deep in the trees, she removed her boot, pulled out the stone, and tapped it three times.

"We are trekking the perimeter of the Caxaven and Arcaeles woods and headed toward Drodour. This is where we believe the Vaenir is hidden. We should make it there in three days." Mirevra took a breath and silently counted. Only two more messages were available after this one. She thought long and hard about what she wanted to say and looked closely to make sure the two Arcanen women were not nearby. "We lost Roman to an unknown enemy. He is buried well within the woods, beneath the trees as he would have liked..." She paused again, closed her eyes, and silently battled with herself. Should she continue with what she wanted to say? Would the Veravant consider it a sign of weakness?

Mirevra looked through the feathery branches at the sky and imagined the lovely druid somewhere with Bagah's mother. A place unburdened by death, *if* such a place existed. She once more siphoned a deep breath and continued. "Be gentle with Tilly when you tell her this news. She loved her brother." The assassin's breath shuddered. "We all did." Not giving herself time to regret the words, she tapped the stone thrice and pushed it deep into her pocket before stomping back to camp.

On the sixth day, the sun beat down on them with newfound strength. By late afternoon, Mirevra's cheeks were red enough to be considered kissed by Deleon, Goddess of fire. Bagah, whose skin was the fairest of the group, did not burn at all, as the sun had little effect on his thick skin. Bagah raised his face to the cloudless sky and smiled. He loved the day and all it offered. He walked next to the coach that held Shiln, Heral, and Neeps while Beldon and Lars sat on the driver's box. Mirevra noted that the two men had not shut up since the guilds left camp that morning. Mirevra shifted as her mare clomped on the beaten path and frowned. Lars was right. Beldon would make a fine Nelimen. Mirevra knew it was not in Beldon's nature to do wrong to others. But the Ring needed a cleric, and the Veravant paid him handsomely for his abilities.

Beldon had once mentioned his family. Of course, not their names or where they resided, but Mirevra deduced they were the reason he had joined the Fox guild. Probably the only reason. He would not leave a well-paying job for the notoriety of being a hero. Most clerics did not find coins where their power was needed, save the Sun Criers, who seemed to only help *after* being paid. The clerics who served under Raenin worked for free; the white fire was a blessing, and blessings should come at no cost. Beldon might be a good man, but that did not deter him from reality. He—and his family—needed coins to survive. He would do what he must. Still, she heard the excitement in his questions as Lars told stories of Nelimen's heroic feats. She allowed herself a smile as she watched him behave like an enthusiastic child, full of wonder.

That sweet moment soon came to a halt.

Bagah raced forward, threw up a hand, and Lars pulled the reins back hard to stop the coach. Mirevra kicked her heels into the mare's ribs and was soon at Bagah's side. "What in the Murks is that?" Beldon called. About thirty paces ahead of Mirevra and Bagah, a figure clad from head to toe in black leather stood in the middle of the path. Their form was lean and sculpted and displayed well by the leather that wrapped tightly around their body. Onyx studs coiled around a snug helmet. Sharp hooks curled off the figure's elbows, making them appear like an insect or worse.

"It looks like Degolian," Mirevra whispered to herself, but Bagah heard her and grunted in agreement.

"If the Lord of Death and Sorrow ever did walk the lands, he would look exactly like that," he said. They both knew Degolian of the Murks, the Lord of Death and Sorrow, who was not given the title of a god, was said to be clad in black and not appear as fully human. He was master of the Murks, the place of torment. Mirevra had always assumed it was where she would find herself when death finally arrived. Now, she swallowed hard and wondered if Degolian had come to collect. Had she died in her sleep? Was this the end?

"What is it?" Shiln asked as she stepped from the coach. Her hands were already illuminated. "What is *that?*" Mirevra glanced back at the sorceress for a second, then cursed beneath her breath. *A second is the difference between life and death, Mirevra!* Sure enough, when she whipped back around, the figure was gone. She whirled to Bagah.

"Did you see where they went?"

Bagah did not move. He did not blink or even breathe. Mirevra shoved her friend's arm. "Bagah, answer me!" But she got no response. "Beldon, come heal him, quickly!" Then she realized Beldon was also frozen. As were Lars and Shiln. She ran to peer inside the coach. Even Heral had succumbed to the paralysis. This was no mere Binding or Clanging Spell. This was something far worse.

Slowly, Mirevra turned in a slow circle and studied her surroundings. No wind moved through the trees. Indeed, the birds above them hovered in space. Just as she realized what Arcanen magic was at play, she was blasted to her back. Instinctively, she hopped back to her feet and drew a short blade. She knew it would be a rough fight and that the odds were stacked against her, but there was nothing else to do, not against Tempust Scavengers.

The Tempust guild was known for one thing—meddling with time. They could hold life still for short bursts. However, doing so made them weak. Stopping time for one minute would exhaust them for at least an hour. The Tempust had stopped time now, likely long enough to rob the Ring and Nelimen blind. Yet somehow, their Arcanen was not working against Mirevra. She would think about that later; now, all she could do was scan the path and the trees. A shadow moved to her left, and she swung wildly, her blade slicing through the air. Again, to her right, with the same results. This play continued till Mirevra was panting and cursing between clenched teeth. "Fight me, you coward!" Though she shouted, no one answered. Beneath their bandages, her fists ached to be used.

'No, little Fox. Use blades to quell your enemy. They will work much better,' she heard the Veravant opine. But for the first time, Mirevra did not give a damn what the Veravant had said. She flung her weapon to the ground and squeezed her hands into tight fists, the bandages around her knuckles pulling taut. She stilled her breath and tamed her heartbeat. Briefly, she closed her eyes and listened. The thing about Tempust Scavengers was they always failed to account for the crack in their spell. While everything was frozen, everything was also silent. Mirevra listened intently, and when she heard the pad of careful footsteps, she did not waste a second. She swung an elbow back, then twisted to face her opponent. Her elbow slammed into her opponent's hard leather armor, and they staggered a few steps. It was just enough. With her arms extended before her, Mirevra launched herself, wrapped her hands around her enemy's neck, and squeezed as hard as she could.

Her opponent's back hit the earth with a hard thud, and Mirevra could hear their breath gurgle behind the mask. She shoved her thumbs deeper into their throat until she heard them cough. "Good, you sack of shit. I hope it hurts," she muttered. She was pushing all her weight down through her arms when a tickle of air hit her nose. She smiled grimly.

Time was starting up again, albeit slowly, and by the time the others were free, this Scavenger would be long gone. Although she knew her enemy could not answer, Mirevra still demanded answers. "What are you wearing?" Scavengers were not known for their ostentatious attire; most wore ratty clothing, linens, and torn wool, and this one was clad in fine leather, indeed. "How did you know anyone would be in these woods?" A strangled cough and wheezing were her only answers.

"Do you work for the lich?!" Mirvevra's anger spiraled as she demanded answers, yet she refused to let her enemy speak. A haughty misstep. Her opponent pulled up one hand and brought it down swiftly so one of their hook-like adornments scratched Mirevra's side. She hissed; her waning strength was enough for the attacker to break free. Still, Mirevra smiled. Time was encroaching upon them, and she knew her enemy was about to fall wormlike to the floor. Against the might of all seven of her group, this bug did not stand a chance. The Scavenger kicked Mirevra clean off, darted for the tree line, and Mirevra gave chase. The yellow leaves swayed in the wind now, and the birds began to fly.

Mirevra heard Bagah yell. She heard Shiln's distant murmurs, but the Scavenger did not stop, and neither would she. She was practically on their heels as they ducked and dodged tree limbs and boulders. She waited for her opponent to give in to exhaustion. Eventually, they did. When the Scavenger stopped, Mirevra crashed into them, and the force of the collision sent them tumbling down a slope near a ravine. As soon as her body was back in her control, Mirevra straddled the spiked Scavenger again and raised her fist in the air.

"Try and stop this," she said. She practically foamed at the mouth as she landed her fist into the side of their face. A laugh erupted from behind the black fabric. Sickly and cool, this laugh was followed by a female's voice.

"It does not matter if time yields. The lich is moving–time means nothing," the female said. Mirevra nearly fell over. She laid another punch into the covered woman.

"You do work for the lich!"

The woman made a noise that sounded more like pleasure than pain. "I do what I must."

Mirevra wanted to smash the woman's face in. She side-eyed a rock just an arm's length away and almost reached for it. But first, she needed answers.

"What would your guild say?"

Another insidious laugh.

"I belong to no guild. Not anymore," the woman said and then reached up slowly to grab her helmet. Mirevra snatched the rock, ready to bring it down on the strange enemy at any given moment. The woman only pulled the leather far enough to reveal her lips, red and swollen from Mirevra's strikes. They twisted into a contemptuous smile. "I have not belonged to anything in quite some time. I am exiled. I am alone."

Mirevra blinked, the rock wavering in her fist. "A Wolf," she breathed.

"At your service," the woman mocked.

"I should kill you now and put an end to your pathetic life," she said. The lips straightened into a line.

"Perhaps," the Wolf retorted, "But if you must, do so quickly. I would rather face death by that rock than at the hands of the lich." Raising the rock higher, Mirevra used her free hand to grab the Wolf's chin and hold her head steady.

"Why were you in these woods? What did you want from us?" A full smile revealing mostly straight and white teeth appeared.

"You are not the only ones wise enough to ask the Tajeh for answers. They led me to you after much... *persuasion,*" the woman laughed. "I wanted the book. I must find the blade if I wish to preserve my life."

"We seek the same goal, then," Mirevra breathed. "For we, too, want to stop the lich. All of our lives hang in the balance." When the Wolf laughed again, it was stark, brutal, and full of disdain.

"It is not death that I fear, you vacuous girl. Death has been my only companion since the day I was exiled." The woman swallowed, her smile vanished. "Once marked a Wolf, your name is a scourge upon the earth. I could not find a guild to accept me. I could not find a business to offer me work. *Murks,* even dingy little inns knew my face and turned me away. I became nothing."

Mirevra snorted. "I know what becoming a Wolf entails," she said with no sympathy in her voice. "A dismal punishment for being a traitor to one's guild."

The Wolf's head moved in Mirevra's hold. "Kill me now, or I will be back to seek the blade."

Mirevra clutched the rock tighter. "It does not matter who finds the blade! So long as it is not the lich or those who would do his bidding!"

"You poor thing," said Wolf. "Such beautiful eyes, and yet they do not see."

A muscle in Mirevra's jaw feathered across the surface of her skin. "Spare me your riddles, and I will consider sparing your life," she snapped. The Wolf's gorgeous lips spread into a broad smile.

"A wish, vacuous girl," she spluttered, fatigue bleeding through her words.

"A wish?" Mirevra asked. "If a wish is what you seek, you waste your time looking for the blade. You would have better luck praying to Rashawe."

"When a god ignores the cries of his people for too long enough, they will take their fate into their own hands," the Wolf ranted. Mirevra scoffed at the very thought of it. *Fate.* "The Vaenir offers more than glory. I am not the only one. You are leading them straight to the blade–"

"Leading who to the blade?" Mirevra bit out each word, squeezing the Wolf's chin so hard that her nails dug into bronze skin. Then, she felt the body beneath her wobble. The woman cackled as a bright purple light illuminated her entire form.

"I am not the only one," the Wolf repeated. "They are exiled. They are alone." Her leather-bound body burned brighter and brighter until despite what Mirevra believed was possible, it disappeared before her eyes.

Mirevra was left straddling nothing but dirt and rocks. Her heart thundered.

It was a dizzying walk back to the coach, where she found the others unparalyzed and in quite the frenzy. They did not spare a moment for Mirevra to gather her thoughts, instantly bombarding her with question after question. Only Bagah stood apart, not weighing her down with inquiries she did not know how to answer.

"It was a Wolf," Mirevra said when she at last had a chance to speak. "I do not know her name, for their name no longer exists." She relayed what the Wolf had said before her body vanished. Shiln shook her head.

"That makes no sense. And neither does the Tempust Arcanen not affecting you. Are you immune to a Warlock's power?"

"It could make sense," Neeps interjected. "The Veravant is a Warlock himself. Perhaps he taught her how to combat it."

"If I had had enough time, I could have countered the spell," Shiln said, stepping on the halfling's sentence. "It just happened too quickly. Heral, was it you? Did you help Mirevra?"

"I was busy with other things," Heral answered quickly. "I did not see the Scavenger at all. By the time I came to, Mirevra was sprinting into the trees." Shiln scratched her head and looked next to Beldon.

"Did... Did *you* counter the spell?" Shiln's voice rose in disbelief. Beldon waved his hands.

"It was not me."

Lars looked at Mirevra intently. "Do you have Arcanen?" Even as he demanded an answer, his damned eyes made her bones squirm.

"Of course, she does not," a voice called from the trees. "Arcanen magic requires patience, and Mirevra has none of that to spare."

Mirevra whirled, a wild look in her golden eyes. A smile begged to be released, but she would not allow it to form until she confirmed that she was not hearing things. Tilly emerged from the trees. Her willowy body was hidden beneath an oversized brown tunic, and her loose trousers were tucked into untied boots. It was not an illusion. Mirevra's smile overpowered her face. Her friend had come to her rescue.

The sorceress had returned.

The Mountains of Drodour

~~~~

For a solid five minutes, Tilly and Mirevra were inseparable. The Fox sorceress all but ignored the others as she explained how she had countered the Wolf's Tempust spell from the trees. "The Veravant came back to the den and told me that you all were hopelessly lost without me," Tilly said, her large hazel eyes flaring. "I told him that much was obvious," she taunted her friend. "He sent me immediately and said that all of you needed the extra help." Tilly finally looked over Mirevra's shoulder to study the group, and the assassin's heart dropped. She placed a hand on Tilly's arm.

"I am sorry you could not see him," she consoled. "He will be missed beyond measure." Tilly blinked. Her plain face, so much like her brothers, was blank.

"Who will be missed beyond measure?" she asked, and her eyes met Mirevra's again.

Mirevra drew back her chin. "Did the Veravant not... did he not tell you what happened?"

She studied her friend's face, but Tilly's expression was perfectly stoic. Never one to show too much emotion, she now seemed devoid of it.

"Where is my brother?" Tilly asked in an even voice.

"Tilly," Mirevra began in a soothing tone. But the sorceress broke free of Mirevra's gentle hold and marched towards the coach to question the others. None of the Nelimen answered. They stood quietly and watched as Tilly rounded on her fellow Foxes.

"Where is Roman?" Bagah only looked at Mirevra while Beldon's face grew heavy. He lifted his hands.

"Tills," Beldon said, extending his hand.

"Roman! Roman? Where are you?" Tilly called out as she circled the coach. "ROMAN?!" she shouted into the trees. At that, Shiln stepped forward.

"I understand you are in pain, but please remember we do not know if we are alone in these woods! We must stay quiet–" Shiln urged, but Tilly would have none of it.

"Roman!" Tilly cried out again and again, her alabaster skin now crested with worried sweat. Mirevra saw the dreadful reality piecing together within her friend's mind and watched as Tilly's gaunt expression stubbornly refused it anyway. After more frantic calls, Tilly stomped toward Shiln. "Which one of you did it, then?" Her hands were lit with the Arcanen hue. "Which one of you killed him?!"

Mirevra dashed over, holding out a hand.

"It was not them, Tilly. It was not any of us."

The Fox sorceress shook her head, her hands glowing brighter. "No! It was one of them. I can feel it."

"No, Tilly—"

"*I can feel my brother, Mirevra!* His blood is on one of their hands!" Tilly's eyes were glassed over, and her nose grew red. "How could you let this happen?"

"Wh–what do you mean–" Mirevra stuttered as she felt her entire being submerged in cold.

"He left you in charge, Mirevra! The Veravant sent my brother on a mission with you at the helm. And now he is dead?"

The fighter rubbed her sore knuckles; there was nothing she could say.

"Surely you are not blaming her for the death of your brother?" Lars' voice cut into the silence, and Mirevra watched as the Nelimen approached Tilly with his arms folded. Tilly's eye twitched as she faced Lars. "Mirevra was deeply upset—more than anyone—by Roman's loss," he said. Mirevra tried to ignore the embarrassment that threatened to drown her. Not only had she wept tears for the dead, but others had seen her. Lars had seen her cry.

"Who the fuck are you?" Tilly's voice was venomous. Her hands gleamed brighter with every step Lars took. Heral appeared from around the coach. Her eyes emitted a tiny flare as they pinned the Fox sorceress.

"No one special," Lars said plainly. "But I too have lost someone I deeply cared for. I know the pain you–"

"I do not care to hear your sob story, Nelimen!" Tilly shouted. "My brother was better than anyone you lost. He did not deserve death. He was always meant to bend it!"

"Aye," Lars spoke calmly, approaching her with steps lighter than a cat's. "You are right, he did not deserve the death that came to him.

But it came anyway," Lars said and looked almost sick. "It took our friend, too." Shiln lowered her head, muttering a silent prayer for their fallen ranger.

"H–ho–how did it happen? How did he die?" Tilly asked, her voice finally breaking. Mirevra noticed her friend's hands were shaking. Lars was close now, only two steps away.

"We don't know," he admitted and paused midstep. "We have hidden enemies; you just protected Mirevra from one of them. We search for something of great value, and it seems the word is spreading." Tilly still shook. Lars reached out his hand gingerly, not yet placing it on her shoulder, and said, "Your brother died serving the Ring. He died serving Estellian. Do not let it be in vain. Help us locate the blade and finish what Roman could not. Help him save us all."

His hand landed on her skin, but Tilly did not pull away. Instead, she dropped to her knees and released a guttural cry into her palms. No one rushed her. No one said a word. She cried painful, gut-wrenching sobs for more than an hour. Afterward, she disappeared into the trees to mourn in silence. No one followed her.

Night fell and blanketed the sky. Mirevra lay on her back with her arms behind her head, staring up at the moon and stars. The cool, pale light of the white orb splashed over the tree canopy and the stars twinkled like diamonds on a delicate necklace. Yes, the night was a woman indeed. Mysterious and beautiful. Mirevra was not spooked when Tilly finally joined her side, laying a weary head on the assassin's chest.

"Why would he send me here without telling me?" Tilly croaked. Her voice was soft, but her words landed like a boulder rolling from a cliff. Mirevra stroked her friend's dry, hay-like hair.

"I do not know," she answered in earnest, still gazing at the stars. It was not right of the Veravant to send Tilly to aid them without caring how or when she would learn of her brother's death. He could have told her, if not out of kindness, then at least out of loyalty.

"Do you truly not know what killed him?" Tilly asked softly, stealing the fighter's attention away from her treacherous thoughts.

Mirevra inhaled a deep breath of the warm summer night air.

"I do not," she admitted. "Bagah and Lars were in the woods. They both swore they could not see what attacked. A wisp of wind, a ghost, perhaps. It could have been anything." She thought of how hours earlier the Wolf had disappeared, her physical body evaporating into the incorporeal world. "We do not know the stretch of the lich's power," she added. "If it was even of him. Who can say?"

Tilly shifted, placing her hand beneath her cheek on Mirevra's rib cage. "I do not trust them," she said quietly. The stars twinkled and gleamed like Heral's eyes.

"Who?"

"Any of them," Tilly stated firmly and shuffled to find comfort. Another deep breath, and Mirevra nodded.

"That is to be expected," she murmured, a wayward part of herself thrashing within. She did not want to trust the Nelimen either, and yet something deep within her did anyway. She waited for the itch to return so that she might cut that soft and foolish part from her chest and be done with it forever, but it did not appear. She heard Tilly whimper and placed an arm around her small friend.

"I drank some Faerabidia," she announced, knowing this would cheer Tilly up.

At once, the sorceress lifted her neck and craned to meet Mirevra's eyes.

"You did not," she laughed.

Mirevra clicked her tongue. "Not willingly, of course. *Tricked* would be the better word. Worst experience ever."

Tilly giggled a hefty amount before resuming her position on Mirevra's ribs. "Well? Did Audrina visit you?" Tilly asked and Mirevra only grunted. "Come now, tell me! Did she reveal anything? They say that is how it works."

The stars winked, the moon glowed dimly. The memory of the bridge resurfaced–Mirevra remembered the night she crawled out of the water and onto dry land. She had been so young; she did not know where she was. She did not know which direction was east. She had clung to that word *forever* like it might save her or at least tell her which way to go. It had not. No one had. She had spent her first night alone, crying beneath a willow tree while the same moon looked down on her with pity.

"She told me to beware of the Wolf," Mirevra said, forgoing the traumas of her youth. "She said it was closer than I knew."

Tilly nodded without raising her head. "It seems she was right. What was with that armor, anyway? Did you see the spikes on her arms? Strange, that was."

Mirevra knew that Tilly spoke of the Tempust Wolf, but her heart felt heavy. *I am not the only one.*

The assassin could make no sense of it. Was there another Wolf after them? A thick lump formed in her throat. The night sky, a beautiful woman, seemed to whisper and hum above her. She thought of Lars on that hill. She had wanted to kiss him. She had longed to entangle her body with his and let him take her then and there on that grassy knoll. She thought of Shiln on their last day in Estunder and the way they had smiled at each other as if they were almost friends. She thought of how she trusted Neeps with the book the Tajeh gave to her, how Heral had saved her life and given Bagah a gift, even if it was one Mirevra did not like.

Last, she thought of the Veravant and his brown eyes raking over her naked form. *'You are mine, little Fox. Forever.'* She was betraying everything she knew. Hearing Tilly snore, Mirevra smoothed back her hair and considered the warning. An alarm bell clanged in her spirit. It would drive the assassin mad all night and she would not be able to sleep.

She didn't hate the Nelimen. She was angry at the Veravant. Mirevra did not know who she was anymore.

Maybe... she thought with a cold chill spreading over her limbs; *maybe she was the Wolf.*

Two long days dragged by as the party traipsed through Droudor. The guilds thought they would have reached the mountains by now, but they loomed far off in the distance like the jutting ribs of a giant carcass the gods could use to pick their teeth. Reaching them meant traversing territory that was not an easy one to trek. The ground was uneven, with undulating jagged rocks and hills reaching as far as the eye could see. Eventually, they had to abandon the coach, for there was no path for the gig. They traveled light. Each member of the team had only one flask filled with water and a few rations. Neeps was most displeased about leaving the coach behind as his short legs struggled to keep up with the group's pace. Finally, Bagah lifted him onto his mighty Teruk shoulders, even as the halfling tried to resist, and they made their way further into the unclaimed territory.

Drodour was a conundrum. Half of it appeared to be a hellish, rocky landscape, but beyond was a gorgeous tundra punctuated by valleys and pools of spring water. Although she was tired, Mirevra could not help but be awed by the landscape. Drodour was the only place in all of Estellian where Mirevra's travels had never taken her. Stories claimed there was nothing in Drodour but death and hollow cries. Kallias had all but destroyed this province, leaving nothing but dust behind in his wake.

She wanted to ask Bagah if the rumors she had heard spread in small hamlets and towns she frequented were true. In the last dregs of night, she had heard townsfolk whisper about Drodour. Claiming it was actually home to legends and demons. Mirevra wanted to ask, but she would not. She had clocked Bagah's expression more than once since they crossed into Drodour. From his face, she could tell this place was nothing more than a bad memory, and the mountains in the distance only served as tombstones for his fallen family.

Bagah had returned to their gravesite. Mirevra spent much of the trek wondering what it would be like for her to stand again on that viaduct above the Murky Lakes. What would she feel? How would she act? Though she had been in Sardek a few times on missions, she had not stepped foot in the city of Rale since that tragic day. She had not seen the black castle or the dark ivy growing over its six spires in over a decade. The black and gold banners that snapped in the wind were merely a fading dream at this point. After long thought, she decided if she ever saw the bridge again, she would destroy it.

A Fallen Sword

Afternoon was the worst time, specifically when the sun reached its peak. The heat spared no one–the air was thick and languorous. Mirevra's tongue felt too dry and cried for moisture, but they all rationed their water carefully. Bagah had warned the only freshwater sources were in the fresh springs of the valley, so they each took a tiny sip per hour and let the tepid water sit on their tongue. Mirevra pitied the horses. She could see their steps growing shorter and slower and heard their breaths more labored. She dismounted and refused to ride her mare any longer. Bagah, with Neeps on his shoulder, led the charge, swinging his club freely to his side. Heral followed them, then Shiln, Lars, and Beldon leaving Mirevra and Tilly in the back.

Eventually, two horses showed signs of colic and fell to their knees. Mirevra would not watch them die but the group refused to let Shiln or Beldon try and intervene. They could not waste their Arcanen on an animal, no matter how much they all might like to. Tilly used a simple cantrip to offer the horses some grain of peace–that they would feel no pain as they closed their eyes for a final time. They left the horses on the rocks, their unmoving bodies a reminder of what they would soon face if they did not find the Vaenir. Night fell once more, and the lot drew straws to see who would take the first watch. Mirevra and Neeps were the unfortunate winners.

The first two hours were silent. Neeps stayed at his post and tinkered with the vials Beldon and Lars had given him in Estunder. Mirevra sat at her post and did absolutely nothing. Eventually, she called out to the halfling. "Thank you."

"I am sorry?" She heard the disbelief in Neeps' voice.

"For reading the book. It would have taken me ages. Bagah even longer; Beldon would not have had the attention span for it. So, thank you," she said. The halfling snorted.

"My pleasure," he lazily offered in return.

"What are you working on now?" She almost smiled at Neeps' expression and how he looked utterly bewildered by her interest. He glanced down at his glass jars and then back to her.

"Um," he started. "I am just fiddling with a few ingredients. Why do you ask?"

Mirevra rose and plopped down next to him. Neeps jumped, which caused Mirevra to laugh loudly. Tilly shifted in her sleep, and Mirevra lowered her voice. "You need not worry. I won't bite."

Neeps scoffed. "I am not worried, especially not of your bite, Fox," he said brashly, then lifted a greenish elixir. "Not when I have this on me, anyway."

Her golden eyes locked in on the liquid that shimmered even in the dark.

"What is it?"

Neeps sent her an incredulous glare but soon realized her interest was genuine. He rolled back his shoulders. "Do you truly want to know?" he asked, and Mirevra nodded like an eager child.

"Acid," Neeps whispered with a grin and clinked his fingernail against the glass.

"Acid," Mirevra repeated.

With a nod, Neeps swirled the bottle. "*Potent* acid. Pour this on someone, and they will burn alive. No amount of Raenin's white fire could save them from its agony," he explained. Mirevra gulped at how roughly Neeps handled the tinctures. He did nothing to assuage her anxiety as he pulled the next one from his bag. A deep red concoction, thick like blood. "Crimson Fury," he proclaimed proudly. "Pour a little of this on the ground and watch as all Murks breaks loose."

"What does that mean? All Murks break loose?! Is it a portal to the afterlife?" Neeps stared at her pedantically before shaking his head.

"No, that is not what that means. I was saying that as an expression. You do understand what an expression is, do you not?"

"I am teasing, halfling," Mirevra smirked. Neeps was not amused. "Go on, tell me what it does then."

Carefully, Neeps placed the vial back into the sack and pulled another out. "I guess you will just have to wait and see," he said. Mirevra grunted with dissatisfaction. Patience was not her virtue. "You already know this one. Heartbeats, remember?" The halfling laughed, but Mirevra did not. She scowled as she remembered how the poison coursed through her veins. Ignoring her distaste, Neeps plucked another out. "Though, now that you mention it, I *do* have something or another," Neeps got lost in his own thoughts as he held the last vial out on his flattened palm. Another green liquid, but not the sludge color of the acid. This potion was a wild viridian, deep and hypnotizing. "This is what I like to call the Relirantur. It is my most prized tonic."

"Will I have to wait and see what it does, or are you going to tell me?"

Neeps tapped a finger against his chin. "Let us just say, if you need to leave a place in a hurry, *this* will come in handy."

"It will transport you? How?" Neeps scrunched his nose at Mirevra's question; her eyes were transfixed on the deep green liquid.

"Drink it, and you go somewhere else."

"Do you choose where to go?" She nearly ripped the bottle from his hands. He pulled it to his chest and shook his head.

"That all depends on who administers it," Neeps beamed proudly. "If you take a swig yourself, it will portal you to wherever you are thinking. Oh, there might be a few hiccups and bumps along the way, but you will arrive in one piece. If someone else administers it? Well, let us hope that they are thinking of somewhere pleasant."

"Indeed," she hummed, then nodded her head. "Wonderful how you make these things. It is practically Arcanen what you do," Mirevra said and saw the glint of pride on Neeps' face. She sighed. "I wish there was someone with your skill within the Ring. I cannot tell you the number of times I could have used the... Reli–the Rally?"

"The Relirantur," Neeps corrected, stuffing it back in his pack.

"The Relirantur," she repeated. "Thank you for showing me these things." The corners of Neep's mouth pulled down as he nodded.

"Thanks for being interested," he answered. Mirevra returned to her assigned post and kept watch in silence. Finally, she woke Bagah and Lars for their watch and curled herself next to Tilly's sleeping form. She closed her eyes and, in her dreams, saw a dark mass twisting before her. The castle in Rale loomed in the background, taunting... beckoning. Gold eyes and fire.

Bagah yelled her name from somewhere in the distance.

And then he was yelling it closer.

Closer.

Closer.

Her body was shaking. Her eyes peeled open.

Bagah *was* yelling her name, shaking her awake.

At once, she was on her feet. The swells of early morning light lined the sky, and she saw the threat before them. "What the fuck," she breathed, only half awake. She no longer had to ask Bagah if the rumors of Drodour were true as she gazed at the nasty mob of creatures making its way toward them. None of them were taller than Neeps, the skin a strange waxy yellow, and their extended forearms ended in large, clawed hands. They stalked forward on all fours, snarling and swiping their hideous claws; some tore into one of the horses. The animal's screams and the gore were unbearable. Mirevra heard a whistle and looked up to see Tilly standing on a high hill, her palms ablaze. She swirled her hands in a violet fury and gritted her teeth. Her hazel eyes grew shades darker, the unkempt brows above them knitted in keen concentration. Tilly threw her palms forward, and a shock wave of power blasted several of the beasts back.

They yelped in pain, one falling limp to the ground, but the rest only grew more agitated. Tilly began working her hands again to cast another spell while Shiln released a deep fog from her palms, and in tandem, Neeps threw a vial. The poison fog and potent elixir exploded, everything in its radius was absolute carnage. Four of the wretched creatures fell howling in pain. Bagah sprinted toward the others, his club swinging high above his head. Mirevra tightened the bandages around her knuckles and ran after him. Her dagger whined as she unsheathed it, and she kicked her legs as fast as she could to try and catch up to her friend.

Bagah swung his club in a circle and brought it up beneath one of the beast's chins, then deftly brought it back above his head to crush down on another's head. Two of the creatures ran toward Mirevra, and with one leg extended, she slid forward on the gravel as the creatures dashed right past her. They released horrific, barbaric yips and yaps as they turned back toward her. But she was on her feet again, and as one ran to her, she jumped, bringing down a fist loaded with all her rage. Flesh met bone, the beast wailed, and she drove her dagger deep into its chest.

She did not tarry but pulled out her dagger, tossed it in the air, and caught it in her other hand. She faced the next beast, sliced clean through its throat, and kicked it away. Bagah had demolished several more, and the evidence lay lifeless at his feet. Somehow, Lars was there too, a sneaky bastard, slicing his own path through the horde. Mirevra felt claws dig into her arms, her legs, and her neck as the creatures swarmed, but she did not stop swinging, or her dagger relent. They had almost claimed victory when she heard Lars curse loudly from ahead. She scrambled up a hill to see what he stared down.

Another one of the cursed beasts. Only this one, the colossal mother, was at least five times the size of the others and glared up at Lars with a bloodthirsty sheen in her abhorrent eyes. Lars glanced at Mirevra and Bagah with a rough smile and widened eyes that pleaded for aid. He could not face it alone, not with all the cuts he now boasted under his torn tunic. The two Foxes immediately ran down the hill, Mirevra's bandages soaked in crimson, Bagah's club wet with flesh. The beast swiped its gigantic talons at Lars, who masterfully dodged and parried with his own blades. He clipped the monster's hide, but it was not enough. The creature exposed its fangs and squealed, angrier than hurt.

A firebolt blasted into its snout before it could wreak its revenge on the rogue. Mirevra whipped her head around to see Heral standing behind them, a weary look in her eyes. Heral did not even look at the creature she fought; instead, she gazed worriedly at the sky. The sun was rising, and she seemed to be counting down the seconds for it to peek above the horizon. Bagah swung next, then Mirevra. They connected with the creature's flesh, but their blows did not seem to make much of a difference. From the corner of her eye, Mirevra saw Shiln and Tilly trying to conjure enough Arcanen for their next spells. Beldon stood a good distance away with his glowing, white palms ready to mend at the first call for help.

"Lars!" Neeps called from the top of the hill. The rogue twisted, and a sack came flying through the air. Mirevra regained her breath as Lars caught it, *barely,* and pulled out a vial. Crimson Fury.

"Back up!" Lars shouted at Bagah and then, "Get out of here!" to Mirevra. He threw the vial against the rocks.

It burst, spraying the stone with red. Mirevra wanted to take Neeps up on his offer and *wait and see.* She did not have to wait long. Soon, she was mesmerized as burgundy vines emerged from the stone and began rapidly twisting, coiling, and hissing. Quickly, violently, they struck like snakes and grabbed onto whatever they could find. One vine sprang toward Mirevra, but Lars caught her up by the waist and pulled her back before it could snatch her up.

"It will kill you," Lars breathed roughly into her ear. "Fury vines suck the life out of whatever they touch." Mirevra pushed against his arm, but he did not release her. Instead, he carried her back up the hill, where she watched in horror and excitement as the vines broke out everywhere the elixir touched. The monster clawed at some of them, but the sentient plants wound their way around its forearm. Another arm of the plant wreathed the creature's leg. Eventually, the giant beast became so wrapped and tangled within the Fury's hold it could not move. Life drained from its body, leaving nothing but a deflated, shriveled husk in its wake. The ravaging plants continued to seek other life to grab hold of. Finding nothing else to siphon, they released high-pitched whines and fell back against the rock, dead.

Lars finally dropped her when they reached the other side of the hill. She stood next to several piles of dead creatures, back-to-back with Lars, ready to fight more. Beldon hurried over and placed his hands on both their bodies. Soon, their gashes, scrapes, and resulting pain vanished. Tilly and Shiln's hands were both alight.

"Do you see anymore?" Mirevra heard Shiln call.

"No," the sorceress answered breathlessly. "Whatever they were, it seems we killed them all."

"Dragels," Bagah coughed in response, shooing Beldon away when the cleric tried to heal his cuts. "Demon-like creatures that protect the mountains."

"Protect the mountains from what?" Neeps asked, letting out a heavy sigh of relief when Lars returned his pouch. Bagah turned his nose towards the craggy peaks far in the distance.

"After Kallias uprooted this land, the dragels emerged. Created, bred, conjured? I cannot say. My mother told me about them."

"They would have been nice to know of *before* we journeyed here," Neeps chided, shuffling his bag around until it rested snuggly against his hip. "Care to fill us in on anything else your mother told you about this place? You know, before we go any further?"

"There are things within the mountains that do not wish to be disturbed," Bagah grumbled almost under his breath.

Neeps threw his hands up, his eyes wide. "Oh, *beautiful!*" he yelped. Heral stared at Bagah, and Mirevra realized it was not apprehension that marked her features but instead, *intrigue,* as if the prospect of another threat from the mountains beckoned to her.

"What about you, halfling?" Tilly asked forcefully. "I saw what your elixirs do, and yet you store them recklessly in your bag! Perhaps you are a greater danger than the dragles!" Neeps immediately countered, and everyone began to quarrel. Mirevra stayed silent, her eyes trained on Heral. The woman had lifted her face to bask in the now-risen sun, and her hands clenched and unclenched as the light beamed across her skin. Lars appeared at Mirevra's side, and despite the sweat, dirt, and fatigue on his brow, the damned rogue smiled.

"Well, that was fun. Say, do you still have my water flask? Unless you are too attached to it now? From all the sentimental memories," he said.

Mirevra rolled her eyes, retrieved the flask, and shoved it into his chest. "Here," she said harshly. Though it was true, she did not know why she had held on to it when she carried her own pouch on her belt.

Lars chuckled, that dark, silken noise she hated more than she enjoyed.

"I saved your life, Viper. *Again*. You are welcome." He sipped from the flask. Mirevra eyed him up and down. *True,* but he had also picked her up, again, without her consent.

"Thank you," she said, then landed a punch in his arm. He nearly spit out the small sip of water.

"What in the Murks was that for?" He was coughing, but the corners of his mouth curled upwards. Mirevra shrugged.

"Sentimental memories."

The group was rattled; they were tired and thirsty and too worried to sleep. Mirevra patted her mare's neck–the only horse left– knowing her mount would likely not make it much further. Sadness weighed on her heart and pulled on her ribs. She saw too much of herself in this horse, marching forward on a mission with no idea of the destination or outcome. They had nimbly escaped death, but Mirevra had a sinking feeling that fighting off the strange, clawed creatures was only the beginning. Death lay in the distance and watched them from above the mountains. She felt its cold stare on her skin.

"How much longer until we reach a water source?" Shiln asked. Her stride was less determined than usual. The heat had slowed her.

"Close," Bagah assured her. "We will be in the valley soon." Again, the half-breed led the way, his club replacing Neeps on his shoulders. A significant incline rose before them. The mountains were indeed close, and Mirevra was thankful.

"You know much about this place for never having been here," Heral called out. Bagah looked over his shoulder at her. "Your mother must have told you many stories," she continued. Bagah remained silent and only nodded before turning back. But Mirevra caught a flicker in his eyes–Bagah was hiding something.

"I just want to know how long *soon* is," Shiln interrupted. "I feel like I am choking on gravel."

"Can one of you magic folk at least conjure up some water? What good is having all these Arcanen wielders if all die from dehydration?" Lars complained.

"What good is having a rogue who does not know how to be quiet?" Tilly bit back, wiping her clammy brow. "Do Nelimen know how to do anything but whine?"

"Do Foxes know anything other than to insult?" Shiln offered hastily in response, a smile playing at the edge of her lips. Tilly snorted.

"Afraid not. That much is in our blood."

Mirevra grinned at Tilly's answer, and Lars turned to face her, wearing a half-smirk of his own.

"That is very true," he agreed.

Bagah held up a hand, gesturing to the group to stop. They did so immediately. Was it a threat? Another horde of dragels? When she joined Bagah at the crest of the incline, Mirevra thought she might cry.

They all stood shoulder to shoulder and breathed in relief. A valley waited below. Pools of fresh springs scattered across the dale, which was strewn with colorful larkspurs and tall, damp grass. At the edge of the vale, the base of the mountains jutted high into the heavens. It would be a staggering feat to climb those, Mirevra knew, but that was a problem for later.

They had made it to water. They had made it to the mountains of Drodour.

The Divide

~~~~~

Gods, water was so fucking good, Mirevra thought. She splashed it over her face, removed her tunic, and plunged in. The cool moisture soaked into her skin, immediately diminishing the sun's heat. Thank Rashawe. Thank Vaste and whoever else could be responsible. She vowed to never take the privilege of wetting her mouth for granted again. Both guilds drank their fill, soaked their bodies, and filled their water skins. Her mare lapped more water than she had ever seen a horse ingest before, and Mirevra was glad for it. "Murks, we might actually do this," Lars whispered to himself. The broad male was drenched, and his torn, black tunic clung to his body in ways that made Mirevra irrationally suffused with lust. His dark hair was soaked and stuck to his brow, the nape of his neck, the stubble on his jaw. Heat flushed through her body when his gaze caught hers. She lanced away, but alas, it was too late.

"Careful, Viper," he teased. "I can feel your stare burning right through my shirt."

Mirevra scoffed.

"Good," she said quickly in response. "I would be doing you a favor, then."

"Indeed," Shiln agreed, and the women huffed a laugh together. The ground rumbled, and amusement ceased. "Oh, gods. What now?" Shiln asked, her sharp eyes wide with panic. Neeps clutched his satchel to his chest as the ground shook again. The horse flung its head, puffing rough breaths, and stepped back from the springs. The earth trembled harder.

"Bagah," Heral said calmly, her face not betraying fear. "Did your mother tell you anything of this, by chance?" Bagah rose from his haunches, water dripping down his lips. His brows furrowed.

"The Tremors," he announced as if the others would know what he meant. "I have felt them. Only once. We must go."

"Go where?!" Tilly cried out, steadying herself as the ground quivered once more. "Is there a place this shaking cannot reach?"

Bagah shook his head. "It is not the shaking that should worry us," he said. Mirevra took cautious steps to stand by Bagah. She rested a hand on his shoulder and narrowed her stare.

"Tell us," she urged. "What are these Tremors?"

"I did not think this would happen with all of us present," he answered. "Such is unusual."

"Godsdamn it, Teruk! Is the ground about to split in two or not?" Neeps squealed. His tiny body juddered roughly; the sound of clinking glass came from the sack clutched in his arms.

"No, the ground will not cleave. This is not an earthquake. It is a means to divide us. It is Arcanen–"

Heral's eyes flared.

"What does that mean, Bagah?" she asked.

"It means they know I am here," he answered with a wistful gaze towards the mountains.

Mirevra fell forward and collided with the earth in one swift, harsh thud. She cursed, pushed herself up slowly, and rubbed her throbbing chin.

"What the–" she started, but her words were stolen away. The ground had stopped wobbling. Everything was calm. But Bagah... where was Bagah?

She turned to face the others, her eyes filled with terror. "What is this?!" she demanded. Lars and Tilly stood before her, their expressions just as disoriented. "Where are the others?" Mirevra shouted. Bagah had vanished. Shiln, Beldon, Heral, and Neeps were gone with him. Even her mare was nowhere to be seen. *Where had they gone? Were they dead?* Lars scanned their surroundings and smoothed back his wet hair with both hands.

"I have no fucking idea," he said. He called loudly for Heral, then Shiln. There was no answer.

"Tilly?" Mirevra's voice shook as she looked at the sorceress. "Was this a spell?" Tilly's brows drew together.

"I do not know of one that can rip souls from where they stand," she admitted. Mirevra remembered the Wolf in the woods. How her form had disappeared from beneath her hold. "And one that would cause the earth to quake? It is unheard of," Tilly continued. "This is a power I do not understand. It is some kind of separation Arcanen–"

"Why would someone want to separate us?" Mirevra asked desperately. Lars continued to call out for the others but to no avail. Tilly only shrugged.

"I do not know, Mir." Then, a scarlet flush crept up her face. "Whoever, *or whatever,* did this must think we are easier to defeat if divided."

Hours and hours passed, the sky darkened, and the stars appeared. Still no sign of the others. Mirevra's heart wrenched with involuntary thoughts. She had placed her hand on Bagah; she had felt him beneath her skin...and then he was gone. Maybe *forever.* She shuddered at the word, the confusion of it all. The three decided, glumly, to trek towards the base of the mountain and begin their climb. What else could they do? The group was gone and none of those remaining knew this land by any measure. The mystery of Bagah and the group's disappearance would have to wait. Mirevra knew she would have to store her worries and woes somewhere deep in the back of her mind, where the memories from the viaduct and the look in her father's eyes had been sequestered for years. The Vaenir was still out there somewhere, and it was still their mission to retrieve it.

They had quite the distance to go before the incline steepened, so they simply hiked towards the tallest of the mountains in silence with Tilly's glowing palms dimly lighting the trail. Lars took up the rear. Mirevra cursed the uneven ground, and worried that more creatures might be hunting them. But she tried to calm her mind by being thankful for what she could be. Tilly was a fierce sorceress. They had enough water to last for a few days. And Lars was...here. Actually, Mirevra was unsure if this was something to be grateful for. Though, he *had* saved her life twice now. She gulped down a heavy lump in her throat and prayed there would not be a third time. Her own leather pouch of water sloshed against her thigh. But she did not dare drink when thirst beckoned. The night was cool, thank the gods, and she needed to save the water for the heat of the day. Tilly curved around a large deposit of fallen rock, and Mirevra moved to follow, but Lars grabbed her hand. She almost drove her fist into his cheek, but he was quick. He pushed her against the base of the rock and held a hand over her mouth, then pushed a finger to his lips.

'Be quiet,' he mouthed. Despite herself, Mirevra listened. Her golden eyes glittered in the dark. Lars gestured for her to stay put and crept around the rock. His feet fell silent on the earth like the pads of a cat's paw. With steps as predatory as a feline ready to pounce on an unknowing mouse, Lars adroitly made his way around the rock pile. Mirevra kept still until she heard Tilly scream. Then, with one fist raised and her dagger drawn in her other hand, she rounded the bend faster than she had ever moved. She could barely see, but after a few blinks, her eyes became mildly accustomed to the dark, and she made out three silhouettes. Without stopping to differentiate between them, she lurched at the tallest one and wrapped her arms tightly around their neck.

"Struggle, and I will squeeze harder," she whispered in their ear.

"V–Vipe–". She loosened enough to give him one breath.

"Lars?" she whispered. He tapped her arm twice, and she felt him try to nod. She released, and he doubled over with a strong cough, then pointed ahead. Tilly's palms were building light now, offering Mirevra enough illumination to see the threat. The black leather, the hooked arms. *The Wolf.* Mirevra's jaw tightened, and her muscles flexed with rage. She thrust forward, but Lars pulled her back and flung himself forward. "Damn you, Lars!"

"One of us has to make it to the summit!" He did not look back as he shouted. His blade was free of its sheath in an instant. He flourished it artfully before swinging it down in an attempt to cut the Wolf's leg. The Wolf blocked Lar's blade with her elbow hook and planted a hard punch into Tilly's face. Mirevra growled, a purely feral sound, and was ready to lunge, but Tilly met her eyes even as she wiped the blood from her lips.

"Go to the blade, Mirevra," Tilly yelled. "Go, now!" An order. A promise.

Lars swung again, finding purchase against the Wolf's ribs, and Tilly's hands were bright enough to cast a spell. As primal as Mirevra's need to fight was, she knew it was not time to argue. Lars and Tilly were right; the Wolf also sought the Vaenir. This is the price of it all, she reminded herself. This was the mission. As she saw Tilly raise her hand to blast a spell, Mirevra gritted her teeth a final time and spun on her heel. She had no idea where the sword was, but she danced through debris and rock, skidded through gravel and dirt, and found a place to plant her boot on the mountain. No more trekking, she thought. The climb begins.

Mirevra ascended through the night. She did not fall; she did not falter. By the time she reached a small ledge sticking out from the mountain's side, her arms felt like jelly, and her legs ached. Pain smarted through her spine. She lay on the ledge and heaved deep breaths.

Tilly was gone.

Lars was gone.

Bagah was gone.

She was now utterly alone.

"Where are we?" Heral called out and rubbed her brow. She patted down her person, making sure she was still in complete form. She looked around for the others, who were nowhere to be found, and then for Bagah, who was staring out at the foaming shore. She took one look at the coastline and drew a deep breath. "Oh," she said quietly and flanked Bagah's side. "It is the Ripper Sea." Bagah nodded in silence, and after a good while of the quiet consuming them both, he turned his chin slightly in her direction.

"How can you tell?" he asked. Heral gazed at the line far in the distance where night met the dark ocean waters.

"I sailed it. Three years ago," she said, pointing at the vast horizon. "From the Cold Lands."

"You are from there." Bagah said. It was not a question. Heral was unlike anyone or anything he had ever seen before. It made sense she was not of Estellian either.

"I am," she answered openly.

"What brought you here? Are the Cold Lands and its people as miserable as they say?"

Heral chuckled under her breath "Surely you, half-Teruk, do not believe the rumors of the masses?"

Bagah raised his nose to the air. "I suppose it *is* common for those who do not understand something to diminish it," he said softly. Their words were hushed. The only sound was their own breaths and the crash of the sweeping waves hitting the sand. Salt and humidity filled their senses.

"Or maybe they understand perfectly, and they are simply engulfed by fear," Heral proposed. She took another deep breath. "That which should be revered is, instead, often outcast. Lest those in power here might actually face a worthy opponent."

Bagah released a humorless laugh. "Are you suggesting that the Teruk and the Cold Lands are more powerful than the High Crown?"

"I am not suggesting," Heral said. "It is true. This is why you and I live in the shadows of others. If we keep our heads low, we believe they will not see us, but they do. Their eyes are always on our skin; they know our faces, likely better than we know our own. They are terrified of us, Bagah. We are not just the weeds in their gardens that need to be pulled. We are the rain and storm. We are the soil and the earth, the light and the fire." Bagah felt a gentle hand touch his shoulder and turned his eyes to meet it. Slowly, his eyes moved up her arm, her fair neck, past her full lips. Yellow met emerald. "Soon, my friend, they will learn that they cannot snuff us out," Heral said. "The more they fan the flames, the higher they will grow."

Bagah let the feel of her hand on his skin melt into him. He relished the mix of emotions it gave him. "For what it is worth, I like you with or without this," Heral said, and though she touched his nose lightly, Bagah's heart raced. She drew back her hand and cocked her head. "What Arcanen was this, Bagah? Who would want to divide us?"

"It was only meant to separate me," he admitted. "I am not sure how you ended up here." Heral leaned her head back and looked heavenward.

"Fate has a way of stitching things together," she mused.

"And ripping things apart," Bagah scoffed. Heral laughed softly and turned to face him. She crossed her arms over her chest, and swallowing, he mirrored her stance. "My mother told me many stories of Drodour when I was a child, but I know more than I ought to about this place because...I came back here after...after my mother died; I wanted to come home. There was nowhere else for me on this cursed earth." Heat flooded Bagah's chest. "In truth, I wanted to come here and scale the mountains so that I could see all of Estellian, the land that hated me so fucking much, and throw myself from the ledge."

Heral's subtle smile was filled with understanding. "Legend says that the Teruk will return to the rock in death," she said. "That the mountains are the souls of the Teruk and Xadaet, long passed on. Perhaps deep down, you only wished to return sooner."

Bagah's brows rose, and his eyes widened. "You know of the Xadaet?"

Heral pushed back her auburn hair, and she laughed into the wind. "I know much more than that, *Habie Nok Pelar.*" Son of the Rock.

"How–" Bagah began, but Heral shook her head.

"Let us discuss what you know first, friend." She took his hand in hers, and Bagah blanched. He had never held a woman's hand save for his mother's. "You came back to die, and yet you live. What happened last when you were here?" Heral kept her eyes fixed on his as she waited for his answer.

Bagah's lips trembled, his palms grew damp, and he prayed their clamminess would not deter her. He did not want her to let go.

"I returned to Drodour and slew many creatures and foes. I was closer to the mountains than we were today, but not by much. Then, the tremors started. One moment, I was there, and the next, I was here. I was…"

"In Darasheem," a sturdy voice called from behind them and finished his sentence. Bagah did not turn with Heral, for he already knew to whom the voice belonged. Heral's eyes sparked with the color of flame and sun, but not from fear.

"Darasheem, the city of the Mountain," she breathed as if she were speaking of a myth. A massive Teruk with long brown hair and deep yellow eyes bounded toward them, a giant flail in his grasp. The male laughed and nodded.

"Correct you are, *Mecarwea,*" he said easily. "But before I ask you how you know of our home, I must first ask you how you know my son."

Heral whipped her neck to face the half-breed. "Bagah?"

Bagah's face crinkled, and his nose scrunched as he turned to meet the Teruk's unwavering gaze. He siphoned a deep breath.

"Hello, Father."

The Jedarei and The Zonderi

※

Bagah walked silently behind his father, not daring to look over at Heral, who watched him. There were many questions he would need to answer, many more to which he could not. When they finally reached the base of the mountains, closer to the shore than the valley, his father walked to the mountainous wall and spoke in Teruk, then placed a giant hand flat against it. Bagah snuck one glance at Heral, surprised that she did not show any sign of fascination or bewilderment when the wall cracked open and revealed the entrance to a cave. Nor did she seem disconcerted when the rock wall closed behind them, trapping them inside. Her eyes danced in anticipation of what awaited them in the City of the Mountain. Darasheem.

Bagah had only seen this place once. Light blue fires danced wickedly in sconces, illuminating the carved alcoves around the city, seeping Darasheem in a pale glow that reminded Bagah of the blue spruce trees found in Tuvaria. The overwhelming smell of figs and fire was the same as he remembered. There was a low hum that permeated through the thick mountain air, a steady beat, a pulse.

"What is–" Heral began, but Bagah's father interjected. He turned his body, larger than his son's, and faced the pair.

"*Saenirth Nok Pelar,*" he said, and though his voice was low and scratchy, his tone was affable, even polite. "Heartbeat of the Mountain."

A chill ran down Bagah's spine. Saenirth was indeed the beating heart of Darasheem. It was composed of the souls of Teruks—full and half-blood—who preceded him. These were the ever-thrumming spirits that forever watched over their home. Heral was right; their legends did speak of their kind returning to the rock in death. Bagah felt the connection to the ground, sturdy and stable and immovable, too strongly for it to not be true. If he closed his eyes and concentrated, that low, pulsing sound would grow and grow until all he could hear was the faint voices of Teruk, who no longer walked the earth. But he would not do that now. Not today. There was too much at stake to grow comfortable.

Bagah kept his head low, but Heral was transfixed. Her gemstone eyes scoured every inch of the city guarded by rock. Its sheer size, which covered the entire base of the mountain, the carved stairs that spiraled towards the mountain summit, peaking so high it was lost within a nebulous mist that could be mistaken as the night sky. A massive rock pillar rose from the middle of the city. It was buried deep within the earth and traveled as high as the eye—even the Teruk eye—could see. Something rumbled within it, but what, Bagah was unsure.

Droplets of moisture hung thick in the air as the grumblings of the Teruk language were muttered by many tongues. Darasheem was not a city that saw visitors. Its denizens who watched them walk by had many things to whisper, especially about Heral. Bagah heard them call out to the goddess Radina and was unsurprised. Heral was, in fact, the most beautiful woman he had ever seen.

"Hundreds," Heral whispered to herself, her hand landing on the nape of Bagah's neck with a gentle squeeze. "There are *hundreds* of surviving Teruk here."

"Yes," Bagah breathed. There was an unsettling feeling in his stomach. A bundle of nerves stuffed in a glass jar, sliding too close to the edge. Being here should have brought him joy, but the glass cracked, and the memories resurfaced. If he stayed too long, his sins would shatter him.

"You said nothing about survivors," Heral said, her brow furrowed. "Why would you hide this?" Bagah did not meet her stare. He could not tell her why; his cowardice would not allow him to confess. The truth was he had not told his father what became of Everarda. *How could he?* Gegaret blamed the Sardek army for his wife's death, and Bagah preferred it stayed that way. The half-breed was also acutely aware that he was not the only coward here. The glass jar shook.

"Bagah is not one for talking," his father said with a robust laugh. "A rather peculiar trait, as his mother and I did not teach him silence. That much is certain."

As they walked through the lines of homes and shops built of wood and stone, Bagah tried to calm his nerves. Hearing his father speak of his mother was its own special kind of torture.

"I do not understand you, Bagah," Heral said softly and he dared a glance at her. She was still taking in the city, but her cheeks had turned red, and her brows slanted toward the bridge of her nose. "How can you hide from all of this? Your home, your family." Heral's words hit him like daggers. "When so many of us long for such things. You should not take it for granted, Teruk."

Gegaret grunted in agreement. "Last he was here, I told him the very same thing," he said. Bagah wanted to use the club to fight his way out.

The rage was peeking through, wondering what all the commotion was for. They approached the Liertiaen, home of the second in command to the Xadaet. Here was where the *Zonderi* resided, the title his father claimed.

The Liertiaen, the largest home in Darasheem, was sculpted entirely out of the rock. Smooth edges, soft as silk, curved and twined into a large dome. Gray stone mixed with white sediments gave the residence a glossy sheen. The blue light shone from within the rock abode, flickering down upon the large limestone table that filled the entire entry. Once they were inside, Gegaret gestured to it. He offered them food and drink, a wash, and a prayer. Bagah was reluctant to even accept water, but Heral found the provisions most gracious. She regarded the steamed fish straight from the Ripper Sea as nothing short of a delicacy.

They were silent as Heral ate, but Bagah was well-versed in the language of eye contact, and his father's stare made his skin itch. Finally, Heral pushed her plate of food away and pressed her back into the rock chair. "So, I suppose we should start answering questions now?" Gegaret snorted.

"A woman who is straight to the point?" He shook a finger at her and smiled. "I like this one, Bagah. How did you manage to seduce her?"

Bagah nearly choked on his water. He was not used to having a place for the liquid to travel, and it leaked from his nose. His father scoffed harder. "I see you have a new embellishment. I am glad your mother is not alive to witness it. She always found the human nose... Oh, what is the common tongue word for it? Ugly? *Lackluster?*" Gegaret rubbed his broad chin. "Ridiculous?"

Heral hummed in laughter. "Your wife and I would have gotten along," she mused. "I, too, find human features *stale.*"

Gegaret frowned at Bagah. "Tell me, how did you get that nose of yours?"

"Instead, let us discuss why your *habie* and I are here," Heral shifted the conversation with authority and ease. Bagah wondered if that was part of her strange Arcanen, too. "There is a lich that threatens Estellian." The Teruk straightened immediately.

"A lich!?"

"Gerreland Nerth's soul, according to The Maji," Heral said. "It split in two when he tried to pass to the afterlife. One part lich, another part a holy weapon he named the Vaenir."

Gegaret grumbled. He knew Gerelland Nerth's weapons all too well. The blades and armor had helped the Root Puller achieve an unbalanced victory. Gegaret was there the day Kallias struck Drodour. But, regardless of voting to go into battle, he did not fight himself; instead, he sequestered as many Teruk as he could into the City of the Mountain. The refuge of the Teruk. Bagah could not look at his father without the unfettered anger and disappointment returning. Gegaret had hidden hundreds who could have helped tip the battle in the Teruk's direction. Forcing them to remain silent and hide from that day on.

"Using a codex given to us by the Tajeh, we were able to pinpoint a rough guess of where the Vaenir is," Heral said. "Bagah seemed almost certain that it would be found in Drodour, so here we are. We were assisted by more hands, that is, until whatever that spell was separated us."

Gegaret muttered in Teruk, then lifted his chin. "That is most unfortunate. We did not realize that Bagah..."

"That I did not come here for you?" Bagah interrupted. A hushed silence followed his remark. Heral observed the two men closely, the slight shake in Bagah's fingers, the frown spreading across Gegaret's face. "Because I did not, Zonderi. I came here with my own guild to oppose the lich. We were well on our way to accomplishing our mission when the Xadaet separated us." Gegaret said nothing as his son angrily pushed away his clay mug of water. "There is no telling where the others have found themselves."

"You cannot reasonably hold me responsible for the Xadaet's decision–" Gegaret began but ceased when he caught his son's expression. Sharp and full of ire. "Bagah..." the name rolled off his tongue slowly. Their matching eyes, Bagah's only slightly less yellow, did not relent. Only a few fine lines around Gegaret's brow and mouth gave away that he was older. It was clear the two were related, but had Heral not known their dynamic, she would have assumed they were brothers. Teruks lived long enough for it to be possible.

"You could have left me in the valley. The Zonderi has great influence, remember?" Bagah said. "You convinced the Xadaet not to bow to the High Crown, and now look what has become of you."

Hiding like a milksop within the mountain.

Gegaret's nostrils flared. Bagah's glass jar slipped closer to the edge. "Do you blame me, *habie*? Is that what this is?

"*Blame* is not the word," said Bagah coldly. His father rose and huffed.

"We did not know the Crown would strike so soon. How could we? Not even the Xadaet foresaw the Gerelland blades!"

"Perhaps now is not the time to resolve family quarrels," Heral cut in as she rose. She was tall for a human woman, even by the Teruk's standards. "You have learned why we are here, and although there is much more I would like to discuss about Darasheem and your position, I think we can all agree the most pressing matter at hand is the lich." Both males were quiet, not unusual in the presence of the fierce woman. "What we need is to find the Vaenir. We must ensure the lich or those in his bidding do not find it first, and then we move on to the next concern."

"Trust that my issues with my father are not a grave concern," Bagah seethed.

"I was not speaking of your issues with your father," Heral snapped, and those damned green eyes pierced him so sharply he almost felt the prick of a phantom blade in his side. "The Sardek army has laid siege to multiple cities of Caxaven, and they will likely move to Sanica next. I know of a few Teruk colonies that hide there as well. If Dern can claim them, they will move to Drodour. And after that, they will no doubt set sail for the Cold Lands."

Bagah stared at Heral in bemusement. "How do you know so much about the Teruk?" The question came swiftly from his mouth before he could stop himself. Bagah had at first mistaken Heral's keen interest in him as a petty curiosity. He was a half-breed living amongst humans; it was not unusual that she would want to know more. However, as their time together grew, he had foolishly mistaken her attention as something else, something that could never be. Disappointment weighed heavy on his shoulders, and he felt them sag. Heral had never truly wanted to know him. This woman could speak in his native tongue. She knew of Darasheem and the Xadaet. Her hand in his only moments earlier no longer carried much excitement. "Who are you?" he asked.

Gegaret folded his muscular arms. "The Xadaet has spoken of you, *Mecarwea*," he said matter-of-factly. "You are The Dame."

Bagah was transported back to the night in Beretina when he had first seen Heral. Before the Nelimen attacked and kidnapped them.

The Dame of Disaster, she had said.

A cold smile overtook Heral's features, and Bagah saw it clear as day. Her eyes morphed from a solid green, the dark moss after rain, to a fiery yellow. Two raging suns. "I am she."

Bagah glanced between Heral and his father multiple times. Who was the Dame? How did Gegaret know of her? Before he could ask, a Teruk female with long, ashy braids plated into multiple strands rushed into the room and bowed hastily to Gegaret.

"Forgive me, Zonderi. I did not mean to interrupt," she said in Teruk, and Gegaret responded in the native language.

"What is it, Niemi?" The woman looked up.

"Commotion here on Develdeon. Ledge twenty-six. We thought it might have been a Sunbird, but it was a human. Someone is trying to reach the summit."

"Human?" Gegaret repeated.

Niemi nodded. "Kirek says it is only one woman." Gegaret rolled his shoulders and tipped his chin back, examining Bagah.

"One from your guilds?" Bagah tensed. Maybe the spell had not cast out everyone? There was hope.

"Did they get a good description?" It was Heral who spoke now, her Teruk perfectly fluent. Bagah clenched his teeth.

Niemi started, taken aback by a human woman speaking their old language. She nodded. "Gold hair, gold eyes," she said. Heral and Bagah whirled to look at each other.

"Mirevra," he breathed and could not help the force that tugged on the edge of his lips. His mouth curled into a smirk. "We think the Vaenir will be found at the summit. She is going to find the blade," he said in Teruk.

"She will not reach the summit," Gegaret assured, stepping close to the entry of the Liertiaen. "The mountain wall is too steep. She will need to go through if she wishes to go up." He glanced at his son. "We will help her." He dipped his head towards Niemi in a wordless order, and at once, she rushed out the entry. "I will have it taken care of, Bagah. You may go and join whoever this woman is. Judging by your smile, I assume you consider her a friend. The Dame will come with me."

Bagah now had a less-than-favorable decision on his hands. "Why should Heral go with you? We were both sent here to retrieve the blade; her Head has ordered–"

"I serve no Head," Heral said promptly, following Gegaret. "I have no master." Bagah could only blink. Was she saying... Did she mean?

"You're a Wolf?" The inquiry was uttered so weakly that Bagah did not know if anyone heard it. But she did, of course. Heral spun around to meet his gaze.

"Not a Wolf," she said. "I have never pledged to any cause other than this." She stepped towards Bagah, placing a finger beneath his chin. "The bargaining chip was that the Ring had a half-breed. One who could lead me here. I sailed across the Ripper Sea. I found you. I found Darasheem." Bagah did not understand her and realized he rarely did. He pressed his mouth into a thin line of well-hidden hurt. She had used him.

"But what of the Vaenir?"

Heral shrugged. "It seems your friend is well on her way to finding it. Estellain is in her hands now. It is up to us to face the threat that comes after."

Gegaret made a rough noise from behind her, and she looked over her shoulder to him, then back to Bagah. "There is much that you do not know, Bagah, but trust in this: I came here to help the Teruk. To gather numbers in the coming rebellion. Your freedom is not lost. There are others from beyond the sea."

"The Xadaet has looked forward to meeting you," his father said. "We should not keep them waiting much longer."

"Indeed," Heral chimed, dropping her finger. "You may choose Bagah, but you must do so quickly. You can go with Niemi and find Mirevra. You can make sure the Vaenir falls into the right hands and save Estellian, or you can come with us and begin dealing with the next concern." Her chin motioned towards Gegaret. "You have stored away much anger for your father; that much is clear. But he is not the only one you hold such rage against, Bagah. I can see it warping your bones. You are full of the same anger for yourself, and it is suffocating you, burying you far beneath the earth." Her eyes roared. "That pain does not have to remain there, so deep down, You can bring it out. You can hold it to the light and let it taste the sun and be healed."

Bagah was still for a moment. This woman knew too much about the Teruk, about *him*. "What are you?" he asked.

"We do not have time, Bagah," Heral dismissed the question. "You must choose your path now," she said and turned back to Gegaret. Bagah was torn by indecision. With the lich on the hunt for the Vaenir, the world was still threatened with oblivion, and his friend, his dearest friend, was on the mountain. Alone.

But something deeper called to him, past his confusion, past the glass jar. His mother's voice. Soothing, calm, and undeterred by the madness. Bagah squeezed his eyelids shut, and his heart pounded against his ribs like fists of rage and sorrow. He took in a long breath. He let her voice reach him, let it thrum through his veins. He heard her clearly.

"One of rock and one of fire."

Bagah opened his eyes. He had made his choice.

The Messaging Gem

~~~~~~~~~~

Her eyes slowly cracked open. At first, she could not remember where she was–her mind was too groggy. The air was thin, and the clouds were far too close to her face. Mirevra blinked. She was on the mountain; she was in the sky. Beneath her was a tiny lip of rock, just enough space to walk several steps before careening down to imminent death. Birds soared nearby, their loud calls had woken her up. She brought her torso forward, placed her hands flat on the ground behind her, and struggled to inhale a full breath.

She imagined this was what it must feel like to have wings, to be an eagle, not a Fox. As Mirevra stood, she prepared herself to brave the heat she would surely feel being this much closer to the sun. Instead, the cool of the previous night seemed to bleed into the morning. Humidity welled around her. Perhaps it would rain. Any other day, she would thank the gods for the downpour, but now, so far above the ground, she withheld such gratitude. Mirevra prayed to the gods they would keep the mountain and her path dry. But when had they ever accounted for her needs?

The summit still peaked above the clouds. She had not yet reached it, and she did not know how she was going to. How far did this mountain extend into the heavens? Behind her, there was nothing but a mountain wall. It was jagged but not enough for her to find a foothold. She wouldn't be able to continue her climb. It was too steep. She placed her hands on her hips and thought. Perhaps she could use her dagger as a pick or carve out niches for her feet, but who was she to believe she could cut through pure stone? Nonetheless, she would have to try. Options were few, and Mirevra knew that as much as she felt like a bird, she could not fly. She would have to be cunning and light on her feet.

Reaching into her boot, she pulled out the Messaging Gem. Only two messages remained, and though she did not want to, she tapped the rock thrice and whispered. "I am alone and do not know where the others are... an unknown Arcanen separated us. Others seek the blade, including a Tempust Wolf. Last I saw her, she and Tilly were fighting, and I am not sure of the outcome. I may be the only Fox left. I am standing on a ledge on the highest mountain in Drodour, the Develdeon, uncertain of my fate. I will try to climb, as we believe the Vaenir is at the highest summit. But it is risky, and I have no tools. If you do not hear from me again, know that I tried. Please, know that I only wanted to serve you and give back what you once gave to me." *In that dingy cell, all those years ago. Life. Freedom.*

She buried the Gem into the deepest part of her pocket and huffed. *She was going to fucking die.* She knew it, but even still, she marched with unfounded confidence and vigor toward the wall, raised her dagger, and began chipping away.

The highest she got by the end of the first day was a few feet–if that. She fell twice, one from only a few steps high and the second from about twelve. Her back slammed against the rock and knocked all the breath from her lungs. There was no way to climb it. There was no way to retrieve the Vaenir. She had failed. She tried to lift herself, but her back was in searing pain, and the rest of her body pulsed with an insatiable soreness. She had to rest and try again tomorrow. And the next day. And the next, if she must. She would not climb back down; she would not leave without the Vaenir, even if that meant not leaving at all. She closed her eyes and panted until, eventually, her heart slowed, and the night spread across the sky like ink in a pool of water. Mirevra was exhausted. She needed rest and lots of it.

Hours passed, and dreamlike images began to dance in her mind. *'It does not end here,'* she heard her mother say. Then, the subtle mist of memory hardened into a solid picture. Her mother had wrapped Mirevra in a blanket and began throwing food into a bag. Her father watched the door, two blades in his hands. When her mother finished packing, she dropped to her haunches and held a young Mirevra's shoulders. *'We will find a way out, my Yahelle.'*

'What if they catch us?' Mirevra recalled her fragile voice. She was so young. Her heart was still forged of unbroken glass, the world had not yet kicked and bruised her. She did not understand why they needed to run.

Her mother smiled tenderly.

'Death is not the end either, Yahelle. Even if they take us from this home, the gods will welcome us kindly to our next.' Mirevra remembered when those words meant something to her. Now, she had to be convinced there was an afterlife. She did not know that she believed in a place of such peace, at least, not for her. For anywhere her soul could travel was bound to be burdened by suffering.

'*We must leave now. They come swiftly,*' her father said from the door. Mirevra's mother hugged her tightly, then pulled her wrist. The blanket dropped. Mirevra was cold. Rain pierced her face like liquid arrows. They had planned to go east. Her father said he had a half-sister there who would give them shelter, but they left too late. The Sardek guards shouted, and their horses galloped down the cobblestone streets. The viaduct appeared. The haunting memory played again and again. Her fingers slipped from the stone's edge. '*Forever.*'

When she hit the water, it felt like Vaste had cupped her within his palms, and she did not immediately rise to the surface. She sank. Down, down, down. She was weightless, and she did not think. It was the last time Mirevra had ever felt genuine serenity. She could have drowned, and she might have been better off for it. Eventually, Vaste hoisted her back to the surface, and her small head broke through the seal of water and poked out for air. The rain hit her face once more.

She awoke to the morning rain hitting her face upon a mountain's ledge. She gasped in a way all too reminiscent of her memory of breaking free of the Murky Lakes. That day was many years ago, a moment she had tried her hardest to store away in the hidden parts of her mind. A locked door never to be opened again. Her pocket burned, but she ignored it. The rain hit her face, and Mirevra smiled. She was going to die, but at least she would not die at the hands of the sun and its relentless heat. She could close her eyes and pretend Vaste was holding her again and maybe find the serenity that once belonged to her. Her pocket throbbed, searing her thigh, and she realized it was not the phantom sting of her own conscience. The Veravant had sent her a message, and more than that, he had used the last of them to speak to her. Her heart roared within her chest. It was an unexpected gift that he cared enough to say something in the event that she might never return. She plucked the Gem from her trousers and held it to her ear, her eyes squeezed shut, and her lips pressed firmly together in anticipation. His voice rolled over her senses like warm honey and silk.

'Little Fox, little Fox,' he said, and the hair on her limbs rose to greet his voice. *'I was kind enough to not make a fuss of your last message when you told me where you were going and that Roman had died. I could have punished you then, little Fox, that you would waste a message on something so trivial. Instead, in my generosity, I sent you Tilly. I left the den unprotected to foster your fragile wants and needs.'* Mirevra felt her stomach sink. This would be no heartfelt farewell. He would not wax poetic or tell her how proud he was of her for getting this far. His tone was vicious. He used the last message not to console her but to reprimand her. In her final moments, the last thing she would hear was his disapproval. *'I find myself reminiscing on when I saved you from that prison so many years ago, how I offered you a new life, a home to call your own. I gave you freedom, Mirevra. I gave you purpose!'* Tears welled; her vision blurred. She had owed him so much, and she had failed. *"I am on my way to Drodour to collect the Vaenir myself since you have proven that you could not. Out of everyone, I expected more from you, little Fox. I am sorry to learn I was wrong. Sleep well, Mirevra. To the Ring we serve."*

The Gem turned gray in her fingers, but she still held it to her ear. There had to be more. She refused to believe those would be his last words for her. She shook the stone and tapped it over and over. She shouted that she was sorry, that she was angry and cold and miserable and alone. She screamed into that damned rock, deep and guttural sounds erupting from her chest. He could have been generous to her in her last days. He could have said nothing at all! Anger swelled in her belly, but her chest felt on fire. With all of her might, she threw the now ordinary rock from the side of the mountain and cursed it as it fell. Then, she drew her dagger. Her stomach grumbled with hunger and nerves, but she spat and stomped to the wall. Over and over, she brought her dagger down, chiseling away at the stone, small nick after small nick. Then she used the dagger as a pick to lift herself, to climb one step, then another. Her attempt was as futile as the day before, but she refused to quit. Her body would have to drop to the ground as a lifeless corpse before she stopped.

Each time she climbed, she fell. Each crash hurt worse than the one before. It filled her with an unbounded fury. She let the anger fuel her as she drove her blade into the mountain with newfound strength. *I expected more from you. I expected more from you. I expected more from you.* She had expected more from herself, too. She should have stayed with her father that night on the viaduct. She should not have let him toss her in the water. She should have fought and fought and fought until her hands bled and her own throat was cut. She should have taken one of those Sardekian officers with her as she fell and drowned him in Vaste's wrath. Mirevra stabbed at the rock as if those guards were in front of her now, and tears mingled with rain stained her cheeks. *Forever, forever, forever...*

"Stabbing the mountain now, are we? Tell me, Viper, what did it do to piss you off?"

Mirevra spun so quickly that she wobbled. Her eyes grew double their size, and her body was rendered entirely immobile as she watched Lars pull himself fully over the lip of the ledge.

He was covered in dust, blood, rain, and sweat. Still, those gray eyes found hers even through the mist and storm, matching the sky behind him. Mirevra was immobile for a moment, not able to process his form in front of her, only a few steps away. Her mouth curved into an incredulous smile, and though she did not feel the blade slip from her hand, she heard it crash to the ground.

"You... You made it?" He might be an illusion, of this she was not certain. The air was thin, her mind was tired, and the Veravant and her own memories had been devouring what was left of her sanity. Perhaps she was already dead. Yet she found herself stumbling towards him till her hands met his flesh, and she squeezed his shoulders. "You are real," she breathed. "You're really here... but how? Are you all right?"

Lars cocked his head. "I'm fine. Are you?" he asked, but she buried her face in his chest without answering. She had not been alone for that long, but after the Veravant's words, it felt like an eternity. She pulled her face back enough to say, "Tilly."

Lars shook his head. "She is not coming up the mountain."

Mirevra's cheeks burned. "She is dead." It was not a question; she was merely letting reality sink in and pull her down. Lars placed his hand in her wet hair, steadying the base of her skull even as her weight sagged.

"I don't know that for sure," he said, and Mirevra's golden eyes seemed to lighten a shade. "We were fighting that woman, and time stopped for a moment. When I came back to my senses, they were both gone. I do not know how much time passed or what happened. And I certainly was not going to wait to find out. I just started climbing and prayed to Rashawe that I would find you up here."

So then, Tilly might still be alive. And maybe Bagah and Beldon, too. Mirevra did not like to hope for such things, but in her weakened state, she could not help herself. She hoped and hoped and hoped with everything in her and put her forehead to his chest again. She tugged at his ripped tunic. It was little more than scraps at this point. "This shirt is utterly ruined, Ruffles." Mirevra said with a breathy chortle. "When I meet the gods, I shall thank them for this one small miracle." She felt his chest rise and fall with laughter. "And then I shall curse them because they left me here with only *you* for company."

She pulled away and smiled at him, shoving her palms against his chest playfully. Even with the rain between them, she caught that halfway smile. "There is no way to the summit. We climb back down or we..." her voice quavered, and she realized in that moment it was not imminent death that scared her most... it was him. It was the way he was looking at her. "Or we die here together," she finished with a gulp.

"Well, if this is to be our fate," he breathed as he brought his thumb to her lip and wiped off a droplet of rain. "It is not such a bad way to go." His thumb remained on her lip. For the very first time, Mirevra did not think so little of that word. Fate. Maybe this *was* her fate; maybe it had been from the very start. The gods had always wanted her dead, it seemed.

"What a sick showcase of the gods' humor this is. The criminal and the *hero*, left to die in the clouds," she scoffed. Lars chuckled darkly, and the smell of vetiver washed over her skin. "I suppose there is nothing left for us to do, then," she added.

"I suppose not," he murmured in agreement before dropping his thumb from her lips to her chin. "Nothing to do, except this." Mirevra did not jerk against him as Lars brought his lips to hers. At first, she thought about ramming a fist into his cheek, but she did not. Instead, her arms found their way around his neck, and she did not resist still when he gathered her further into himself. For five years, Mirevra had not kissed a single soul. She had gone to bed with the Veravant hundreds of times, and not once had their lips met–not once did she betray an ounce of her pleasure. *To be damned with all of that,* she thought as Lars' tongue found hers. *To be damned, everything.* Mirevra felt her eyelids flutter, and even that tiny movement made her heart pound. This was a rough, passionate kiss between two opposites of the same coin, facing the end together, hungry and desperate to feel something before their souls were claimed.

Lars had told her she had a choice once, and she had not believed him. But at this moment, there was *nothing left* to believe. There was only him.

His mouth pushed deeper into hers as he wrapped one arm tightly around Mirevra's waist, while the other still held her head and guided it in raw movements. Maybe half the day had gone by, maybe two or three, but she did not care. Her last day spent trying to climb this damned mountain would not end in her wallowing in pity. She would allow herself one petty ounce of joy before the rock quelled her.

When Lars shifted his head to reposition their kiss, her eyes slit open a fraction, and she jolted. She did not see Lars anymore but the Veravant. *He* was kissing her, and though his mouth did not move, she heard his voice anyway. *'I expected more from you, little Fox.'*

Mirevra was losing her mind. She pushed his body off hers at last, but it was Lars again. Black hair, gray eyes. The Veravant's mirage was gone as quickly as it came. The two stared each other down with wordless pants until, finally, Lars spoke.

"Is something wrong?" Mirevra shook her head. She had thought the kiss would break her free from feeling the Veravant's disappointment, or that it might have shaken off the last remnants of his hold on her. But she was wrong. She still owed him.

Lars stood with heavy breaths, awaiting an answer. Mirevra turned to face the mountain and took the last swig of water from her leather pouch. "No. Nothing is wrong. I simply realized I am not ready to give up," she said and tried to pay no mind to the handsome, proud smile that was etched across his face.

"I am going to need you to help me climb the wall, Ruffles. I am going to need you to help me get this fucking sword."

The Ash of Hands and Many Mouths

Bagah did not see anything he recognized as he trailed his father and Heral up the carved stone stairs. The staircase clung to the side of the mountain and was wide enough for a Teruk's broad body, but Bagah still felt uneasy with the lack of railings. His steps were cautious, and his breathing steadied. He was not used to being so high. Heral moved up the steps like liquid, unconcerned with the fear of falling. Bagah grew more envious of her with every push of his leg. She was not afraid of the mountain; she was not afraid of anything. Worse, she was not afraid of using his feelings as a rope to pull herself up where she needed to be. She was brutal in that way, using him to find Darasheem. Bagah ascended in silence. Though he had never seen these surroundings, he somehow found them familiar. A previously dormant place in his soul shuddered when he stopped his thoughts, the humming heartbeat matched his own. Perhaps it was the Saenirth.

Bagah might not have known this place, but this place certainly knew him.

After an endless quest up steep stairs, Gegaret finally placed his hand against the wall and muttered under his breath. Again, the rock split into a gaping entrance for the trio to pass through. They stepped into a hollowed-out portion of the mountain, surrounded by darkness. Bagah could still make out most of the cavern; he sensed Heral could, too. The cave was shrouded with sharp, fang-like ice that hung from the ceiling like a threat. Bagah understood the warning; they were in the mouth of the beast, and they would do well to not forget it. The only sound was the dripping of moisture running off those fangs, the blood of its last prey, Bagah thought. He had never felt like prey before, and yet, in this place, the thought plagued him. The air was thick and sour and hard to breathe. Gegaret reached for a lone staff leaning against one wall of the humid chamber and gripped it firmly. He spared one glance and a quick smile for his son before tapping the staff against the floor.

Boom, boom, boom, boom.

Slow, steady thuds echoed throughout the cave. Bagah realized his heartbeat had slowed to match this new beat. He straightened and held his chin high. The mountain seemed to whisper in his ear. *The Xadaet* it sang in a haunting tune. *The mystic of the Rock.*

From overhead, a dark purple and blue mist, the color of bruises and black currants, gradually appeared and covered them like a blanket of dusk. But soon, the mist changed into a swift, cyclical pattern. This cyclone of vapor coned till its tip touched the ground. *A tornado*, Bagah thought. *A furious, hungry wind.* He had heard of these tearing through unlucky villages but had never actually seen one. Not until now. Heral's hair slapped roughly against her face, and her body braced itself to not be thrown back by the strong winds. Bagah's body was stationary, but even he felt himself involuntarily rock on his heels. Water slashed their faces, and the air became even more challenging to breathe. A quick look behind him showed the opening had been closed and there was no way to leave this place. They were stuck in the baleful storm until it ceased or until it claimed them. The half-Teruk lifted a hand to shield his squinted eyes and tried to focus on the violet whirlwind. Its shape was warping. First widening and then thinning until the gusts slowed. When it was calm enough for Bagah to drop his hand, the mist was taking another form.

A silhouette, tall with broad shoulders, stood cloaked by the steam. The fog was a cloud-like cowl, hiding their face from the trio before them. Gegaret and Heral dropped to one knee and bowed their heads, but Bagah stood like a rogue thread poking out of smooth fabric. The form in the veiled mist said nothing, but Gegaret cleared his throat repeatedly until Bagah looked at him. "Kneel before the Xadaet, Bagah," he said through gritted teeth. Bagah's eyes widened as he dropped to one knee. He wanted to apologize and explain that he was unaware of most Teruk traditions, but before he could speak, the Xadaet's voice filled the cavern.

"We do not hold fault in the boy," said the voice, and Bagah's mind flared with frenzied thoughts. The voice was soft and light, an amalgamation of different tones. A dark, booming male, a child-like squeak, and an old crone's warble were all in those words. They did not all speak simultaneously; the elder female's voice was first, and the others followed as if they were its shadow, trying to keep pace. Bagah kept his head lowered and stared at the ground. *"He does not know who we are. He does not know our way."*

Even with his eyes on the cave's floor, Bagah could feel the Xadaet's stare. He watched as the mist curled towards him and dark tendrils of black smoke wound around his ankles. *"Yes, we sense the rock within him. Yes, we do,"* the voices whispered. *"But something else lives in him, too. We can feel it."* That mist crawled up Bagah's leg, and he ground his teeth. Cold air wrapped around him, and Bagah did not favor the cold. The voices hissed as the smoke pulled away from him, as a hand would after touching something too hot. He dared look up only as the mist coiled back into the cloaked silhouette. He saw Heral's eyes flashing in wonder. *"Why have you summoned me, Zonderi? The mountain is at rest."* The Xadaet sounded curious, not angry, and Bagah felt some relief. For all he was told, the Teruk worshiped the Xadaet and not the other way around. Everada had mentioned the Xadaet was the protector of their people, and not much else.

"The mountain should be stirred," he said evenly. "The Dame of Disaster has come for us." With a wild howl, wind whizzed around them. The excited air sent gooseflesh up Bagah's arms. He lowered his gaze again.

"Then let her speak. The mountain has waited decades for her arrival," the vociferous echoes proclaimed. Heral rose to her feet, her head still lowered in submission.

"And I have waited just the same," she said. "But now, I come to you with news of the Cold Lands and the rebellion in the West."

A shuddering breeze blew past them. *"How many?"* The voices sounded closer together now.

"At least seventy," Heral answered, and Bagah's brows furrowed. "Perhaps a hundred if the *Yedaelsh* can gather them."

At that, Bagah looked up. The *Yedaelsh* had been the legendary leader of the Teruk army. A fierce Teruk who had not cowered before

Kallias or his army. But Bagah's mother had told him the *Yedaelsh* had died in the Sardek attacks. How did Heral know—

"How many in Sanica?" The voices crooned.

"Over one hundred more, that I know of," Heral said steadily. Indeed, she must not be afraid of anything, Bagah thought. There was no waiver in her voice.

"Two hundred and forty-seven of Darasheem. If we move quickly, we can collect more from the outliers of the Sardek kingdom." Gegaret added.

"Hmm," the voices mused. *"Do we trust that they will stand to fight? One born to the life of servitude does not always know how to leave it."*

"They are Teruk. They will leave it if they know it is a chance for true freedom," Gegaret replied. "But someone must go and share the truth and make them see."

"Yes," the words were drawn out like a snake hissing. *"Who then shall we send?"* Gegaret looked between Heral and Bagah.

"Bagah," he said, and though his voice was almost firm, there was a shake to it. "Will you go?" Bagah shifted, and his breath hitched.

"Will I go where? I do not know what any of this means," he said. Heral turned to him.

"Almost fifty years ago, Kallias attacked the Teruk lands. He thought he had won that fateful night. He was sure of it. He soured the minds of the Teruk he kept in captivity. He poisoned their hearts, tortured them, starved and beat them. After decades of this depraved conditioning, they will now only fight for the High Crown; they do not know anything else," she said. Bagah swallowed hard. He already knew this much. "But Kallias did not know the strength of the rock," Heral continued. "He did not realize the might of the Teruk. A sword, especially one of a greedy king, cannot break a mountain." *Thud. Thud. Thud.* The pulse had returned, and Bagah's heart again matched its beat. "When the Root Puller ambushed Drodour, it was grim, but thanks to your father, many were saved."

Bagah's stomach churned in protest. No, his father had been a coward! He had not stood and fought! He had run away like a dog with its tail between its legs! Bagah glanced at his father and saw Gegaret's sad expression. "Others sailed to the Cold Lands," Heral explained. "That is where I met them. My kind took them in, we worked together and understood one another. Your story is not far from my own. The High Crown is an abomination. It must be thwarted, Bagah. The Crown must be returned to whom it was destined by the gods to wear. The Teruk are not the first to be unwelcomed in these lands," she said. Her eyes were now flames. "And we do not deserve a life of hiding, Bagah. You and I? We do not belong to the shadows."

Bagah heard the mountain susurrate and the Xadaet's many voices trilled in agreement. But he focused on Heral, how her chest rose and fell with her passionate words and the heart that roared within her. This passion seemed to call to him. It lulled his senses into a fixed calm. "A rebellion, Bagah," Heral thundered. "It is time to fight back against the Crown. We belong to the sun."

"Send me." Bagah heard the words leap from his mouth as if he had no control over them. But every fiber of his being had meant them. His veins bulged, but they were not black with rage. They were red and hot. It was a fire that coursed through him now.

The mountain shook. Loose rock and ice skittered down the cave walls, and dust rose in plumes like when an old rug was swatted against a wall. A low rumble rang for a seemingly endless time.

"*The Mountain is awake,*" the Xadaet exclaimed, whorls of dark blue and purple smoke twisted and danced through the air. *"Develdeon lives."*

As the mountain shook, Mirevra and Lars held on to each other for dear life. Their attempts to continue the climb had gone as expected: dismally and to no avail. They had not let the impossible stop them from trying, though. At one point, the assassin stood on Lars' shoulders. He threw her as high as his muscular build allowed on another attempt. That did not work, either. How could it? They were two pebbles trying to reach the top of a tree. Now, the tree was rocking, vibrating with fury. At first, Mirevra feared it was the same Arcanen that had separated the guilds in the meadow, but as the two remained on the ledge, she wondered if the mountain itself was collapsing. She prayed to Rashawe that he would not let the tumbling debris demolish them. After a few minutes, the shaking stopped, and she found herself still entwined in Lars' arms. Rashawe must have answered. They were still alive and breathing, and she saw a crack in the mountainside. Mirevra stumbled backward as it split further, and Lars stepped in front of her body to act as a barrier whilst the crack widened into an opening. She peered over his shoulder as a blue light spilled out from the yawning mouth, and a Teruk woman with long gray braids stalked out. The woman held her hands before her; she was not a threat. Thank the gods.

She babbled in Teruk, but Mirevra caught a few words she recognized. "She says her name... her name is Niemi," Mirevra tried to translate for Lars and knew she would not get very far. Unless Niemi started to curse, they likely would be here for days. The Teruk was tall, sturdy, and full-blooded. Her yellow skin and lack of a nose were devastatingly familiar, and Mirevra's heart squeezed as she thought of Bagah. The woman's large brown eyes were wide with hope of understanding. She was trying to help them, Mirevra surmised.

Niemi spoke faster, and more Teruk words blended together, sounding like utter nonsense. Finally, she paused to take a breath and closed her eyes. "Bagah," the Teruk said. *"Bagah!"* Now Niemi was pointing to the opening in the rock. Bagah must've been inside.

Mirevra did not hesitate and started towards the entry impatiently. Lars pulled her wrist and she turned to face him, the fighter gleaming in her eyes.

"Are you sure?" Lars asked her, and Mirevra nodded, all too excited at the prospect of seeing Bagah again. Still, the rogue looked hesitant.

"Summit," Niemi said slowly as if unsure how to pronounce the word. The Teruk pointed a finger heavenward, where the mountain's top was coated in clouds. "Summit," she repeated, then pointed to herself, then back up to the sky. "I go...summit."

"Summit," Mirevra echoed with an emphatic nod. "Bagah, summit. The Vaenir."

"Vaenir," Niemi repeated and pointed to her sheath. A long sword that nearly scraped the ground hung from her belt. "Vaenir!"

Mirevra spun to face Lars. "Bagah must've found a way!" She released a deep sigh of relief, hope rippling in her chest. *Bagah was alive.* Wherever he went, wherever he was, he found a way to the summit. "This Teruk knows of the Vaenir. We must follow her."

Inky black pools spilled over moody gray skies as Lars' pupils dilated. His brows lifted, but not from enthusiasm, Mirevra could tell. There was something in his gaze that made him appear lost. "So, we can still find the blade," he murmured. "Are...are you certain you still want to do this, Viper?"

Mirevra stared at him. His doubt made her suddenly feel heavy and unsure. How could he not be excited? Not moments ago, they had been wholly doomed, stranded on the lip of a mountain, and now luck was pouring over them from a heavy cup; she could not fathom why he sounded disappointed. Part of her wanted to grab him by his shoulders and shake him from this mood. Another part, perhaps the more significant portion, wanted to kiss him, take his hands in hers, and whisper reassurance. She did neither. Instead, the Veravant's voice played like a sickly tune stuck in her head. She spat on the ground.

"I am positive," she confirmed. "This is the only reason we are here, is it not?" Lars did not speak, but his tight jaw and knitted brows argued all the same. Mirevra gazed at him silently until she saw a single flake of snow land on his cheek. She snapped her head back and felt more flakes hit her face, lifting a hand as the soft snow landed on her palm. This snow was not cold, though. It felt like dust against her skin. It did not melt. Instead, when she rubbed her fingers, the flakes left a dark stain. "It is not snow," she mused. Lars stared at her fingers and then answered her knowingly, the pieces of the Tajeh's codex snapping together like a puzzle in his mind.

"Ash."

As hard as Mirevra tried to communicate with Niemi, the Teruk woman could not explain, in enough comprehensible common tongue, why ash littered the ledge just outside the opening. From the earnest look on Niemi's face, Mirevra was sure the woman wanted to help. The Teruk had led them into the mountain's opening, and they now stood in a vast, cylindrical room with stairs spiraling up, up, up—and down, down, down. Bright blue fires burned in the stone sconces lining the room and the stairs, illuminating the chamber in an enchanting glow. It was ungodly hot within the rock walls, and Mirevra tried not to stare at Lars' chest as he removed the rest of his torn shirt to cool off. Sweat crested his brow. Mirevra studied his tight shoulders, curled fists, and the muscle feathering in his jaw and frowned. Perhaps the hero had not enjoyed the journey so far; perhaps heroes, unlike criminals, were unaccustomed to having so little at their disposal.

"Bagah," Mirevra said slowly to Niemi. "Where..." she began, then gestured around the cavern. "Where is Bagah?" Niemi blinked and tilted her head. "Bagah..." Mirevra said again. "BAGAH?"

"*Bagah,*" Niemi echoed and pointed down the stairs. Then she lifted her pointer finger upwards. "*Vaenir.*"

"Oh, what the fuck," Lars practically spat. He ran a hand down his face. "We are getting nowhere with this. Maybe we should go back outside."

"Bagah?" Mirevra asked, ignoring the shirtless male's complaints, and pointed down. Niemi nodded.

"*Ich, Bagah,*" the Teruk woman said, pointing down the stairs. "*Bagah li Zonderi. Testch Nu Zul Xadaet.*"

It was nothing but incoherent babbling to Mirevra's ears. Bagah, she knew, of course. Ich, she had heard her friend say. She had assumed it meant 'sure,' but maybe it meant 'yes?' Xadaet, she had heard when Bagah spoke to the Tajeh. Something about his father not being one? Oh, gods above and Murks below. This was a disaster. Niemi grabbed Mirevra's arm and shoved it upwards. "Vaenir," she said. "Vaenir Nu Hele!" From the Teruk's wide brown eyes and strained tone, Mirevra knew she was communicating something urgent. Vaenir Nu Hele.

"Vaenir," Mirevra said and placed a hand on the hilt of Niemi's blade. "Hele?" Then she brought her upturned palms to chest height and shrugged. "Hele?"

"Ich, Hele! Li Nok Develdeon!"

Lars chuckled in defeat behind them, but Mirevra did not relent. She nodded rapidly and cupped Niemi's hand in hers. Develdeon was the name of the mountain. Bagah had told them the tale.

"Hele? What is Hele?" Mirevra asked. The Teruk blinked as if she could understand the human by gazing at her long enough.

"Hele..." Niemi said, drawing the word out. "Hele!" She pointed upwards again. "Deleon! Hele, Deleon!" Mirevra arched her brows. *Deleon, goddess of sun and fire.*

"Deleon... sun?" The assassin released the Teruk's hand and spread her arms above her. "Sun?"

Niemi huffed a harsh breath and stomped her foot. So, no. Not the sun, then. *"Deleon,"* Niemi said with gritted teeth. *"Hele, Deleon."* Her round eyes inspected their surroundings, and the corner of her mouth quirked up. Pushing past Mirevra and Lars, Niemi ran to the wall and pointed at the blue fire. *"Hele,"* she said evenly. *"Hele."* She held her finger near the flame, hissed, then pulled her hand back to her chest. *"Hele."*

Mirevra nodded.

"Hele. Fire," she said, drawing out her words as realization dawned. The ash, the cloudy fog hiding the mountain peak, the earth trembling and shaking. It all began to make sense. Total, horrific sense. Mirevra looked at Lars.

"What?" The rogue asked, folding his arms over one another.

Mirevra let out a long, weary breath and meandered towards him slowly. She rolled her right shoulder, which was tight from days of climbing.

"It seems I was wrong about our fortunes changing, Ruffles. This is not just any mountain," she explained with a sigh. "It is a godsdamned volcano."

The Scorn and the Skin

※

Of all the things Mirevra found herself ungrateful for, to her surprise, the shirtless rogue was not among them. She was glad that she was not alone. She was glad it was Lars with her. As they climbed toward the volcano's peak from the inside, the smog became unbearably thick. It stung Mirevra's eyes; it flooded her nose and mouth. It lingered in the back of her throat, and she could not comprehend how something could taste so sharp yet utterly bitter all at once. She and Lars coughed hoarsely and tried their best to cover their mouths as they ascended. Mirevra wondered how in the Murks they would navigate the vent of this fiery beast without getting themselves killed. But Niemi apparently knew these stairs and chiseled hallways from precise memory. Mirevra reassured herself that the Teruk had no doubt walked this route many times and somehow survived. She longed to ask their guide when the last eruption occurred, or the next was due. Instead, she mumbled fervent prayers to Rashawe that Bagah would appear. She then prayed to The Maji that They would translate for her.

"I have never seen a volcano before," Lars said weakly from behind her. "All I know is that they leak fire and melt cities. So, the chances of us making it…"

"The chances of us making it this far were already slim," Mirevra interjected. "The odds of us defeating ice mages and dragles and scaling the *inside* of a mountain? Exorbitantly low. Yet, here we are, a Fox and a Nelimen being led by a Teruk to the apex of this spear. We have defied the odds this far," Lars said nothing in return. "Look here, Ruffles. We always knew this mission would more than likely end in death, and still, we took it on," Mirevra said without turning around. "That does not change here; that does not change now." She clamped her mouth tightly shut as she finished the sentence. She heard him chuff, and a smile spread across her face. If she could do this, if she actually retrieved the Vaenir, she would make the Veravant eat his words. She would have him fall to his knees before her as she delivered the blade to his hands. He would kiss her knuckles and pray for forgiveness; likely, she would give it to him. So long as he understood the trade. The blade for her life. She would not owe him anything.

What she would do with her life apart from the Ring, Mirevra did not know. Another problem for another day. She glanced over her shoulder. "If you want to turn back, I will not blame you," she said truthfully. "Though I will most assuredly judge you as a coward," she added. Lars chuckled darkly, and Mirevra found herself grinning before turning back to Niemi, who had stopped walking. The Teruk swiveled her large form, now looking at the two guild members with a hint of a smirk.

"Develdeon," she said, pointing towards a small alcove an arm's stretch away. *"Summit. Vaenir."* Mirevra saw narrow stairs, much steeper than the ones they had been climbing, nestled in the nook. Niemi then moved her extended finger from the tucked-away stairwell. *"Nu belitea vor vorae,"* she said with wide eyes. Mirevra heard Lars sigh.

"Oh gods, please tell me you know what she said this time," he beseeched. "Or surely I will throw myself from this volcano and end our suffering sooner."

"Vorae," the assassin repeated, ignoring the rogue's weak attempt at humor. She searched within for why the word rang so familiar. "Bagah would say it when he wanted a break after a long task," she exclaimed. "Vorae."

"Vor Vorae," Niemi stated again, pressing her palms together and leaning her cheek against them. She feigned sleep, even faked a snore. Opening her eyes, she wagged her finger back and forth between Lars and Mirevra. *"Nu belitea, vor vorae."*

Mirevra turned her chin and called over her shoulder. "I think she is saying we ought to rest before ascending the summit."

Lars scoffed. "Really? I think she is calling us impish fools," he said.

He flanked Mirevra's side and braced two tight fists on his hips. "She is probably bidding us a final farewell before we become the latest ingredients in volcano soup."

Niemi blinked, awaiting a response. Mirevra offered her a single nod and pointed to the left. *"Ich, vorae."* Her accent was terrible, but her words sufficed. Niemi seemed more than pleased with the answer and began descending the stairs without another word or glance. The Teruk must be all about business, then, Mirevra thought. No time for small talk. Lars clicked his tongue as Niemi descended, shaking his head as if their only lifeline had escaped their grasp. And likely, it just did.

"That is it," he stated. "We are going to be soup." Mirevra frowned and offered an impassive shrug.

"Probably."

Their resting spot was a hollowed-out section of the mountain, no, the volcano. It was little more than a tiny cave with two fur hides thrown lazily upon the earth floor. Only one blue fire lit the small cavern, washing it in an ethereal hue that reminded Mirevra of the ocean at night. She took a deep breath, relieved it was not as smoky here. She pointed to two large imprints in the dirt and deduced that Teruk rears made them. Mirevra sucked on her teeth. "This must be where the Teruk usually guard the summit," she said.

Lars bobbed his head in agreement. "It is a wonder they left and let a pair of strange humans take their shift? I cannot imagine why they would leave this place, cozy as it is...," Lars pondered sarcastically. The volcano grumbled as if the gods were showcasing their wicked sense of humor again. A slight vibration buzzed at their feet, and Lars flashed a rictus grin. "Oh, well, there is your answer."

Mirevra rolled her eyes and began to spread the furs out wide. "She knew of Bagah and the Vaenir. There is only one logical explanation. Bagah is here, and he told her about our mission." Once one fur was flattened, she slid it away from the other and then plopped down with her arms draped over her bent knees. "Why he did not come with Niemi is a different question." With pursed lips, Mirevra rocked her head from side to side. "One that I do not have the answer to."

Lars mirrored her actions with the remaining fur, only he lay on his back. "Probably because Bagah is smarter than us," he said. "He is likely somewhere safe while we are up here, taking a graveyard shift. Literally."

Mirevra did not bite down her laugh but let it fall freely. "I am still processing that there are more Teruk who live. In Drodour, no less. The High Crown will not be pleased to learn this," she said.

Lars splayed his hands across his chest, drumming his fingers lightly. "I am still processing that kiss," he said. Mirevra's entire face glowed red. Even the blue firelight could not hide her blush. Lars chuckled. "Perhaps if I got another, my mind would be refreshed."

"I thought we were going to die," Mirevra protested, her golden eyes squinted. Lars drew in his chin, narrowing his eyes to look at her down the bridge of his nose.

"I still think we are going to," he said, waving his boots playfully at her. "Maybe our kiss saved us last time? We should try again." The assassin bared her teeth.

"Doubtless, I only lived because the gods pitied me and that I had been stricken with such insanity as to kiss you. Our fortunate escape was due to their charity."

"Mm," Lars hummed. "Insanity suits you well, then." The broad male hoisted himself up on his elbows. Mirevra twisted her face into her usual scowl. She reached for her leather pouch to quench her dry mouth but found it empty, then looked to him. Lars flashed a crooked grin. "Needing a favor, are you?"

"A small sip," she said, holding out her hand. Lars held his waterskin and swung it gently so Mirevra could hear the water splash within it.

"How about…" he said, and his voice trailed off. "A fair trade?"

"I am not kissing you again, Ruffles. Come off it." Lars sat up and put a hand to his chest in feigned offense.

"First of all, I was not going to ask for one," he said. "However, you need to stick to what you know, Viper. Either get better at lying or stop altogether," he smirked. "Besides, try as you might to deny it, I know for a fact you enjoyed yourself."

Mirevra gagged exaggeratedly, then allowed a small, barely-there smile to tug at her lip. "Fine, Ruffles. You win. For a drink, what do you want from me?"

"I want to know the story of how you joined the Ring."

Mirevra's eyes widened. This was certainly not what she had expected. "Why?" It was all she could think of to say. Lars' jaw ticked.

"A hero's curiosity, let us call it," he said smoothly. Mirevra did not believe him for a second, but her tongue was dry, and her throat stung from the smoke.

"The Veravant found me some years ago," she said. She would not tell him where or how. "He helped me out of a... *situation,* we'll call it. After a few test runs, stealing things mostly–which I am very good at–he declared I had what it took to become a Fox. I went under initiation, and that's it. Since then, I have served the Ring," she said, throwing up her hands in a theatrical flourish while bowing her head. "The end." When she peeked up, Lars' face was anything but amused.

"Well," he said finally. "Thank the gods that you can fight better than tell a damn story."

"There is not much of a story to tell," she countered. Lars shook a finger.

"Nonsense. There is *always* a story to tell," he said with a sardonic smile.

"You sound more like a bard than a rogue sometimes. I hope you know that," she japed.

"You only need to expand your story and not spare the details. For starters, *why* are you so good at stealing? A life born in poverty, I assume. Unless..." He stopped and eyed her up and down. "Unless you are incredibly well off and love crime that much." Mirevra snorted. Lars rubbed his chin. "Did you steal for a purpose? A family back home?"

"I have no family." She regretted saying it as soon as the words left her tongue.

"See? There! That is how you begin a real story," he said, then handed her his water, but withdrew it a bit before she could grab hold and raised an eyebrow. "I suppose I cannot barter with you to tell me anymore?" Mirevra lowered her head, thankful that he did not press. Instead, he offered her the water, and she took a generous swig. Half the flask was left, and they would need to save it for tomorrow when they entered the fiery belly of Develdeon.

"What about you?" she inquired with a softer look. She hugged her knees to her chest and wrapped her arms tightly around them. "What is your story?" Lars drank quickly, then sloppily wiped his mouth with a loud sigh.

"What is in it for me if I tell you?"

Mirevra's smile slipped. She had only her dagger to offer. Or another moment of passion.

"I could..." she began, and her voice trailed off as she gazed around the empty alcove. "Not kill you in your sleep?" There was that dark chuckle again.

"Oh, in that case, I will tell you anything." Lars teased, bringing his torso forward to mirror her position. He shook his head and ran a hand through his black hair. "What do you want to know, Viper? I will count the kiss as my favor." Her cheeks bled warmth, and she cursed them. *Do not blush,* she seethed internally. She countered her embarrassment quickly, tilting her head back till her chin was pointed at him.

"When we were at the Tajeh's rectory," she began, faint memories of their drunken forms atop a hill melded once again. Maybe she had already asked him this? But alcohol had made the moment fuzzy, so who could say? "They said something about an oracle–"

"The Oracle of Hawthorne," he said slowly. "I went to see a man in Arcaeles by that title. He was part of a traveling group of Arcanen Seers, and I wanted to learn something promising about my future. I did not get anything of the sort, though."

"When did you go to him?" She was more interested in his answer than she cared to admit to herself. Lars' eyes turned that dark, stormy gray as if clouds were ready to crack and unleash a downpour.

"Long, long ago," Lars answered. "When I was still an adolescent. Before I met–" he stopped and looked down at his boot, picking at nothing with his thumb and pointer.

"What did the oracle say?"

Lars glanced at her, and she spotted his wicked little grin. "I am afraid that is all one kiss will get you. You'll have to offer something new if you want more."

"A terrible deal," Mirevra pouted, her face contorted into a crumple of disdain. She thought about the Tajeh again, how they swapped a tale for a tale. With a large sigh, she placed her palms flat on the ground at each side.

"I was not born into poverty. I grew up in a lovely estate with my mother and father," she said, and Lars lifted his face to meet hers fully. "I was incredibly well off for a time, as you said. But that time was short-lived. That time is a bleeding portrait in my mind. The colors are distorted and smudged; only a small portion of my life's painting remains carved into memory." She scanned the cavern's walls, her mind trying to piece together specific images it had not thought of since she hit the water. She felt a hand on her thigh but did not look at it.

"What happened to your parents?" She did not know if it was the story's weight or if the cave was shrinking, but Lars' voice seemed louder. Her eyes did not leave the far wall.

"They died. Perished in a fire." She could not tell Lars the truth. That her parents had been hunted down and slaughtered on a viaduct. All because of their name and the blood that coursed through their veins. "A competing merchant of my father's set our house aflame." It was another lie, but regardless, Mirevra felt her chest crumbling. Mentioning her father out loud? Lifting his memory from her chest and out into the world, she had not realized how heavy it would feel.

"My gods," Lars breathed. "Why in the world would they do that?"

After King Dern's father died, the young king grew paranoid, she desperately wished to say. *He convinced himself that the Vethari line would try to regain their throne. After Kallias usurped King Syhther's crown and killed him, his wife, and their two young boys, Sardek thought that might be the end. But Dern would not settle. 'A small flame can grow. It can burn down a city! It can melt down a crown! All of them must be wiped out. Kill every last Vethari.'*

They came for her family without warning.

There was no time.

"My father was good at business. The merchant feared my father could easily take all the buyers he wanted and stomp out the merchant's trading entirely," Mirevra said. The lie spilled from her lips as if it were the truth, and when she finally met Lars's stare, he appeared to believe her. "Petty nonsense that cost their lives," she said coldly. "Only I escaped."

"And the merchant?" Lars asked. His voice was far from the playful, cocky one she was used to. It sounded primal, almost animalistic. "What became of them?"

Mirevra shrugged. "Still living, still selling." *Still ruling the High Crown and burning cities to the ground.*

Something flickered in Lars' eyes, a violent fork of lightning streaking across the billowing storm clouds. Mirevra's chest heaved in deep dips. She had not realized how shaky her breathing had become. The hand on her thigh squeezed.

"The oracle told me I would lose my first love at the hands of another," Lars said, and she knew it was a mercy confession. He had sensed her discomfort and meant to shoulder some of it. "Then he told me I would lose another by my own hands." Sadness clouded his features.

"The Tajeh said you suffered a great heartbreak," she gulped. "They said your love is dead."

"Aye," Lars answered and took another small sip of water. "That she is." Mirevra was at a loss for what to say. Her heart beat faster and faster.

"Was the oracle right?" She swallowed and asked despite her apprehension. "Did she die at the hands of another?" She felt a tightness in the air. Something uncertain was suspended above them and she could see how his body stiffened and jaw clenched.

"She did," he eventually said. Mirevra heard not deep sorrow in his voice but unfiltered anger. "There was a man who could not stand my happiness. He took her from me to prove that he could." Fury swelled in Lars' every breath. "And he did."

"What was her name?" Mirevra asked, then brought trembling fingers up to cover her mouth. She did not remember her mind urging her to ask; the question leaped from her throat. She also did not recall extending her hand, but there it was, resting atop his. Lars examined their hands before looking at her.

"Illiyana," he said, and for a fraction, his lips quivered. "Illiyana Feyl." It was a beautiful name. The assassin was sure it belonged to what had probably been an even more beautiful woman. Lars looked pale. He likely had not said that name in quite some time. "After she was taken from me, I was lost," he continued. "I had no home. My heart felt like it had stopped beating. I was falling apart. So, I set sail for the Cold Lands. They say it is an island made of ice, rock, pain, and despair–I thought I would fit right in. What better place to go and rot for the rest of my days?" Mirevra curled her fingers around his palm. "But those lands are anything but cold, Viper. The sun is brighter there, and the hills are lush and green. I had never seen a place so beautiful in all my days." His jaw relaxed, and his eyes lingered on their entwined hands as if they had a map of that new world sketched on them. "That's where I met Heral. She took me in and breathed me back to life in some ways. She was a whole lot to take in at first. Murks, she still is. But she helped me. Heral was dead set on coming to Estellian, and though I pleaded for more time, she dragged me back with her. Next thing I know, I am drunk in a tavern where I bump into a gorgeous patron named Shiln," he laughed. "The following day, I am meeting with Briatriel, pledging to become a warrior. Sturdy as the earth." He lifts his other hand and bares his knuckles to show off the Nelimen ring. "In a rather cruel and shocking turn of events, I survived my heartbreak, and Heral and I became heroes. Did you know we slayed a leviathan within our first week on the job?"

"Everyone in the waking world knows," Mirevra groaned, pulling away her hand. "It was all the Nelimen talked about for years!" She found herself smiling. "Still rather impressive, I suppose," she admitted, and Lars beamed.

"Do you think you will ever be the same after losing her?" Mirevra squirmed as the words came out, but she needed to hear the answer from someone else who had lost everything. Was she bound to be broken forever?

"I do not know," he answered earnestly. "Truth be told, I think I died when Illiyana did... only her spirit got to go somewhere else, and mine had to stay here. I think whatever fragment of my soul was left ventured to the Cold Lands, and all that came back was a shadow." His words hit Mirevra's chest like a flurry of blows. She knew this feeling all too well.

"I think I died too," she whispered. "My soul was ripped apart on a bridge after my parents..." She swallowed. "I did not have anywhere to go, either. I was too young, too lost..." She felt tears build, and a lone one trickled down her cheek when she blinked. "When the Veravant found me, I was a mere corpse parading around with the living. He was the first person to see me, I think. I was not a ghost to him. He recognized my potential; he made me feel like maybe I still had something to give to this world." A smirk played at the edge of her lips. "Or to take from it, at least."

"He uses you," said Lars plainly. Mirevra blinked again, and another tear ran to catch the first. "I have said it before and will say it again," Lars said. "The Veravant does not care for you. He uses you to do things he is not capable of. You are stronger than him, braver than him, too. He is a coward who hides behind you, Viper. And he knows it. We all know it."

"You do not know that," Mirevra countered, but her protest was weak. Soft, even. The Messaging Gem tormented her thoughts.

"I know he does not see you," Lars said, raising his hand to cup her cheek. "He only sees himself. He treats you poorly,"

"You do not know how he treats me!" Mirevra rebuked, though she knew it was not a complete lie.

"I know you treat him as a god." He moved dangerously close, and Mirevra was faced with vacillating wants. It did not feel wild and desperate as it did on the ledge. As Lars closed the distance between them this time, something else thrummed through her. The blue behind his gray eyes seemed to pulse. Thunder rolled in his stare and in her gut. "He should be the one worshiping you, Mirevra."

Tobacco and vetiver filled her senses. A familiar taste nipped at the tip of her tongue as the hair on the back of her neck and arms rose, and her chest pushed forward. She forgot if she was mad or not. There was only a tiny chance this was a good idea. Still, Mirevra could hear Beldon practically singing from somewhere deep in her thoughts. *Always take the chance.*

"One last favor, Ruffles. For saving my life," she breathed into his mouth, which was now so very, very close to hers. "And then I owe you nothing."

"Deal." He had barely said the words before she pulled his lips to hers. She pushed back against his chest but did not lift her mouth from his as she moved her weight. He leaned back, and she slid her knees until she straddled him, his hardened cock pressing against her trousers with fervent desire. Her body ached with sensations, and her muscles trembled. His was a kiss unhurried; their tongues lightly brushed as their mouths moved in tandem. His hands moved from gripping her waist to pulling her tunic over her head. She raised her arms for the cloth to easily slip off and revealed her bare breasts to him. They peaked with desire, beckoning his full attention. First, he stroked her nipple with his thumb, then his tongue. She whimpered when he barely scraped his teeth against them and instantly drew back.

Had he heard that? Fluttering one's eyes and releasing sounds of pleasure were entirely different things. She quickly schooled her face back into a calculated void. Her mouth clamped shut into a bloodless line. "Everything alright, Viper?" Gods. Oh, gods. Even that name coming from him was almost too much to bear. His hands pressed firmly into her back just below her shoulder blades, pushing her body harder against his as he kissed and sucked on her breasts. He pulled back. "Do you not like it when I do that?" His voice was raw and rough-hewn, like the question came from deep in his throat. She wanted to scream *Yes! Yes, I do more than anything!* But Mirevra did not know how to break her years of training, the countless encounters of practiced absence, in a single moment.

So, she nodded, allowing her lip to curl. Thankfully, in times of intimacy, Lars was not one for many words. The subtle answer was enough for him, and he pushed his torso forward into her until her back was completely straight. She lifted her chin, leaving her neck vulnerable, which he instantly seized. His tongue, teeth, and lips buried her flesh, and she cursed beneath her breath. Lars went from ravaging her neck and jaw to lightly nibbling on her earlobe before returning to her breasts. Her features crumbled under the burden of holding back such ecstasy, and she could take no more. With nothing gentle about it, she pushed Lars down flat and began to work at his buckle. The shirt was already gone; there would be no trouble there. Mirevra already knew what awaited her beneath his trousers, and her mouth salivated at the thought of him. His muscles were hard lines down his body, deep divots in a marble carving. Lars released a gratified hiss when his trousers came off. She discarded them with an impatient toss, and they landed on the ground with a faint jingle.

She turned her attention back to him, holding his hard cock in her solid grip, but her fingers could not wrap around it entirely. Gods above and Murks below; no wonder the obnoxious brute was so damned arrogant. Before she revealed her satisfaction, Mirevra quickly dragged her tongue down the trail of hair from his navel to his length and lathered the sensitive tip with her spit. His hips arched forward, and she felt his member throb in her palm.

"Viper," he grumbled. She took the whole of him in her mouth and felt his cock hit the back of her throat. *"Fuck,"* the word was wholly carnal as he gasped aloud. Lars snatched her hair and twisted it. The slight twinge of pain pleased her. She reached one hand to his stomach and clawed her nails into him, the other she used to stroke where her mouth did not fit.

His body convulsed as she bobbed quicker, stopping only to haul her tongue back to the tip. Her mouth was red and swollen from the challenge, and Lars released her hair to put his hand under her chin and lifted her head to face him. She gasped as he popped from her mouth, the moist air swimming around her. "Those eyes," he said with a smile. "I want to see those eyes."

Mirevra let him tug her chin up. He was gentle, unlike the Veravant. Nothing like him at all. Lars guided her to meet his mouth, and their tongues slowly collided again, a delicate dance between unrushed intimacy and unfettered desire. And then, without warning, his arm was around her waist, and he flipped her on her back.

"No," she protested, placing a hand on his chest. "Not like this." Lars' aroused expression quickly turned to worry.

"What is it?" he asked. "Did I hurt you?" Mirevra's eyes were wide. She had never allowed a man to be on top. Her heart thrashed against her ribcage; everything within her screamed to get up. "Mirevra? Do you want me to stop?" She *did* want him to stop; she *never* wanted him to stop. Mirevra grappled with her confusion, her face tormented. When she did not answer—because she could not—Lars brushed the tip of her nose with his. He kissed her lips gingerly, then her chin, her throat, her sternum, and her belly. His kisses traveled lower and lower until he pulled off her trousers. He only lifted his head to meet her eyes once. "If you do not wish to continue, tell me now," he said frankly. "I am a man of little self-control, and this close, I do not know if I can..." He gazed down, then back into her eyes. "I cannot hold out for much longer."

"Then do not," she ordered bluntly. Well, there it was. The answer flew out of her unbidden. She was totally fucked now. Lars licked his lips, and they then curled into a devilish smile.

"As you wish."

Lars gripped the outside of her thighs with his large hands and spread her legs. Mirevra threw her head back as the rogue made good on his promise. He certainly did not hold back, his tongue quickly swirled right on the hood of her clit, his head jerking in a frenzy of fluid movements. Mirevra's body twitched. She bit so hard on her tongue she was afraid it might sever, payback for the many tongues she had cut straight from a man's mouth. Her nose crinkled, her brows knit together. Lars had begun to lick her slowly now, the skin of her thighs pinched in his grasp. He lifted his mouth for a second, the longest prolonged second of her godsdamned life, and uttered the most dangerous words Mirevra had ever heard come from a man.

"Moan for me, Viper."

Mirevra, a tight bundle of frayed rope and a thousand excuses, unraveled. Loud moans of pleasure rang throughout the cave, sounds she had never heard emerge from her throat. Lars exulted in this victory, licking her from her entrance to her clit repeatedly. Just when she thought she could not take it anymore, when she believed the pleasure too much for her body to hold, Lars slipped two wet fingers inside her. Mirevra was swept up in the raptures of complete passion.

Her moans became stuttering screams, and her legs began to tremble. Lars held her steady with one arm, his fingers thrusting in and out as he returned his tongue to massage her clit again. She pulled his hair taut and whimpered, praying she would not faint. His fingers curled slightly and caressed her apex with masterful precision. She could hardly breathe.

Maybe there *was* an afterlife. Maybe she was in it now. Perhaps the gods had found her worthy after all. Lars pushed his fingers in one last time, kissing her warmth gently before releasing her leg. He scaled forward, their faces mirroring each other's, their breathing labored. Mirevra drank in his sharp jawline, his sculpted nose. His thick dark brows, the thin line of sweat coating his creased brow. His eyes, those pools of murky dust bordered by a light blue corona. Lars was beautiful in ways she had not fully noticed before. Perhaps, and unfortunately, the most beautiful man she had ever seen.

"Is this alright?" he asked, his biceps bulging on either side of her face. Heat whirled between their bodies, awaiting her answer. He was on top of her, yet she did not feel afraid. Mirevra did not speak; instead, she nodded, and her flaxen eyes, molten gold, burned with want. The setting sun of her stare met the menacing overcast of his.

He kissed her again, soft and slow. Then, she gasped. A wave of pleasure eclipsed her body as he entered unhurriedly, his rasping breaths filling the cave. Lar's eyes rolled back for a moment, his mouth hung ajar, and his brows deepened towards the bridge of his nose. Most of his weight rested upon one elbow; his other hand cupped the back of her head, careful not to let it touch the floor. Mirevra spread her legs wider, and this time, it was Lars who moaned. Mirevra felt the rest of him slide into her, and she did not know if she made a sound. She could only hear the music in her mind, a symphony of Ocal, Our Lady of Heathers. The goddess was singing to Mirevra, a song created for this very moment. Every muscle of Mirevra's body spasmed in concert. Lars did not move for a minute. Instead, he looked at her with quivering lips and his features tinged with sadness.

"Lars?" Her voice was gentle, a tone she had rarely used in all these years. With the hand that held her, he used his thumb to stroke her cheek softly and gave a gentle nod. Still, his eyes concerned her. But her worries were ripped away as he slipped out of her with one rough movement and thrust himself back in. Her body jerked. Her eyes squeezed shut, her hands flexed and unflexed as he did it again and again and again. Mirevra had never felt something so glorious, and while she relished the pleasure, a small part of her fissured with anger. *Of course, the hero would be great at fucking, too.*

Lars buried his mouth in the crook of her neck, and Mirevra wrapped her arms and legs tightly around him. The sensation of him inside her was so inexplicably good, so unequivocally pleasing, that she barely heard him speak.

"Tell me," he murmured between each drive of his hips. "Tell me, Viper." She opened her eyes, and her heart sank, the command all too familiar. Now, she did not see Lars. She did not hear his voice anymore. Red hair began to fill her vision. Brown eyes and fair skin. The face of a Fox, the face of disappointment. His voice warped, but there it was, in all its silk and honey. *"Tell me,"* she heard again. *"Tell me, little Fox."* Mirevra felt heat sting her eyes; she sensed moisture on her cheeks.

"I belong to you," she said and nearly shattered with pain at her words. "All of me. I belong to you. My mind, my body." The thrusts of ecstasy slowed, but Mirevra continued her pledge. "You own me," she choked out in a sob. "In whatever way you please. *You fucking own me.*"

The pleasure stopped. Lars had pulled out of her. His expression was wary as he cupped her cheek in one hand. The Veravant was gone, and Mirevra had to blink a few times to regain full consciousness. "Wha–"

"What are you saying?" Lars cut off her question with his. Mirevra felt the heat between her thighs pulse, anxious to finish what they had started. She felt the heat elsewhere, too; her mind burned in embarrassment.

"What?"

His thumb caressed her cheek again.

"I asked you to tell me how you felt, and you...Gods, Viper. You..." Lars trailed off, but his eyes darkened in anger. "Nobody owns you, Mirevra," he said through gritted teeth.

She pulled her arms away from his neck and covered her chest. Shame flooded her, and she realized that anger was not the only emotion with a sharp pair of teeth. Humiliation also had a gruesome bite.

"I did not...I did not realize what I was saying," Mirevra began. *Godsdamn it.* She had no idea what to say as he wiped away her tears. She opened her mouth, but before she could finish her pathetic speech, Lars' lips pressed against hers. Pulling back, he tucked a rogue hair behind her ear and smiled.

"I am not him, Viper," Lars said. "You do not owe me anything." Mirevra found a great deal of comfort in gazing at him. The scent of tobacco and vetiver, his gray eyes, and handsome albeit cocky smile. "I would save your life a thousand times over, Viper. There would still be no debt for you to pay."

Mirevra wanted to cry. She wanted to embrace and beg him to continue, but she could not. She instead held back her tears and let Lars slide to her side. She did not fight when he coaxed her head to his chest, played with her hair, and lightly stroked her back. She did not cry as he held her, though she did not understand why he still wanted to be so close now that the deed was over and done with. And she did not argue when he urged her to rest as he told her tales of the Nelimen and the Cold Lands, until she finally slept.

When Mirevra awoke, fully clothed and well rested, she found it was an effort to stomach looking at Lars. There was a sticky clog in the back of her throat from dehydration or embarrassment, she could not say. The previous night had been a whirlwind. She had shared parts of her story and body, pieces of herself she had never laid so bare to anyone. And then she had ruined the entire song before it could reach its heavenly crescendo. All because she could not banish the Ring leader from her mind, because she refused to let him go. The Veravant may have freed her from the chains that held her in that cell so many years ago, but the manacles were still there, only now invisible. She felt them heavy on her wrists each time she tasted a hint of freedom. Mirevra's head ached, the pain centering between her temples, likely from the lack of water and the omnipresent smoke. *Who am I?* The first clear thought of morning, and a rather bleak one at that. Mirevra loved being a Fox. She loved her Ring; they were the only family she had ever known. But they were not who she thought of as she stretched her sore limbs. Her mind was engulfed by one person alone.

"Good morning," the one who occupied most of her consciousness said. Lars was already in his trousers. "I hope you do not mind that I dressed you. I wanted you to savor those few precious moments of sleep."

"That was..." Mirevra gulped down a gummy lump. "Awfully heroic of you," she said with a hint of sarcasm. Lars chuckled.

"It was mostly self-serving. I wanted to watch you sleep. It is when you are at your kindest." Mirevra chortled nervously. She could not get a good read on him, which irritated her. Was the rogue angry that she had squandered their romantic encounter? Frustrated that he had not been able to finish?

She smacked her dry lips, ignoring the mortifying thoughts. "Is there any water?"

Lars hesitated. "A little," he replied, then ran his hand through his tangled morning hair. His eyes scanned the floor. "Mirevra, I have a question."

Mirevra. Not Viper. Gods. Here it came, his disappointment. Lars leaned forward, his eyes were drained. "Do you still belong to him?" The question was accompanied by the shaking of the mountain and a pounding in her chest. Not disappointed, then. Something far worse. "The Veravant," Lars added as if he needed to clarify. Mirevra wrapped her arms around her torso and tilted her head from side to side. Everything in her wanted to scream *NO! He does not care about me! He doesn't care if I die! He did not show any remorse about Roman's death either. Or anyone! Why should he own me still?*

But the truth was not so simple. Every time she kissed Lars`, the Veravant appeared. Any time she allowed herself a moment of hope, the Veravant's voice batted that hope away. Maybe, even though she did not want it to be true, it still was. Mirevra's shoulders rose high as she sighed heavily.

"I do not know," she said and looked away. "I do not have an answer to that question." Lars' mouth tightened. His eyes were weighed down with more than exhaustion.

"You are wrong," he said, his voice low. "That *was* an answer." Another violent shake of the mountain later, he offered her the water skin. "Here," he said in a defeated voice. Only one sip remained. "It is fine," he affirmed with a wave. "I drank a little this morning." She felt a tiny scourge of guilt but took it anyway, swallowing the last bit of water. Perhaps it was some peace offering, or maybe Lars did not need such a thing. Either way, it tasted sour. She chalked it up to her tasting the bitter guilt on her tongue.

The fighter did not enjoy the sorrowful expression that marked both their faces.

They did not speak as they left the alcove or ascended the narrow stairs to the volcano's vent. For the first time, Mirevra missed his incessant remarks.

The Vaenir

~~~

Heat. Despair. Rock. *Hele.*

The summit of Develdeon was all Mirevra had dreaded. Ash fell in violent frenzies from dark, stormy skies; plumes of black smoke enveloped her and burned her eyes. She thought that if Deleon ever walked the earth, this would be her footprint, a deep crater, blazing and charred. Mirevra steadied her breath. They had done it–she and Lars had reached the summit. From the gods' point of view, they must look like two helpless rafts about to set sail on the vast sea towards the eastern lands of Bessere. So small, if you blinked, you would miss them. Larks flanked her as she stood at the bowl's edge, and the pool of bubbling pissed-off lava hissed at them. An excruciating death was only a quick stumble and fall away.

The heat made Mirevra think her skin might start peeling off at any minute, but she knew it would have been worth it if it happened. For straight ahead, glistening like a diamond, was the Vaenir. It was on a small rock platform that rose from Develdeon's stretched belly. *Shining like the godsdamned sun,* just as the book had said. Bagah was right, that Jedarei was right! Here was the fallen sword! Its hilt was pure, black onyx. The blade itself was transparent, yet it glimmered. It was undeniably the most gorgeous blade Mirevra had ever seen. Her heart sank as she wondered if she would ever get to hold it close and admire its beauty. How in the Murks would she get to it? She had not realized she had asked that aloud, but Lars turned to face her with a smile. He plunged a hand deep into a pocket and pulled out a vial. She narrowed her eyes, and then her mouth fell open.

"You sneaky little rogue," she whispered. "You stole the Relirantur!" She did not try to hide her shocked laugh or mask her joy. He nodded and shook the vial, and she playfully punched his arm. "Spending too much time with criminals, are you?"

"One in particular," he said with a wink. Mirevra felt something tight in her chest ease. She had worried Lars' questions about the Veravant had placed a distance between them, but his cheerful smile was back. His flirtatious banter had returned. She felt relief, even standing so close to fire and death. "It should only take a small sip since the Vaenir is right there," he explained, pulling the cork out. "I will be back momentarily."

"Hold on," Mirevra said, her flattened hand held out before her. "Why do you get to use it?!"

"Because I stole it, Viper. And it is in my hands." It was almost too easy to snatch it away; the rogue was hardly paying attention.

"There. Now it is in my hands," she gloated.

Lars' eyes darkened. "Very funny. Now, hand it back."

"No."

Lars bit his bottom lip. "Fine. There is no time to quarrel. Go and come back quickly," he instructed. Mirevra smiled wickedly. She had longed to use this potion since Neeps had explained its abilities. Lars continued, "You must steady your breathing and keep your heart rate relaxed. Once you take a swig, think *clearly* about where you want to go. It is of the utmost importance–"

"I know how it works," Mirevra interjected. "Neeps explained it to me... sort of."

Twisting off the lid, Mirevra smiled. "I'll be right back."

Lars grabbed her hand. "Be careful," he murmured, staring at her fingers. "And please, *do* come back." She understood the words he did not say. *I trust you not to take the blade. I trust you will use the potion to return here, not elsewhere.*

I. Trust. You.

Mirevra did not know if it was a sweet notion or utterly foolish of him.

She wasted no time. One gulp later, she closed her eyes and pictured herself standing on the platform next to the blade. She imagined it in her grip, holding it to the sky. Even in her vision, she felt the Vaenir's potent power. Gerreland's mightiest weapon. Estellian's greatest warrior. Heat almost seared her skin, and Mirevra slowly opened her eyes. A surprised laugh escaped her. She had not sensed movement and her feet had not felt the ground disappear beneath them, but here she stood on the platform. The blade was only a few steps away, glistening on a stone plinth made from the volcano's own rock. She put her hand to her forehead and scanned the slope across the lava lake. She saw Lars standing with his hands on his hips and waved. He did not wave back, and she noticed the apprehensive tapping of his foot.

Then, a pulse began to beat. A current coursed through Mirevra– lightning stitched its way through her veins. The Vaenir seemed to sing. Her eyes wide, she approached the armament. Up close, she saw that the blade was not actually transparent. Purple, green, and blue streams along its true edge wavered like colors reflected in water. The blade hummed again. No, it was not a song, Mirevra realized. It was a call, a plea. It was reaching out to its master, beckoning the lich to come find it. Wailing for the other half of its soul.

Fear struck Mirevra's heart, but she straightened her shoulders. She had not come all this way to quit now. She reached for the hilt and pulled the sword from the earth. Unrestrained power lanced through her hand, chest, and entire body. Her veins constricted, and her eyelids fluttered. Mirevra held the Vaenir up to the heavens, and a crack of lightning split the sky. Ash fell harder now, nearly blocking Lars from her view. She could barely catch a glimpse of him gesticulating wildly.

"COME BACK!" Mirevra could have sworn she heard Lars shout, but the ground wobbled, and she dropped her arm. The Vaenir was still firmly within her grasp, but it felt heavier. The world was shifting. Quickly, she took another small swig from the vial and imagined herself next to Lars. Shirtless, covered in soot. His muscular form, his gray eyes.

"Viper," he said next to her. Before she could peel her eyes open or settle her uneven footing, Lars caught her by the arm. "This damn thing is about to explode. We need to go. Now!" He pulled her towards him as they hurried towards the exit to the narrow stairs that had brought them here. Mirevra felt lightheaded, her surroundings swirling around her. Maybe it was the effect of Neep's potion.

Still, she held fast to the holy blade and let Lars lead her. Faster and faster, they descended the narrow steps until Lars yanked her into the cavern they rested in the night before.

"Is it safe here?" she asked, and her head throbbed harder.

"I have no idea," he panted. "But we cannot outrun it. This is our best bet."

"I still have this," Mirevra lifted the vial of Relirantur and cursed at herself. In the wake of all the excitement, she had forgotten to replace the cap. Most of the liquid was gone, likely staining the thin stairwell. There was only a sip left, enough for one person. Not two. Lars cursed, then shook his head.

"We will wait," he said plainly, taking the vial from her. Mirevra was happy to relinquish it, for she did not want to decide which of them would live or die. She did not think she could. Develdeon rumbled its fury; the ground shook and vibrated relentlessly. Lars led her to a corner of the cavern, where she curled into his arms and buried her head in his chest. She waited for the worst, fully anticipating the scorching flames would swallow her up as punishment for a life poorly lived. The sword continued to drum deep rivulets of power in her palm. If she wanted, she could cleave the entire rock in half. Perhaps she could keep the fire at bay, but she did not try. Mirevra remembered what the Tajeh had said about a human not being meant to wield such a weapon. She and Lars huddled, washed in fading blue lights, and let Develdeon bleed out its wrath.

Mirevra estimated that at least an hour had passed before the quaking stopped. In the sudden silence, she suggested the calm could be a feint, that Develdeon could be readying to fire up another eruption. "Then, we need to be quick about leaving," Lars urged. Mirevra agreed, but she lifted a hand as he stood, gesturing for him to wait. She felt queasy and weak.

"Not yet. I need a little more time," she pleaded. She knew that time was something they did not have, but she could not make herself stand.

"Here, let me hold the Vaenir. It might be easier for you–" Lars started, but Mirevra showed her teeth and hissed.

"No. I will not let it go." Her words sounded more venomous than she had intended, and she blamed it on the quaking earth and intense heat. The blade had to stay within her grasp. It was her chance, her only chance to.... A laugh overshadowed her thoughts. The laugh was not the dark, arrogant, and charming one she had grown so fond of. This one was filled with contempt. She lifted her eyes just enough to see Lars shaking his head.

"You still want to give him the blade," he said. It was not a question; he clearly already knew the answer. "That is why you refuse to hand it over."

"I..." Mirevra struggled to find a suitable answer. "It is mine to give him." Lars huffed roughly.

"After everything, you would truly still serve him?" He moved away from her. "I guessed you would, but it does not take away the pain."

"What does it matter?" Mirevra coughed. "The lich will fall no matter who wields the blade. We have it, Lars! We hold the sword!"

"You do not understand what he is doing," Lars sneered, his bare chest heaving in angry pants.

"And you do?" Mirevra snapped.

"Yes!" Lars cried, his eyes wide. "He is a terrible, greedy, merciless–"

"I care not for his character!" Mirevra yelled, and the ground beneath them groaned. "He is the Veravant! The leader of the Ring!" Her voice broke. "I serve the Ring, Lars."

"You act as if there is no choice," Lars said, shaking his head.

"There *is* no choice," she said, choking out a hoarse cough. When she caught her breath, she squeezed the weapon tighter. "The Veravant gave me a command, and while I still live, I must abide by it."

"Or what, Viper? What in the Murks do you think will happen if you do not?" Mirevra scooted toward the cave exit, dragging the sword behind her.

"I will not defy the code. To the Ring I serve. Or suffer to become a Wolf. They are exiled. They are alone," she recited. Lars was on his feet and she longed to stand herself, but did not have the strength. But if she had to crawl out of this gods-forsaken place, she would. Mirevra could see in Lars' face all the things he did not understand. He did not understand why she had to do this. He did not carry the weight of her debts. She would not defect; she would not betray her guild. Not until the Veravant granted revocation. The Vaenir was her bargaining chip. When she gave it to the Veravant, he would have no choice but to wipe the slate clean. Lars' footsteps grew closer, and she seethed.

"Do not come closer, Lars! You must let me do this! I beg of you!" Mirevra's pleas were unfiltered cries of pain and need. She could have been calling upon Rashawe himself. "I beg of you," she rasped. "I will deliver this blade, the Veravant will slay the lich, and Estellain will be free. *I* will be free."

"You still do not see," Lars said. Something in his voice had changed. It was even lower and darker. "It is not the victory of slaying the lich he wants, Mirevra. That is not what he longs for."

Mirevra stopped squirming long enough to regain her breath. "What are you talking about? He will use this weapon to reunite Gerreland's soul and destroy the lich for good. Estellian will be saved." Lars stood before her, blocking the exit, a deep look of pity plastered across his handsome face.

"No," Lars' voice shook. "He will hand the Vaenir over to the lich." Mirevra could barely see now. Her heart crashed against her ribs, and pain seared through her spine.

"Are you mad?!" She thought she was shouting, but her voice was waning, barely more than a whisper. "Why would the Veravant willingly hand over the most powerful weapon in all Estellian? To the very creature that could destroy us all, no less!" There was silence, save for the low grumblings of Develdeon.

"A human cannot wield the blade. It is useless to him as a weapon," Lars explained quietly. Mirevra hardly heard him over the volcano's rumbling. "If he finds the Vaenir for the lich, however, he will be granted whatever he desires. And you cannot imagine how dark his desires are, Viper." Mirevra had no fucking idea what Lars was babbling on about. The smoke must have drained his mind of any rational thought, the same way it was siphoning all of her strength now. She wheezed as she pushed her words out.

"Why do you speak as if you know him?" Even talking was beginning to take too much energy. "You have never even met him." Lars did not answer, so Mirevra pressed him. "And how do you know anything about the lich? Granting desires? What in the Murks does that mean?" Even as her energy dwindled, Mirevra remembered all the times Lars had insulted the Veravant. Why? And now this information about the lich? Lars sounded eerily like the Tempust. *'A wish. The Vaenir offers more than glory.'*

Pain smarted through her ribs at the thought. Lars still had not answered her.

"How do you know, Lars?" She demanded, each word laced with poison.

"Well? Do not keep the poor girl waiting. Answer her." A familiar female's voice rang through the cavern. Mirevra jerked her chin up to see the black leather of the Wolf. The shapely woman held a blade straight under Lars' chin.

"Lars?" Mirevra nearly choked. The rogue stood perfectly still, careful not to be sliced as the mountain wobbled. The Wolf let out a crisp laugh.

"*Lars?*" She practically gagged. "Is that *really* the name you chose?" The Wolf turned her masked face to Mirevra. "I tried to warn you," she said. Mirevra attempted to pull up the Vaenir in defense but could not. The world was no longer level; her head was spinning.

"What does she mean?" Mirevra asked weakly.

"Pay her no mind, Viper," said Lars. "She wants the blade for herself. For the wish the lich will grant her."

"And what about you, *Lars?*" The Wolf laughed. "Will you tell me you sought the blade for anything different? Have you had a change of heart?" Lars growled, but the Wolf continued. "Did her cunt make you a better man?" Now she cackled. "Please. Did you not learn well enough last time?"

"Don't say another word," Lars seethed. "Or I swear it, I will slice your throat."

Mirevra could barely follow their conversation. "What is she saying?" No one answered her.

The Wolf pressed her blade deeper into Lars' throat. "I think if anyone will be doing the slicing, it is me," she said.

Mirevra's fingers twitched. Through her disorienting pain, she recognized the itch. Insatiable.

"Tell me, *Lars,* what will you wish for, hmm? It cannot be for your life back. I mean, you went through all that trouble! Sailing to the Cold Lands and finding an Enchantress. Changing your face! This look would afford you a new life on its own," the Wolf said as she inspected him closely. "Ah, but every pinch of Arcanen leaves its mark. I can still see the blue behind the gray. Oh well, it is still impressive."

"I swear, Zain, I will let you leave with your life if you end this now," Lars growled. Mirevra used the itch for violence to fuel her and pushed herself into an unstable, rickety stance using up every ounce of her strength. The Vaenir hung heavily at her side.

The Wolf used her free hand to tap her chin. "But if you will not use the wish to clear your name—because you apparently have a new one—what else could it be? Why go through all of this..." Behind the taut, black fabric, Mirevra saw the Wolf's brows rise. "Gods. It cannot be! You want to bring her back." Lars' lips curled into a snarl, and the Wolf sighed in disbelief. "That is it. You want to bring back Illiyana?"

"How does she know about Illiyana? Lars? Tell me what is happening!" Mirevra shouted and pulled the sword up as high as she could.

"Vacuous girl," the Wolf snipped. "His name is not Lars. Tell her!" She pushed the blade, and blood began to seep down his throat. "Tell her your true name, Wolf."

Mirevra gritted her teeth and lunged for the woman, but the blade was heavy, and the world tilted on its side. She stumbled, and the Wolf released Lars to block the charge.

Kaven Hiring

It did not go as Mirevra planned, but it worked well enough. Before the Wolf could turn again to face him, Lars kicked his boot into her back. With a rough release of air, the Wolf flew forward and landed hard on her face. Mirevra collapsed; she could no longer stand. She watched as Lars straddled the Wolf and turned her body to face him. The Tempust snarled through blood-soaked teeth. "Even if the lich could bring Illiyana back, she would not recognize you," the Wolf spat. "You are not the same person, Cage."

Mirevra's stomach flipped.

Cage?

Cage.

Cage Mastrosis.

The Wolf of the Ring.

"You were her friend, Zain. For that, and what you did on the docks, I will not kill you now," Lars said as he pulled the almost empty Relirantur vial from his pocket. "But get in my way again, and I will show no such mercy." Zain licked her bloody teeth and smiled.

"Show Illiyana the mercy that Calfaren did not, Cage, and let her rest in peace. It would be wrong to bring her back to this," Zain crooned. "And tell me, how do you plan to explain to her that you have fallen for another?" Lars ignored this question and lowered the vial to Zain's lips. "Will he kill her too, Cage? Which will you bring back then?"

"Enjoy the Murks, Zain," Lars fumed. He shoved the remaining Relirantur into her mouth, then covered her eyes with his palm. "Right where you belong."

An instant later, the Wolf was gone.

But one still remained.

The Wolf

✥

She had been such a fool.

Her palm pooled with sweat, and her thoughts crashed like viscous waves, not sparing her a chance to catch her breath. Her vision warped, and her ears rang. The Wolf of the Ring. Could it be true?

Lars, *Cage,* turned to face her. He dropped the empty vial and fell to his knees. "I am sorry," he choked out. His body split into two, three, and now four forms. She tried to blink away the blurriness but to no avail. As her heart thundered and her head roared, Mirevra gasped for breath. Another vial fell from his pocket and shattered. "I had no choice," he said, his voice like smoke. The ungodly realization dawned on her like a brutal kick to the gut. He had not only stolen the Relirantur from Neeps... and he had certainly not offered her his last sip of water as a kindness. "You were going to give him the blade," he said.

That gods-forsaken heartbeat poison now surged through her veins. Her pulse quickened as she contemplated his betrayal, sending her into a worse frenzy of pain. She lay limp on the ground as he walked towards her; though she thrashed and kicked, it was not enough to prevent him from taking the Vaenir.

"Viper," he said coolly beneath his breath. Even as his shape contorted before her, she could still make out his eyes. Full of sorrow. *Full of bullshit.*

Mirevra hissed. "Do not call me that, you bastard!" Pain lanced through the sinews of her neck. "Wolf!" She spat. So much hatred and anger swam through the marrow of her bones that she finally understood Bagah, for she could see nothing but red.

"Just listen to me," he pleaded, his voice breaking. She would do no such thing!

"You liar!" Mirevra screamed, her remaining strength teetering. "*You* are a Wolf! You betrayed the Ring! You wanted the Vaenir for yourself! You, you..." Her mind scrambled to recall his conversation with the Tempust Wolf. Agony swelled in her chest. The poison was overtaking her. "You work for the lich."

"No," he corrected immediately, then shut his eyes. "Well, yes. But not in the way you think."

"Traitor," she snarled. "Traitorous, backstabbing, liar." Nausea crawled up her throat as more cruelty came to light. *Oh gods.* "It was you! You were the reason the enemy was always one step ahead. You led the mages to us."

Lars, Cage, *The Wolf* looked down at her. His shoulders lifted and fell with a large breath.

"Yes," he admitted. "But that was before...Viper, you must understand, the lich was never going to let this many people–"

"What happened that day in the woods?" Mirevra asked quietly, and he stumbled back. Deep lines creased his brow, and his nostrils flared.

"Viper."

"Did you kill them? Did you kill Roman?" She whimpered, but not from the poison's pain. He looked down at the Vaenir and swallowed hard.

"Yes."

Mirevra felt tears streak down her cheeks. Her racing heart sank deep into her stomach. No. No, she could not believe it. "You," she said. Words. Words were so hard to find. Everything in her mind scattered; each thought was a glass shard. "You killed him?" She saw Tilly's hazel eyes filled with tears. "You killed Jardin, too? Oh, my gods." The bile rising in her throat was not far from her tongue now. "You did all that, and you still let me... You let me..." Vomit spewed across the cavern floor as she remembered how he had touched her, kissed her, and stroked her cheek. She had allowed his body over hers. She had trusted him. She had been such a fool.

Now, he stood before her, gripping the Vaenir and frowning. "You still belong to him, Mirevra. I cannot let you give him the blade. Believe me, I–"

"Fuck you," Mirevra condemned him. "Fuck you and your godsdamned lies." Her head was searing with unfathomable agony. Her damn heart would not stop fluttering and racing. "You lied to me. You murdered my friend. And then *you fucked me*. You poisoned me! Nothing you say means anything, you godsdamned traitor! You defected from the Ring. You are a Wolf," she spat again at his feet, though she had no real idea of whether it landed anywhere near him. She looked up and thought she saw a tear run down his cheek.

"I am sorry," he said, his voice cracking. "You do not know what he wanted me to do." The Wolf dropped to his haunches and leaned his weight against the Vaenir. Mirevra desperately longed to grab the blade and use it to kill him. Fuck the lich. Fuck Estellian. Fuck everything.

"Living in exile, existing as the damned, that is its own kind of torture, Mirevra, but it was nothing compared to the loss of Illiyana. *That* was true exile. I did not know how to breathe without her," he said. His voice, along with his face, swam in and out of her consciousness. "I told you I died when she did, and that was the truth. But I never told you who it was that killed us," he said with a strangled sob. "The Veravant, Mirevra. It was him."

Mirevra squirmed. Her breathing was now slow and labored. She knew death was not too far away. She felt the warm touch of his calloused palm against her cheek. "I set out to resurrect Illiyana by the only force on earth powerful enough to do so. I hoped it would bring me back from the dead, too, but you see, someone else had already raised me. Someone showed me that my heart could be healed. I am alive again because of you."

Her eyelids had flitted shut at the sound of his voice. Still, his smell consumed her.

That damned familiar scent.

And the memory finally snapped into place.

Her first night as a member of the Ring. The Veravant had shown her the cot she would sleep on for the remainder of her time in the guild. He had warned her of the Wolf it had once belonged to. That was the first and last time she had heard of Cage Mastrosis. But she had faintly smelled him each night in the threads of her pillow.

Tobacco and vetiver.

"Kill me," she rasped. His hand was still on her cheek, but she could do nothing to swat it away. "*Kill me,* you coward."

"I am not going to kill you."

"A grave mistake," she managed. "For I will not stop until you are..." Each word grew heavier and heavier. Her tongue felt swollen. "I will kill you..." She could not finish, though her fingers still ticked with rage. She heard a long sigh.

"One lost by another's hands," he said. The warmth on her cheek disappeared; his voice was fading away. *"One lost by my own."* She did not know if what she heard was his footsteps leaving, if the Develdeon had erupted once more, or if Degolian Murks had come to take her away. She did not know if the Wolf was still there, and she certainly did not feel the many tears that slipped down her cheeks as the world around her went dark.

She awoke with a crippling pain in her right ear. Smoke hung like thick curtains in the cavern, but she could see two black silhouettes within the mist, only a few steps away. One broad, strong, and wide. A Teruk.

The other was tall, lithe, and toned. "Hello, little Fox," he said, stepping into view. Another cruel figment of her imagination, she thought, as the Veravant bore a primal stare into her. The viridian blade hanging off his hip contrasted starkly with his all-black attire. Red hair covered both shoulders. His golden helmet was held between his arm and waist, staring at her like another set of eyes.

Shame and guilt heated her cheeks. How long had she been asleep? Where had Cage fled to? The Vaenir was long gone by now. *Fuck.* The Veravant did not deign to lower himself to her level but towered above her like a looming tree. He drummed his fingers against the hilt of his

Gerreland blade.

"I hear you met an old friend of mine," he said coyly, then threw her a small pouch of water. It slapped against the ground, moisture spilling from its tap. She did not immediately reach for it, though her dry throat and cracked lips beseeched her to. The Ring leader smirked, and Mirevra felt like a Fox again, one caught in a trap, forced to look at the hunter who had captured her. The Veravant's sharp features hardened.

"Get up," he ordered. "We have a Wolf to catch."

Acknowledgments

I want to thank the entire club for being here tonight. I would like to thank Pinot Noir and coffee for helping me write this; I'd truly like to thank my dice for being both god sent and troubling little bastards.

Of course, I have to thank BOOKTOK and BOOKSTAGRAM for always championing me and my success.

To my husband, to my mother, and to all my friends... I love you all more than words could ever say and you make my world go round.

I'd also like to thank the song, "Miracles Happen," for being the driving force behind every project.

I hope you all had fun, know that I'm halfway through book 2 (the final book) and it's absolutely going BUCK. (that is millennial slang for awesome)

I love that I can write whatever I want here because I'm self published..... Pee pee. Poo poo.

See? I can just do that. Lol. I can write *anything*. There are no rules, man, we're lost.

So, I guess that means I'd like to thank myself. I'm awesome and anyone who thinks otherwise is wrong.

Okay. Bye!

Printed in Great Britain
by Amazon